SIREN

SIREN

TARA MOSS

AUSTRALIA'S NO. 1 CRIME WRITER

MAX
CRIME

Published by

MA CRIME

an imprint of John Blake Publishing Ltd,
3 Bramber Court, 2 Bramber Road,
London W14 9PB, England

www.johnblakepublishing.co.uk

First published in 2009 by HarperCollins*Publishers* Australia
This edition published in 2010 by John Blake Publishing

ISBN: 978 1 84454 281 6

British Library Cataloguing-in-Publication Data:
A catalogue record for this book is available from the British Library.

Design by www.envydesign.co.uk

Printed in Great Britain by CPI Bookmarque, Croydon CR0 4TD

1 3 5 7 9 10 8 6 4 2

Papers used by John Blake Publishing are natural, recyclable
products made from wood grown in sustainable forests.
The manufacturing processes conform to the environmental
regulations of the country of origin.

MA CRIME series commissioning editor: Maxim Jakubowski

OTHER BOOKS BY TARA MOSS

Fetish

Split

Covet

Hit

Tara is the author of five bestselling crime novels published in sixteen countries in ten languages. Writing has been a lifelong passion for her; she began penning gruesome 'Stephen King-inspired' stories for her classmates when she was only ten. Tara enjoyed a successful international career as a fashion model before pursuing professional writing, first earning a Diploma from the Australian College of Journalism. She began writing her debut novel, *Fetish*, when she was just twenty-three. Her crime novels have been nominated for the Davitt and the Ned Kelly awards. She has a star on the Australian Walk of Fame: the first person so inducted for services to literature.

Not a writer to rely solely on imagination, she has toured the FBI Academy at Quantico, spent time in squad cars, morgues, prisons, labs, the Supreme Court and criminology conferences world-wide, taken polygraph tests, shot weapons, conducted surveillance, flown with the RAAF, and acquired her CAMS race driver licence. Tara recently earned her PI licence, and was set on fire by Hollywood stunt company West EFX and choked unconscious by Ultimate Fighter 'Big' John McCarthy for her research.

Born in Victoria, BC, Tara is a proud dual Australian/Canadian citizen, and divides her time between Sydney, Los Angeles and her hometown in Canada. She is a UNICEF Goodwill Ambassador, as well as an ambassador for the YWCA and the Royal Institute for Deaf and Blind Children.

Visit taramoss.com

To New Beginnings…

siren

— noun

1 a device that makes a loud prolonged sound as a signal or warning: a *police siren*.
2 *Classical Mythology.* One of several sea nymphs, part woman and part bird, who lure mariners to destruction by their seductive singing.
3 a seductively beautiful or charming woman, esp. one who beguiles men.
4 a woman who is considered alluring or fascinating but also dangerous.

Security is mostly a superstition.
It does not exist in nature.

HELEN KELLER

PROLOGUE

A brief glow peeked through the curtains, washing the crowd in crimson light, before the little theatre plunged into shadow. There were murmurs, and then renewed silence, ears straining for sounds beyond the curtain.

Shhhh ...

It was late in Paris, and the infamously unsavoury streets of Pigalle were dark, though anything but quiet. Tucked away inside the venue at the end of Rue Chaptal, the audience was fully immersed in the claustrophobic atmosphere of Le Théâtre des Horreurs. Men and women sat quietly in their seats, some holding hands, some sitting tensely with crossed arms, all overlooked by a pair of two-metre carved angels hanging above the neo-Gothic wood panelling of the interior. In the stygian darkness, the angels seemed to glow with a sickly green light, the origins of which were not clear. The theatre had once served as a church, but those gathered this night had come to find entertainment in acts of iniquity and horror, not divine solace. Rather than lighten the spirits of those present, the ghostly angels added to the sensation of a tomb-like proximity with death.

A stark spotlight hit the darkened stage, and a delicate dancer emerged into the pool of light, toe first, as if stepping into water. She was dressed in the corset, fishnet stockings and top hat of burlesque tradition, her *chapeau* set at an artful angle atop a wavy platinum-blonde wig: a nod, perhaps, to the nearby Moulin Rouge. The eyes of each silent audience member followed the fragile beauty as if mesmerised. She held aloft a painted placard, which in elaborate script declared the final ghoulish act of the evening's program:

Le Baiser Dans La Nuit

With a wink for the tourists, she turned the placard over to reveal the English title printed on the other side:

The Final Kiss

In moments the young woman had vanished, and the red velvet curtains parted. The audience found themselves peering voyeuristically at a small lounge room in the centre of which a male character — ominously bandaged from chin to forehead — sat grimly while a doctor and a nurse changed the dressings on his face. The young man's back was to the audience, fists clenched at his sides. His laboured breathing communicated wordless agony.

'I've never seen anything as appalling as these injuries,' the doctor was saying to his nurse. 'And I hope I never see anything like them again. Sulphuric acid. *Vitriol.* That's what caused this. An acid attack …'

Acid.

With the patient's back still to the audience, the extent of his wounds was left to their imagination, by now active with horror.

'They happen too often, sir,' the young nurse replied through a voice half swallowed by revulsion. She was dressed in the black-and-white uniform of her profession, a Catholic red cross emblazoned on her cap. From her unnerved expression, it was clear she was deeply troubled by the patient's appearance.

'Light … light burns my eyes,' the man complained sullenly, naked of his bandages. A number of audience members craned their necks in hope of a better view.

'It was so calculated,' the doctor continued, addressing the nurse as if his patient was not there or perhaps was not even fully human. 'Often with this kind of attack, the perpetrator throws the acid from too far away or too quickly, or they lose their nerve and their hands shake. But in this case, it was done with absolute precision.' The doctor stabbed the air with a quick, violent motion, and one could clearly imagine the acid's terrible trajectory. 'Every drop hit the intended target — Henri's face.'

The young man's hands clenched again. Still he did not turn.

'The attacker had a very cool head. Exceptionally cool,' the doctor finished.

'He wanted to maim him,' the nurse commented nervously.

'*He?*' the doctor rebuffed. 'It was a lady.'

Low murmurs rippled through the audience.

'Our patient Henri's estranged fiancée,' the doctor explained with disgust. 'Should've given her the death penalty

… a great performer in court, so I hear. She got off lightly … probably free already. He forgives her. If anything, he helped her get a light sentence.'

The nurse appeared moved. Her mouth hung open as she considered Henri's magnanimous response to his attacker. 'Love!' she declared, and looked off into the distance melodramatically, her gaze above the audience, her large eyes catching the light. 'To forgive like that! No desire for revenge. Just forgiveness! Underneath the pain, you must have great peace to forgive like that …' The admiration was clear in her voice.

Finally their patient could take no more. He moaned with discomfort, and in strained syllables begged them to hurry with the changing of his dressings, and leave him alone. They hastened their care, and eventually the door shut with a gentle click.

He was alone.

Henri struggled to his feet, swaying slightly from the effects of opium and whatever pain his drugs could not dull. He faced the audience, head heavily bandaged, with only slits for his eyes, nostrils and mouth, a look reminiscent of *The Invisible Man*. He was an image of pity and horror, simultaneously a victim and something from a nightmare. Standing before them, seemingly lost in dark thoughts, he looked to his watch and then felt for something in his dressing gown pocket. Once, twice, he checked for it, and finally held the object up to admire its quiet violence. Light revealed it to be a vial of some substance, made clear by a strain of violin to be a force of destruction. He slipped the vial back into his pocket and looked at his watch with impatience.

There was a knock at the door.

Enlivened, Henri moved across the room, then paused,

bandaged head bowed, his hand lingering above the doorknob. A laboured breath, then he turned the knob and stepped back. There emerged from the doorway an actress of startling, ageless beauty. Her presence was felt throughout the theatre, as if the collective heart of the audience began to beat faster. This was Bijou, the infamous scream queen, the face of the troupe called Le Théâtre des Horreurs. Her shoulder-length hair was ebony, and framed an exquisitely formed face of large, expressive eyes, smooth pale skin and high cheekbones. She wore a silk dress that draped elegantly over her curves, cut on the bias.

She stood rigid, reluctant to enter.

'Is it …? It is you! At last!' Henri cried, recognising Jeanne, his estranged fiancée, through his damaged sight. This was the woman responsible for his agony and disfigurement, the woman he loved so much that he had forgiven her and helped her avoid a harsh sentence despite the irreversible damage she had inflicted on him. How would it be to see her now? And how would it be for her to view her gruesome handiwork? Gently, Henri convinced the woman to enter. She took three steps in, and he closed the door.

'I'm so glad you agreed to come.'

'It's the least I could do,' she managed, her voice quavering.

'You're trembling. Am I so disgusting?'

'No, I'm cold,' she lied, eyes riveted to his bandaged face.

'If you removed my bandages you'd be horrified. People shudder when they look at me. Give me your hand. I want you to touch me … I'm a thing without form … or name. I have suffered … and I'm scared,' he told her.

'I didn't want to hurt you!' she blurted, though clearly this could not be true. She recoiled from him, and inched her way back towards the door.

'You're shaking. I can understand why. But don't worry,' Henri told her, his voice even. 'Relax.' He coaxed her away from the door and did his best to put her at ease. He asked her what she would do now that she was free.

'I don't know. Look, I need to get going. I have to see my mother. She's expecting me,' she said.

'Stay a few more minutes. I beg you. I have missed you.'

He gestured to his couch.

Jeanne sat stiffly, and Henri took a spot near her. It was she who had done this to him, and she could not even look.

Henri leaned in. 'You'd never agree, but … I want to kiss you,' he told her frankly. 'There … I've said it. *One kiss. The last time.* I'd be so happy, and I'd ask nothing else from you. You could go.' He was close to her now, only inches from her face. 'Would you let me kiss you?'

The audience shifted uncomfortably in their seats, some peeking through laced fingers.

'All right, just don't hold me so hard,' Jeanne pleaded. 'Let me go!'

'I'm going to punish you!' Henri cackled triumphantly, pulling the vial from his pocket.

There followed magnificent screams, and gasps from the audience, perverse yet familiar music to the carved angels leering overhead.

Jean-Baptiste had heard all this before.

The little troupe Le Théâtre des Horreurs performed two short Grand Guignol plays a night, interspersed with vaudeville acts, including a magician, sinister twin contortionists who doubled as actors in the plays, and a titillating burlesque dance. They were now performing the concluding scene of violence in *The Final Kiss*, and soon the shocked audience would applaud, the curtains would close, and Jean-Baptiste's lover would invite him back to her dressing room, for pleasure and carnal seduction, as she did most evenings. She was the troupe's undisputed star, *Bijou — La Femme Assassinée*, billed as 'the most assassinated woman since Paula Maxa', the darling of the Grand Guignol's heyday: variously attacked, tortured, shot, strangled, hanged, raped, devoured by a puma, electrocuted, poisoned with arsenic, whipped, stabbed, cut into pieces, executed by the guillotine, terrified by supernatural horrors or buried alive every night to the exquisite horror and morbid delight of her audience.

As Jean-Baptiste watched, the ex-lover she had disfigured was enacting his carefully planned revenge.

The final kiss.

Some in the crowd would be familiar with the gruesome 1912 play by Maurice Level, and those who were not would have sensed the nature of the horror to come. Every play in the Grand Guignol tradition promised violence; it was only a matter of *when* and *how*. Versions of the revenge tale had been performed countless times in the very same theatre back in its glory days as the Théâtre du Grand-Guignol, but, a century after the play was written, the shock value of the genre had diminished. Gone were the days when royalty would brave the wrong side of town to sneak a glimpse of the shocking performances and experience a frisson of ghoulish terror. No longer could an enterprising promoter drive the press wild by claiming to need nurses on call during the show to care for the frequently fainting audience members. To Jean-Baptiste's knowledge, no members of any royal family had snuck in to watch Bijou. No one in the audience had yet fainted.

Still, the plays retained their infamy and their power to unnerve and disturb. And most importantly for him, they were to provide his promised introduction to the stage.

Jean-Baptiste was twenty years old, and had dreamed of being an actor ever since, aged eleven, he'd attended a production of *Le Malade Imaginaire* with his parents. It had been the applause that had grabbed him — such exhilarating praise — and when the opportunity to be the one in the spotlight emerged, he had jumped at it. That it was his new lover who had encouraged him was all the more exciting. She had spotted him waiting tables at Chez Paul, and assured him he had 'the look'. He was a handsome young man, with wavy blond hair and a classic nose, and was regularly in receipt of compliments on his beauty. The first role she had in mind for him was from the play *The Ultimate Torture*, where he would have the significant role of D'Hemelin's colleague Gravier, but not many lines. Despite his dreams of fame, he had no acting experience, but his lover promised he would be eased into bigger parts, eventually taking over the lead roles, currently played by an actor named Michel, right now inhabiting the disfigured and less-than-magnanimous Henri. Michel had been a fixture with Le Théâtre des Horreurs for numerous years. Jean-Baptiste wondered if he and the rest of the troupe would accept his addition.

And so, with hopes of stardom, Jean-Baptiste waited patiently for his lover to be tortured for the pleasure of the audience, so that he might see her backstage when it was all over.

'Do you honestly think I got you here for a cosy little chat?' the disfigured Henri shouted. He had removed his bandages to reveal the full horror of his disfigurement to the horrified audience, and his even more frightened former fiancée. The effect of a simple nylon stocking and painted sponge gave his wounds a lifelike quality, the horror of which was enhanced by sickly-green stage lighting.

'… To say nice things to you? To beg you for a final kiss? You've lost all sense of reason if you think I could ever forgive you for what you did to me. I will take my revenge!' he cried, and with this held Jeanne down, triumphantly pouring the liquid from his vial directly onto her beautiful face while she thrashed violently beneath him like a wounded snake. It was an eye-for-an-eye revenge he could never have enacted had she been incarcerated for life.

'We'll be the perfect lovers … we'll be *made for each other*! You're like me now …' he declaimed maniacally.

'Like me! Like me! Like me!'

Love, it seemed, was not always beautiful.

It was well past midnight, two hours after the curtain call.

Tipsy and spent, the aspiring actor Jean-Baptiste was sent out to the streets of Pigalle to make his way home, seen off by his lover with a lingering kiss and the promise of more lovemaking to come.

'*Bonne nuit, mon chéri …*'

One foot in front of the other, the young man thought as he slid out the theatre's stage door into the narrow cobblestone street outside. *One foot in front of the other …*

Cool night air shocked his warm cheeks. The crowds for Bijou's show had long since dispersed, and the little cul-de-sac was still. There was the faint smell of perfume in the air, either hanging around his nostrils after his lover's final embrace, or wafting down from a nearby open window. He could hear the main strip still buzzing with revellers a few blocks away, near the Moulin Rouge: the rows of sex shops, brothels and the Musée de l'Érotisme. Pigalle would not settle just yet.

Jean-Baptiste's feet traced a weaving, wandering path, and it took some measure of concentration for him to stay in motion across the uneven cobblestones. Such was his absorption that when he was approached in the alley beyond the theatre, he took some time to notice he was not alone. His footsteps in his stiff new leather shoes, already irregular, were joined by other, softer soles; a lighter, quicker step. He expected them to pass, but the footsteps stopped with his.

He turned just in time to see the outline of a figure haloed in a streetlight, thin and cloaked in black.

'*Bonsoir*,' he managed to say, feeling expansive and friendly to the world in his post-coital stupor, but nonetheless confused by this unexpected company. *Do I know you?* he thought to say, but did not utter. His brain and tongue felt sluggish. He stumbled and went over, letting out an animal-like grunt of surprise, and it was some seconds after his elbows had jarred painfully against stone, breaking his fall, that he realised he had been pushed.

'Hey!' he began, but before the words left his lips, they were cut off by an excruciating burning, something like a liquid fire hitting his mouth. His instinct was to shield himself from the source of this fresh agony, but it was too late, the fire was everywhere: dark, acrid and smelling sharply of vinegar.

Choking.

Writhing on the ground, Jean-Baptiste clawed at his face and felt his palms burn as they too melted. *Acid! Just like in the play. Only this is real, this is happening.* Behind eyelids shut against a bright kaleidoscope of pain, he recalled vivid flashes of Henri's face in *The Final Kiss* — the primitive stage makeup with its appearance of festering death, layers of raw skin and exposed bone — and he knew in that moment that he was melting, his face was melting, he was becoming that thing on the stage, the creature stripped of humanity, the living monster. Screams reverberated through his body and into the alley, infinitely more jarring than the trained shrieks of his lover Bijou on her stage.

That famous scream seemed hollow now, unconvincing, a pale imitation of the shriek that emanated from the deepest part of him, shredding the passages along which it passed, from his burning lungs to the melting hole that had once been his beautiful mouth.

CHAPTER 1

To Makedde Vanderwall, the clear asphalt curves of the Federal Highway were a most welcome sight.

With her slender, leather-gloved hand, she gripped the throttle of her motorcycle, the road opening before her unsullied by snarls of traffic. Despite being weighed down by more than the usual amount of supplies, woman and motorcycle cut briskly through the air as one creature, bringing with them a satisfyingly thunderous roar. Mak had fitted her motorcycle with aftermarket pipes, and their throaty tones still excited her, no matter how many times she turned the key. It was a clear February day for her ride; the blue Australian summer sky nearly cloudless. Mak hoped that was a good omen. She needed a good omen. She had ruminated on the implications of this particular ride for many long nights, and now that she was finally making the journey, she wished only for greater certainty about her decision, and for greater luck in her future.

With adrenaline pumping from the strong coffee she'd downed to counter lack of sleep, Makedde followed the highway as it arced past Lake George, an ancient basin known by indigenous Australians as Werriwa, meaning 'bad water'. It emptied and filled in cycles, and had taken many a life through drowning when its waters were full. But today it looked to be bone dry, and it again occurred to Mak that Australia was a place of extremes. Certainly her life in Australia had been consistent with the theme.

No more extremes. No more bad luck.

When Makedde rode her motorcycle there was little room for meandering thoughts, which was precisely why she favoured it. There was much she didn't care to think about. She'd spent far too much time on painful debate, argument and the endless weighing of options. Now was a time for action.

Sharp corner, gear down, drift right, look through the turn, lean …

Makedde — or Mak, as her friends called her — executed the turn confidently, and anyone observing the young woman could not have guessed that she had not so long ago survived a stunning motorcycle crash. Her previous bike had been totalled. She was lucky to be alive. But her late mother had been fond of the old adage about 'getting back on the horse', and so Makedde had wasted no time. Her new horse was a 900cc Triumph Scrambler. At least she had given up riding twitchy sports bikes that did wheelies at intersections and required her to hunch over the petrol tank like a spider on a windshield. She now preferred what her father called 'those handsome British bikes'. Her particular handsome bike was a retro model, with knobby tires, plenty of chrome, a long flat seat and upright handle bars. It had no shortage of guts or beauty, and when she had ordered new leathers — the old ones having practically disintegrated in the crash — she had chosen black with an old-style sports stripe through the jacket, something Steve McQueen would have approved of. In fact, she would have looked just right burning down the Federal Highway wearing goggles and with a white scarf trailing behind her.

Mak's thick dirty-blonde hair wrestled free of its ponytail and blew back into tangles at her shoulders, having escaped from her stiff jacket collar. Somewhere across her consciousness danced a brief thought for the wild mess of knots she could anticipate when she dismounted in Sydney. Within her helmet, a stiff current of air came through the vents, by turns refreshing and stinging. She squinted as a speeding truck passed her, turning the air momentarily gritty and foul. It pulled her into its wake before she hunkered down and steered back into position, a touch of moisture running from her eyes to sweep back across her temples. *Moisture. Not tears.* And then the road was clear again.

Big trucks like those had once frightened her. Now, very little did.

The addiction to riding was closely linked with the sensation of complete freedom, and that palpable liberation seemed appropriate as Canberra fell away behind her, along with another of her failed romances. Makedde rode with a few valuables, her toiletries and a couple of changes of clothes quite literally strapped to her back, the rest of her belongings packed in boxes and headed for storage. It was only a four-hour ride, but this particular four hours had been a long time coming, and her sense of direction was even clearer now that she could negotiate it, smell it, ride it.

New beginnings, Makedde Vanderwall told herself, staying focused on the road. *New beginnings …*

★ ★ ★

Hours later, with the sun low in the sky on a warm Sunday evening, Makedde was exhausted, dishevelled, and smiling.

She had arrived.

With a relaxed roll of the throttle she pulled into a suburban lane in the inner-city Sydney suburb of Surry Hills, an area of warehouse conversions, and rows of terraces and brick apartment buildings with wheelie bins lined up at the kerb. She flicked her visor up and geared down, looking left and right to pinpoint the address she sought.

Loulou's place. Here it is.

Loulou was an eccentric makeup artist friend she had met in Sydney back when she was working as a fashion model. She was letting Mak stay in her apartment while she and her on–off muso boyfriend Drayson rocked out at a music festival in Byron Bay, and Mak planned to crash there for a couple of weeks while she looked for her own place. She hoped that finding a one-bedroom rental would not prove to be too tedious.

Mak pulled up to the kerb and cut the engine, flicked the stiff kickstand into position and set the heavy bike on its support. At over 180 centimetres, she swung her long limbs off the bike in one smooth and practised move, like a roundhouse kick. Grabbing hold of her full-face helmet with both hands, she tugged it off, leaving red imprints across her face in patterns like warrior paint. A mild breeze felt cool against her perspiring skin.

Mak could imagine her friend's feverish dialogue — *Darling! Sweetie! It's so good to see you!* But she was alone. Even without a welcoming party, Mak really was happy to be back. She had not realised how isolated she had been without her girlfriends, and being back in familiar Sydney reminded her of the friendships she had put on hold. 'I knew you wouldn't last long in Canberra, sweetie,' Loulou had announced on the phone when Mak told her. Perhaps she was right, but Mak had winced at her friend's comment regardless, wondering if it had been so obvious that her relationship with Andy had run its course before she had even made the move. Before her arrival, Mak had not spent time in Canberra — an ordered and visually stunning city filled with sensibly dressed public servants, overwhelmed by the presence of Parliament. All people and things had seemed unnaturally tidy to Mak, as if it were a Utopian catalogue.

Mak looked around her. There was nothing Utopian about this.

She loaded herself up with her backpack and overflowing panniers and walked towards the concrete steps of the industrial-looking apartment block, fishing the keys out of Loulou's mailbox and letting herself in. The interior hallways of the building were all polished white concrete and tall ceilings. It was stylishly lit, and struck Mak as slightly eerie in its minimalism. Mak made her way down the echoing concrete corridor on the ground floor, in search of Apartment 101. The scent of curry permeated the hallway. Someone was cooking Indian. She found the door of Loulou's apartment towards the back of the building, and let herself in. There were more polished concrete floors inside, covered with shaggy pink throw rugs. Exactly Loulou's kind of décor. There were movie posters adorning the walls: *Moulin Rouge, La Femme Nikita*.

Mak carefully put down her stuff on the floor with a strained groan, then dialled her friend to let her know she had arrived safely.

'You made it!' were Loulou's first words.

'Hi, Loulou. Thanks for letting me stay.' Her words echoed strangely through the apartment.

'Sorry I'm not there, darling. I can't wait to see you in a couple of weeks!'

But if you were here, I wouldn't have a bed.

'That's okay. I'm glad I can stay. Have fun in Byron. I'm happy things are going well for you two,' she said of Loulou's romance with Drayson.

Drayson had been the latest of Loulou's greasy-haired musician boyfriends when Mak had moved to Canberra. A week after meeting him, Loulou had packed up for Melbourne to cohabit with him, but her relocation had lasted just one tumultuous month, even worse than Mak's failure in Canberra. Loulou had lost her previous apartment thanks to that impulsive move, but had found this one after a short stint on a friend's floor. The break-up had been followed by on-and-off interstate couplings since, and things looked to have well and truly picked up again.

'I always kinda liked Drayson. He doesn't say much, but he seems sweet,' Mak admitted, although she always felt he was a bit more stoned than was helpful. 'I like the way he looks at you.'

'Oh, Mak. He is *soooooo* good in bed,' Loulou confessed. 'He does this amazing thing with his tongue —'

'Hello!' Mak jumped in. 'I don't think I need this information, but thank you. Especially as I am newly single, unless you have forgotten already.'

'Here he is … Oh, I'm being dragged away …' There were muffled sounds, and something that sounded like sucking. 'Darling … make yourself at home. Love you!'

The call ended.

Mak shook her head and smiled.

She set about taking in her temporary surroundings.

The apartment was tight, but with the tall ceiling it was more than liveable. Through large windows she could see an unkempt communal garden out the back, overwhelmed by low-lying branches, overgrown weeds and dry grass. The kitchen-cum-living room was an open space with a TV, coffee table, furry couch and a couple of stools pushed against the kitchen counter. There was more than the recommended amount of pink.

Mak moved down the short hallway that led to two doors, and pushed the right one open to find a small bedroom with a double bed, and a window looking out to the garden. A closet was bursting with Loulou's colourful outfits. She was a woman for whom neon, fishnets and all manner of synthetic fabrics were forever in fashion. Mak spotted men's shirts in one corner and a rockabilly-style jacket hanging on the closet doorhandle. There was a pair of men's pointy black shoes next to the bed. It looked like Drayson had been spending a bit of time at the apartment.

She stepped back into the hall and pushed the opposite door open. It was a bathroom of plain white tile, small enough that Mak guessed it would be possible to shower, use the toilet and brush one's teeth in the sink simultaneously.

Two weeks. Well, you'd better make yourself at home.

She returned to the bedroom, and looked the room up and down before piling Drayson's things in one corner and hers in another. There was no hanging space left in the closet, but Mak had brought only two small panniers of clothing, which amounted to little more than some T-shirts, jeans, a suit jacket and skirt, two LBDs — little black dresses — and her briefcase. She hung her nicer things carefully from the window fastener before peeling off her leathers with a sense of relief, and heading for the shower cubicle.

Mak was eager to scrub off the seven months and 288 kilometres.

You did it. You aren't going back.

An hour later, Mak found herself frowning in Loulou's living room, a cooling cup of tea in her hand. A few feet away, her bike leathers were depressingly sprawled over a plastic chair, in the form of a deflated man. She could hear echoing footsteps in rooms and hallways on floors above. A dog barked outside. Her mobile phone was ringing on the coffee table.

She ignored it.

How many moves in the past five years? Four? Five? How many more in the next five years? she wondered.

She was getting tired of her life being perpetually uprooted. This time she had packed her things in a flustered rush once she'd made the final decision to leave. She'd tried to get everything done before there was a confrontation with her lover upon his return from overseas. She didn't want a fight. She didn't want any more fighting.

Beep.

Beep.

Beep.

Mak listened to her phone's persistent cricket-like cry with a distinct lack of enthusiasm. It might have been her Sydney friend Karen Mahoney, a cop, checking in on her recent relocation. But it might be her ex-lover, Detective Senior Sergeant Andrew Flynn, who had just touched down in Australia after his latest stint at the Quantico FBI Academy. Andy was the man she had temporarily moved to Canberra to be with and precisely the one person she didn't want a call from.

No more fighting.

It rang and rang, and when finally she capitulated, it had rung out. With strained breath, Mak flipped the phone open to check, and at the sight of the name on the display, a little knot formed in her stomach.

Andy.

There would be no comfort there. Not now and never again. Mak closed her mobile phone, put it back gently on the coffee table and tried not to look at it. She tried not to imagine what she would say if she called him back. She tried not to imagine *him* — tall, dark-haired and masculine — arriving at the door and kissing her deeply.

Fuck.

He was back after a three-week trip, and part of her missed him. She had known it wouldn't be easy. Not at first. This was something she had to do, and anything worth doing was hard, wasn't it?

Beep.

Beep.

Beep.

Oh, for godsake, Andy! Leave me be!

Exasperated, Mak picked up her mobile phone and again checked the caller ID. To her surprise, it was an unlisted number. She sat cross-legged on the furry couch and gathered herself before answering, suspicious that her former lover might be calling from another number so she would answer him, and have to listen to his limp explanations.

'Yes?' Her voice was tentative.

'Mak Vanderwall?' came a familiar drawl. Only her friends knew her as 'Mak'. It was not Loulou. It didn't sound like Karen.

Mak paused, unable to exactly place the voice. Her eyes went to the windowsill, where a wind-up toy hula girl stood at rest, arms raised above her head in wait for the next opportunity to dance. 'Yes, this is Mak.'

'It didn't quite sound like you,' the familiar woman's voice purred.

Marian Wendell!

'Oh, God, you scared me. How are you? I got in not even …' she looked at her watch '… not even two hours ago.'

Marian Wendell ran a private investigation agency. Mak had done some PI work for her the previous year, and by the time she'd left there had been a little too much focus in the local papers on one particular investigation of Mak's. She now wondered if perhaps she had followed Andy Flynn to another city as much to try to save the relationship as to distance herself from the investigation and the controversy it caused.

'I was going to call you tomorrow …' Mak continued guiltily.

Marian had a new assignment for her, and right on time, too. Apparently, the client had asked for her specifically.

Makedde had previously plied her height and natural good looks in the modelling industry, catwalking around the world to pay her way through her PhD in forensic psychology. Now that she finally had her doctorate, she found it ironic that she wasn't even working in the field, which wasn't to say that psychology couldn't be useful in this new trade. Her involvement in private detective work had begun innocuously enough, with a bit of banal administrative stuff for Marian's agency, but the next thing Mak knew she was getting her Certificate III in Investigative Services and becoming one of Marian's part-time investigators. Every step she took towards starting her psychology practice seemed impeded in some way, yet investigations pulled her in like a magnet. It was not the occupation she had chosen, but it sure seemed to keep choosing her. Certainly the casual psych tutoring she had picked up at the Australian National University in Canberra had not encouraged her to find similar academic work in Sydney. Teaching a semester of 'Introduction to Methodological Design and Statistics' to first-year students was excruciatingly tedious, and not very helpful for her pocketbook.

'Nine-thirty in my office.'

'Nine-thirty? Okay,' she heard herself saying. 'Uh, Marian, who is this client who asked for me?'

'I'll see you in the morning. It's good to have you back.'

Mak hung up the phone and ran a hand through her mane of long dark-blonde hair, her fingers catching in a tangle at the ends.

Back to investigations.

CHAPTER 2

With considerable haste, Mr Nicholas Santer departed from his palatial London home at the hour of five a.m. while his wife of seventeen years slept soundly in her own bedroom, on her own floor, in a separate wing of the house. He had packed several valuable items from his private safe including £20 000 in hundred-pound notes, his father's medals and watch, and a small Rembrandt ink sketch no larger than his fist, which he hoped to sell on the black market.

He had not bothered to say goodbye.

Nearly twenty-four hours and over 1000 kilometres later he was snoring in a rustic farmhouse south of the town of Vézelay, France, his dreams assisted by a now empty bottle of fine cognac. As the bottle from his impressive cellar had been steadily drained, so also his worries and strain had dissipated, along with the feeling in his limbs, his lips, his face. He was tingling and warm by the time he nodded off, stretched out on a couch he barely remembered buying years before, surrounded by white dust covers, a half-unpacked case and an overflowing ashtray of cigarette butts that he could no longer see through the blur across his eyes. His 52-year-old body slumped in inebriated rest, but even in his dreams his mind was active with worry. He imagined himself in a huge wine barrel, running like a mouse on a wheel, a heavy briefcase of money in his hand. In his nightmare everything depended on him running and never stopping.

Running … running …

A bead of acrid sweat rolled down his temple.

With distaste, the man watched the bead of sweat move down Santer's face. Santer did not realise it, but he was not alone.

The sweat was puzzling to the man who stood silently over the snoring, sweating, murmuring Santer. The room was not particularly warm; in fact, it was winter in Burgundy, and the old farmhouse felt like an icebox, not a sweatbox. It had been no colder in Russia, his last stop.

Santer let out a grating snore, and at this Mr Hand squinted.

Luther Hand had found him easily. One of the things he specialised in was finding people. And what he did to the people he found paid very handsomely. For five or six figures, Mr Hand — Luther, or 'The hands of Lucifer' as he was sometimes called — would remove from the food chain any politician, policeman, dignitary or despot, witness, waitress or lover, troublesome competition or troublesome colleague his client nominated. He was what the industry called a 'cleaner'. He cleaned up problems for anyone with pockets deep enough to pay for his services. His job was simply to follow instructions, and to remain invisible. As a cleaner — a hitman — he was adept at delivering death using knives, axes, blunt instruments, rope, poison and chemicals. He had fine firearm skills at close and middle range. His sniper skills were excellent. He had successfully staged fatal drownings, robberies, suicides and accidents, and had also arranged terminations where the hit appeared precisely what it was — to make a point. He was a flexible and near flawless operator, unfussed by codes that restricted others to eliminating only male targets, or members of particular 'organisations'. He did not belong to any crime family. He had no loyalties. He did business, and that was all it was. He was professional, unattached and virtually untraceable, and anyone on his list, whether man, woman or child, would be dispatched efficiently, and according to any special instructions. With these attributes, Luther Hand had gained a reputation over six years as a valuable and successful component of the international crime community.

Generally, Hand was one or two closely guarded steps removed from the client he served. They never met him, and it was not his job to ask why the names ended up on his list. More often than not, he received background on the individual mark, but he did not require reasons for the call upon his services. This mark was different, however. Santer had pissed off an impressive number of ruthless people, and had come to the attention of more than a few members of Luther's trade. If it had not been Luther, it would have been someone else cutting his throat that night.

Luther adjusted his latex gloves, gripped Santer's floppy chin in one steady hand, and drew the sharpened blade of a hunting knife across his neck from his right ear to his left. The mark was so drunk that his body barely flinched at the intrusion of the blade. There was a gurgling sound as the trachea opened up and air rushed out. In seconds, torrents of blood flowed from the wound and down his chest. The cut was deep, and the skin sagged as it hung open, giving the dead man the look of a fleshy jack-o'-lantern, head thrown back against the couch cushions, a giant, oversized red smile slick across his neck. Luther briefly thought of pulling the tongue through the wound to create a 'Colombian Neck-Tie', as it was called. But he didn't see any reason to bother with such flashy creations. It was not in his instructions, and if he did everything properly, there should never be anyone to witness his handiwork with this mark. Instead, he set to work transferring the body to the garage for the next vital stage. Mr Santer needed to disappear, something he had not so successfully achieved in his living moments, and so Luther's work was not over yet. He spent the next hour focused on the task of dismembering the mark over thick sheets of plastic in the garage next to his new car, a maroon BMW, with bright yellow British plates. It, too, would need to disappear. When the body was dissected into enough pieces — eighteen in all — it fitted into a chest. Luther locked it and by torchlight buried it in the back garden amongst the dead flowers.

It was early morning when Luther stripped the BMW of its books, plates and valuables, and drove it to nearby Vézelay. The black-market dealer was waiting for him at the edge of town at six. He was Italian and Luther had dealt with him before. He counted the notes carefully. The transaction was quick, and in minutes Luther had ten thousand euros in cash. The serial numbers would be filed off Santer's car, the paint changed, perhaps even the interior. Untraceable, the new car would be resold to an Italian businessman for four times what Luther was paid for it, still somewhat less than its retail value. He returned to the farmhouse and gathered up the valuables Santer had fled with. They were best hidden on the property for now. It would not do to travel with such easily traceable items. He replaced the dust covers in their original positions, cleaned up the blood and superficial evidence of recent activity, and closed the place up.

It was a beautiful area, he reflected.

Remote.

Luther might like to return to such a place, if ever he found someone to share time with. Perhaps he could send his mother to a place like this. There would be many cottages and farmhouses in the area, all of them affordable to a man of Luther's means. But he couldn't be sure his mother would even recognise him. Or accept him. She lived in Australia, where he had grown up. She had not seen him in years. But she would like a place like this, wouldn't she? She had been on his mind a lot lately.

Luther stepped out into the fresh air, showered, cleaned and satisfied with his work. Without a tip-off, Santer would not likely be found for some time. There was no one alive who'd be the least bit interested in getting in touch with the authorities regarding his absence. Scotland Yard would be left to their own devices, having to search every one of Santer's nine properties that stretched from the Bahamas to the English countryside. He doubted they would care that much. And if they did, and if he was found, no one would be very surprised that he had met a grisly end. He'd certainly seemed to be asking for it.

The client would be pleased to know that Santer had taken a permanent vacation. He would let his agent, Madame Q, know the job was done. With something like the contentedness of job satisfaction, Luther turned on his phone and sent the agreed message to signal the success of another job.

COMPLETE.

He had a message waiting on his phone, and it was not from Madame Q, but from a hired contact in Australia.

At the sight of the name, his countenance changed. His throat tightened.

URGENT NEWS ABOUT CATHY DAVIS, the message said. CALL ME.

CHAPTER 3

Running ... she was running as fast as she physically could. Running ... muscles burning ... *I must save her!*

Mak wore a uniform, a police uniform, but it was too big for her and the arms and legs were long like an unbound straitjacket, cuffs dragging across the ground of her dreamscape, tripping up her feet. It was her father's police uniform. 'Mom!' she tried to say, and the word came out like her own name, and bounced from the edges of the surreally lit corridor, echoing back into her ears again and again, fading. *MAK ... Mak ... mak ... mak ...* Room 101. She had arrived. Mak broke into the hospital room, door flying off its hinges in a flash of splinters. Inside, the room looked like a bedroom in a cabin. It was familiar. *Horrible.* A hospital bed stood at its centre. Her mother, Jane, was strapped to the bed, wrapped in tubes that moved in and out of her nose and mouth and twined themselves around her limbs. She was still alive. For a too-brief moment Mak felt a weight lifted. She was in her mother's presence. *Jane Vanderwall. Mom.* But there was another figure in the room. A man stood over her mother with a scalpel. He did not hold it as a surgeon would; he held it like an icepick, ready to drive it down. *I must stop him!* Mak was just in time, and she tried to get the gun, but her arms were useless. The straitjacket was tied, and she wriggled uselessly like a worm, wrestling with herself, frustrated, impotent.

A strange moan escaped her lips, and the man with the scalpel turned to look at her.

He was grinning blood.

Mak knew his face. It was Damien Cavanagh.

Mak woke on Loulou's mattress with a gasp, exposed and short of breath. At some point during the previous hours of restless sleep — shifting in the dark and missing the distant sensation of a warm male body next to her — she had remembered that the boxer shorts she wore had once belonged to Andy, and had tossed them aside as if they were cursed. Now her naked body was slick with a sickly sweat, sheets pushed down and twisted around her ankles. Her heart pulsed like a drum.

Mom.

Makedde folded her knees up to her chest.

Damien Cavanagh.

She turned on her left side.

Andy.

Now she was face down, body positioned like a rock-climber, one knee up near her chest and the other straight, a hand extended to touch the cool wall.

A shiver.

Her head was abuzz with thoughts of her failed romance, and the failed, dangerous case she had been involved with before leaving Sydney. *Andy.* She shifted and sighed. *The*

Cavanaghs. Mak finally rose, and paced the small bedroom a few times, then returned to bed, stretching herself across the mattress like a starfish, her long limbs reaching from corner to corner. Loulou's alarm clock glowed the early hour of 4.53 a.m., which seemed painfully uncivilised. There was nothing helpful about being awake at this time. She was not being productive, and she would feel horrible in the morning for her meeting with Marian.

Close your eyes.

Sleep.

But her mind was too active. Sleep would not come.

There was one sure-fire way to clear her mind, and it did not involve staring at the ceiling. At a quarter past five Mak crept into the basement garage of the apartment building, where she'd shifted her Triumph after unpacking. She was clothed in a full set of dark leathers, helmet in hand.

This is the way to reacquaint myself with Sydney.

She threw the silver cover off her bike and put the key in the ignition, pulled the choke out and started it up, filling the garage with a thunderous roar and the fumes of her exhaust. After a short while she pushed the choke back in, and the engine began idling nicely. It was satisfyingly loud. She belatedly hoped she hadn't woken anyone on the lower floors. She zipped up her black leather motorcycle jacket to the collar, pulled her helmet on and flicked the visor closed. Now warm, the bike rolled off the kickstand willingly.

Ah, Sydney streets at night … It had been a while.

After midnight the city streets opened up. It was a motorcyclist's dream: the city without cars, the roads welcoming and free, the occasional headlights in the far distance on long roads. Freedom.

She pulled out of the garage and headed in the direction of the CBD. It was, as she'd expected, a corporate ghost town. The buildings in the central city were modern rectangular monoliths — many forty or fifty floors apiece — their windows now but dimly lit. Streetlamps lined empty footpaths where businesspeople would begin gathering again in a couple of hours. Mak ripped across the bitumen on her sleek machine, crossing white lines at will, leaning into corners, the wheels gripping the road as if they had claws. George Street, Elizabeth Street, Macquarie … She circled near the giant white shells of Utzon's Opera House, beautifully lit up, as an icon ought to be at any hour. A security man stepped out of his booth to peer at her. With a roll of the throttle she was back up the road, then passing the wharves of Woolloomooloo, boats bobbing up and down, water shimmering in moonlight. She slowed through Kings Cross, still abuzz with groups of revellers at that late hour. Neon lights glowed, spruikers invited groups of men into their strip clubs, and revellers exited nightclubs to stagger home via the kebab shop. A thin woman in very high shoes and an even higher hem swayed and beckoned to passers-by. Mak flicked her visor up to take in the sights and sounds, then kept on her way.

Gradually her tension disappeared into the play of throttle and gears, the sound of her engine and the feeling of the wind through her helmet. Makedde sped through the dark streets, content in her concentration. She found a good pace down Kings Cross Road, and made a little detour to Kellett Street, where, she'd read, a bloody showdown of razors and guns had occurred in 1929 between the rival gangs of underworld queens Kate Leigh and Tilly Devine. *Prostitution. Prohibition-*

era booze. Tonight, a few scantily clad women with hard faces loitered about neon doorways. No blood on the streets. She turned her bike and headed out past Rushcutters Bay Park, picking up pace again. Her bike flew along the streets, not planning her path, and when she reached the hill on New South Head Road she geared down.

Go on.

Darling Point. She was being pulled towards it. And there could only be one reason for that. She turned onto Darling Point Road, passing the former home of Nicole Kidman, and the gate where a bug had notoriously been discovered, supposedly planted by a paparazzi photographer to monitor the movie star's comings and goings. Mak rode slowly past the homes of Sydney's sleeping multi-millionaires, and before long she saw the familiar high stone wall and gates of the Cavanagh house. She geared down to second, then to first, her bike purring between her legs.

The Cavanaghs.

The Cavanaghs were one of the most powerful, rich and influential families in Australia. And they had ended up being the focus of Mak's last investigation. Her failed investigation.

Frowning, she imagined them sleeping soundly on Egyptian cotton sheets in their safe, luxurious abode while others took the blame for the deaths of those who got in their way. The Cavanagh heir, Damien, still lived in his parents' palatial home. Born into all that money, he wouldn't have to worry about things like rent, like making a living, abiding the law …

His powerful father protected him, and it seemed there was little anyone could do about it.

Perhaps.

Makedde drifted in slow circles with the engine purring low, and then braked directly across the street from the front gates of the property. She could not see the house over the stone walls, but she knew it well. She had bluffed her way inside Damien Cavanagh's swanky thirtieth birthday party there shortly before everything had spilled onto the front pages of the papers, and before her departure to Canberra for doomed love and temporary escape. To fake her way in, all it had taken was some cubic zirconia, a chauffeur-driven luxury car and a couture gown with a distractingly high split. It had probably helped that she could still pass herself off as a supermodel if she needed to; she would use those looks where necessary while she still had them. Looking the part had worked to get her in, but had also got her spotted by the wrong people among those hundreds of rich and influential guests — people who wanted her dead. The fireworks, the expensive champagne, the long corridors bedecked with priceless artwork — it had been the opulence she had expected, and more. But it was no better than a very salubrious crime scene, and that birthday party had feted a sick young man who'd managed to successfully avoid being charged with sex crimes, drug possession, murder and perverting the course of justice. Few, if any, of the guests could have known that, of course.

Mak knew.

There was a lot Mak knew.

'*These are very powerful people, Mak. You can't just go accusing them of murder.*'

Andy, her cop ex-boyfriend, had defended the way the police were handling the case. That was ridiculous. How much evidence did the police need?

The Cavanaghs were protected, and not just by the high walls surrounding their luxurious home. They had their power, their influence and their teams of lawyers and spin doctors. Mak would like nothing more than to bring them down. She just wished there was a way.

Something will come, something … Something will slip …

They could not be impenetrable forever.

Mak snapped her visor shut and sped home through the dark Sydney streets, feeling no greater pull to the arms of Morpheus than she'd had before she'd left.

Hours later, Mak was on a bus bound for Marian's office, eyes puffy, stifling a yawn.

She crossed and uncrossed her legs impatiently, tugged on her pencil skirt so it would cover her kneecaps, and tapped her pointy stiletto absent-mindedly. Instead of reading her paperback, she was fidgeting with her nails, staring blankly out the window, wrestling with the adaptations necessary for her new life.

Her prime reason for staying in Australia was no longer a going concern, but she was not sure she wanted to return to Canada, the country of her birth. And she was about to be drawn back into PI work, despite her intention to become a forensic psychologist. This wasn't what she'd had in mind for her life, but she'd always been adaptable enough to use the opportunities that came her way. *Maybe just a few jobs with Marian and I'll apply for that job at Long Bay Correctional, and make a career for myself there?* Mak didn't yet have enough money saved to open her own practice, a situation her stint in Canberra had not improved. That meant scraping together some extra cash working for Marian, or going back to her old model agency to try to drum up some catwalk or photographic jobs. But imagining walking into Book Model Agency gave her a rush of insecurity. Modelling was increasingly unlikely work for her, she knew. Despite the politically correct sound bites of those in the fashion industry, models over twenty-five were not in demand unless they were already famous brands, like Kate Moss or Elle Macpherson. In Australia Mak might arguably be *infamous* in some circles, but she was certainly not famous. Being snapped on the courthouse steps was not exactly good for one's portfolio.

Ugh. Body odour.

Someone's smell drifted up to her nostrils and Mak rubbed her nose. *Terrible.* She had opted to take public transport so she could wear something businesslike for her reintroduction to Marian Wendell, instead of her tomboyish motorcycle leathers. Already she wondered why it had seemed important to dress up. Marian knew her well enough. Perhaps after her hiatus she wanted to feel like she was 'going to work', the way normal people did.

Who was she kidding? She was anything but normal.

As if to emphasise the point, Mak felt plastic brush against her bare elbow, and her edgy survival instincts kicked in. But it was only a silver-haired woman manoeuvring her shopping bags next to her. *No threat there.* In seconds the bus braked, and she was pulled a few centimetres across the seat towards the woman's shopping before the vehicle came to rest and let a new passenger on. It was an odd-looking man. He wore his few strands of hair in a greasy comb-over, and had on a woolly turtlenecked sweater with a pilled business suit, a choice that seemed more than a little out of place for the warm Sydney weather. Had he been wearing a long coat, she might have ducked for cover. In Mak's experience, people wearing long coats in summer generally harboured weapons. As it was, she watched the man in the periphery of her vision as she pretended to read her novel. He walked past her and took a seat nearby. His appearance made her uneasy.

You are paranoid.

The doors of the bus hissed closed with a familiar hydraulic sound, enough of a sensory cue to temporarily transport her back to her early twenties, to New York City, hearing that same hydraulic sound as she fought a horrible man with a similar penchant for comb-overs to the man on the bus. She had been living in a model's apartment in a modern high-rise, and arrived home from a shoot to notice someone dressed in a tracksuit near the bell panel. The instant she unlocked the glass lobby door to go inside, the man leaped on her, groping her breasts and trying to push into the building. Self-defence classes had taught her well, and she shouted with all her might and smashed her umbrella into him like a nightstick. But he persisted, and each time she managed to get him back outside the doorway — beating his prying hands out of the way with her umbrella — she would try to slam the door closed, and instead hear that horrible hydraulic hiss, the door fighting against her urgency. Mak and her attacker struggled violently for what seemed like five full minutes before she managed to close the maddeningly slow hydraulic door, finding safety in the lobby on the other side of that locked pane of glass, exhausted and in shock.

You are a psycho-magnet.

Thankfully the past several months, though emotionally trying, had not offered up any fresh psycho-magnet stories. But she wondered how much longer this respite from the bizarre would last.

'Hey … you're that woman from the papers, aren't you?' came a male voice.

Mak looked up. It was comb-over man. She had sensed that he would be a problem. She really didn't wish to engage with him, especially as she was trapped, at least until the next stop.

'It *is*. I thought it was you,' the man persisted, pleased with his discovery. He continued to stare at her, expecting a response. He had caught the attention of several other passengers, who were now doing the same.

Though seemingly crazy, the man had recognised her from the press coverage of the Cavanagh case. Her involvement had been widely reported in Sydney, she knew, but she had hoped people would have forgotten. Didn't they say it was 'today's news and tomorrow's fish 'n' chips wrapper'? She'd hoped that the better part of a year would have made it all blow over. Evidently not. Not in the mind of the public, and certainly not in her own mind. The Cavanaghs had not left her thoughts. Or her early-morning motorcycling routes …

Outside the bus windows she recognised the buildings near Marian Wendell's investigation agency. Frankly, her stop could not come too soon. She took the opportunity to stand and move away from her unwanted inquisitor.

'Yeah, you're that private eye chick,' the man said to her back as Mak stood waiting impatiently for the doors to open. 'I reckon those rich people did it,' he added. 'You can just *tell* they're guilty.'

Makedde stiffened.

Guilty. Yes they are. I know they are.

She disembarked with her head down. 'You must have me confused with someone else,' she lied, more for the benefit of the other passengers than for the strange man who had clearly pegged her. She felt eyes on her as she stood at the kerb and the doors of the bus closed with that hideous hiss.

Next time you'll ride over on your own wheels, under the anonymous shield of a helmet, she promised herself. But if she was going to work for Marian, she needed a car.

Mak waited for the traffic to clear, mentally shaking off the encounter. The bus dawdled away down the busy street, and she stood alone on the side of the road near Bondi Junction, looking across to the three-storey, seventies-built concrete box that had been Marian's office building for decades. The traffic eased and she dashed across clutching her black leather purse to her shoulder, stiletto heels clicking on the uneven surface. Despite her reservations about returning to investigation work, a smile found the corners of her mouth as she pushed the lobby door open and stepped inside. It seemed she had missed the place more than she'd thought. The old office block was a thing of curious, kitsch beauty, from the over-abundance of brown and yellow tones right down to the faux wood panelling in the lobby. It was a feast of tacky 1970s delights. In the seven months since her last visit to Marian, the rather tired green-and-yellow carpet had been replaced with something in an inoffensive modern grey. Perhaps no one made reams of yellow and green diamond-patterned carpet any more.

The old lift took its sweet time, as always, but soon enough she arrived at Marian's agency on the second floor. She read the words on the door, and took a deep breath.

MARIAN WENDELL INVESTIGATION AGENCY
PROFESSIONAL PRIVATE INVESTIGATIONS

Here goes.

A chiming bell announced Makedde's arrival. She let herself in and closed the door behind her.

'Be there in two minutes,' came a familiar and immediate shout from the main office down the hall.

Mak located one of the spy cameras and gave it the thumbs up for her boss's benefit. She was aware that the offices were fitted out with all kinds of surveillance equipment, and that Marian could watch everyone entering or leaving from the comfort and safety of her desk chair.

The carpeting outside may have changed, but nothing inside the investigation offices had, not even the magazines in the waiting room, many of which were now several years out of date. *The Australian Women's Weekly*, *Woman's Day* and *National Geographic* respectively boasted stories on Olivia Newton-John's personal life, Angelina Jolie's 'shocking!' weight loss and the plight of radio-tagged deforestation-tracking tarantulas. There was even an old, dog-eared cover of a fresh-faced Princess Diana, smiling with her prince. Mak was sure she'd already read every page of every story during previous visits to the waiting room, so she left the glossies alone, and picked up a section of the local paper.

Jack Cavanagh.

She blinked. A metal taste rose in the back of her throat.

Jack Cavanagh was the patriarch of one of Australia's richest and most powerful families — the very same family the stranger on the bus could just 'tell' was guilty. The Cavanaghs were unavoidable in Sydney, influential as they were. They owned buildings, real estate, businesses and media. In this instance, Jack Cavanagh was pictured doing a deal on the front page of the business section.

Mak's eyes narrowed, anger rushing to the surface of her thoughts.

'Don't look at that,' Marian Wendell snapped at her.

Mak dropped the paper like a reprimanded puppy, and got to her feet. 'Whatever do you mean?'

'I'm serious, young lady. You'll want to steer clear of them,' Marian warned her, looking stern. 'It's good that you've been out of town for a while, and out of their way.'

Mak recovered herself. 'Well,' she said, 'it feels kind of good to be back, I have to say.'

Marian Wendell smiled inscrutably.

The older woman was a vital sixty-something, and could cheat the years when she wanted to, which was always. She had a helmeted mane of auburn hair that would do any country singer proud, and though her clothes were a touch outdated, they were expensive and well tailored. Her days of skulking around filthy back alleys to get information for her clients were a distant memory. Today she looked businesslike in a midnight blue suit with a striped silk blouse, the bow oversized and elegantly covering her neck. Mak was glad she'd made the effort to look presentable herself. For a woman of diminutive physical size, Marian could be formidable. She wielded great influence in her field, and certainly she had Mak's respect, though her agency was by no means one of Australia's biggest. Such titles were left to the giant corporate investigation companies that dealt in big-money cases — insurance fraud, corporate espionage. Marian managed to earn a good living in her less glamorous niche of deadbeat dads and cheaters. Female clients were unquestionably her strong point. There were a lot of women out there who wanted a 'private dick without the dick', so to speak.

'It's good to see you,' Mak continued.

She couldn't resist giving her boss a hug and air-kissing her neatly on both sides of her face in the European style, as had become her habit after years of working as a model in Paris and Milan. In this case the friendly gesture required considerable stooping. Marian, birdlike next to Mak's exaggerated Scandinavian proportions, looked up at her for a moment after their embrace, and Mak imagined her thinking that this odd young investigator of hers was some kind of giant albatross.

'Come on,' Marian said, starting towards her office.

'You know, some of your magazines are getting pretty old,' Mak commented as they walked down the hall. 'I can pick up some new ones for you if you like.'

'Don't bother. Nothing ever changes.'

Mak laughed. 'Well, actually, Marian, you have one of Diana there that is decades old already. A lot has changed since that happy little cover photo was taken.'

They'd arrived at the investigator's office. 'Faces and names change, but the story is always the same,' the older woman replied, deadpan. Mak wondered if she was serious.

Certainly nothing had changed in the personal offices of Marian Wendell. The handsome Art Deco nymph was still positioned on its square display table in front of Marian's prized painting depicting the Rainbow Serpent of the Aboriginal Dreamtime. The crystal vase was stocked with fresh yellow roses. The ceramic aromatherapy oil-burner was doing its soothing work from the corner of Marian's wide desk. The rows of filing cabinets were still stuffed with past cases, some of them quite colourful from what Mak had heard, and neat files covered every surface. Naturally, the photo of Marian's beloved late husband, Reg, still took pride of place in the room. Reg had been somewhat older than his bride, and had passed away a full two decades earlier. He had been her intellectual match, Marian had once confided — a true soul mate — although Mak wondered if such things existed. Though it had been twenty years, Marian had never remarried. Marian's personal life, like her office and her wardrobe, was an immaculately kept time capsule.

'Take a seat.'

Mak did. She looked out the window and then at the painting, and finally at the floor. She fidgeted with her hands.

Ah yes, time for the post-mortem.

Mak found herself uncharacteristically nervous, anticipating a brutal dissection of all that had gone wrong in Canberra. She had procrastinated about telling Marian that she was coming back to Sydney, and Marian no doubt knew that. She had not felt ready to explain things, she supposed. Not until she was on that open road and riding away.

Mak gazed determinedly at the Sydney cityscape outside Marian's window, inwardly bracing herself.

'Where are things at between you and the cop?'

Andy.

'It's over,' Mak said with resolve, not looking at her interrogator.

Marian had guessed. She paused, watching Mak swallow heavily. 'Good then. I'm glad you're back,' she continued, and, after another beat, cut to the point. 'The case I have for you involves a missing person.'

'Okay,' Mak blurted, relieved by the change of subject. She could hardly believe she'd got off so easy.

'It's a legit case.'

'Great,' she said, again too fast.

All of Marian's cases were legit, but she always let Mak know she had checked into them. It was one of her important rituals. Checking the legitimacy of a client searching for someone was a very real issue in investigation work. Some people had good reasons for disappearing. Countless obsessed ex-lovers and angry loan sharks tried to enlist a third party to find their victims for them … victims who sometimes ended up dead.

'The subject is a young man. Your client is his mum.' Marian took a file from a stack next to her, put it in the centre of her desk and placed both hands on it thoughtfully. 'He's a teenager,' she went on, closing her eyes as she often did when recalling information. 'Well, he's nineteen. Still lives at home. Name is Adam Hart. It's been nearly a week and there's been no sign of him. His mother is concerned, so she called us.'

Mak took out her notepad and at the top of a fresh page wrote the name ADAM. 'Surname spelled with an EA or —'

'No E,' she was told.

ADAM HART

'Your client contact is Mrs Glenise Hart. I've made an appointment for you to see her this afternoon.'

Makedde nodded. 'Single mum?'

'Widow,' Marian explained.

After a beat, Mak asked the obvious. 'You said on the phone that she asked for me specifically. Do you know why? How did she hear of me?'

Marian seemed strangely unprepared for the question. A thought flickered behind her amber eyes. 'Why wouldn't a client ask for you?'

It was clear evasion.

'I see,' Mak said. She frowned as her mind ran through scenarios. 'So … she asked for me …' She paused, hoping for more, but her boss was not biting. The old 'finish my sentence for me' trick was one that a surprising number of people fell for, but Marian, of course, could not be so easily led. Mak decided to drop the subject for the moment. 'Are there any known risk factors associated with this boy? Depression? Drug use?'

'Mrs Hart described him as introverted, but was adamant he was not suicidal. And thankfully he hasn't shown up in a hospital emergency room or at the bottom of The Gap.' *The Gap*. Sydney's most notorious suicide spot. 'She insists he would never do drugs, and she thinks he doesn't even drink.' Marian relayed this last bit of information with a touch of incredulity. Few parents would want to imagine their child experimenting, but that hardly meant that drugs or alcohol weren't factors. One thing that private investigation work illuminated was the staggering amount of deception within families. It was frightening what parents did not know.

'What do we know so far?' Mak prompted.

Marian's eyes closed again. 'His pushbike is missing, as is his wallet.'

Bike. Wallet. Frankly, this sounds like a very boring case, Mak thought.

'I don't suppose his toothbrush is also missing …' Mak added cheekily.

'This one's not necessarily that easy.'

But it probably is. 'Does he own a car?'

'No car. No licence.'

There would likely be no listed property for someone his age, and with no car to trace it looked like Mak was going to have to do a lot of door knocking. 'I assume a formal report has been filed with the police already?' she said.

'Yes. Apparently Mrs Hart reported it last week.'

'Right.' Mak wondered if the police had any good leads, and who she might casually ask about it. Not Andy, that was for sure, and his former police partner Jimmy Cassimatis would probably not be of much help either. Thankfully, she had other friends in the force, if it became necessary.

Marian pushed the file across to Mak. 'Your instructions and info.' She leaned back in her chair and let out a tiny, elegant sigh. 'Somehow I can't imagine the cops committing much time to this. Twenty-two people go missing in this state every day. This boy is not underage, not high-risk. He has no record. He hasn't been caught up in any crimes or foul play in the past.'

Marian was right, of course.

'I've arranged for you to see Mrs Hart around three.'

'Thanks.' Mak wished she felt more enthusiastic. She needed the money, but the idea of door knocking to find an errant nineteen-year-old seemed like pretty dull stuff.

'Do you have a car?' her boss asked.

A car would be more convenient for transport than her beloved motorcycle, and certainly would be a more realistic option for any surveillance that might eventuate. Private investigation work often involved sitting patiently with tightly crossed legs in a car with the lights off and the window rolled down.

'No car.'

'I'll get Sarah to organise one.' Her assistant.

'Nothing too bright this time, please.'

The last rental the agency had organised had been bright orange, which was not a colour particularly good for blending in. Magnum PI's red Ferrari would never have been good for blending in either, but that was television for you.

Mak became aware that Marian was watching her face carefully.

'You're a good investigator, despite the reservations you have about it.'

She opened her mouth to defend herself, but said nothing. She would not bother trying to deny it.

'Be thorough with your notes and procedures in case this one turns out to be a criminal matter,' Marian cautioned her, perhaps sensing Mak's confidence that Adam Hart was a standard runaway. 'I hope this kid's all right, but ... we don't know that yet.'

Makedde stood. 'I will.'

'And try to stay away from *him*.' *Andy*. 'You gave him his second chance already. It's time for you to move on.'

She smiled. Only Marian would be so bold as to offer personal advice to someone as stubborn as Mak. Mak performed a mock salute in response and left Marian to her files.

'And stay away from those other people too,' Marian added when Mak was halfway down the hall. 'They are no business of yours ...'

The Cavanaghs.

Don't worry about that, Mak thought as she stepped into the hall.

And wondered.

CHAPTER 4

Four Rolls-Royce Trent 900 engines propelled a hulking A380 Airbus through clear skies far above the Indian Ocean.

Inside the aircraft, over four hundred passengers slept soundly with their blindfolds, travel socks and trays of food, imagining through twitches of sleep their touchdown in Australia. At the front of the plane, one man sat awake and alone in his first-class suite, head bent solemnly. His shoulders were nearly too wide for the fold-down bed, his size forever an issue, and for the moment he sat up in his seat with his eyes closed, awake and pensive. His muscled and knotted form felt even heavier than usual, his neck as stiff as steel. A light but constant headache had plagued him since boarding at Heathrow. Though he was in his late thirties, and considered himself worldly, he was wrestling with his first experience of true grief.

Luther Hand had lost his mother.

He would soon be arriving in Sydney, a place of personal significance. It was the place of Luther's birth, the place of his transformation from boy to man, and man to killer. He had all but left Australia behind him since, reducing it to little more than a fragment of a humble hidden past he did not discuss and avoided reflecting upon. His failures were there, the realities of his humble beginnings were there, and now, with his mother gone, he would have no reason to return. The last of his real past would have turned to ashes, slipping forever into the unknown; the only woman who ever loved him, gone. His trusted contact in Sydney had been the one to inform him of his loss. Even he had not known Luther's true relationship to Cathy Davis — only that Luther left money for her every month. According to his contact, she had returned to her Redfern apartment with her groceries, and tripped on her porch, cracking her skull open on a garden gnome. The thought filled Luther with anguish and a sense of regret and failure.

His mother had not yet turned sixty, but had suffered the health of someone much older. She had lived hard in her youth. Luck had been a stranger to her.

Mum.

Sydney was also the location of Luther's only failed contract of the past six years, and the circumstances and target of that failed job came to the forefront of his thoughts as he prepared for arrival. The target had been, of all things, a beautiful woman. He had underestimated her resourcefulness and luck. She did not know him and had never seen his face, but he knew her well, and regarded her with special interest. The enigma of the one hit who had escaped him seemed to loom profoundly as the plane hurtled towards the geographical place of their encounters, where it had been his job to follow her and, later, to kill her. They had scuffled in a darkened hall, a messy exchange. And he had soon after witnessed her crash her motorcycle to what should have been her death: a clean kill for his client, attributable to mere accident, no one to blame, no investigation. But this unusual woman had survived.

She had broken Luther's nose with her motorcycle helmet. He had not bothered to have it fixed.

Makedde Vanderwall.

Luther wondered where she was now, and if ever chance would have their paths cross again.

CHAPTER 5

Jimmy Cassimatis was gnawing anxiously on the end of a warm Mars bar, and gripping a styrofoam cup of coffee, postponing the inevitable. That morning a couple of boring cases were sitting on the detective senior constable's desk — a burglary at some rich guy's house in Macleay Street; a fatal hit-and-run. But the visit he was about to make was in relation to an older case.

A death knock.

Not one person in the department liked to be stuck with a death knock. There was no gratification in informing a member of the public that their loved one was dead. And Jimmy, who for all his long years in the department regularly pulled the short straw, was two blocks from the address where he would have to tell a Madeline O'Connor that her missing husband, Warwick, was dead. And this death knock was going to be particularly ugly. There had been somewhat of a bungle in forensics.

Skata. Fucking forensic fuck-ups …

With that death knock but minutes away, Detective Cassimatis was more than happy for the distraction of this phone call from his mate and former police partner, Senior Sergeant Andrew Flynn.

'Well if it isn't the big shot,' Jimmy drawled into his mobile phone. 'I wondered if I'd hear from you this *year* …'

Jimmy hadn't heard from Andy in weeks, not counting an amusing postcard sent from the Quantico Marine Base in Virginia, the town just outside the FBI Academy where he'd been holed up in some kind of exchange program with the FBI. The postcard pictured a smiling blonde pin-up straddling an aircraft gun, Hanoi-Jane-style, wearing nothing but a pair of brief stars-and-stripes hotpants with two superimposed red stars demurely covering her impressive DD bare breasts at the nipple. Just the kind of postcard Jimmy appreciated. WISH YOU WERE HERE, the caption said. Well, that was exactly what Jimmy wished. Especially now. He kept the postcard in the squad car glove compartment, and occasionally referred to it using an improvised double entendre or two in an attempt to induce some personality in his new police partner, Rhys. *She could blow me … away … with those weapons of mass destruction.* So far, these attempts had not worked.

'Mate, it is so good to hear from you,' he said, meaning every word.

'I can't talk long,' Andy interrupted him. 'I'm just on the highway …' The phone was crackly and Jimmy cupped his ear with one meaty hand to better hear his friend's voice. It was the same hand that was holding the Mars bar, and a bit of melted chocolate smeared his neck like a wound. 'Any chance I can crash at your place tonight?' Andy was asking.

Jimmy had made the words out fairly clearly over the din of traffic and static, but he was mighty surprised to hear them. 'Of course, mate. Of course. You're always welcome at our house. I'll let the missus know.' She would spew at him about the late notice, but she liked Andy, so he hoped she wouldn't whinge too hard. 'It can be a bit loud with the little ones, but you are most welcome.'

Jimmy was delighted he would see his friend and former partner in person again after so many months, but he was confused. Andy had moved on to a bigger job. It was Federal. He was now an important figure at the serial crime unit in Canberra and consulting on big investigations. If he was coming to Sydney, why was he driving? Why wasn't he flying in business class? Why wasn't he being put up at some fancy hotel?

'Crashing at my place? They pull your budget already?' Jimmy joked. 'I knew they'd eventually figure out you got no talent.' He could say it confidently because it was so very far from the truth. Andy Flynn had cracked some of the biggest and most famous cases in Australia in recent years. And he had paid a heavy price for it, too.

'Jimmy, Mak left. She was gone when I got back. She said she'd be gone, but ... I didn't think she'd really do it.'

Skata.

'Oh mate, that sucks dogs' balls.'

In Jimmy's eyes, Makedde Vanderwall was pretty cool for a chick. Plus she was a former *Sports Illustrated* cover model, for godsake. But she was a handful. Andy seemed only to like the stubborn ones. His ex-wife, Cassandra, had been full of fire, too. Theirs had been a tumultuous relationship, to say the least. And Jimmy had thought he and his wife had some serious fights.

'I'll be round to drop my bag off in a few hours,' Andy explained. 'Thanks, mate. I'm driving ... I gotta get off the phone.'

'Yeah, it won't do for the police to pull you over. See you when you get here.'

Jimmy hung up and frowned. They'd split again? It seemed like yesterday that the two were in love all over again, and she was moving to Canberra to set up house with him.

Jimmy resumed interest in his Mars bar and before long it was nothing but a sticky wrapper. Rhys had been drinking some energy drink, and he chucked the empty can in the bin. He was the type who liked to spend time in the gym. He liked getting 'ripped'. Jimmy didn't understand him. They drove the two blocks to the O'Connor house, and Jimmy felt especially heavy as they walked up the drive. He was worried about Andy, and he was almost as worried about this death knock.

After several raps on the door, they were faced with a scowling woman in her late thirties. Her hair was askew, and a bit greasy through a grey part. She stood her ground in the doorway, a cigarette dangling from her lower lip. 'Whaddya want?'

'Are you Madeline O'Connor?'

'Who's askin'?' When she spoke, the cigarette wiggled slightly. Her arms were crossed, and a deep crease divided her forehead into hemispheres.

Skata. 'I'm Detective Cassimatis, and this is Detective Morrison,' Jimmy explained with an unusual level of patience. 'May we come in?'

'I've already spoken with you guys.'

She had.

'There has been a development. We'd like to come in, Mrs O'Connor.'

At this the woman stepped back from the door, and gestured down a hallway towards a small kitchen. She moved past them and pulled a chair out for herself with a screech, sat and leaned heavily on her elbows. An ashtray made a pungent centrepiece on the table, and she tapped her cigarette against the rim, building a greater pile of grey ash. With thinly veiled hostility, she waited for what they had to say. Rhys and Jimmy pulled chairs out for themselves and sat down.

'I'm afraid we've got some bad news, Mrs O'Connor,' Jimmy said.

This was the part he hated the most. The look on people's faces when they first discovered that their *husbands/wives/children/parents* would never be coming home again.

Mrs O'Connor put her cigarette out, crushing it in the ashtray, where it joined its discarded twins, twisted like white corpses in the ash.

'Your husband, Warwick O'Connor, is dead. We are sorry for your loss.'

Madeline swallowed. Her lip trembled slightly. 'When?' she asked. Her hand reached out for the crumpled cigarette, and then retreated.

'His body was discovered in his burned-out vehicle,' Rhys said, joining in. 'He was identified yesterday from dental records.'

'*In his car*? That was him in his car this whole time?' she cried.

Her husband's burned-out car had been discovered seven months earlier in a massive shipping yard. They had been able to establish ownership through the serial numbers and registration, but the badly burned and decomposed human remains found in the trunk could not be so easily identified. The only hope had been a dental match on the corpse's teeth. As Mr O'Connor was missing, and it was reasonable to fear that it might be his body in the car, the match should have been made months earlier. However, O'Connor's teeth had been inexplicably 'misplaced' for over six months. Jimmy had no idea how.

'That body! It took you seven months to find out it was my honey! Seven fucking months!' she screamed, enraged. Her eyes bulged, moist and on the edge of tears.

'We do apologise, Mrs O'Connor. We understand this must be difficult for you —'

'*Difficult!* He was murdered and you took seven months to identify him!'

Her words hung in the air.

'In these circumstances, a positive identification can take a great deal of time.'

Jimmy had seen the car, and the charred corpse in the trunk. What remained of Mr O'Connor could probably fit in Mrs O'Connor's ashtray. His eyes drifted to the smouldering mess, and, seeing images of burned bone fragments and teeth, he quickly looked away. She wouldn't need to cremate him.

'We are sorry for your loss, Mrs O'Connor,' he repeated.

Her husband had been no hero. The police knew of Warwick O'Connor long before his burned-out car — and corpse — turned up. He had been a run-of-the-mill thug. And around the time of his disappearance he had been implicated in the violent stabbing of a young woman named Meaghan Wallace. But now he was dead, and his wife was understandably angry about the circumstances of his identification.

'Fucking pigs,' Madeline bellowed.

Nice.

Under different circumstances, Jimmy might have snapped back. But he couldn't. It was a death knock so he was on extra-good behaviour, something somewhat foreign to him.

'Is there perhaps someone you could call?' Rhys suggested. 'Any friends or family who might be able to come over —'

'Fuck off, pigs!' she screamed. 'Get out of my house!'

'We'll leave you to your grieving, Mrs O'Connor,' Jimmy said, managing a lacquered composure in the face of her insults.

They left the widow cursing and crying into a fresh cigarette.

CHAPTER 6

Andy Flynn sounded like he was standing in a stadium being circled by revved-up monster trucks.

Makedde held her phone to her ear, frowning. She regretted having answered the call, but she could not bear the thought of ignoring him any more. Somewhere she heard diesel brakes. She cupped the phone more tightly.

'How are you?' her ex continued, sounding distracted. 'Look, I'm just near Goulburn.'

'Um, Goulburn?' she repeated, not quite masking her alarm.

Goulburn was a small city in south-eastern New South Wales, nestled between Canberra and Sydney. Her ex had no relatives there. Unless some serial killer had recently been busy in Goulburn and he had been sent there to do a profile, there was only one reason Mak could think of for him to be there.

'I'll be in Sydney in a couple of hours,' he confirmed.

Mak's stomach shrank to a small fist. He was taking a pit stop in Goulburn because he was coming to see her. This would be the confrontation she had been avoiding. 'I see,' she replied, trying not to encourage whatever he had in mind. She was not ready to see him, and she knew it. She wanted to settle in first. She wanted to get her strength back.

'I need time.'

'We haven't seen each other in three weeks,' he snapped back.

There followed an excruciating silence: him not asking to see her, and not asking her to come back, let alone convincing her in some romantic manner that she was mistaken in leaving him. She had become used to silences like those in recent months.

'I ...' he began, and his voice dissolved into static.

Mak's ambitious effort to move to Canberra and make a home with her on-and-off lover had been a disaster, by any measure. In the more than five years they'd known each other, it seemed that every time they made a serious commitment it triggered yet another breakdown in communication; he would hit the bottle or bury himself in work even more than usual, or worst of all, they would begin having flat-out hideous fights on a weekly basis. Moving in together in a new city had always been destined to be too much for them. To his credit, Andy had reasons for difficulties with commitment. His wife, Cassandra, had left him, and their bitter divorce battle had been interrupted when she was slain — a murder that in part seemed to be aimed at getting to Andy, who was the profiler tracking the killer responsible for a string of previous violent murders. Mak did not even need to be a psychologist to understand that such things were not easy to get over. For all his brilliant abilities in the field, Andy was riddled with issues of guilt and personal failure. The fact they had launched into their affair shortly before Cassandra was murdered probably did not help things. It was as if their union had been hard-wired for problems from inception.

After much soul-searching and one final fight that somehow felt more emotionally devastating than all the other fights combined, Mak had come to the conclusion that their problems weren't ones she could fix. It simply wasn't going to work, and she had to get on with her life. It would not be easy at first. She had known that.

And here it was, not being easy.

'Andy, I thought we agreed that we both needed some time to heal.' She spoke with a steady voice. The difficulty was that she sensed she still loved him, perhaps even desperately at times. But they simply didn't work, she reminded herself. She didn't need to get pulled back into all that tumultuous emotional impossibility. Too much had gone wrong, and she no longer believed it could be made right. The last thing she needed was to see more of him while she was vulnerable and they were both still hurting. It was hard doing the right thing as it was. Already, his attempt to come to see her gave her a dangerous glimmer of hope for some romantic reunion that she didn't even want. She just needed to stay away from him for a while, until such emotional traps were no longer so potent.

'… Sydney … you …' His voice was crackly, his words making no sense.

'What was that? You're breaking up,' she replied, annoyed.

'The re—p—tion is bad— this stretch—o—road. I —'

The line went dead.

'*Oh come on!*' she shouted to the cramped bedroom, and pocketed her phone, tense. She paced back and forth, feeling ready to punch something.

Don't get sucked back in … Don't …

In a week she would feel better. In a month she might even feel okay, she told herself. *This feeling is temporary.* There was no need to be dramatic. Break-ups were never easy at the best of times, and when exactly was the best of times, anyway? She could easily find more jobs with Marian, and she could probably get herself a date or two if she wanted the distraction. She had things to do. She was thirty, she had her PhD and there were no excuses. For much of the past year she had been foolishly focused on saving the last of their floundering relationship. She was not going to spend any more energy on that losing battle.

Mak resisted the urge to call her ex-lover back.

She had a rental to pick up, and background information to check on her case. That Andy was on his way to Sydney made no difference to that.

Mak had work to do.

It was right on three o'clock as Mak Vanderwall arrived in St Ives, a middle-class suburb on Sydney's leafy North Shore. She pulled up in a rented dark blue sedan outside a pleasant faux-Tudor two-storey house, the home of Mrs Hart and her missing son. Mak walked towards the house with her full briefcase of tricks.

One of Loulou's lines came to mind. '*You are like … Jane Bond!*'

Mak did not exactly feel she was living the life of a James — or Jane — Bond. Instead of an arsenal of high-tech gadgets and fast cars, she was prepared for her rather routine assignment with a notepad, compact digital camera, pocket dictaphone, packet of tissues and slimline laptop. Her car was an anodyne rental — thankfully not orange — rather than an Aston Martin. In the movies you never saw a private eye doing paperwork, printing out statements and getting signatures, but that was precisely the sort of thing that took up most of the job. And then there were the exhaustive reports that had to be filed, the tissues to hand to the upset client, the door knocking, the uneventful hours of surveillance. But Mak did have her own tricks. On this occasion she wore carefully chosen smart-casual clothes — a pair of dark jeans, rubber-soled black boots that she could run, jump fences or attend decent restaurants in — a bit like a modern, feminine version of the gum-rubber shoes worn by 'gumshoe' detectives of early days — and a lightweight suit jacket she'd had fitted with a small microphone, unobtrusively installed where a button would normally be. This last detail was near enough to the stuff of Bond that she didn't dare tell Loulou for fear her friend would not be able to stop talking about it. It was a trick she had been told about by an experienced investigator and former undercover cop, Pete Don, who had lectured during her Certificate III course in private investigation. She could ensure her all-important contemporaneous notes were absolutely accurate by transcribing such recordings, but most importantly, if ever there happened to be a debate about her professionalism in handling a particular situation … *voilà*. Proof of professional conduct, pure and simple. It was a precaution to cover her arse. Recording for that purpose was perfectly legal and acceptable so long as she didn't broadcast the recordings to anyone else. You never knew when a routine job might turn to trouble.

'Hart household, first interview,' she said and gave the date and time for the benefit of her button.

She knocked.

The door of the family home opened, and Mak was met by a woman in her forties, her face crumpled into a sad smile. 'You must be Macaylay. I'm Glenise Hart.'

The two women shook hands, and Mak felt the hard edge of diamonds on the woman's fingers. Her baubles were the size of small doorknobs. By now Mrs Hart's eyes were moving speedily over her, measuring her up as she stood in the doorway, a stranger. Perhaps Mak did not fit her image of a private investigator, or perhaps this woman wanted to know at a glance that she had hired someone capable of bringing her son home safely. Adam Hart's mother was a fair few inches shorter than Mak and wore a pair of light pleated slacks and a brown, round-necked shirt with a simple gold pendant. Her hair was cut politician-short, her smooth skin ruddy from the summer heat. Mak imagined her face would be pleasant under normal circumstances, but now tension bubbled behind the eyes. It was clear she had not been sleeping well. According to the file, she was a widow, and worked as a teacher. That was a lot of bling for a teacher.

'Thank you so much for coming. Please come in, Macaylay,' the woman politely murmured.

Mak smiled, ignoring the mispronunciation, pleased that she had passed the first test. She handed Mrs Hart one of Marian's business cards as she stepped inside.

Although Mak was only really interested in one room of the house — Adam's bedroom — she smiled graciously throughout a tour of the ground level of the home and yard. Mrs Hart was clearly houseproud, and everything appeared very tidy and well kept. The tour ended in the living room near the front door, where Mak was invited to sit alone with her briefcase on a loveseat. Mrs Hart sat opposite her on one end of a long, empty couch. A low coffee table separated them.

'Would you like some tea, Macaylay?'

'I'm fine, thank you. Actually, my name is pronounced Ma-kay-dee,' Mak said, gently correcting her. 'But you can call me Mak if you prefer.'

'Oh, I'm sorry.'

'Please don't be. I get it all the time. Actually, I don't know what my parents were thinking, giving me a name like that.' Mak smiled broadly, which seemed to help her client relax. She took out her notepad and placed it on the coffee table. 'Glenise … may I call you Glenise?'

A nod.

'I know you've been through a lot in the past week, and you may have gone over most of this with the police already, but it would be very helpful for me to hear your view of what's happened. Please don't leave any detail out.'

Glenise took a breath and sat forward. 'Well, I guess you know that my son, Adam, has disappeared,' she began, her voice strained, as if the mere mention of the subject made her throat close up. 'I don't know what could have happened. I am really concerned.'

'I understand. Can you tell me a bit about yourself to begin with?' Mak prodded, encouraging her. This sometimes made for an easier entry than the problem at hand.

However, her client's first statement was anything but light.

'My husband, John, was an accountant. He was killed at work. He hailed from London originally …' The woman spoke in a rush, as if to get her wretched story out of the way as fast as possible.

Mak's eyebrows went up. 'Oh, I am sorry for your loss.'

'You might well ask how an accountant dies at work,' Glenise continued. 'Well, he fell thirty-four floors down the elevator shaft. It was stuck between floors for over an hour, and rather than wait he squeezed himself out of a tiny gap and jumped to the lower floor, which would have been fine except that he fell backwards into the shaft, and …' She trailed off. 'That was two years ago.'

'I'm so sorry for your loss,' Mak repeated, temporarily stumped. *And your son has been acting out since?*

Thinking again of those diamonds, Mak guessed there had been a substantial pay-out.

Now widowed and single, her son, along with her teaching career, appeared to be Mrs Hart's whole world. Though an adult at nineteen, Adam was described by her as a 'good boy', upstanding and pure. She painted a suspiciously simple picture of an innocent, thoughtful son, inexplicably missing.

'We are very close,' she insisted. 'He did not run away. He didn't,' she repeated. To her, this seemed to be an important point — that he had not abandoned her. Mak was sure that the police would already have suggested the possibility to her, to be met, no doubt, with the same firm denials. 'The police said they can't do much until someone hears something from him, but what if he's out there somewhere needing my help?' Her eyes clouded with pain and bewilderment.

When citizens are not satisfied with what the law is doing, or able to do, private investigation agencies like Marian's often come into the picture, Mak reflected. The predicament was more common than people realised, until they themselves became somehow embroiled in trauma. Mak knew she would probably do the same were she in this woman's position. Despite having a respected cop for a father, her faith in the law was limited. As it was with many of the police officers she knew. Mak suspected she too would insist that her child was faultless in his or her own disappearance, that everything was utterly normal and harmonious except for this one sudden, unexpected incident, and that the police were not doing enough. None of these assertions was necessarily true, however. And Makedde had to disregard such statements in favour of facts, none of which she had yet ascertained.

'Adam doesn't drink, smoke or do drugs,' Glenise said confidently, almost challenging Mak to contradict her.

A nineteen-year-old who never even drank a beer would indeed be a rare find, Mak thought. She was about to ask another question when Adam's mother abruptly got up from the couch and walked away. Mak wasn't sure if she was too upset to go on and was leaving to compose herself, or if she had just remembered something.

'Just a moment,' the woman murmured as an afterthought in the doorway before disappearing from view.

Mak waited dutifully on the loveseat. She took the opportunity to quickly jot down some notes, before taking stock of her surroundings. There was an older-style tube TV against one wall, increasingly rare even in lower-middle-class households. There was a model ship on the hearth, of the type Mak's dad had once been interested in constructing. Perhaps John had made it before his fatal elevator ride. Landscape prints adorned the walls. Glenise had lots of books stacked on her shelves, and rows of family photographs propped up in frames on every surface. Mak got up to take a closer look.

Well, hello there.

On the mantelpiece were pictures of family milestones that one might expect — graduation, birthdays, school presentations

— and images from other gatherings. There was also a striking photograph of a well-built young man reclining on a sandy beach with his shirt off, skin glowing, his hair sun-kissed and wavy. It could have been an advertisement for something luxurious like cologne, so handsome was the young man.

Adam Hart?

'That was taken in Noosa two months ago,' came a voice behind her. Glenise had returned with a notebook in her hand. 'He's sweet, isn't he?' She hovered in the doorway then disappeared into the kitchen without another word.

There was a rattling of dishes and the whine of water coming to the boil. After a few moments, Mrs Hart returned with a pot, some biscuits and glasses of water on a large lacquered tray. She put her notebook on the seat next to her, and poured Makedde some tea that flowed from the spout the colour of molasses. *You'll be up for hours*, Mak predicted.

'Thank you. That's very kind,' she replied graciously. She took her place on the lonely loveseat again, and picked up her pen and notepad. 'May I have that photograph to copy?'

'Yes.' Glenise nodded and closed her eyes for a moment.

'Adam looks quite athletic. Does he play much sport?' This was more than a way of simply building rapport. Mak needed to find out whom she could canvass about his disappearance. Team-mates? Classmates? Friends? Neighbours?

'Oh, no. Nothing like that. I tried to get him interested in joining some clubs but he's not very social.'

Does 'not very social' mean 'depressed'? Mak wondered.

Glenise explained that Adam had not played organised sport since early in high school, and that he was not in touch with any of his school friends now. He was a natural athlete, she said, but never used his gifts. His only nod to athleticism was his cycling, which he appeared to do mostly to get to university and back. It kept him fit, and meant he didn't feel the need for a car. Again Mak wished he had a car or something equally traceable. His bike was missing, which meant that whatever happened to him, he appeared to have at least left the house voluntarily. But that didn't mean he was voluntarily staying away. *Am I going to be knocking on doors all bloody day, with nothing else to go on?*

'If you could provide me with a description and a serial number for the bike, that would be helpful.' It would be *something*. Mak took a sip of tea. It tasted as strong as it looked. 'I have a few more questions,' she continued, her pen poised.

Glenise nodded distractedly, her fingers unconsciously straying to her notebook.

'Has your son ever run away before?'

'No!' Glenise declared, fully alert now, her hands forming fists. 'He hasn't run away. He's a good kid.' She paused thoughtfully. 'Not that he's always been an angel. But if I find out he's run away …' She trailed off and her fists tightened, a wellspring of anger becoming apparent. 'If he's run away I'll take him straight to the police! A night in jail would teach him a lesson!'

This sudden change in tone was jarring.

'I understand you must be very concerned about him,' Mak said soothingly, 'but it's not illegal to run away — if that's what he's done. He's nineteen for starters, so technically he can go where he pleases.'

Glenise appeared momentarily stumped by this obvious fact, and reddened.

If Adam ended up in the hands of the correctional authorities, Mak doubted it would give him the kind of lesson his mother hoped for. Jails were often nothing more than a school for delinquents to learn how to become better delinquents.

'I didn't mean that literally,' Glenise explained. 'Of course I would never want my son in jail.'

'Of course,' Mak agreed. She waited a moment for the older woman to regain her composure before continuing. 'Does Adam have any tattoos, piercings or other identifying marks?'

'Certainly not.'

'Does he have a mobile phone?'

'Yes. I haven't found it.'

'Passport?'

At this Glenise frowned for a moment.

'I checked, and it's still where I always keep it.'

So no travel plans.

'His wallet?'

Glenise shook her head.

'Does he have a credit or debit card we might be able to trace?'

'He had a credit card for a while, but he couldn't keep up the payments, so I made him cancel it. He's on a family card now. A MasterCard.'

Okay, that's something.

'Has he been using it?'

Again, a shake of the head.

'So you haven't noticed any unusual activity on it? No purchases you can't recall making?'

'No.'

Mak pressed on. 'It would be helpful if you could give me a full list of Adam's friends, as many as you can think of, even if there are a hundred of them.'

'There won't be a hundred.'

Thank God. 'That's fine,' Mak said. 'Just give me a list of all his regular contacts, when you are able. I know it may take a while, but it would be very helpful. Most of these sorts of cases are solved that way. Often, someone knows something. A romantic partner might know a great deal, for instance. Is Adam involved with anyone?' Makedde asked. 'A girlfriend, or …?' She left her query open.

'He isn't seeing anyone.' The reply was swift.

'No one that you know of then?'

'No.' Glenise was definite.

Mak frowned slightly. Was there something Adam's mother was uncomfortable with? 'No recent partners?'

She shook her head.

Mak felt her client shrinking away, and decided to move on to another subject. 'Now, if you can, I'd like to hear your view of things. You last saw Adam on Tuesday at dinnertime, I understand. Is that correct? What was he wearing?'

Glenise surprised her by opening her notebook up about halfway through. It was not a notebook at all, Mak saw, but a diary. The year was embossed on the cover. She had sprung up and left Mak alone so she could fetch her diary. This was a good sign, even if the timing seemed odd. Glenise was the meticulous type. This could be helpful.

'He was wearing a dark blue hooded sweatshirt and jeans,' Mrs Hart recited, as if reading from a textbook. 'He came home from uni, and then said he was going to eat in his room. He took his dinner upstairs. He wasn't there in the morning.' She paused and, when she spoke again, Mrs Hart sounded as if she was barely keeping her emotions at bay. 'He didn't come down for breakfast, and he wasn't in his room.' She referred again to the pages before her. 'At seven-fifteen a.m. I discovered he was missing,' she said dolefully.

So he could have left any time that night.

'You sure keep a thorough diary,' Mak commented.

'Always,' Glenise replied with a touch of pride.

'Does Adam keep a diary as well?'

Glenise frowned. 'No. I don't know. Well, he used to ...'

'Did he often eat alone in his room?' This had struck Mak as odd; did it mean he and his mother had been fighting? It was antisocial, to say the least.

'He's a teenager.'

Mak nodded, and made another note. LOOK FOR A DIARY

'You know, Kevin recommended you very highly,' Glenise said, quite to Mak's surprise. She looked up from her notes.

'Kevin?'

'You did such a good job with Tobias that I hoped you could help me,' Glenise added.

Mak twitched at the mention of the boy's name, and the fingers of her right hand gripped the seam of her jeans, nails curling up to stab the stitches. Kevin was the name of Tobias's father.

Tobias? How would she know anything about Tobias and Kevin?

'You know Tobias Murphy?' Mak asked calmly, managing a decent act of masking the impact of the connection.

'Oh, the Murphys are a lovely family. They moved in down the street earlier this year.'

Mak felt a rush of uneasy adrenaline surge through her.

Okay, you now have my attention.

Sixteen-year-old Tobias Murphy had been wrongly arrested for his cousin's murder. It was all part of the same complex and sordid investigation that led Mak to uncover Damien Cavanagh's involvement in the suspicious death of an underage girl. Mak's investigation resulted in Tobias being cleared of any wrong-doing, even if she did not quite manage to bring the Cavanagh heir to justice, or cause much more than a ripple in the wealthy Cavanagh family's privileged, important lives. She often wondered how Tobias was doing after being released from police custody and reunited with his biological father. The thought that he had so narrowly avoided spending his life imprisoned for something he was innocent of sent Mak's thoughts quickly into territory Marian would not approve of. Injustice had a way of invigorating her. Of course the case had long since departed her professional domain. She had been sternly and repeatedly warned to be sensible and steer clear of any further involvement for her own good, perhaps even her own safety.

Mak was smart, but not always sensible.

This was the connection Marian Wendell had been hesitant to mention. The Cavanagh case was the reason for her recommendation. Mak had sensed that her boss was holding something back.

'Are Adam and Tobias friends?' Makedde asked with deceptive calm.

'Oh, I think they've got to know each other a bit.'

The two boys would be a couple of years apart by Mak's calculation.

'Have you spoken to Tobias about Adam's disappearance?'

'Not personally,' Glenise said. 'I've not seen him around lately. I spoke with Kevin about it, of course, and that was when he recommended you.'

It was natural enough for Tobias's father to recommend Makedde's services. He had not been her client, but the outcome of her investigation had been good for the Murphys, and it was not as if the average person knew a lot of private investigators. Mak had thought the door knocking in this case would be depressingly ho-hum. Adam might best be located by speaking to a lot of his friends, associates and neighbours, as more often than not someone somewhere knew something, and it was only a matter of time and perseverance. But perhaps while speaking to the Murphy family she could gently find out if they knew anything she didn't about the Cavanaghs, and where the case against the scion of one of Australia's most powerful families had stalled …

CHAPTER 7

His motel room was cheap.

The young man stood in its centre, clothed only in his underpants, and glared at the locked door with disdain. A truck drove by on the nearby road. He heard some stranger cough. He would not sleep well here. He had not slept well for days, and tonight there would be no respite: of that he felt certain. The faint smell of deodoriser and stale smoke permeated the thin walls, the carpet and the papery sheets he did not look forward to sleeping between. This was in no way a step up from the caravan outside.

In three strides he traversed his tiny quarters to the spartan bathroom. At least the mirror was large, the corners of it fading away to a non-reflective grey. He stared himself down with a dark, unhappy gaze. There was a crease between his brows that displeased him. Even when he tried his best to relax his forehead, his frown remained like an ineradicable watermark. He leaned in until he was centimetres from the glass, staring at his reflection, obsessively tracking the undesired lines beginning to form on his fine face that once had been so smooth. He noted each new sign of age with acute anxiety: the creases that extended from the sides of his nose to the corners of his lips like the mouth of a ventriloquist's doll; the lines that fanned out from his eyes like spider's legs; the hairline that others denied was slowly, irreversibly receding. He cursed the fact he had not acquired a single one of the youthful genes that should have been his birthright.

One red apple.

One piece of rye toast. No butter.

One tin of tomato soup.

One pinch of salt, but only a pinch.

Salt made him retain water. He couldn't afford that. He studiously avoided animal products, too much sodium, cholesterol, oil.

Twice a day he was in the habit of carefully tallying his intake. It kept him in line. It meant he did not make mistakes.

For a moment the young man stood side-on to the mirror and studied his unclothed shape. His sinewy muscles were keeping well, the skin on his chest still taut, tanned and smooth. He sucked his stomach in until it pulled back against his ribcage, giving him the narrow waist he was praised for. He was once told it was his low body fat that made him appear older than his years. Nonsense.

'*Ebanatyi pidaraz,*' he cursed under his breath, words he would never say aloud in front of his family.

Being constantly uprooted like this made him edgy. He felt unbalanced, discombobulated, alone. The travelling made him weary. He felt older than his years, that was true. He felt old.

Bijou … Bijou … Bijou …

She had taken another lover. Why? She was getting on in age now herself, though no one seemed to guess it. She was still beautiful, still the star attraction of the troupe, their driving force. She possessed him like no other ever could. It mattered not that he was rejected from her bed for now. She was inside him. Inside him. Inside him. And he inside her …

And she was not going to get him out.

Still fixated on his reflection, he reached blindly around the edge of the basin until he found what he wanted. He raised his black eyeliner pencil to his face. A little unsteadily, he drew its sharpened point across the seam of his lashes, giving him the lined eyes of a sinewy jungle cat.

Bijou.

This new boy might be in her bed now, but things could change. He could make things change. He would never be far away.

And he would be watching. Waiting …

CHAPTER 8

'Hi, you've reached Mak. Please leave a message …'

Andy Flynn hung up his phone without saying a word. He felt the urge to throw the thing against the wall and break it into small, useless pieces. He was back in Australia, in Sydney again, a short distance from Makedde, and still they were at an impasse. She knew he was in town and yet she was not answering his calls.

Fuck it.

He looked across at the neatly stacked turquoise towels at the foot of the single bed he was perched on, and suddenly felt an extreme tiredness. He had driven from Quantico, Virginia, to Washington, then flown from Washington to Los Angeles, and Los Angeles to Sydney, and Sydney to Canberra. He had arrived home to find that his live-in girlfriend had done precisely what she'd said she would. She had moved out. The house had been neat and empty. She had not left a note.

And then he had driven here. He could be forgiven for feeling weary.

Beyond the door, Andy could hear the chaotic, comforting sounds of family. Only the family was not his own, but that of his former police partner. The Cassimatis marriage had survived Jimmy's long hours in squad cars, his absences, and even the unveiling of his infidelities. Andy's own marriage had survived precisely nothing. And his wife, Cassandra, had not even survived their bitter divorce. She had been sliced up by the Stiletto Killer like some kind of sick present, as a cat would leave a dead bird at the end of the bed. It was precisely because Andy was working the case that the killer had gone for her. It was Andy's fault that Cassandra was dead. He had not joined the police force to be the *cause* of murder. And after all that hell, he had really thought he could make it work with Makedde — if he could make it with anyone. She was not bothered by the morbidness of his work as a profiler of violent serial criminals. Her father was a retired cop. She understood the job, the hours. Sure, she had been a model for many years, but she wasn't precious or self-absorbed. They really had something, but it had gone wrong yet again.

To make it worse, they had fought over professional issues as well as personal.

The Cavanaghs.

They had not seen eye to eye on what had transpired in Mak's last Sydney assignment, and she had been bitter at his lack of support.

If only she knew his real reasons, things might have been different.

Sorry, Mak. Sorry.

Andy looked listlessly round Jimmy's spare bedroom and tried to gather his thoughts. The room appeared to be used for storage of anything that didn't fit elsewhere. There were a few cardboard boxes along one wall, a television that looked like it didn't work, and, taking up precious space, a home gym. It was hilarious to Andy to imagine his former police partner even knowing what such a thing was. The man was perpetually out of shape and overweight, and his doctor had him on blood thinners. Still, there it was, complete with bench press and various pulleys.

There was a knock, and the door opened.

'Papa!' a smaller Cassimatis yelled, and Jimmy slipped inside and shut the door behind him as if keeping back a wave.

'Mate, never have kids. They'll suck the life out of you!'

Andy laughed. They had this kind of exchange from time to time. It was an unconvincing display, especially given the naked look of fatherly pride in Jimmy's eyes. He had four children now, between the ages of fifteen and ten months. Andy was childless.

'What did Bill Hicks say? That kids are naturally smarter than we are, because he's never met a kid who was married and had children.'

'Yeah!' Jimmy declared. 'They've got it worked out. Beat up kids in the schoolyard, come home, get fed, yell at their dad. Kids have it made.'

Jimmy's boys were at the age where they still idolised their father, and swelled with pride at the knowledge that their dad was a cop and carried a gun. It gave them cred at school. It was cause for boasting, for a couple more years anyway. Once the boys started going to parties, it would be different.

'So, mate, you wanna find some beers tonight after dinner? Maybe hit the local? Or …' he winked lasciviously, 'we could check out the shows.'

He didn't mean the Opera House.

'Uh, I'm seeing Mak tonight,' Andy told him. 'Maybe after.'

'Okay, mate. Sure,' Jimmy said, clearly disappointed. 'That's okay. I have to go in and check on some stuff at work, anyway.'

The reality of what he had returned home to filled Andy with a mix of rage and grief. He didn't know what he would do when he saw her; he only knew that he needed to.

'Maybe we can do a work-out, too,' he managed to joke, gesturing to the rusting equipment.

Jimmy cracked a smile. 'Fuck you.'

CHAPTER 9

Mak pocketed her phone, and held back a strange sensation of drowning. Andy's name had come up on her caller ID and she had not answered. It was not the time or place. But already a series of unwanted memories had begun flickering below the steady surface of her professional focus.

Dammit.

'I'll show you upstairs,' Glenise Hart told Makedde, and the women both rose from the couches on which they'd sat and discussed the disappearance of Adam Hart for over an hour.

Makedde was led towards a staircase at the end of the main hall, and as she ascended at the woman's heels, they passed more framed family photographs. Lots of smiling. Lots of sunshine. Mak's heart lurched a little at the thought of all that broken cheer.

'When did you notice that Adam's bike was gone?' Mak asked.

'Not until I spoke to the police.'

'He kept it in the garage, or somewhere else?'

'Sometimes along the side of the house. It's a safe neighbourhood. I don't know where he'd left it that night.'

As Glenise had not been awakened by the sound of the garage door, Mak thought the bike had probably been parked beside the house the night he disappeared. She would need to take a look at the spot.

They reached the top of the stairs. An open door revealed a tidy bathroom with a toilet and bath. Glenise moved to the next door down the hall on the right and placed her hand on the doorknob.

Mak interrupted her. 'If it's okay with you, Mrs Hart, I'd prefer to have a look at Adam's room alone, and then I might ask you to take me through a few things.' It was better to take an objective look first, so as not to be led into the same false conclusions others might have fallen into. 'I'll be a while. I'll be careful with his things, I promise.'

'Okay.' Adam's mother stepped back with something like a whimper of rejection, before padding softly down the carpeted stairs, shoulders slumped.

'Thank you,' Mak called, but she was already out of view, and there was no reply.

Who is Adam Hart?

Makedde Vanderwall took a breath and entered Adam Hart's bedroom with as clear a mind as possible. She found herself in an average-sized room with off-white walls and a window with a leafy outlook. Immediately the neatness of the room struck her as odd: all perfect files and books stacked so precisely they were practically colour-coded. There was a single bed in the corner, made with an almost military precision. It brought to mind her days as a naval cadet back in Canada; from age ten to thirteen, she'd gradually gained confidence along with semaphore and Morse code skills as she rose through the ranks to chief petty officer, in charge of a parade square of kids. A tightly made bed was given strange value in cadets. '*If I can't bounce a quarter on it, you get fifty push-ups ...*'

Mak moved first to the window. It unlocked easily and slid open far enough for a slim person to fit through. With a half-hearted jiggle the flyscreen came away. She peered out, feeling the fresh evening summer air on her face. It was a single-storey drop to the ground beside the house, but there was a wooden ledge above the kitchen window — part of the fake Tudor design — and a drainpipe within reach. She could shimmy down it if she wished. Adam could have got out this way. Or someone could have got in. She replaced the flyscreen and closed the window.

How often did you sneak out, young man, and for whom? Do tell ...

The décor in the room was minimal. There was a single large poster over the bed, a black-and-white illustration in traditional Victorian sideshow style, advertising the Jim Rose Circus. It depicted five characters, each engaged in a different bizarre performance. The central figure was a strongman type, tied up with chains and struggling atop shattered glass. Floating to his left was a man in a suit with a tube up his nose. The tube ran down into a big syringe containing some presumably sinister substance. Below him, a traditional sword swallower posed with a smile, the handle of the weapon protruding from between gleaming teeth. On the right-hand side of the poster was an oddly proportioned clown breathing flame, and below him a male figure struggled with a heavy weight that dragged his tongue down to his waist from an overstrained piercing. The poster proclaimed enticingly:

THE JIM ROSE CIRCUS
SIDESHOW FREAKS!

The images were set against a giant stage curtain, and brought to mind the dark sideshow world of Tod Browning's subjects. Mak squinted at the poster, intrigued that Adam had chosen this over a poster of, say, a scantily clad Jessica Biel or a Suicide Girl. Perhaps his mother wouldn't allow anything too racy in the house. *Was she controlling?* Mak wondered.

She set about searching the room.

Stacks of DVDs were set neatly against one wall, one upon the other from the carpet up: kung fu movies, foreign films, black-and-white films, fantasy. He was a *Star Wars* fan. There was an inexpensive-looking guitar in the corner closest to the bed, the make of which Mak did not recognise.

He had a medium-height chest of drawers filled with the usual socks, underwear, jeans and T-shirts, all neatly folded. There was also a four-shelf bookcase filled with carefully ranged books. She read titles off the spines: *English as a Legal Language*, *Professional Practices*, *A History of Accounting and Accountants*.

Riveting stuff, Mak thought.

But there were also copies of Kerouac's *On the Road* — well thumbed — *Ringolevio* by Emmett Grogan and *Shantaram* by Gregory David Roberts. There was a dichotomy between the young man's field of study and his interests, if such tales of adventure and rebellion against the system were anything to go by. There were also a lot of philosophy books, a number of which appeared to have unbroken bindings, and a thick book of Bob Dylan songs.

Hmmm. What about drugs …

In one smooth manoeuvre Mak dipped to the floor on one elbow and swept her eyes under the young man's bed. A guitar case, empty. A fat dictionary.

Nothing. Not even the swirls of fluff and dust you'd expect to find under any bed, especially a nineteen-year-old male's.

She sat on the edge of the bed and contemplated the space. *What nineteen-year-old keeps their room this clean?* She slid her hand under the mattress and searched for contraband: porn, marijuana, a flask of alcohol, a little black book, a tell-all diary … something interesting, anything. Perhaps Adam was like Andy's old police mate Jimmy Cassimatis, harbouring a collection of trashy weekly nude magazines with their HORNBAG NEXT DOOR contests? It might not help to find Adam, but it would at least be amusing.

Again, nothing.

With its neatness and sterility, the room was almost a blank space. This was disappointing for Makedde's purposes, to say the least. It was certainly not the messy jumble of unwashed gym socks and *Ralph* magazines she'd expected. Was this extreme tidiness the result of a strict upbringing? His mother was a schoolteacher and she did seem to like to keep things orderly and under control. *Or was Adam expecting someone like me to come along*? Mak wondered suspiciously. Either he had recently tossed a lot of belongings out and purposely tidied the place in preparation for his departure, or he routinely spent a lot of time keeping everything organised. Or — and Mak suspected this was closest to the truth — Glenise Hart had tidied her son's room in anticipation of Makedde's visit.

Mak stood up and felt something hard under her foot. She rolled her boot to one side and saw she was standing on a single coin — or rather, half of one. It was an American quarter, and it looked like a bite had been taken out of it. She examined it from all angles. The edge seemed to have been crushed by something, but the rest of the coin was unscratched and unbent. She placed the quarter on the bed and frowned.

A coin out of place. You missed that one, Glenise, she thought suspiciously.

She pocketed it for later, then took out her digital camera, checked that it had a fresh, correctly labelled memory stick, and began to take the first photographs for her new case.

When Makedde emerged from Adam's room thirty minutes later, she felt only the tiniest step closer to knowing who he was.

She moved into the hallway and looked both ways. There was some movement in the kitchen directly below, a cupboard closing, the rattling of china, the shriek of water coming to the boil again. She stepped into the bathroom. It, too, was spotless. The towels were dark. There was a mirrored cabinet above the sink. She opened it, hopeful. If it were anything like hers, the shelves would be overflowing with toiletries, vitamins, toothpaste oozing out of tubes.

Anti-psychotic medications, party drugs, bags of condoms, what have you got for me …

There was a small tub of hair gel. Deodorant. Toothpaste still in a box. *Boring*. Mak opened the cupboards under the sink and found nothing but neatly folded towels, a rubber plunger. *Nothing*.

Makedde readied herself to face Adam's distraught mother again. What had she learned? Her son was tidy. He read novels and watched DVDs. He liked *Star Wars*. He liked the Jim Rose

Circus. And he had a strange coin. He most likely entered and exited his room through the window and down the drainpipe. But why? Mak descended the stairs wishing she'd discovered something more tangible, something to give hope that Adam would soon be returned to his mother, but of course it was far too early for results.

Glenise was waiting for Mak at the bottom of the stairs.

'More tea?' she asked.

'Oh, thank you,' Mak replied, not at all meaning it. 'But I should get going soon.'

Tea was poured and Mak returned to her place on the lonely loveseat, smiling gently. She hadn't had to use the tissues yet and she hoped the meeting would not turn to tears now. Adam's mother sat across from her, expectantly. She seemed to have gained some composure. Her posture was stiff and proud.

'I was wondering ... does Adam's room look any different than normal to you?' Mak asked.

'Not really.'

'You didn't perhaps clean it?' she suggested gently. If Mrs Hart had cleaned the room to make it presentable for her and for the police, it was an extremely counterproductive thing to do.

'Oh no. I wouldn't do that. He has to clean his own room.' Glenise held her gaze, and her answer was direct. Could the orderly teacher's pride allow strangers to sift through her only child's untidy room if it had been a mess?

'It's very well organised in there,' Mak observed.

'Oh, yes,' Glenise replied, swelling with pride. 'Adam's a very neat boy. I didn't raise any slob.'

Mak smiled. 'You certainly didn't.' She took a sip of tea for the sake of diplomacy, but she had spent enough time in this pleasant, fractured home with its antiseptic grief. For the moment there was nothing more she could accomplish.

'Before I go, may I have a look at where Adam kept his bike? You said he sometimes left it alongside the house?'

'Of course.'

Mak gathered her things, and Glenise led her out the front door. The suburban street looked different in the slowly waning daylight, the houses beginning to be bathed in purples and greys, the shadows growing longer. They walked around to the side of the house, overgrown with green grass. Mak dodged a spider web, and was struck with images of Glenise Hart mowing the lawn alone, working in the garden alone, shopping for groceries alone, cooking for one.

'He often kept it here. But it's gone,' Glenise said.

There was less than two metres space between the Harts' house and a tall fence separating the property from next door. Mak could see wheel tracks through the grass, but it was hard to say how recently they'd been made. She again spotted the drainpipe that extended up to the roof, past Adam's window. Had Glenise never noticed that her son conveniently parked his bike at the bottom of it?

By the look of that photo on the beach, Adam would certainly have had interest from the opposite sex. Or both sexes, actually. But Glenise had denied he had a girlfriend, or any 'special' male friends. Right on cue, Glenise reached into her pocket and presented Mak with the photograph from the mantle.

'Oh, thank you.'

'Bring him home to me,' the woman said.

Mak nodded. 'Don't worry.'

They walked back to the front of the house, and Mak left

her client with her arms crossed, silhouetted by the glow of the slowly sinking sun.

'I'll be in touch again later this week,' Mak assured her.

'He didn't run away,' the woman said once more, adamant.

Mak thanked her for her hospitality, neither legitimising her belief that her son could not possibly have run away, nor refuting it. But the way that flyscreen had come off made her think it had been removed many times before.

'I was just wondering, has Adam ever travelled to America?'

'America? No.'

Mak supposed he could have got the coin anywhere. 'If you could get that list of Adam's friends to me as soon as possible, that would be helpful. Thanks again for your time. I know this is hard for you. I'm confident we'll find him.'

The early evening air felt refreshing as she gained distance from the house, and from Mrs Hart, who stood in the doorway watching. The hire car engine started with a splutter. It was not the most glamorous exit, Mak reflected, but as she drove away, she felt lighter.

CHAPTER 10

Lush red theatrical curtains were pulled back to reveal a nearly bare stage. Off to the right, a small band assembled, looking artfully dishevelled in tatty tuxedos — a guitarist and an androgenous-looking drummer surrounded by her kit.

The round drum was painted in old-style lettering.

LE THÉÂTRE DES HORREURS

A drum, lonely for other instruments, rolled its rapid rhythm, and on cue two young women appeared, both petite and dressed in classic burlesque attire: blood-red corsets, fishnets and tiny velvet hats set over the side part in their tightly curled blonde wigs. The makeup gave them the look of goth twins, their lipstick black, skin white. One pushed a cart like a restaurant trolley; the other carried a vintage-style placard:

ARSLAN LE CONTORSIONNISTE

The audience watched as the woman with the placard shimmied her way across the stage, striking little poses and making gestures in Bettie Page pin-up fashion — a smile here, an eyelash-heavy wink there — ensuring the placard was noticed by all. She daintily placed it on an easel stage right and joined her twin.

The audience waited, anticipation palpable.

Finally, the wheeled trolley was pushed to the front of the stage. On the trolley sat an ornate box not even half a metre wide, about the size of a minibar or large overnight bag. With lace-gloved hands the two attractive women stroked the box lovingly, making clear something of value was inside.

'*Arslan le contorsionniste,*' came an announcement in exotic-sounding French. '*Amoureux tordu …*'

The women gracefully reached down and locked the wheels of the cart so it would not move, then stepped away in their stiletto heels, blowing the mysterious object fond kisses and disappearing from view beyond the vaudevillian curtain.

The box sat centre-stage on its elevated cart, unmoving.

Again, the audience waited.

A full minute of suspense followed, seeming like an impossibly long stretch of time, the lone drummer tapping out a low roll. Finally, a striptease beat began, the guitarist strumming exotic, sensual sounds, and centimetre by centimetre the doors of the box opened, as if they had a life of their own.

Oh!

The audience collectively gasped as one hand appeared, and then another. Incredibly, a full-grown man was emerging from the box before the stunned audience, the empty space beneath the cart making it clear that this was no trick. Arslan the contortionist had not just appeared from a trap door under the floor, or from a hidden container within the trolley. A whole person had folded himself into that box, and he now rose, extending one arm and then the other, stepping out, unfolding himself limb by limb, and making a show of unfurling fingers and toes and placing his spine back into a more natural, upright alignment.

He stood.

Amazing ...

Despite fitting in the box, this was no small man. He was exceedingly lean and sinewy, but well muscled, and looked at least 180 centimetres tall. He wore his slick hair parted to one side, and sported a 1920s-inspired thin moustache, curled up at the edges, a look which added enormously to the sense he had been transported from an earlier era, the ornate box his time capsule. His skin was the colour of milk chocolate, his bright green eyes rimmed with kohl. In ballooning white boxers and black socks pulled taut with old-fashioned sock suspenders, he posed, chest out, like a silent-era movie star caught in a particularly risqué moment. The creature on the stage grinned, and raised an eyebrow lasciviously, as if performing for the intimate pleasure of a lover. He curved one leg around the other, looping it once, twice, three times, locking it around his thigh, shin and ankle, seeming to will his bones to rubber.

Amoureux tordu. Twisted lover.

The young man in the back row folded his arms and smiled, delighted by the riveting spectacle. Watching this act for the fifth time, he was still amazed by Arslan the Contortionist's impressive flexibility and theatrical flair.

As the act came to an end he applauded along with the crowd, and felt the soft wings of butterflies building up in his stomach.

The next act was a crowd favourite. It featured the classic French beauty pictured in the program — Bijou, 'the most assassinated woman since Paula Maxa', starring in a famous play of the Grand Guignol.

It was a gruesome tale of love and revenge.

Le Baiser dans la Nuit.

The Final Kiss.

CHAPTER 11

Mak pulled up to Loulou's apartment block with a sense of lightness. She was into the work. Her mind had a task to focus on, a puzzle. She was in Sydney. It was the beginning of a new beginning. For the first time in months, her failures did not seem to be clinging quite so closely.

She stepped out of the rental car, and stared at something on the road behind her.

No.

Andy's car.

Her stomach fell. The timing was terrible.

Andy's red Honda was parked on the street outside the building, and the sight of him waiting there for her pulled everything out of focus. Mak felt panicked in an instant. *How could he know where I'm staying?* Mak could make out his dark silhouette behind the wheel. Her heart lurched at the sight.

Andy. Not now.

After his earlier call, bad reception and all, she'd realised he wanted to see her, but at the apartment? Unannounced? Like this?

She had not expected to feel so thrown by his proximity. It was too soon to see him. Makedde strode across the footpath, up the stairs and to the front door of the apartment block, briefcase in hand, barely breathing. She tried to keep her thoughts sober, and listened intently. As she fished her keys out there was the sound of a car door closing and footsteps behind her. She felt, as much as heard, Andy's approach.

'Mak … We need to talk.'

'I agree,' she replied, looking resolutely at the keys in her hand. She didn't want to look at him. Yet. She stuck the key in the street door and opened it.

'You weren't answering your phone.'

Mak had switched her phone off, hoping the problem would go away for a while. Yet here he was. Her jaw felt tight, her stomach uneasy.

Get this over with.

They stepped inside the echoing hallway of the apartment complex and made their way to her temporary abode like a couple attending a wake. The stark corridor seemed to Mak to stretch for miles, the white concrete and harsh lighting oppressively institutional. They reached the door of Apartment 101, and in a tense silence she let him in. Only once she closed the door behind him did she allow herself to acknowledge the man she had spent much of the past five years with. She turned to faced him.

Andy.

Just as she had feared, she found the sight of him pleasing. He wore faded jeans, and had rolled up the sleeves on a collared shirt wrinkled from the long drive. If he'd been working, he would have worn a suit, she knew. He had driven to Sydney for her, she was now certain. Her eyes ran over his features, and took in the familiar face with its strong jawline and handsome but imperfect features: the slightly crooked nose, the generous mouth, the scar on his chin. His face was shaded with stubble, circles under his intense green eyes. His dark hair was full, and only slightly greying at the temples. Andy's naturally strong build was impossibly appealing to her. He had always possessed an indefinable masculinity that she found compelling. And then there was the height — with Mak being so tall herself, it was not every man she was forced to look up to, as she was now. Even in such unpleasant conditions, she found him magnetic. Frustratingly, that had always been the case.

There was love there. There had always been love there. But it was flawed love, deeply flawed. *He's just familiar. That's all. We are like a bad habit for each other.*

'I see you wasted no time finding me,' she challenged him, looking up to meet his eyes. 'Does the whole police department keep a file on me these days, or did you just send someone to follow me yourself?'

He said nothing.

How arrogant, Mak thought, her anger temporarily pulling her out of her vulnerability.

Neither spoke for a few minutes. They looked at each other at brief intervals. Andy's gaze drifted over the floor, around the room. Mak experienced uncomfortable flashes of their years together, like an unwanted sensory slide show — places shared, words spoken, touches, lovemaking. He took a step closer and she didn't back away. Images of him naked lingered in her mind, and she felt herself becoming slightly — inappropriately — aroused. It had been a while since they had been in each other's presence, and this growing concupiscence surely stemmed only from the appealing familiarity of his presence, the knowledge of sexual compatibility. Their sexual chemistry had always been strong. Had pheromones driven their doomed attraction to each other? Was simple, pathetic biology to blame? Surely it wasn't love. Love was not supposed to be so hard.

Her eyes drifted to Andy's muscular forearms, then his hands, held tightly at his sides, and then up to his face. Once her eyes met his she couldn't break his gaze.

Okay, I want to scream.

Am I still in love with this man? Fuck!

Fine. Let's get on with it, she thought, and broke the moment of tension. She dragged a stool away from the counter and sat on it backwards, her legs open like a man's and her arms resting on the low seat back. Andy took a seat next to her. Makedde took a breath and looked ahead, searching for words to begin the conversation they needed to have. She wished she did not feel so conflicted. It was not a good moment to feel conflicted.

'It's a pretty small place,' he remarked.

'Yes, it is. But it's just fine,' she replied defiantly, looking at him with something more like anger. If she hadn't gone to Canberra to be with him she would not now being staying at a friend's place and living out of what she could fit in a couple of panniers.

'You have to stay away from them,' Andy stated flatly.

Mak sat up straight, unsure of his meaning. '*Them*?'

'The Cavanaghs.'

'I'll do what I want, Andy,' she replied crossly. This was not exactly the way back to her heart. They had fought often over the issue of the Cavanaghs, and it had possibly been the straw that broke the back of their relationship.

'Mak, listen to me. Stay away from the Cavanaghs.'

'I am,' she responded.

'No, you're not,' he admonished her. 'You were seen sitting outside their Darling Point home on your motorcycle.'

Mak's mouth hung open for a moment. *What?* That had been after five in the morning. She was seen? Had she been followed?

'That is ridiculous. I just drove past the place. I may have slowed down for a moment or two. I didn't do anything.'

'Mak, stay away. Please.'

Anger coursed through her like a red mist. He was talking to her like her father, the ex-Detective Inspector, might. She was not a child. There was no crime in riding along Darling Point Road and looking at houses. This was outrageous.

'Just trust me. You need to stay away from them.'

She sat stiffly, arms folded. 'Are you quite finished?'

'What happened with us?' he asked suddenly.

What happened with us? Mak felt unreasonably crushed by the question. She could feel his eyes on her as she struggled for a reply. 'I shouldn't have to explain it to you. You were there,' she managed to say with something that sounded like decisiveness. 'We fought like cat and dog, and you always found a reason to be overseas and not call. We'd both had enough.'

Their final phone call had left her weeping alone through a sleepless night, a pathetic display she did not intend to repeat for anyone or anything. Ever. It had seemed in those dark moments that she had never before felt such a deep stab of pain. She had long believed she could never go through anything more heart-wrenching than the death of her mother, so how could the breakdown of a romantic relationship compare? She had felt angry at herself for considering the comparison, and yet the pain was so fresh and confronting now, she wondered if she had underestimated the depth of her feelings for Andy. Mak had watched helplessly as her mother slipped away. But in this, she was less helpless. Yes, the relationship was flawed, but she had taken the responsibility of pulling the plug herself. It was the weight of that responsibility that made it all the more agonising, especially now they were face to face again. She could feel the logic for ending the relationship beginning to slip under the weight of emotion.

Don't push me.

'What are you going to do here?' Andy pressed. 'Work at that investigation agency again?' This wasn't a friendly question, but an accusation, a challenge, rousing her anger instead of her grief.

Just because Andy, like her father, was a decorated police officer, didn't mean that Mak wanted to join their ranks. She was perfectly happy with her career choices. This was another issue they had fought over many times. A lot of police didn't like private investigators, and arguably the only people Andy liked less were defence lawyers.

'Yes,' she said. 'I'm working for Marian and I'm fucking good at it.'

Pull yourself in. You are angry and emotional. You'll regret this later.

Their reunion would have been better in a public place, somewhere she would have to keep it together, and was less likely to be overwhelmed with the unexpectedly powerful emotions that were welling up in her. She could feel herself being caught up in the drama. Months of anger and disappointment and hurt were bubbling to the surface. Years.

'I didn't mean it like that,' Andy told her. 'Honestly. You can work where you want. Look, Mak …' He held out his hand. 'I've missed you.'

'Don't say that,' Mak replied. She did not accept his gesture.

'It's true. Look at me, Mak. *Look at me.*'

She did. Their eyes locked, and despite herself, her heart cracked open an inch.

'I love you.'

Oh, God, he loves me. Or something. Get me out of here.

He had always had such trouble saying those three words, *I love you*. And now he could say them? Now? There was an intensity about him that seemed new to her. Where was this passion before he left? Where was this look in his eyes when she was in Canberra, wanting so desperately for things to work? Where was this passion when he was over in Quantico again, not even bothering to call after their fight, and she was packing her things to leave him?

'I've missed you so much,' he went on. 'I …'

His eyes seemed to burn intensely as he spoke. They were bloodshot, vulnerable, huge. Her eyes passed over his lips as they trembled slightly. At this display of vulnerability, she felt some part of her let go.

Dammit, Mak, don't fall for it.

She needed him to leave. She needed to keep him at a distance for a while.

In an instant he had Makedde in an embrace, her head resting in the hollow of his neck, lips just millimetres from his warm skin. His scent was intoxicating.

Fuck.

'Andy, it's over.' She said this softly, her eyes shut.

Her heart was not cold to him at all in that moment, not as she wished it to be. There was an ache building in her, a physical ache that soon became unbearable, and she moved closer to him, an automaton. *Watch out.* Running her fingertips over the top of his hand seemed to relieve the ache, but only momentarily. She began to stroke his hair, her mind still caught in a confused attempt to remain safely distant while their bodies moved ever closer together. He leaned into her, head down, his face at her shoulder, dangerously close to the swell of her breast. Perhaps if she just pulled his head into her chest, let him rest there, it would all pass. They could hold each other for a while, reconcile their failure, prepare to move on. Just because it was over between them didn't mean they couldn't love each other still.

'Andy,' she said, mustering some strength. 'I want you to go. *Now.*'

CHAPTER 12

Adam Hart's heart jackhammered in his chest with an uneasy mix of excitement and fear.

It will all be okay …

He was in a back alley outside a down-at-heel motel in a inner suburb of Sydney that was not familiar to him, approaching a parked caravan with his nerves high. It was Bijou's temporary home, currently detached from the tour bus that carried the Théâtre des Horreurs performers from venue to venue, city to city. Her little oasis was a hired vintage Airstream, sitting strangely like a chrome toaster in the dark alley, reflecting streetlights and shadows. Somewhere close, he heard a generator power up with a soft hum. One of the streetlamps was out, glass on the ground crunching under his feet. It had not surprised him to discover that she would not travel in the back of the bus with the band, contortionists, illusionist and dancers. She was a star, and she would not bunk in cheap motels, either. She had her own realm. That only seemed fair. And when he was permitted to be within it, cocooned in his lover's world, it was like no pleasure he had ever experienced.

He was moments away from that world now.

Please let her like this …

In his pocket, Adam had a pearl necklace. It would look beautiful on her, and she would surely love it. They were real pearls, he knew. He held in his hand a bottle of wine he hoped his lover would approve of. He had gone to a pub with a bottle shop a couple of blocks away, and the man behind the counter had recommended it. At a sheltered nineteen — *nearly twenty* as he liked to remind himself — Adam was not yet sophisticated about such things, but he wanted to learn, needed to learn. He had paid nearly $40 for the wine, double what he had hoped to spend. But when he worried about such things he wondered if those were his father's thoughts he heard, not his own.

He would make his own decisions now.

Adam passed the bus that the troupe travelled in. It appeared unoccupied. The final Sydney performance had been a success, and they would be moving on tomorrow to the next venue. He would go with them.

It will be okay. It will all work out …

Adam checked his wrist for cologne with one anxious sniff. The scent was pleasant, spicy. It seemed a grown-up thing to wear. He had scraped some money together to buy the small, expensive bottle, hoping to impress Bijou. Despite his best efforts, he was quickly running out of cash, but he did not want his lover to know that. She was used to the finer things — jewels and silks and sparkling bottles from the Champagne district of France. The least Adam could do was arrive at her door with a bottle of decent wine, even if it broke the bank. Besides, he had other ways to get money if he really needed to. He hoped he wouldn't have to stoop to that level, but right now, his world being what it was, he was not ruling anything out.

'Okay,' he murmured under his breath in a muttered mantra of determination. 'Okay …'

The truth was Adam had never wanted something so badly. He'd never wanted *someone* like this. The thought of having time alone with the woman he had fallen so deeply — and quickly — in love with had thrilled him all day, and he felt a certain fear at the mere fact of his intense longing. Would he scare her off? Would he disappoint her?

What had she seen in him during that first show he attended? He had been in the second row, alone, mesmerised, and when the lights came up and the crowd began to disperse, he was tapped on the shoulder and invited backstage. He had not known what to expect. Certainly he could not have expected to be invited into this divine woman's dressing room.

'Jean-Baptiste …' came a whisper from the shadows, stopping Adam in his tracks.

He whirled in the direction of the voice. *What?* 'Who's there?'

A man leaned in the shadows between the Airstream and the bus, cloaked in darkness, only the tip of his slim, straight nose illuminated in the streetlight. It was a member of the troupe, Adam figured. Perhaps it was the illusionist, Lucien? His conjuring was amazing. Adam had watched his act five times already, and looked forward to seeing it at closer range.

'Oh, hi. I'm Adam!' he said, stepping forward with an eager smile. 'We haven't really been introduced,' he offered, and bravely extended his free hand into the darkness. After a few seconds he realised his handshake was not going to be accepted. Feeling awkward and intimidated, he retracted his hand and put it in his jeans pocket. His eyes adjusted to the light slowly, and soon he could make out the shadowed eyes of the man standing before him. 'Lucien?' he ventured, pronouncing the name badly, sounding younger and more Australian than he had intended.

'It's amazing what you do. You're world class. I'm a bit of a magician myself, actually —'

But before Adam could finish speaking, the strange man squinted balefully at him and walked away. Perhaps he didn't speak English as well as Bijou, Adam thought.

He was left standing alone outside the Airstream, holding the bottle of wine, flustered and embarrassed. More than any other moment of the past week, he felt the urge to find the nearest phone and call home. His mum would be so worried about him. He sometimes imagined her torment, and it was almost enough for him to ring her up. But he didn't want that. He didn't want that life. He couldn't go back now.

And what would his lover do if he phoned home? She would reject him; she would think he wasn't even a *man*. She would think he was a scared little boy. He had only been with one other woman, and she was certainly nothing like Bijou. Her approval meant the world to him. What would she do if he said he had to go home? What if the disapproval he sensed from the other members of the troupe rubbed off on her, and she decided she didn't like him any more? The thought stabbed at him with unbearable insecurity.

Oh, Bijou.

The young man paced for a few minutes, stomach churning. He did his best to gather himself before returning to Bijou's door. He knocked, his heart still beating far too fast for the calm he wished he possessed. As he waited, he exhaled into his palm, checking his breath, and ran a hand over his blond hair, patting it down. His palms, he noted, were sweaty. His body was out of control. A horrible feeling. Uncool.

Just a little longer … and then when you call home you'll have news to be proud of. You will have proved yourself. It will all work out.

There was a faint rustle and the door opened.

Bijou — *La Femme Assassinée* — stood in the doorway, wrapped in a long, elegant silk robe.

At the sight of her, Adam fought for a moment to breathe.

Bijou had lit candles inside the Airstream, the space behind her glowing with warm haloes of light. A gentle waft of her scent curled into his nostrils and settled somewhere in his groin. The mere sight of her aroused him. He was both excited and embarrassed by this visceral, physical effect. He felt helpless before it.

'I … I got you a necklace,' he said, awkwardly pulling the string of luminous pearls from his pocket.

'*Mon amour*,' Bijou murmured in a sweet-smelling whisper. She leaned forward and pressed her warm painted lips to his mouth, leaving her mark on him, possessing him. She took him by the hand and led him inside, closing the door behind him.

Adam Hart's anxieties left him at once.

In the darkness, the man watched his former lover with this new boy, this child of a man, and his eyes narrowed to slits. In the pit of his stomach something hateful and pitiful squirmed. He had felt it before. He knew what it was.

Jealousy.

He would do what he had to do to destroy it.

CHAPTER 13

With shaky hands, Mak sat up and untangled the sheets that had wrapped themselves tightly around her body.

On the windowsill Loulou's alarm clock glowed: 2:35 a.m. Mak was alone, edgy and now viciously awake. She had convinced Andy to leave. She had pushed him out the door and locked it, then cried herself to sleep. *The last time. That is the last time you will ever cry yourself to sleep over him, or any other man.*

But she was restless now. And awake. As her disorientation faded, she realised that something had woken her.

The front door.

There was a footstep. The front door creaked and clicked shut. Someone was definitely there, in the apartment. It was not her imagination. *Shit.* Mak made out the sound of one set of footsteps, not two. It could not be the lovebirds Loulou and Drayson back ahead of schedule …

This is bad …

Immediately, Mak snapped into her well-honed survival mode. With silent stealth, she rolled out of Loulou's bed, arriving in a crouch on the floor and picturing in sharp relief every dimension and object in the dark room. *Set of keys to hold in my fist like a weapon. Alarm clock wire. Knives in a rack in the kitchen — too far. Sliding window one foot away. Garden courtyard beyond.*

There was a noise like something hitting a wall, a rustle of metal, then footsteps approached. *No time.* In seconds Mak had rolled under the bed with the apartment keys in her right fist and one of Drayson's pointy black shoes in the other.

The bedroom light came on.

Mak squinted.

She had only a sliver of vision. The intruder was a man of slim build, with dark hair, wearing jeans and a leather jacket. He was alone. He had his back to her. Strangely, he was leaning casually against the closet door and kicking off his cowboy boots. The leather jacket landed on the floor.

What the …?

With his boots off, he turned towards the bed and began undoing the snaps of his black collared shirt. Mak blinked, still gripping her makeshift weapons, though less tightly. The man's shirt came off to reveal one tattoo after another, illustrating an attractive, toned torso. A large belt buckle, in rockabilly style, cinched his jeans and he unbuckled it with one hand as he tossed his shirt with the other. A face emerged from beneath the crown of rocker hair, a face framed by a familiar quiff and a pair of black-rimmed glasses.

I don't believe this. I don't bloody believe this …

'Bogey …?'

The sound of her voice startled him. He jumped back a metre, then fell into something like a ninja stance, eyes darting in all directions.

'Bogey, it's Mak,' she explained from the safety of her hiding place.

'What ...? Where are you?'

'Don't laugh ... I'm under the bed. I thought you were an intruder.'

He bent to look for her, but she stopped him. 'Don't look! I'm not wearing any clothes.' Her words hung in the air, surreal, and she began to laugh. 'This is so ridiculous! Sometimes I hate Loulou, I really do.'

'Mak? Are you okay? They didn't tell me you were going to be staying.'

'Loulou didn't tell me *you* were here!'

There was either a massive miscommunication somewhere, or Loulou really was a scatterbrain. Or playing Cupid.

'I think this is yours,' Mak said, and held the pointy black shoe out from under the bed as a kind of peace offering.

'Oh, Mak. I'll get you something to put on. I'm so sorry.' She watched the lower half of his body rush off and appear a few moments later accompanied by a fluffy pink robe. He placed it next to the bed, careful not to look at her.

'I'm not sure if this is my colour,' Mak said, still under the bed — relief, bewilderment and a certain excitement coursing through her.

CHAPTER 14

Tuesday morning the summer sun beat down on Lara as she traversed the alley with an armful of boxes and a heavy satchel thrown over her shoulder.

She had already packed her drum kit and personal belongings on the tour bus, and now she halted before the steps of the star performer's gleaming Airstream, hoping to have a chat. She needed to discuss a problem with the glamorous Bijou, presently leaning languidly against her trailer door, shaded from the sun in a silk slip and robe, a cigarette balanced elegantly between the fingers of her right hand.

La Femme Assassinée.

Bijou was fully made up and bejewelled, even though it was morning, as if she thought she might be living in a black-and-white film and had to forever be ready for her close-up. While the rest of the troupe had been eating at a nearby café and packing their things, she would have been powdering, scenting and painting herself. Bijou was never seen without makeup, and she never ate before midday. Breakfast was vulgar, she was often heard to say.

'Tell me you're not going to,' Lara said.

Bijou took a drag of her cigarette, and smiled slightly.

The two women were a study in contrasts. Lara had been born and raised in America and divided her time between Venice Beach, California, and Paris when the troupe was not on the road. Bijou, however, was born in Paris and was proudly, demonstratively French — if arguably from another era. Lara had none of Bijou's affectations. She wore her hair cropped short, and preferred to dress in baggy jeans and T-shirts when not performing in her mannish stage tuxedo. Bijou, on the other hand, would never be seen in anything less than the attire of a star. The concept of casual dressing was anathema to her. Thankfully, she had long ago given up complaining about Lara's lack of feminine glamour. It helped that Lara did not like men, and there was no competition between Bijou and this much younger woman. Bijou reserved her scorn instead for the troupe's other two female members, Gia and Yelena, who it seemed were never thin enough or pretty enough to live up to her demands.

Lara and Bijou shared an unusual relationship that defied conventional labels. In fact, most of the troupe could be described in such terms. Few on the outside would understand their dynamic. But one thing was clear: Bijou was the star, the senior and founding member of the troupe, and had the final say in all of the big decisions. And she held the purse. Her absolute authority was rarely questioned. Lara was the only member of the troupe who would even dare to delicately enquire about Bijou's decisions, or choice of company ... which she was questioning now.

The packing up was being finalised before the drive to the final show of their Australian tour, and while Bijou was wasting time with her cigarette — and Lara was waiting for a response — the rest of the troupe was doing the heavy work. Lara was becoming impatient.

'Don't do this again,' she pressed, the satchel weighing heavily on her shoulder. The petite performer only flashed her beautifully painted eyes at the younger woman in response, then turned her gaze to observe the well-built young man walking towards them, the subject of Lara's comments. The boy had the moronic beauty of youth in abundance, Lara had to concede. His hair was blond and thick, his body lean, fit, and precisely formed. He had been in the company of the theatrical troupe for a full week. For Lara, this was seven days too many, but the star performer clearly thought otherwise, and no doubt would have her way. Bijou was no dummy. She spoke fluent English and Russian, in addition to her native French, and yet when it suited her she would feign misunderstanding. '*Comment? Je ne comprends pas.*' Or, as with this conversation, she would simply choose not to respond. Bijou had no peer in the art of getting her way.

'Brisbane? For one show? Why bother?' Lara complained, before he was in earshot.

And certainly not Paris …

At that moment the young man approached bearing a styrofoam cup of coffee.

Bijou had sent him to fetch a café au lait, her morning beverage of choice. It would be pretty hard to find coffee she liked once they hit the road again. Adam must have sensed he was being watched. He looked up with an eager smile, his eyes directed towards the object of his flagrant crush, who for her part returned his gaze with an encouraging nod and a flick of the tassel of her robe.

Merde.

Lara shook her head, not finding the words to express the frustrated thoughts cycling through her brain.

The young man waved in their direction with the enthusiasm of a child, and sped up his pace. Bijou, having remained silent all this time, only smiled mischievously. '*Pourquoi pas?*' she said.

Why not?

And then Bijou, the infamous scream queen, the assassinated woman, vanished into her trailer, leaving only the teasingly beautiful scent of L'Air du Temps, and the whirl of silk robe in her wake.

CHAPTER 15

First thing on Tuesday morning Makedde Vanderwall sprinted to the bathroom to avoid her accidental roommate, Bogey Mortimer.

Thirty minutes later she emerged, composed, fresh and perfumed, wearing a blouse and pencil skirt, heels in hand, hair tamed and makeup applied, the slight puffiness of her eyes the only clue to the draining and near-sleepless twenty-four hours she had experienced. She wished she could have put her alarm forward by an hour or two, but she was eager to meet Tobias Murphy before he left for school. It was still too early in the morning to call Loulou, who would no doubt be sleeping off another night of holiday festivities in Byron. Mak would have a few choice words with her later.

She padded quietly across the polished concrete floor of the hallway, unsure if Bogey would be awake. After only a few steps, her nostrils knew the answer.

Coffee.

Bogey was in the kitchen, preparing breakfast and working the coffee machine like a barista. He turned when she approached. 'Hi,' she watched his mouth say, mesmerised. He gave her a slow, friendly smile. 'You obviously don't need beauty sleep. You look great.'

She felt herself grow a little taller with his compliment. 'Hello, stranger,' she replied, and immediately regretted the cliché. She still felt somewhat off guard in his presence. The couch was a little dishevelled, a doona thrown over one end. 'I hope you slept okay.'

'I slept just fine. Espresso or latte?' he asked.

'Oh, I'd love a latte. Thank you.'

'I think there's enough milk,' he replied, tipping the carton. 'I made you some toast and eggs. I hope you don't mind scrambled?'

'Perfect.'

Heaven. Is this heaven?

Mak had not seen Drayson's friend Bogey Mortimer in almost a year. Back then, she'd had rather a crush on him. He was attractive, artistic, sensitive, interesting. She had convinced herself that he had seemed appealing because she and Andy were having problems — and Bogey was so different to the jaded, stoic cop that was Detective Andy Flynn. In the time since she'd last seen Bogey she had wrestled with her relationship with Andy and finally moved to Canberra to make it work, only to watch everything between them dissolve into misery and petty bickering. That once promising future was gone. She knew the reality of the loneliness and frustration the relationship held for her. It was over.

And here he is. Bogey. I can't believe it.

'You still hanging out in strip clubs for a living?' he quipped, plating their breakfast.

Mak laughed. 'Not lately. But I'll have to make a return.'

Shortly after their first meeting in Melbourne, she had dragged Bogey along to a lap dancing club called Thunderballs when a case had led her to contact a particular dancer at the club. Bogey had agreed to be her fake boyfriend, so she wouldn't arouse too much suspicion in the male-dominated environment. She recalled how he had sat nervously tapping his foot and wondering where to look while a dancer named Charlotte tried to wiggle her way around Mak's probing questions, quite in the buff. Memories of that shared moment brought a slight grin to her lips.

'You still designing coffins for bikie gangs?' was her comeback. Once a coffin-maker in small-town Australia, Bogey had moved on to designing furniture, but not before his services had been enlisted by the Coffin Cheaters gang, who'd had him make coffin-shaped eskies and tables for their club-house when he was a teenager. In return, they had marked him with a number of wild tattoos.

'No coffins this week,' he replied good-naturedly.

She sat on a stool and he served her, leaning over her for a moment to put her plate down. He smelled like honey and amber incense, and her attention lingered on his scent, before the lure of food drew her to her plate. The eggs looked perfect, and steamingly hot. Mak herself was domestically retarded. She could barely cook toast. 'Thanks, Bogey. This looks fantastic.'

'My pleasure. I thought you could use some caffeine and sustenance.'

That I can.

After breakfast she led Bogey into Loulou's bedroom. 'I really am sorry about the mix-up. I put your things over there.' She pointed to one corner of the room.

116

I touched his underwear. I folded goddamn Bogey Mortimer's underwear without even knowing it.

'It's no problem, really. I'm the one who's sorry. No one wants to wake up like that.'

Mak left that one alone.

'I had to drive back to St Kilda on Saturday for a couple of extra things from the shop.' He had a boutique furniture shop showcasing his own designs.

That would be why she hadn't been disturbed the first night.

'You must be exhausted from all that driving.'

'I like driving,' he said, and she remembered his beautiful vintage car. Who wouldn't enjoy driving that?

Standing so close to him, her heart sped up. Or maybe it was the fresh caffeine. She remembered watching him take his shirt off. Tattoos. Skin.

Loulou, dammit. You could have prepared me.

Bogey leaned down and picked up the folded pile of his things. Her eyes clapped on his form a touch too long — the curve of his muscles, the back of his neck — and when he stood up again, she looked down at her feet.

Awkward. This is awkward.

'Thanks again for breakfast. You are so thoughtful. I am so sorry to eat and run, but I have a case,' she said abruptly. 'Perhaps we can catch up later? I'd love to hear what you've been up to.'

She turned on her heel and headed out, still not quite believing the night she'd had.

CHAPTER 16

He'd only just finished breakfast, but Detective Jimmy Cassimatis was already keen for a snack.

He fished around in the top drawer of his desk and found it littered with crumbs, balled paper, mangled staples and the Mars bar he sought. Again the thought came into his head.

This place sucks since Andy left.

To say that he missed having his partner around would be an understatement. Since Flynn left for his lofty new post at the serial crime unit, the department had gone down the tubes. He had no real partner in crime now. The losers he'd been paired with did not count, including the latest, Rhys. Drifting in a daily grind of violent arseholes and paperwork, Jimmy was not finding life rewarding. But it was worse to see Andy so listless. The sight of it somehow ruined a fantasy of Jimmy's.

Lamenting his life, and perturbed that he'd already eaten most of his daily ration of Mars bar before eight-thirty — his doctor had him on blood-thinning medication and rations of his favourite foods — he did not hear his superior, Detective Brad Hunt, until he was on him like some rabid dog.

'You better tell Flynn to get that woman on a leash,' came the snarl from over Jimmy's shoulder.

Jimmy was unprepared, and dropped the chocolate bar onto his bulging belly. It did not have far to fall.

'Ah, woman?' Jimmy mumbled.

'Your mate's girlfriend is back in town, isn't she? Vanderwall?'

Jimmy opened the top drawer of his desk, plonked the remains of his chocolate bar inside and closed it with a squeak. He couldn't enjoy his snack in Hunt's presence.

Jimmy crossed his meaty arms. 'Huh?' he replied, purposely vague.

Detective Senior Sergeant Bradley Hunt was a royal annoyance. He had an exaggerated chin like a hero in a Marvel comic, and at present he had that chin tilted high, looking down his nose at Senior Constable Cassimatis as if he were a rookie. *Fuck you, I've been here longer than you, knob jockey.* Despite having done much less time in the police force, Hunt had rapidly risen above Jimmy's rank. Jimmy was not a fan of Hunt's. And Andy's departure had meant that Jimmy had to put up with the likes of Hunt on a more regular basis.

'Macaylay Vanderwall is back in town,' Hunt stated.

It's Makedde, you idiot.

Jimmy had no intention of confirming the fact. Mak and Jimmy had their differences, and she and his best friend had only just split, but he had a soft spot for her. Always had. The last thing he had any desire to do was feed information about her or Andy to this halfwit undeserving arselicker. For starters, it was none of his business where she was. But most important, the guy was a royal tool.

He could feel Hunt's eyes burning into the back of his head. He was waiting for a reply.

'Yeah?' Jimmy muttered. 'Oh.' He unfolded his arms and hunched over his small desk, pretending to take an interest in his paperwork again.

'She better not try to pull any more stunts like last year.'

Stunts? Like nearly getting your mates charged with murder? That kind of stunt, you arsehole?

Jimmy said nothing. He was no good at office politics, but he knew enough not to say what he was thinking this time.

'She's been hanging round outside their house. The Cavanaghs. On her motorbike. I can't imagine what she's trying to prove.'

Oh, Mak. Mak, Mak, Mak …

Makedde had attracted trouble for as long as Jimmy had known her, but she had really put herself in it when she had decided to set herself in the sights of one of the most powerful families in Australia. Why she would be baiting them now, he could not imagine either. It had been Jimmy himself whom she had called in a whisper from inside the Cavanaghs' palatial Darling Point mansion during Damien Cavanagh's lavish thirtieth-birthday celebrations the previous year, to say that she had 'happened across' the room where a hapless Jane Doe had been killed some days earlier. Sure, Makedde had all the right answers in the subsequent interrogation — how she had come to the A-list party as a guest, and it was only when she happened across the room with a particular Brett Whiteley painting on the wall that she realised it was the same room that matched video footage of the crime scene. But all her cleverness wasn't going to keep her safe if she kept making trouble for herself.

Mak had not been on the guest list. She had known exactly what she was doing. But all that was over last year. What did she think she was doing now?

'If she knows what's good for her, she'll go right back to the States where she came from.'

'Detective *Cunt*, she's Canadian, actually,' Jimmy corrected him quietly, under his breath.

'Did you say something?'

Jimmy stood, pushing his chair out with a scraping sound across the floor. He walked off with his paperwork. 'I said I need another coffee.'

Hunt watched him go. He didn't bother to congratulate him on his breakthrough in the Macleay St burglary he'd been so keen for them to solve.

CHAPTER 17

Mak turned onto the road to St Ives, distracted, her hands gripping the wheel too tightly. She was thinking about Andy. He had saved her life once, years before. She had really believed in him then. And now? Now it was over. There was much hostility and hurt between them.

Horrible.

And then there was Bogey.

He was in town for a week for meetings to sell his new furniture range. After getting over the shock of their initial reacquaintance, she was starting to quite like the idea of him being there. Who wouldn't like a home-cooked breakfast? A compliment? A handsome face to wake up to? She hoped he didn't leave, now that he knew that Loulou and Drayson had double-booked them at Loulou's little apartment. Would he stay on the couch?

Don't rebound.

Humphrey — or Bogey as he preferred to be called — had been the focus of some considerable romantic thought for a spell the previous year. He was unlike any man she had met. In addition to his previous life as a coffin-maker, he had played guitar in Drayson's band, Electric Possum, and even worked as a masseur. He had a small shop in Melbourne where he designed and sold his own handmade custom furniture, and was getting his hands into more than just pine. In fact, he'd got his hands onto her, too. It had only been a platonic massage, of course. She had complained of a backache, and he had graciously offered to help. But those hands had been memorable. Never mind that she had touched herself that night with a private lust coursing through her, and had taken mere minutes to shudder to guilty orgasm with the thought of those hands of his. She was still living with Andy at the time, so there had been no room to explore that particular romantic possibility.

Things were different now.

Here it is.

Mak slowed down. She found herself feeling uncharacteristically anxious as she eyed the Murphy family's stucco home. She passed the Hart household not eight doors down. Glenise Hart didn't appear to be at home, and the street was quiet except for a man in a cap pulling up to the kerb half a block away, and a little kid running around a yard with a puppy.

Try to keep it about Adam. For now …

She genuinely wanted to do the best possible job with Adam's case. She wanted to find him quickly and safely. The rest was another issue. That she hoped to be dealing with soon …

Mak got out of the car, adjusted her jacket — and 'button' — and looked over her shoulder. She walked towards the house, feeling all the moisture evaporate from her mouth. She knocked, and stood gripping her briefcase in a trembling hand. She swallowed hard.

He's just a kid. Like any other.

An attractive woman of about forty opened the door, blonde and smiling pleasantly.

'Hi. I'm sorry to bother you. Is Mr Murphy in?'

'Kevin isn't in at the moment. I am his wife, Linda,' she said, still smiling, only now there was a flash of curiosity there, concern even.

'Hi, Linda. It's lovely to meet you.' She extended a hand, and Linda took it. 'My name is Makedde Vanderwall. I'm a private investigator.' She braced herself for whatever response this introduction brought.

The woman's jaw dropped. 'You are ... *her*? Wow! Makedde!' She said Mak's name perfectly. 'It's my pleasure to meet you. Please, please come in.'

Mak stepped inside and followed Linda down a hallway of plush carpet to a cream-and-brown kitchen.

'I'll get you some tea.'

'No, thank you. Just water.' Mak had already decided she wasn't interested in tea any more. If she hadn't had so much of Glenise Hart's tea, she might have just gone to bed, instead of feeling wired and emotional and coming dangerously close to sleeping with her ex.

Linda handed her a glass. 'I've heard so much about you. Kevin is so grateful. Really. What you did for Tobias was incredible. You gave him a new life.'

Mak smiled. She found herself feeling proud. 'I was wondering if I could possibly meet him. Is Tobias here?'

'Sure. I'll get him. I'm sure he'll be happy to finally meet you.'

It was, in some ways, extraordinary that the two had not already met. She had been instrumental in his release from custody, and in clearing his name. He had been a street kid, and he had a chance at a normal life now, in part thanks to her investigative efforts. Mak shook her head. She had been back in Sydney only a few days, and already she had a job and she was finally meeting Tobias. She was doing fine, even if things were tough in her personal life.

There was movement in the hall. Eventually a figure emerged. *Tobias.* Mak was pleasantly shocked by his appearance. By her calculation, a year had passed since he was put on the path to rehabilitation, but already Tobias looked nothing like the photographs she had seen in his file. He had put on weight. He had got a haircut. And underneath all that long greasy hair that used to obscure his face, there was a normal, if fragile-looking, seventeen-year-old.

'Hi,' the boy said.

Tobias wore grey school trousers and a white shirt, so different from his ragged, dirty street clothes. His hands were dug deep into the trouser pockets. He looked at Makedde for only a moment, and then stared down at his bare toes, as if they held some great interest.

'Tobias. It is really nice to finally meet you.'

'Please sit down and talk with Makedde, Tobias,' Linda said, gesturing to a chair.

'Could I perhaps speak to him alone for a few minutes?' Mak said to his stepmother in a low voice. Linda nodded and smiled. 'Just don't make him late for school.'

Tobias and Makedde sat side by side in the colour-coordinated kitchen. It would be somewhat of a contrast to the soup kitchen he would have eaten in at the city mission. When he used to eat. Heroin did not do much for the appetite.

'How is it here, Tobias? Do you like it?'

He nodded. 'Okay. Good. Yeah.'

'You look pretty happy.'

'Yeah.' This seemed an honest response. Perhaps it was the shy version of jumping up and down and screaming with joy because you are no longer locked away for murder.

'That's really good,' Mak said gently.

He looked up at her and searched her face for a moment. 'They said that you went away.'

'I did. Just to Canberra for a while, but it didn't work out, so I'm back to work here in Sydney again,' she replied.

Although he was seventeen, Tobias seemed, in some ways, younger. His heavy drug use and the problems of street life, and no doubt his emotional traumas as well, seemed to have slowed his social development subtly. He was introverted, but there was something more as well, a kind of hesitation and bewilderment in his manner.

'Did you miss your mum?' he asked her.

Makedde's throat tightened. Her mother had died of cancer when she was a teenager. Why would Tobias know anything about that?

'Is that why you came back?' he continued, when she failed to reply.

The penny dropped. 'I'm from Canada, actually, which is why I have this funny accent. I get back to Canada to visit my dad every year, but my mother passed away when I was about your age. A bit younger, actually.'

Her hands were so swollen and puffy. Warm, puffy hands, and the sound of the respirator …

Tobias frowned, as if he might have said the wrong thing.

'It's okay. It was a long time ago for me.' *Like yesterday.* 'I'm sorry about *your* mum.' She knew that Tobias's mother had suffered with severe, debilitating depression for a number of years, and had killed herself a couple of years earlier. 'It must have been incredibly hard to lose her.'

He nodded barely perceptibly at this acknowledgement of his huge loss.

'I'm really glad things are going well for you now, Tobias. Really glad.'

'Thank you.'

Mak felt strangely touched by the conversation. She had touched a life. *His life.* All those silly private investigations with rotten cheating spouses and rip-off artists trying to pretend they had whiplash, and here she had really done something. She had changed a life in a tangible, positive way.

'I'm not actually here to talk to you about all that stuff. I'm trying to find out about Adam Hart from down the street. You two are friends?'

'A bit.'

A bit? 'You know each other a little?' she suggested.

He nodded, which could mean anything from close friendship to a single conversation.

'When did you last see him?'

'A while ago.'

'A week ago?' she pressed.

'Longer.'

Mak felt fresh disappointment weigh on her. 'How recently?' she said, still trying.

He shrugged his shoulders again.

'Was he in any trouble at home?'

He stuck his lip out and shook his head.

'Are there any people you can think of who don't like

Adam? Enemies?'

He shrugged again.

'Can you think of any reason why Adam would want to leave home, Tobias?' She leaned in slightly, and watched his face carefully.

'Again?' Tobias asked, and Mak straightened up.

'Yes. Again.' *Again?* 'When was the last time?'

'With his girlfriend,' he said, as if it were obvious.

Her heart sped up. 'Oh, you mean ...' Makedde trailed off, and waited for him to fill in the blanks. After a few seconds of silence, he did exactly what she had hoped.

'Patricia,' Tobias said.

'Yes, Patricia,' she agreed, wondering who Patricia was and when she could speak to her. 'What is her last name again?'

He looked blank. Perhaps he had never been told Patricia's last name. She didn't want to lose him on that point. Adam's mother would certainly know who she was, but why hadn't she told Mak about her, and that her son had left home before? Was it because she thought everyone would assume he had done the same thing again? That was, in fact, exactly what Mak was doing.

'How long ago was that? It was only ...' She trailed off again, expectantly.

'Ages ago.'

Perhaps yesterday was ages ago. It was hard to tell.

'Since you moved here?'

He nodded. *So less than a year ago.*

'And Adam told you about it?'

A nod.

'Do you remember what he said?'

He shook his head, perhaps deciding he'd said too much.

'Tobias, I noticed you're on Facebook.' She had done some internet searches. 'You and Adam are friends on Facebook, aren't you? Do you think you could hook him and me up? I wouldn't get him in any trouble, I just want to chat with him. You know, he is nineteen, and if he doesn't want to come home he doesn't have to. I just want to chat.'

Tobias appeared to think about this for a while. 'Sure, I can hook you two up. If he's checking his messages and stuff.'

'Oh, that would be very helpful. Thank you, Tobias.'

He perked up a little, and even offered a very small version of a smile. 'What's your handle?'

Mak blinked. *Handle?* 'I'll, uh, send you a message tomorrow, and we'll do it that way. I'll just go by my name.' It was best to deal with these two honestly from step one. Anything else could be seen as disingenuous. She had to gain Adam's trust.

'Cool.'

'Yes,' Mak thought. *Very cool.*

CHAPTER 18

There is another man.

Andy Flynn sat at Jimmy's kitchen table, resting heavily on his elbows. His face felt puffy and he thought his eyes might close up again at any moment. He had made an ill-advised stop at a pub in Surry Hills after Mak threw him out of her apartment, and when he had returned to her door he had seen another man arrive.

Him.

Andy did not know the man's name, but he was familiar. He was some kind of rocker. Andy needed only to observe him approaching the apartment block at three in the morning to know that Mak was with him — that he was there for *her*.

He is the other man. That's him. There had to be someone else, he had reasoned.

Andy was not a man who cried, but driving back to Jimmy's he had pulled the car over suddenly, and wept like a madman against the steering wheel on the side of the road. The experience had unnerved him, and no less now as he looked back on it after a few hours of broken sleep. He wondered if he had finally gone over the edge.

Cassandra, and now Makedde — the women you love — they leave you. They always leave you. You are cursed. You are poison …

'You look like shit,' Jimmy said. His mate was smiling at him as he spoke, but Andy spotted the look of genuine concern in his eyes.

'Thanks. I'm sorry if I woke anyone. I got in pretty late.'

'No, mate. Everyone in this house sleeps like the dead, except me,' Jimmy told him. 'I've never been much of a sleeper.'

Few cops were. The odd hours and the focus of the job gave a person plenty of reasons not to sleep well at night.

'So what's the deal? You bang her, or what?'

An image of Makedde's arched back sprang to mind. 'Shouldn't you be at work already?' Andy retorted.

'You *are* the job,' Jimmy said, in long-drawn-out syllables and a voice much deeper than his own natural tone. He pointed at his mate with an extended index finger, then pulled the 'trigger'. 'Bang!' He slapped his chubby hands together.

'Yeah, some hitman you'd make,' Andy murmured humourlessly.

'I been already to headquarters and come back, mate.'

'Jesus. I did wake late.' He looked at the digital clock on the microwave and saw it was nearly nine.

'Some of us have *real* jobs,' Jimmy quipped, Andy's job being of much higher rank, status and pay than his own.

'Look, I gotta say, that cunt Hunt really jerks me off. He is *very* bloody interested in your Makedde.'

She's not my Makedde now. If she ever was.

'What do you mean?' Andy asked.

Jimmy walked to a cupboard and pulled out a tin with a lock on it. 'I mean he knows she's back in town,' Jimmy continued. 'And he seems a little too interested.'

'What do you mean by a little too interested? Like he wants to stalk her? Ask her out?'

'Probably both.' Jimmy pulled a ring of keys off his belt and opened the lock. He pulled a Mars bar out.

Andy could not believe what he was seeing. 'You are joking. You actually lock away your Mars bars?'

'You don't have kids. You wouldn't understand.' Jimmy unwrapped a corner and took a bite. 'What Hunt said was that she "better not start stirring shit up again" or something to that effect.' He was speaking with his mouth full. 'He meant the Cavanaghs.' Jimmy sat and the chair creaked under his weight.

'Can we not talk about her right now?'

Jimmy frowned. There was an awkward pause.

'I had a beauty come through this morning. You know that burglary down in Macleay Street?'

'No,' Andy answered flatly.

'Well, some rich prick got his fancy house robbed on the weekend, and apparently there was hundreds of thousands of dollars' worth of jewels and shit there. "Woe is me, I only have five million dollars left," and all that. Hunt was all over it, pushing everyone to make the guy who did the place. And guess who gets to look a genius this week?' He grinned proudly and raised his hand.

'Um, you.'

'I found a pair of leather gloves in the yard, discarded. And yup, they found the index finger and thumb on the right glove matched prints in the house, and inside the gloves were a couple of full handprints, with perfectly usable fingerprints. What a moron for tossing the gloves at the crime scene. And for using hand cream before he put his gloves on. *Skata*. He must've been some kind of metrosexual robber.'

'They just don't make criminals like they used to,' Andy said darkly. He felt bad about it, but he was not in the mood for Jimmy's humour, and he was no good at pretending.

Jimmy was silent for a while. Andy wished he could have been more enthusiastic for him. His mate really did need a professional break like that. How many robbers use hand cream? Prints had been lifted from inside gloves before, but it was still fairly rare. It had never worked in any of his cases.

'Anyway, I just came for coffee and to see how you doin'.'

'Thanks, Jimmy.'

Nearly fifteen minutes passed, with Jimmy staring at the newspaper and Andy staring into the bottom of a second bad cup of instant coffee.

'So,' Jimmy finally said. 'You bang her, or what?'

Andy gave him a look that froze him.

'No, mate,' Andy finally said, pushing his cup away. 'It looks like she's banging someone else already.'

CHAPTER 19

The grounds of the Eastern Suburbs Memorial Park Crematorium were hot and still. At eleven o'clock the February morning sun was already vicious, casting crisp shadows and bright rays across the pale Art Deco chapel in which a small service was underway.

Three people occupied the little chapel, one of them in a coffin.

At a modest podium, a pastor read a passage from Psalm 23. 'Yea, though I walk through the valley of the shadow of death, I will fear no evil: for thou art with me; thy rod and thy staff they comfort me. Thou preparest a table before me in the presence of mine enemies ...'

The pews were empty save for a solitary hulking figure, hunched at the shoulders. The killer Luther Hand sat alone in a dark suit, his hat held in his scarred hands. His head was bowed, his eyes closed. He was not sure if he had ever in his life cried, and as such he was slightly perplexed by the moisture collecting in the corners of his eyes. Tears? His tears? His eyes had seen violence; violence committed by his own hands, and by others; violence done to tear at and scar his own face, his head, his oversized body, which lived on like a battered monolith. But tears? His eyes had not been blurred by tears.

'We say goodbye to Cathy Davis today, knowing that she is in a better place …'

Luther's grief at losing his parent and only living relative was compounded by the enforced distance he had kept from her in the decade before her death. He had long ago made a professional decision that kept him from having her — or anyone else — intimately involved in his life, and as he prospered in his lethal trade, he had disappeared from her completely. She had believed him dead, and from a distance he had watched her grieve for him. At first he had felt it a small sacrifice, but he had soon grown to be tormented by it. With the nature of Luther's work, it had been safest that Cathy Davis knew nothing of him, and that they had no ties. He would never have forgiven himself if something had happened to her because of him.

Sooner or later, the loved ones of killers met a horrible end. Luther knew that.

And there was one other reason he had disappeared from her life. Perhaps it was even the real reason. Cathy Davis would know, in one glance, what her son had become.

The phone in his pocket bore a message from one of his main agents, Madame Q.

PRAGUE. DOUBLE. 24 HOURS.

It was another contract. He had accepted it not minutes after arriving in Sydney.

Killer.

Luther had become a killer, and his mother would have known it, just looking at him — the fine weave of his suit, his watch, his car, his scarred face, his hands. His eyes. He spent much of his life in transit, a global citizen with no real country, no loyalties, no ties. The men and women he killed trailed behind him like ghosts.

His mother would have seen them.

The pastor continued with Ecclesiastes. '… A good name is better than precious ointment; and the day of death than the day of one's birth …'

The day of death.

Luther's mother had not been religious, and he was not raised to be familiar with the Bible. For all his close proximity to death he had never heard such a sentiment before. Certainly he had been there at the end of many people's lives, but none of them had seemed desirous of their end. The pastor's words meant little to him. They offered no comfort. They did not reflect any reality he knew. He had lost the one woman who loved him, the only person who loved him, the only woman who knew his name. What help could words be?

Australia now seemed to encapsulate not only his humble beginnings, but all of his failures. With his mother now gone, there was no reason for him to return.

The music rose to a crescendo, and with only the pastor — a stranger — and Luther to watch, the curtains were closed on the alcove at the front of the room, and the coffin was rolled into a cremation chamber that would burn his mother at over 750 degrees, reducing to a few kilos of bone fragment and ash the body that had borne Luther Hand thirty-seven years before.

CHAPTER 20

'Loulou, I was practically *naked*,' Makedde Vanderwall explained, her phone in one hand and a bag of takeaway Thai food in the other. 'I *was* naked!' Her voice echoed through the hallway of Loulou's apartment building.

'Darling, that doesn't sound like it was all bad. I thought you liked Bogey.'

'Are you stoned or something? Come on, Loulou,' Makedde said, exasperated and fumbling with the keys. 'I knew you'd try something like this. He's a nice guy, yes, but you should have told me. You should have told *him*.' Loulou was notoriously fun-loving and vague, but Mak was amazed that she could not win this simple point. 'What if I had beaned him with a frying pan before realising who he was? You know what I'm like. It could have been a disaster. We could have both spent the night in emergency.'

Mak put the keys in the door. 'Anyway, it's fine now. I think he's just going to sleep on the couch till he leaves for Melbourne. Look, I should go. He could be home. And I've got Karen coming over for a quick lunch catch-up. I'll say hi to her for you. Just keep enjoying Byron, and remind me to kill you when you get back …'

'Love you, sweetheart!'

'Ugh. You too.' She hung up and shook her head.

Loulou.

Mak let herself into the apartment and the door clicked shut behind her. It was the middle of the day, and the apartment was light with sunbeams. The garden looked green and overgrown beyond the windows. It was quiet.

'Bogey?'

There was no answer.

The couch was tidy, the cushions neat, and there was no sign of the doona or Bogey's things. For a moment her chest tightened with the thought he had gone back to Melbourne already, or found another place to stay. She had bought a bit of extra Thai in case he was home. It had been nice of him to cook her breakfast. Their meeting had embarrassed her, but she didn't want him to leave.

Ten minutes later there was a buzzing at the door panel, and soon Mak heard her friend make her way down the echoing hallway to Loulou's door. Mak opened it with a smile.

'Karen, it's so great to see you.'

The women embraced.

Karen looked, and felt, thin. She was a detective constable working homicide, and Mak had first met her at the gruesome crime scene of her friend Catherine Gerber's murder years ago, when she'd first arrived in Australia — the same crime scene where she'd met Andy, whom Karen had been working with. It looked liked work had been tough for the curly-haired redhead lately.

'I have to say a big congratulations to you again on your promotion to detective. That's really brilliant,' Mak told her.

'Thanks.' Karen had worked hard to earn it, particularly being one of the younger officers in the department.

'Come in, come in. I got us some Thai.'

Twenty minutes later, Loulou's small living room was strewn with dirty dishes, napkins, flimsy wooden chopsticks, and plastic tubs reddened in splatters with remnants of sweet chilli sauce. Karen and Mak were curled up in opposite corners of the comfortable furry sofa, finishing the last of their lunch.

'I've checked with the morgues,' Mak said, continuing the brainstorming over her missing nineteen-year-old. She was more familiar with such places than most. Her detective inspector father had first taken her to a morgue for father–daughter bonding when she was twelve. 'No one of his description is listed at the hospitals either. I don't know where he is, but I doubt he's lying under a stiff white sheet anywhere. It seems to me that he shimmied down that drainpipe and ran away, but I guess I can't be sure. It would be pretty awful for his mum. I don't think she has anyone else.'

Makedde pushed a lonely prawn around a cooling bed of flat noodles, feeling the weight of her own loneliness, despite the company of her friend. 'And if he's not okay, I don't want to be the one to tell Mrs Hart that her son dropped the wrong acid and has turned up as a John Doe somewhere,' she continued. 'God knows that happens enough.'

'I thought he didn't do drugs?' Karen piped up.

'Exactly.'

She took a sip of cold water. It moved down nearly to the base of her belly. She had not eaten enough. She would have to be careful not to lose too much weight on what Loulou called the 'Divorce Diet'. Perhaps this was the reason for Karen's weight loss?

'Any men on the scene, Karen?'

'Like romance? No.'

They continued eating.

'Sorry about the shop talk, but … you know the case I did last time in Sydney? And the homicide scene you attended?'

'How could I forget?' Karen replied, flashing her customary wry smile. 'It was front-page news there for a while …'

'Well, remember that poor street kid, Tobias Murphy, wrongly arrested for the stabbing? Guess what? Tobias is living down the street from my new client. Tobias's dad recommended me.'

Karen digested her words. 'Really?' She sounded unimpressed. Perhaps, like Marian, Karen wasn't happy about the connection.

'I met Tobias this morning. He's out of rehab and living with his dad and stepmum. It's a happy ending for him, considering he nearly ended up in prison for life,' Mak continued. She strongly suspected that the Cavanagh family was to blame, and resented them still being out there, free and privileged and able to do what they pleased. But she had cleared Tobias. She had done that much.

'It was amazing what you did with that case, Mak. It really was,' Karen told her.

Makedde stared down at the table, and her regrets returned. 'I think we both know the bad guys didn't get caught.'

A frustrated look twisted Karen's features. 'Mak …'

'No, seriously. We both know the Cavanaghs were involved,' Mak insisted. 'Enough bullshit with this thing.'

'There was a full confession from that Aston guy. Case closed.' Simon Aston had been Damien Cavanagh's right-hand man for a time.

'We both know that Damien Cavanagh was there when that girl died, and she was *underage* for godsake, and it sure seemed like they had been pretty intimate with each other … yet he was never even formally questioned? Come on, we both know that isn't right.' Mak was angry. 'He's a monster.'

The problem was money. The Cavanagh family was so powerful, they could evidently protect their son from anything. There had even been video footage placing the Cavanagh heir at the scene. Sure, it was grainy, but Mak had seen it. It was him. The Cavanagh family's heir, right there.

'Maybe you saw Aston in the video, not Cavanagh?' Karen suggested. Simon Aston had supposedly confessed to the killing, and was shortly afterwards found hanging from a chandelier in an apparent suicide. To Mak, he seemed a little too conveniently dead. He would have known a lot about Damien.

'Simon Aston was *blond,*' Mak pointed out. 'And built. The guy in the video looked exactly like Damien Cavanagh. Dark hair, slim build. He had his shirt off for Christsake; there was no mixing them up.'

Karen seemed a little less sure of her position. 'Well, I haven't seen the footage, but they've looked at it and decided it's not Damien Cavanagh. We've talked about this before, and I really don't think—'

'Who are *they*?'

Karen furrowed her brow. 'What?'

'*They* have looked at the video and decided it's not him. Who are they?' Makedde demanded, getting worked up once more over the police handling of the case, and now in front of a police officer, a member of that clique. She and Andy had already fought over the issue many times. Was it to have the same detrimental effect on her friendship with Karen? 'Who *has* looked at the video?' Mak went on, unable to stop herself. 'Because Andy hasn't seen it. *You* haven't seen it. Andy said that Jimmy hasn't seen it, either. So exactly who *has* seen it?'

'Well, Hunt, for starters,' was her friend's reply. 'He was on the case.'

'Ah, Hunt,' Mak said with a hint of incredulity. She raised an eyebrow.

Detective Hunt was Karen's senior. He was politically minded and intent on climbing the ranks. Mak did not like him, or trust him. And like many who wanted to make it in Sydney, he apparently mingled with the Cavanaghs.

'Okay. But others would have seen it too.' Karen screwed up her face. 'You know, Hunt knows you're back, and he mentioned it to me this morning like I would be impressed that he knew.' Karen seemed a little disturbed by the fact, in light of Mak's comments. 'I think you should just drop this stuff. Be careful. The Cavanaghs probably haven't forgotten about you,' she warned.

Well, that's mutual then.

Mak knew she was complaining about something Karen had no power over, but she could not help but continue to plead her case. 'So the death took place in the Cavanagh home, as I managed to prove by getting in there myself, because no one else would try. And there is a man on the video with the dead girl, and he looks exactly like Damien Cavanagh. And he has never been formally questioned? Never a person of interest? Nothing?'

Silence descended on the small apartment. Mak was seething over the injustice and Karen had crawled into her own thoughts. The air was icy.

'*Time takes a cigarette. Puts it in your mouth …*'

The strains of David Bowie's 'Rock 'n' Roll Suicide' drifted across the courtyard, and with the tension temporarily allayed, Karen spoke. 'That murder was one of the more horrible ones I've seen.'

Karen had been part of the team called to the scene when Meaghan Wallace was found slashed to death in her apartment. The victim had struggled valiantly with her attacker, and Karen had been confronted with blood streaked across the walls, the furniture, and soaked into the carpet. Stabbings were notoriously messy, and television shows did not accurately capture the graphic horror of real-life crimes. It was Makedde's strong belief that Meaghan Wallace — who was Tobias Murphy's cousin — had been killed in this horrible manner simply because she witnessed the Cavanagh heir up to no good, and the family was afraid she would go to the police. The witnessing of one death had led to the other. It was a hit.

'Karen, I don't want to put any heat on you, but—'

'Then *don't*.' Karen glared at her with glistening green eyes, the intensity of which gave Mak pause.

She soon regained herself. 'Come on. You used to be a lot more fun with this stuff.'

Nothing. Not even a smirk in response.

'Look, if you just happen to find yourself tying up loose ends with the old Wallace case …' she dared to continue '… and the Cavanagh stuff —'

'Don't even start.' Again, the look was intense.

'All I'm saying is that there might be something obvious that's been overlooked, and if you were to find it, it could be amazing. It would be great for your career.'

'Don't come back to town and immediately start stirring up shit, Mak.'

Mak pulled a fingertip across her pouting lower lip, signifying that she would say nothing more on the subject. For now.

Karen folded her arms. 'Come on, enough talking about work and crap. I want to know. Have you spoken to *him*?'

Him.

'Why won't you speak to him?' Karen's voice was a touch accusatory. She had not even given Mak time to answer. Her red curls trembled like snakes ready to strike.

'We *have* spoken,' Mak said, feeling unreasonably defensive. 'Actually, we've spoken a great deal. We both just need a little space right now. And I don't particularly want to talk about it.'

Karen was adept at interviewing, but with Mak she had met her match. Karen knew Andy well, but she was a loyal friend to Mak, and in this break-up she had to try to be Switzerland. It was not always easy to tread the thin line of impartiality in such matters. Mak sympathised with that. Still, she did not want to discuss her love life with anyone for the moment. She didn't want advice. She didn't want a shoulder to cry on. She just didn't want to talk about it.

'I'll talk to him again, just not right now,' she offered as a way to close the matter. 'I don't have the energy for another emotional face-off — it's too soon.'

Silence.

'You're my friend, Karen. I don't want to fight,' Mak murmured.

'Neither do I.'

But their frosty exchange hung heavily. The reunion was over.

'I better get back to work.'

'Me too,' Mak said. 'I have to see a man about a coin.'

'What?'

'Nothing.'

'Let me help with those dishes,' Karen offered.

'I got it,' Mak insisted. 'It's takeaway. It practically takes care of itself. You should get back to work. It's nearly one.'

She wondered if Andy was there, complaining that she had kicked him out. Perhaps even waiting for Karen's report.

'Good luck finding your boy … Adam.'

'Thanks.' Mak led her to the door, disappointed. They didn't hug. Karen's footsteps retreated, and Mak closed the door.

Shit.

I'm sorry, Karen.

Mak carried the remains of their meal into the kitchen, and tried to compose herself. She ran the tap, and let her hands sit in the warm soapy water once the sink was half full, dishes slippery to the touch, a prawn tail floating at the surface.

Andy. He had left her a couple of new messages, but she wasn't going to call him back. She had not asked him to come to Sydney.

A plate slipped from Makedde's hand and clanged in the sink.

Fuck.

CHAPTER 21

Mak had seen a lot of odd bookshops, but never a place such as this before.

She was the only customer in the shop, and she wandered from shelf to shelf, feigning a sense of purpose as she examined books on the American illusionists Thurston and Kellar, the inventive French magician Robert-Houdin, and the famous American escape artist Houdini, who borrowed the Frenchman's name. She noted books on various illusions, levitations, mindreading techniques and card tricks, and flicked through them with a cursory interest. Many of the shelves were dusty. The shop did not sell the toys and magic kits for children she'd been expecting, but catered for those serious about the art of magic.

A book on lock-picking caught her eye, and she took it off the shelf with an eagerness unrelated to her current mission. She was pretty good with simple locks like handcuffs, but her effort with more sophisticated locks had been abysmal the one time she'd really needed the skill. She could make a three-pin lock look like a seven-pin. Which was not a compliment. She put the book under her arm and continued browsing.

Eventually, the shopkeeper approached her, as she had hoped. 'Is there anything I can help you with, miss?' he asked.

Makedde found herself face to face with a man who could only be a magician himself. His mane of silver hair was slicked back dramatically from the temples and forehead, displaying a distinctive widow's peak and elongating a pleasant face with oversized teeth, presented in a polite and disingenuous smile. The man was dressed in a high-collared coat and slacks, and had the air of one who'd just emerged from one of the dusty books.

'This is a great shop,' she told him.

'Thank you, miss.'

'You're the owner?' Mak ventured.

'I am he.'

'Has this wonderful shop been around for long? I don't know how I could have missed it before.'

The shopkeeper seemed to take umbrage at her question. His smile vanished and his eyes wandered away. 'We are the oldest and most respected purveyor of illusionists' tools, manuals, historical books and paraphernalia in New South Wales,' he explained a little stiffly.

Is that so?

Mak extended her hand. 'My name is Makedde,' she said, to make amends.

He shook it. 'What an unusual name,' he remarked. 'A stage name?'

'No.'

'I am Mr Millard,' he introduced himself majestically, bowing ever so slightly. She imagined him sweeping a top hat through the air as he spoke. He gestured to a large framed poster that hung over the cash register, and there it was, an image of Mr Millard in the top hat and tails he seemed to wish he was wearing. His photograph had been transformed to a grainy sepia tone, giving it the look of an old-fashioned flyer, though his toothy grin seemed not at all convincing for the period.

'Mr Millard, it is a pleasure to meet you,' Mak said, implying in her tone that she had heard a lot about him. 'Can you tell me, do you sell these coins here?' She had brought the cut coin from Adam's room with her, and she pulled it from her pocket.

'Mmm, yes,' he said, with what seemed like mild distaste.

'It's not a good trick?'

'We specialise in rather more *sophisticated* tricks. But yes, I have such coins.'

'Thank you.' Mak slipped the offending coin back into her pocket. 'Do you have a members club perhaps, Mr Millard?'

He lit up. 'Yes, we do. Are you interested in joining?' He moved to the register and took a thick book from under the counter. 'We could use more female magicians,' he told her enthusiastically, opening the book up at a marker. 'There really aren't very many, which is a shame.'

Mak brought the lock-picking book over and put it down by the cash register. 'Actually, I'm interested in someone who I believe may be one of your members,' she told him, and pulled Adam's photograph from her pocket.

He closed the book with theatrical indignation. 'I can't reveal the identity of our members.'

'Of course not,' Mak backtracked. 'Let me explain why I'm interested.'

Playing mind games with this magic shop owner would be an exercise in frustration. But honesty might just work.

'I'm a private investigator helping out a very worried mother who's looking for her son.' She passed him the photo. 'Adam Hart. I think he's probably been in here some time.'

'Good-looking kid,' Mr Millard said, studying the photograph. 'Is he a performer?'

'Probably an enthusiast.'

'Well, all the *real* enthusiasts come here.'

'So he is a member, then?'

'I couldn't say.'

Mak took a breath. This was beginning to get annoying. 'I see. Perhaps he's a member of another magicians' club,' she said, taking the photograph out of his hands. 'Sorry, I've come to the wrong place. Thanks for your time.'

She began to leave, the lock-picking book sitting unpurchased on the counter.

'It's possible he might be part of our membership,' she heard him say as she reached the doorway. 'I'll just check for you.'

Mak turned and flashed him one of her dazzling smiles. 'That would be most helpful, Mr Millard. Thank you.'

If Adam was an active member she could find other people who knew him, who might have seen him in the past week and might even know where he was. She might be able to find additional contact information for him, information on his interests. Perhaps someone would even have a helpful theory on his disappearance?

'I don't have an Adam Hart listed.'

Mak's heart sank. 'Thank you for checking,' she said, defeated. She pulled her credit card out of her wallet and purchased the book.

'Excellent choice, miss. You'll find it most helpful,' he assured her.

'I hope so. You never know when you might need to bust out of a pair of handcuffs,' she joked.

She might find the book helpful, but she sure wasn't finding the coin lead very helpful. Perhaps most nineteen-year-olds had a coin trick or two in their bedrooms.

'Oh, I wanted to ask you one other thing,' Mak said. 'If you were going to conceal something personal in a room — say, some valuables, or a diary — how would you do it?'

'Things are always best concealed in plain sight!' he declared.

Concealed in plain sight?

'You wouldn't want to use padlocks and the like,' he added. 'Locks can be picked. Yes, conceal it in plain sight. That's what I would do.'

Makedde was puzzled by his response.

'Or fake books. You know, like this.' He pulled out what looked like a thick Bible from behind the counter. There was a liquor flask inside.

'That's neat,' she said, and smiled. She'd seen those things a hundred times. 'Thank you. It was nice to meet you.'

Makedde Vanderwall left the magic shop cloaked in disappointment, passing a cork bulletin board covered with flyers for classes from various 'Master Magicians' and playbills for local shows. The words 'Le Théâtre des Horreurs' caught her eye for just a moment, printed in gothic letters at the top of the board.

The Sydney show dates had just ended.

CHAPTER 22

Adam Hart could not remember ever having felt so free.

Destiny.

His world was an exciting new invention of richer colours and greater possibilities. He lay with his beautiful older lover in her caravan, enjoying the feeling of escape as they were driven like a royal couple further and further from Sydney, further from his clinging mother, the dead father who'd left him behind, and far from anyone who might recognise him and burst this bubble of new reality. Le Théâtre des Horreurs was on the move, their tour taking them to Brisbane where they would perform their final Australian show at the Powerhouse Theatre. And he was with them. He was part of it.

The tour bus moved ahead of them, filled with the rest of the troupe and their sets, their props, their costumes, while Adam and his lover luxuriated in style: special, different, cocooned amongst plush silk cushions on a double bed, just as he believed stars of another era would have been. Bijou insisted on having a caravan for herself when she toured, and would not perform without it. He understood her needs. A refined woman, a *queen*, she needed her comforts and privacy.

And she was satisfied with his company. *His company.*

She was nothing like Patrice. She did not criticise him, belittle him, tell him he was immature.

'*Mon ami*, fetch me a soda, yes?' his queen murmured, and Adam sprang up from her side to get her a drink from the minibar-sized fridge. He opened it for her and she took a sip. '*Chaud, non*? Hot.'

The skies outside were clear and blue, and the temperature had risen as they neared Queensland. It was indeed a hot day. She leaned against the open window, her ebony hair and diamond drop earrings blowing back in the breeze. He drank in the sight of her sophisticated beauty with a fresh excitement. She was stunning, exotic. Her acceptance transformed him. He was a man.

For the past five hours, he and Bijou had been able to spend time together uninterrupted by the rest of the troupe. A relief. Despite the giddy happiness he revelled in, the new landscape of feelings, there were problems. Adam felt uncomfortable with the others, particularly the illusionist — or was it the contortionist? — who was strange and seemed always to stare at him a little too long. There was a look in the man's eye that Adam did not recognise. He found it odd, unsettling. Was it curiosity? Hatred? Was he being measured up? Perhaps it was just a culture clash. The man was a foreigner, after all. Adam now tried to avoid him, but naturally they were in close proximity day and night, such was the nature of a troupe on the road. At least the actor, Michel, had exchanged a few brief, friendly words with him before their departure from Sydney. Apart from that brief dialogue, and

Bijou's loving words, Adam had not conversed in his native language for seven days. Perhaps it was that which had begun to give him an aching longing for the familiar, and encouraged a vague feeling of indefinable dread that lurked just beneath the surface of his bliss.

But for now, with the trailer softly bumping along the freeway in the sunshine, and his lover in his arms, it seemed the world had opened to him. Loneliness was impossible. Dread was far behind.

He was finally free, just as he had always wished. He was Kerouac, an adventurer, living his dreams. '*What is that feeling when you're driving away from people and they recede on the plain till you see their specks dispersing? — it's the too-huge world vaulting us, and it's good-bye. But we lean forward to the next crazy venture beneath the skies,*' Kerouac wrote.

These are the days that make you a man, Adam thought.

A man.

CHAPTER 23

At three o'clock on Tuesday afternoon, the self-made
billionaire Jack Cavanagh sat in his opulent fourteenth-floor
office, leaning back from his mahogany desk, his arms folded.

Cobwebs.

Through pale eyes he stared out floor-to-ceiling windows
at the picture postcard view. The Sydney skies were sunbaked
blue, charcoal clouds looming in the far distance. By evening
there would be rain. Despite its changing colours, the view
had become a thing of routine. It no longer impressed him.
Very little did impress him, he realised. He felt removed from
every triumph, viewing his domain of success through a
narrow aperture, a child looking through a tiny pinhole in a
cardboard box so he would not burn his eyes in the fire of an
eclipse.

Cobwebs and tar.

In his quieter moments, Jack had begun to sense that his
heart was slowly filling with cobwebs and tar, and that it
would soon stop functioning completely.

A man known for his drive and business sense, Jack found

He had been on retainer with Jack for the past seven years, since Cavanagh Incorporated had been threatened by the kidnapping of a top-level executive in the Middle East. He was a confidential asset to the company. If Mr White was involved, things were serious. It had not been a good twelve months for the Cavanagh family, so Mr White, *The American*, had been busy.

A red light flashed for line one. Jack took a breath and picked up the receiver.

'Bob.'

'Good day, Jack.' The American was one of the few people who called Jack by his first name. Perhaps it was due to the intimacy of their dealings that this seemed natural. 'I have news on the matter from last year.'

Jack felt the tightness in his chest increase a fraction. Cobwebs. Tar.

Damien.

'Go ahead,' Jack told him.

'Our security discovered a motorcyclist idling outside the gates of your Darling Point home on Sunday night,' The American began. 'It seemed suspicious, so they took down the registration plate number as a precaution. It was an ACT registration, in the name of Makedde Vanderwall.'

Vanderwall.

'The private investigator woman?' he blurted with indignation. Jack knew her well, although they had never met. She had nearly been the cause of his son's complete, irrevocable downfall, and the ruination of the Cavanagh name. He had been relieved when she had moved away from Sydney. It was a great disappointment to discover that her relocation might have been temporary.

'Should I be concerned?' he asked. 'What was she doing there?'

'The motorcyclist parked across the street for a time, looking at the house. That was it. She did not approach. We have no reason to believe that there's anything to be concerned about at this stage, but if it was indeed Vanderwall, then why she would be hanging around your street on her motorcycle, I couldn't say.'

Jack remembered her motorcycle crash the year before. He'd have thought she'd have given that up by now. He couldn't figure the woman out. What did she want from him? He couldn't figure out how to make her go away, without resorting to the types of decisions he was now struggling with. More of the same. More death.

'This morning Makedde Vanderwall visited the Murphy boy. The one who was released from jail,' Mr White went on.

Jack felt his panic rising. 'I can't have her snooping around,' he said, finding a surprising spark of strength in his anger. A minor return to himself. He was frustrated that she could still cause him trouble, frustrated by what she'd forced him to do.

'She won't. We'll be keeping an eye on this.'

'Yes,' Jack said, nodding to himself. 'We have to. Follow her. You know my concerns about letting this issue grab headlines again.' There had been a rather embarrassing front page featuring Makedde Vanderwall running barefoot in an evening gown from the Cavanaghs' palatial home, where his son's extravagant birthday party was being held. There had been talk that she was running from an attacker, which the family naturally denied by way of their legal counsel.

But the attacker had been real enough.

He was a man who went by the name of Luther Hand. Hand had been employed by The American to clean up some messy problems for Jack. He had wisely declined to escalate the situation at his client's property. Nonetheless, it had got out of control, thanks to the photographs taken by paparazzi as Vanderwall fled. The photographers had been there to snap arriving celebrity guests and dignitaries, and they instead ended up with a surprise front-page story. The whole incident was a disaster. It had taken some time to get things to die down. But they had. Jack had made sure there were no repeats of the dangerous party antics that had started the debacle in the first place. He had done what had to be done, and for a while it looked like things might eventually return to normal. But nothing was normal. Not for Jack, anyway.

This news of the woman's return to Sydney was alarming. This was unfinished business.

'Bob, I don't want any trouble from her,' Jack reiterated, again finding some minor rekindling of his old spark. 'What can we do about her?'

'So long as she's in Australia we're limited. Anything that happens to her could easily arouse suspicion.'

Makedde had become publicly linked with the Cavanaghs' troubles. She was bad publicity for the Cavanaghs and their businesses. It would certainly not look good if something happened to her. It was still too soon after the events, still too high-profile. The American was right.

'No, we can't have that,' Jack agreed. 'What are our options? Can we scare her back to Canada, or out of the state?'

'Leave it with me,' White said.

'We can't have any unwanted attention right now, Bob. I thought you said you had a contact in the police force keeping an eye on her?'

'We do. We'll make sure she stays away,' White assured him. 'Jack, we can handle this. We'll protect against the possibility of any interest in the press.'

'You have my faith, Bob.'

Jack paid The American an enormous sum to look after his interests, and to protect him from the knowledge of the grim specifics that task sometimes entailed. Legally, the less he knew the better. Over the years and through a number of crises, there had been very few occasions when Jack had been disappointed with The American's work. He was exceptionally experienced and well connected. Jack knew of no one better qualified.

'I can't afford to have bad press right now,' he reiterated. 'The merger is nearly signed off.' Mr White would already know this.

The conversation complete, Jack Cavanagh hung up the receiver and looked out at the blue sky once more. It had not regained any of its wonder in the interim.

Cobwebs and tar.

Cobwebs and tar.

CHAPTER 24

'Marian Wendell and Associates, Marian speaking.'

Mak smiled. She imagined her boss sitting at her desk, composed, elegant and dealing with files full of sleaziness. What a woman.

'Hey, it's Mak.'

'I was wondering when you'd check in next,' Marian responded. 'Things moving along?'

At an age when a lot of people were retiring, Marian was working harder than most 25-year-olds. And she had the energy for it. She had probably already combed through paperwork on the current investigations, and called her agents for updates. She liked to keep on top of everything happening in her agency, and she rarely missed a trick.

'Yes. I've been busy Face-wasting,' Mak joked. 'You can not only poke people, but super-poke them!'

Nothing. Not even a faint chuckle. And because Marian was a bit of a Luddite, there was a chance she might not even know what Facebook was, let alone Face-wasting, Mak realised.

'There's a social website called Facebook,' Mak patiently explained. 'It's so popular that it's already passé. It has a poke game thing. Never mind. Anyway, I found Adam Hart on it, and I'll try to contact him that way. Perhaps he'll respond. He's nineteen after all. A lot of younger people use it.'

'Oh. Good.' Marian sounded unsure.

Mak flipped her laptop open and went through her notes, getting more serious. 'I met with Ms Hart on Monday afternoon,' Mak told her boss. 'I had a good look through Adam's room, but I didn't find much. I have to say his room seems awfully clean, even for a neat freak. Damn, that is a neat house. His mother said the police didn't take anything, and she didn't clean it up, so … well, it was pretty sparse in there and I wonder if perhaps he knew he was leaving. My guts tell me he's a runaway,' Mak admitted. 'He could easily have shimmied down the drainpipe outside his bedroom window. He's probably been doing that for years before finally taking off.'

There was a pause. 'You know, it's poor form to make up your mind when you don't have the evidence. It makes for narrow-minded investigating.'

Ouch.

Mak knew that. She had been told many times. 'You're right.'

'Good girl. What else can you tell me?'

Good girl.

Mak shook her head. From anyone else's lips, it would sound like pure condescension, but she knew that Marian took her on in a way that went beyond the usual expected professional relationship. This was something a motherly figure might say to a favourite child. Mak found she'd missed Marian's interest in her.

'Well, I found a trick coin in his room, and a poster for the Jim Rose Circus. I believe he may have an interest in magic and performance. I know it's not much, but I'm checking out the local magic shops to see if he was a member or a regular customer or something.'

Marian seemed less impressed with that lead. 'What else?' she said simply.

Mak had something more concrete to reveal. She had spoken to Mrs Hart again and determined the identity of the woman Tobias had mentioned. Her name was Patrice, and she had agreed to see Mak.

'Apparently he took off once before, with a girlfriend of the time named Patrice. I'll be meeting with her later. I'm talking to neighbours. Someone will know something. Also, I could use a little extra cash if anything else comes up in the meantime, Marian. You know, any of those other types of cases I could help out with,' she said.

What she meant was domestic cases. With her model looks, Mak was well suited to getting up close and personal with straying husbands. Being hit on in bars had always been something of a regular nuisance for Mak. In the end she tended to avoid bars and clubs as much as possible. It was funny that now she'd finally found a way to get paid for being hassled. Marian liked to call her the agency's 'Secret Weapon' because of her unique suitability for closing such cases with one step of her stilettoed foot. Mak had a special red silk designer dress she liked to use for such jobs. Not too revealing, not too obvious, but with just enough leg to give an air of 'Are you Mr Right Now?' to a man looking for precisely that. It was just right for the upmarket bars where married businessmen liked to get a few drinks in and try their luck for a one-night stand. She had successfully given her room key to a few husbands — the rule was they had to approach her first — only to have them arrive to be confronted by their wife, and/or their wife's lawyer. It was ugly stuff, yes. But Mak rationalised that it was best for these enquiring wives to have their suspicions checked out before they broke up with their husbands over nothing, or their spouses came home with something more sinister than lipstick on their collar. Like a paternity suit, or HIV.

'Ah, my Secret Weapon is back.' Marian sounded pleased. 'There's nothing around at the moment, but you'll be the first one I call if any stray husbands need getting caught. Things might pick up on Valentine's Day.'

Valentine's Day. Of course. How depressing.

Now Mak sat up straight and prepared herself for her real news. 'By the way,' she added, as casually as she could, 'you won't believe this. But Adam Hart's mother knows Tobias and his family. Isn't that an interesting coincidence? They live on the same block. Adam and Tobias are more or less friends.'

There was a pause as Marian absorbed that little bombshell.

'*You know*,' Mak continued. 'Tobias. The street kid who was wrongly arrested for the murder of that PA, Meaghan Wallace, last year? Well, he's no longer a street kid. He's out of rehab and living with his father on the same street as our Adam Hart. It's such a small world, isn't it?'

'Yes, I knew the connection,' her boss admitted. 'Mrs Hart asked for you, and told me that Tobias's father had recommended you.'

Mak smiled. *And you hoped I wouldn't find out ... so I wouldn't start thinking about the Cavanaghs again. Well, it's too late.*

'I met with Tobias, and he was helpful. He's the one who told me that Adam took off once before, to be with Patrice.'

'You met with Tobias Murphy?'

'I'm canvassing Adam's friends and neighbours,' Mak said with confidence.

'Mak … you are going to be sensible, aren't you?' Marian said. Her tone was grave.

'When have you known me to be anything but sensible?'

Her boss did not respond.

Pete Don, in a lecture in Makedde's Certificate III course in Investigative Services, had confirmed that 'new technology and trends' could be surprisingly helpful tools in an investigator's arsenal.

At the time, Mak had thought it funny coming from him.

Pete was a rather gruff ex-undercover drug squad officer turned private investigator, who'd been beaten so badly in his former post that he had no cartilage left in his nose. It sat in the centre of his face like a formless mound of putty with nostrils. This guy was not someone Mak could imagine slowing down from catching the bad guys, the cheaters and the insurance fraudsters for long enough to even acknowledge the existence of something like a computer. And yet he had stood in front of the class and explained the importance of Twitter, MySpace and Facebook, as if he were a sixteen-year-old emo. And he had been right. It was amazing how many people could be tracked down by something as simple and accessible as a search engine. Once in a while even dead men turned up looking remarkable well, as in the famous case of John Darwin, who faked his 'death by canoe misadventure' in 2002, resulting in a massive-scale sea search, and later had his wife, Anne, claim on his life insurance. A member of the public typed 'John', 'Anne' and 'Panama' into Google Images, and found of picture of the couple posing together in a shot taken four years after his passing. They got six years imprisonment for their trouble. It seemed that nearly every person in the Western world now made an imprint somewhere on the web — whether they wanted to or not.

And so Makedde typed in the name of the person she wanted most to find information about.

DAMIEN CAVANAGH

SEARCH

Incredibly, there were fewer than one thousand search hits for the controversial heir to the Cavanagh business fortune. Or perhaps it wasn't so incredible. Damien's father, Jack, wielded great power, and no doubt had done his best to keep his son out of the press, and firmly out of the public eye since the problems with his 'lifestyle' had erupted. *Parties, drugs, underage prostitutes, murder.* It wasn't pretty. Not that the latter had been publicly proven, but Mak knew better than most. And she was not afraid of the Cavanaghs. The mainstream press were evidently too spooked to write directly about the troubled heir, despite the obviously riveting copy he would make. But internet bloggers could not be controlled, and they seemed to have the most gossip. If their information was correct — and obviously there was no guarantee of that — Damien Cavanagh had returned to Sydney after a six-month sabbatical in Europe and was back to his partying ways, living in his dad's palatial waterfront mansion, estimated to be worth upwards of twenty million Australian dollars. The palatial mansion she had been seen loitering in front of on her motorcycle.

So Damien was back. Well, so was Makedde.

And she was eager to find out just which of his 'old ways' he was indulging in. Bad habits were hard to break. She had a few ideas about how to find out just what he had been up to.

The case. Get to the case you are being paid for.

Now it was Adam Hart's turn to have his internet imprint investigated. Mak had already typed Adam's name in a simple search, and found 125,000 hits from around the world. It was too common a name. When she narrowed it down to Australian hits, she found a link to Facebook, clearly showing the missing boy's face. It had been easy to find him electronically, but would be more difficult, probably, to get a response from her 'friend request', as it was called. If he was indeed alive and well, and able to access the internet, she might get some communication going. To do that, she first had to get him to accept her as a friend. She hoped Tobias could be of help in that regard. It was a bit of a long shot, but if Adam was logging on, he might just reply to her message or accept her Facebook friend request and end up in communication with the very investigator being paid to track him down. In the meantime, though, Mak had access to seventy-five of his Facebook friends whom she could now ask about him. It was virtual door knocking.

Mak flicked through what she could find on Adam Hart, aware that this process was precisely the same kind of search newspapers and other media routinely did every time some kid turned up dead or disfigured in a hideous, national interest tragi-story. They just looked them up and pulled personal photos of them off the social networking sites to accompany the story.

She hoped she could find Adam before that profile photo was printed everywhere, with the caption Found Dead: Adam Hart. Photo courtesy of Facebook.

Beep.

Beep.

Mak's phone rang, and she tensed. She pushed her laptop away and picked up her mobile. It was Karen, calling her already.

'Hello,' she answered. 'Thanks for coming over. I'm sorry if —'

'They finally found the guy who did it,' Karen said abruptly.

'Did what? Who?'

'The guy who killed your Meaghan Wallace. He's been found, so you can stop looking for him.'

Mak digested that. *They found Meaghan's killer?* 'The guy Simon Aston said did it? He said it was a hitman, right?'

'A small-time thug, really. He had a few priors. Was known to police. Probably hadn't done a lot of heavy work before,' Karen told her, while Mak madly scribbled notes. 'He must have screwed something up, though. His remains were found in the back of his burned-out car, charred and badly decomposed. And I do mean *badly decomposed*,' she said. 'From the photos, you could hardly tell he was human. There was almost nothing left of him or the vehicle. It was a miracle they could make an ID.'

Mak locked onto the new information about the case with a rush of adrenaline. 'His name?'

'Warwick O'Connor. Positive ID.'

'So he was in the back seat of a car. Killed? A car accident? What happened?'

'No,' Karen explained. 'He was in the back, as in the *boot* of the car. The trunk, as you Canadian types call it.'

If he was in the trunk, that could only mean that someone had quite literally dispatched the dispatcher. She imagined how terrifying it would be to be trapped in the trunk of a car. A burned-out car? Was it burning when he was still alive?

She shivered.

'When did they get an ID?' Mak asked, suspicious that Andy had known this key information and not passed it on to her. Before his suicide, Simon Aston had confessed to organising a hit on the witness Meaghan Wallace, and had given a name, but the man he pointed to had disappeared. And now he'd shown up dead in the back of a car. How could anyone ever know if he had really been guilty of anything? Dead bodies could not defend themselves.

'After our convo I had a sniff around. As you know, I was part of the original investigation,' Karen explained. 'But it's a closed case now, and nobody told me about this new detail. Jimmy said he did the death knock yesterday. O'Connor's wife was none too impressed that it had taken so long to ID him.'

Mak wondered if Karen's friendship with her had prevented anyone telling her earlier. She didn't want to be a reason for her friend to be ostracised.

'Karen, I can't thank you enough for telling me. I know our conversation got a bit tense … I'm sorry for that.'

'You're back in Sydney, and I'm so glad,' Karen said. 'Just … *be careful*. You seem on edge.'

Mak frowned. Karen had a way of cutting past her defences and saying the most alarmingly apt things. *But what exactly am I on the edge of?* Mak wondered to herself, too afraid to ask Karen's opinion.

'You do know that we can't know if he actually did it, or it was a setup,' Mak said.

There was a pause on the line. 'I know.'

'Thank you, Karen. I appreciate the call.'

Mak hung up, excited by this first glimpse of new information.

So the guy who had been hired to kill Meaghan Wallace, or had been framed for the killing, was now conveniently dead. The guy who confessed to setting it up was also conveniently dead. In fact, every one of the key people involved in the case had ended up dead one way or another.

Except Mak.

CHAPTER 25

Early evening on day two of Makedde's investigation into Adam Hart's disappearance, things were about to get interesting.

Mak was to meet Adam's ex-girlfriend, Patrice, a woman his mother had failed at first to mention, and only grudgingly gave Mak the phone number for, once Mak mentioned her name. It appeared, if Tobias's information was reliable, that she had been quite central in Adam's recent life. Her name was Patrice, not Patricia — Tobias had that wrong — and she was four years older than Adam. She had sounded at least moderately helpful when Mak had called, and was a natural next stop. Hopefully meeting Patrice would give Mak more insight into Adam and his previous attempt to leave home.

Mak waited only a few seconds before the intercom was answered.

'Come on up,' the female voice said as the door buzzed, unlocking. Mak stepped into the building foyer.

Built in the nineties. Decent place. Not fancy.

She climbed two flights of stairs, found Apartment 308, and was about to knock when the door opened.

'Hi.'

Patrice was an attractive young woman. She had a wholesome student look about her: large brown eyes, brown hair held back in a headband, good skin. Mak imagined her in a library somewhere, perhaps having finished a healthy game of tennis with some fetching young man who would let her win.

'Thanks for agreeing to speak with me,' Mak said.

'Sure.'

Patrice sat down at her dining alcove and Mak took a seat opposite.

'I have to leave in about ten minutes,' Patrice began, sounding a bit short.

Okay, so that's how it's going to be.

Mak would have to cut straight to the point, which wasn't always the best way to build rapport. 'I appreciate your time, Patrice. I won't keep you long.'

The young woman crossed her arms. 'Look, I know this is about Adam but I don't see what the point is because I don't know anything.'

Mak nodded. *Great, she has her arms crossed defensively already.* 'You two dated for a while?'

Patrice nodded a silent yes.

'I mentioned on the phone that I'm looking for him on behalf of his mother, and, because you dated for a while and knew him quite well, I thought I would ask you —'

'I broke it off, like, a year or so ago.'

This is interesting, Mak thought. According to Tobias's story, admittedly vague, they had stopped dating no more than seven months earlier. Was Patrice being evasive for some reason?

'I'm not a cop, Patrice, and you aren't in any trouble. I just want to find out where Adam might have gone. I want to make sure he's okay.' There was a nod, something that seemed like a positive sign of co-operation. Patrice even unfolded her arms. 'Where did you two meet?'

'The cafeteria at uni,' Patrice answered.

'And you started dating?'

'Yeah.'

One-word answers really suck, Patrice.

'When was the last time you heard from Adam?'

'Ages ago,' she answered.

Ages ago. What is this ages ago? Does no one speak with reference to the normal passing of time?

'Ages being one month, one week, one day?' Mak pressed.

'*No.*' Patrice seemed cross. Those pretty eyes grew dark. 'Not a day. Like, ages ago. Months.'

When a subject was being difficult in an interview, it was wise to wonder why. Did this young woman have anything to hide? Had she taken a dislike to Mak for some reason? Was she really so rushed? If so, why had she agreed to meet Mak?

'So you haven't heard anything from him in the past week. No notes? Emails? Phone messages?'

'No. Why would I?' Her response was immediate. 'He didn't write about me in that stupid diary of his, did he?'

Mak felt a touch of excitement.

Diary ... There is *a damn diary and I have to find it.*

Patrice opened up a touch. 'Look, I liked the guy, but you know ... he's so *straight*. He doesn't drink. Nothing. He doesn't have a car. After I moved out of home, I just didn't think we had much in common any more.'

Four years was not that much of an age difference, except when you considered that Adam was still living at home and

173

riding a bicycle. Patrice might have found her lifestyle being cramped by her younger boyfriend's limitations.

'Did he leave home? To be with you?'

Patrice bit her lower lip briefly.

'Patrice, it's okay. You can tell me; you won't get in any trouble.' Mak leaned forward sympathetically, and waited for more.

'You said you're not a cop, right?'

'I promise you I am not a cop. I only care about finding Adam.'

'Okay. Look. About a year or so ago, Adam decided to move in with me. Or maybe it was six months ago, I can't remember. Anyway, he knew his mother wouldn't approve, so I guess he just left and didn't say goodbye, which I certainly didn't make him do. That was his idea and I thought it was a bit … dramatic. It only lasted a week anyway. Not even. He is just *so straight*. It would never have worked.'

Mak considered that. 'What do you mean by "so straight"?'

'Like he would never drink or smoke or anything.'

'Pot?'

'Exactly. And I started bugging him about it. Eventually he agreed he would try it. So there is this party at my friend's house and we're all there. Adam doesn't smoke fags, right? So we put some hash in a piece of bread, folded and toasted it. No big deal. Easy. And then an hour later he tells us he still can't feel a thing. He is like, totally sober. So we did it again — another bud in some toast.'

Mak was no drug expert but she could see where this was going. If the drugs were ingested with food, they would take a long time to reach the stomach and take effect.

'Finally it hit, like another hour later, and he completely freaked out. Adam was going on and on about how he couldn't feel his tongue and he couldn't talk. He said his hands were numb and he couldn't breathe. He just freaked out. It was so uncool.'

'You were embarrassed?'

Patrice nodded.

'And then what happened?' Mak prodded.

'At the end of the night we all had to head home, but I'd been drinking, so he was the designated driver. Anyway, we got pulled over by the cops, and this cop, he actually shines his light across the floor of the car, and there it is, the rest of the hash. And Adam is driving and doesn't even have a valid licence. Can you imagine? I thought we were really screwed. Then this cop just gives us a warning to drive carefully and waves us on. Adam went cold on the whole thing after that. He went home to his mother the next day. I broke it off with him after that. I mean, he was acting like a child.'

Mak nodded. 'I haven't found his diary yet. Do you know where he keeps it?'

'I don't know. Used to be under his bed.'

Mak had checked there already. She would check again.

'I doubt his mother knows about it. There's a lot she doesn't know about him. She just tries to stifle his every creative impulse.'

'What kind of other things wouldn't she know about?'

At this, Patrice recoiled.

'You won't tell her any of this, will you?'

'I just want to find him safe. That's my job.' She avoided the issue of disclosure. 'Would there be anywhere else he might hide things, like his diary?'

'Unless he took off with it, I'm guessing it should be somewhere in his room.'

Hidden in plain sight? Mak wondered.

'Thank you, Patrice. That was very helpful.'

Yes, very helpful, actually.

Mak sat on the lonely loveseat and sipped strong tea that she didn't want, as Glenise Hart searched her face for answers about her son's disappearance. Mak wanted answers, too

'Thanks for letting me take another look in Adam's room, Glenise. But first, I need to ask you a few questions about Patrice.'

'*Well*,' Glenise piped up. 'I *was* surprised when you phoned to ask about her. They are no longer together, you know.'

'Yes, she told me. But tell me, what did you think of her?'

'Well, she was a nice girl. But ...' Glenise trailed off. Clearly she had not approved. 'They went out for nearly a year. It was Adam's first real relationship. He suffered over her. I think it was the first time he'd had his heart broken.'

By the look of that photo on the beach, Adam was quite capable of breaking hearts himself, Mak thought.

'What happened?'

'I don't really know,' Glenise said. 'He doesn't talk to me about things like that.' She fidgeted a bit with the pleat in her pants. 'They split up about six months ago. I haven't heard from her since. He didn't talk about it, but I knew he was upset. He lost weight for a while there. He became even more ... introverted, I suppose.'

Mak was finding it hard to reconcile the image of that bronzed beach Aussie with the introvert his mother spoke of.

She wondered if Adam was still not coping well with the split. Or with the death of his father.

'For a while Adam wanted to get back together with Patrice. I try not to interfere in these things,' Glenise said, clearly awkward with the subject.

'And shortly before they broke up, that's when he disappeared the first time?' Mak asked, straight-faced. She sipped her tea.

This bombshell hung in the air for a while. 'Uh. Yes. He left without telling me.'

So he had *disappeared before and you didn't tell me.*

'Do you think he might have done something similar this time?' Mak asked, without directly challenging why Mrs Hart had withheld this vital information. She didn't need to. The woman knew she should have told Mak.

'Absolutely not,' Glenise said. 'That girl is out of his life.'

She blamed Patrice for the transgression. Of course.

'You can't think of anyone else important in Adam's life? Or any other reason he might have left again?'

'No.' She was adamant.

'Well, if you think of anything, please do let me know,' Mak said. 'Anything at all. Any little bit of information could help me find him for you. And on the off-chance, I recommend that you keep an eye on that credit card. Check the transactions daily, if you can.' Glenise sat with her arms crossed, half defiant, half dejected. 'I'll get him home to you as soon as I can, Mrs Hart,' Mak said soothingly. 'Now, I'd like to have another look in his room to see if I missed anything.'

They stood.

Mak walked up the staircase to Adam's bedroom, noticing that Glenise Hart did not follow her this time. Mak was glad for the space.

Makedde began her search of the room again, this time concentrating on hiding places she might have missed. Fake soft-drink cans with drugs stashed inside. Hollowed-out books. As clean as it was, there had to be some trace of Adam Hart in that room, some clue as to who he was and where he might be.

She felt a little guilty and destructive as she lifted the mattress off the bed, flipped it over and went through Adam's drawers like a cop on a raid. Mak thought of the fake Bible from the magic store, and returned to the bed where she had seen a thick, innocuous-looking dictionary. She pulled it out, took a breath and opened it. *Damn*. No hollowed-out middle containing vitally important clues, or even an old flask of whisky. It was just a dictionary. So far her search had yielded nothing new. But then there was his bookshelf. It was so neat. So perfect. She cocked her head to one side, and began pulling each book out one by one, flipping through the pages to see if any notes might fall out. There was a slim volume at the end of one shelf, heavily worn and probably loved. *THE ACTOR'S BOOK OF MONOLOGUES*. Mak pulled it out, once more hoping for private notes or letters. *Was Adam interested in acting as well as magic?* Instead, she found a thin, stiff manual nestled inside. *Magic City Library of Magic, Volume 6*, it declared. *Folding Coin. 'A Beginning in Magic'*. Mak opened the thin tome, and a DVD fell out. *Wild Card*, the sleeve declared, above an illustration of a magician in a turban and bejewelled costume gazing intensely into a crystal ball, surrounded by flying cards, nymphs, bats and dancing figures, all in the style of the early twentieth-century posters of the great magicians Houdini, Thurston and Kellar, and most specifically the turban-wearing illusionist Carter the Great.

THE WORLD'S WEIRDEST AND MOST WONDERFUL CARD TRICK, it declared in smaller type.

So Adam was, or once was, interested in magic and performance. Patrice said his mother tried to stifle his creative urges. Perhaps there were more hints about his interests here? Perhaps there was some link between these interests and his current whereabouts?

She next pulled out a thick hardcover copy of the book *Shantaram*, another tome that seemed to give an insight to Adam's interests and desires, and noticed that the glossy dust jacket did not quite fit.

'Yes!' she muttered under her breath.

It was a journal.

Adam Hart *did* keep a diary, and finally Mak had it in her hands.

She shook her head, delighted, as she flipped through the pages and saw just how in-depth the entries were, though she noted the last one, on the final page, was dated some months earlier. Still, the smell of well-used paper filled her nostrils, and she smiled. Ink. Felt pen. Pencil. This boy was a writer. He had written down *everything* he thought. She would be amazed if the diary did not reveal some valuable clues as to his whereabouts. Marian — and Glenise — would love her for this.

Now she could see the original hardcover copy of *Shantaram*, sans jacket, waiting further along the shelf. She eagerly continued her search, checking for any other valuable finds, and could barely believe her luck when she found another diary hiding amongst Adam's textbooks, this time concealed under a book jacket for a treatise by the German philosopher Hegel.

This made her laugh out loud.

Hegel. Of course.

The philosopher was famous for, among other things, having kept incredibly meticulous journals every day of his life — his 'excerpt mill' he called them.

A coincidence? *No.* This kid was naïve, perhaps, but no dummy.

Mak felt sure she would get a much better feel for what made Adam Hart tick after reading his intimate thoughts. She was not one to fall for card tricks or magic shows. She believed in science and reason. A disappearing act like Adam's could not be without clues. Makedde was determined to find them in his own words.

Only the first hundred or so pages of this journal were filled, with numerous blank pages waiting to receive his new thoughts and ideas. The final page of entries was bookmarked with a colourful vaudeville flyer: 'Le Théâtre des Horreurs', it proclaimed in elaborate gothic-style script.

CHAPTER 26

'Rehearse, rehearse, rehearse!'

It was an hour before their performance for the Brisbane audience, and Bijou clapped her slender white hands together to punctuate each word, as the five younger performers sat in a circle at her feet, their heads bowed. No one dared talk back as their star berated them.

'What will you be like? *Merveilleux? Non.* You are sloppy.' Bijou shook her head. 'Lara, you missed your cue last night.'

Lara opened her mouth to speak, but said nothing. She *had* missed the cue, but only by half a beat.

'If you were better performers, we would have a full house! You never listen to me! Rehearse, rehearse, rehearse. It takes practice to be *magnifique*. Practice!'

'We had a great review in Melbourne,' Michel ventured. 'This tour's been going really well.'

Bijou ignored his valid point as if he had not spoken. 'I've looked after all of you for too long!' she shouted dramatically. 'So long! What must I do? When will you learn? I'm docking your pay this week. All of you. Sometimes I don't know why I bother with you.'

She doesn't mean that, Arslan the contortionist told himself. *She can't mean that*.

She paced around them as they sat on the floor, silent. This was something of a routine for the troupe. Every month or so it came to this. It had been that way for years. Arslan could not remember things having been any other way. This was life. Bijou was the brains behind the troupe, and she pushed all of them to be their best. She pushed them hard so they would be great one day. Without her, what would they be doing? Where would they be? Where would he be without her?

But Bijou was not finished yet. 'Yelena!' she went on. Arslan's sister looked up, eyes wide. 'You're getting plump,' she was told. 'Day by day you are becoming a fat little pig. How will your brother lift you? We can't have you being lazy like this. I won't stand it any more.'

Yelena, though twenty-four years old, still reacted to Bijou's scathing comments as she had when she was little more than a child. She clung to her brother Arslan's arm and wept quietly, hiding her face. Arslan felt her hot tears on his biceps, and feelings of frustration and sadness swelled inside him.

'Honestly, you look like a fat little dumpling out there. It's disgusting,' Bijou snapped. 'Gia, you were supposed to keep an eye on her. Why hasn't she lost any weight?'

Gia sat on her thin hands and said nothing.

Bijou, her still-beautiful face set in a pout, stalked off, her silk robe trailing behind her. The hectoring was over. For now. Arslan squinted darkly as he watched her. The contortionist rarely spoke, even when his sister was picked on in such ways. He understood English and French, but Russian was his first language. Bijou spoke Russian too. She had travelled through Russia as a performer for a time. But Arslan and Yelena had been banned from speaking it. Now he sat in a lotus pose, his arms folded tightly. Yelena's grip on his biceps was beginning to ache.

It was Michel who was always the voice of reason in these moments. 'Arslan and Yelena, your act is tight.'

'She's not even watching. She's too busy with that kid,' Lara complained. She was the rebellious one in the troupe. She always spoke her mind, though perhaps not in front of Bijou.

That kid.

'That kid' was Adam Hart. Arslan, though merely five years older, was envious of the boy's fresh-faced appearance. Bijou had pointed out the lines on his own face. The aging. The slow and irreversible loss of tone. More than that, though, Arslan was envious of Adam's place in Bijou's affections.

He had not at all recovered from being cast out of her bed.

He wanted Adam gone.

Adam waited in Bijou's trailer with an agonising sense of excitement.

His lover had stepped out to attend to business with the troupe, and he had been trusted to remain there alone — an honour. Basking in fresh love, he soaked in the atmosphere of her private space, and decided it was the next best thing to being with her. Every detail spoke of her — the lingering scent of her perfume, her silk-and-lace slip hanging on a doorknob, her gowns and costumes hanging against the cupboard, her makeup and creams on the dressing table. This was a woman of sophistication. Never before had Adam been given the time of day by someone like her.

What will Mum think of her?

It might take some time, but he was sure she would be happy for him and this new love he had found. Yes, it would just take time and some planning. *Amor vincit omnia.* Love conquers all. With a love like this, surely she would see the importance of what he had found. Who cared about age gaps or differences of culture? His mother would understand. And even this strange beginning could be forgiven one day.

A wistful look came over his face as he admired the many magazine covers of Bijou framed in a clever wooden foldout screen she dressed behind. He stepped closer and looked carefully at each one. One cover showed Bijou standing in a white medieval-style gown, with a flowing fabric belt. Another was of Bijou with some ghoulish-looking players performing a dark horror piece. Before she'd left the trailer to rehearse with the others, she'd thrown a silk slip over the edge of the screen and Adam gently pushed it aside to take in his favourite cover of her. In this one she posed, hands on hips, in a burlesque showgirl outfit on the cover of *SHOW*. He could not understand the headlines, as they were written in French. She looked younger, and her dark hair was pixie-short. The paper was faded. He recognised that most of the covers were decades old, but he thought she looked just as beautiful now as she did in the pictures. Even more so.

Adam felt he was in a time of great growth. Once he'd met Bijou he'd realised that he'd never been in love before. What he'd felt and experienced with Patrice paled by comparison. Every moment of his life before Bijou had been nothing, he now realised. It was as if every minute of his young life had been leading up to their meeting. He had never felt anything remotely like this before — this longing and painful need to be near someone.

Adam was overwhelmed.

It was such a glamorous, free life the troupe lived. A life to be envied. Especially Bijou's. She was by far the most elegant and glamorous. She was a star.

Adam ran a fingertip over the stage photos she'd propped up against her mirror. She had a stack of magazines on her makeup table and he flicked through them, aching for her return. Underneath the magazines he found what looked like a photo album.

He opened it, and found it contained a number of newspaper clippings.

COMÉDIEN A ATTAQUÉ, a headline declared.

The string of words made Adam uneasy, though he did not know precisely what they meant. He did not have much French, but he knew that the word for actor in French was *comédien*. And was *attaqué* like the word 'attack'? He flipped the page over and found another clipping slipped into the plastic sleeve on the other side.

It looked to be a scrapbook of the troupe's reviews over the years. He turned the book sideways to read the next page. There was a large picture of Bijou, looking glamorous.

ATTAQUE A L'ACIDE! LA REINE DU HURLEMENT GRILLÉE SUR ENROULER DE SON AMANT

He squinted. Grilled? and *amant* … Didn't Bijou use that word as some sort of endearment when they were together?

His brows pressed together. He looked at the face of the young man in the newsprint. The caption said 'Jean-Baptiste Trevillie'. Jean-Baptiste was blond and young. In fact, Adam himself looked passingly like the young man in the photo.

Jean-Baptiste … He had heard the name somewhere.

A small yellowing photograph fell out of the album. He picked it up.

Bijou?

Adam smiled at this one. It was a happy-looking snapshot. In this photo she was much younger, and there was a little boy by her side. He was dressed in a leotard and was folding his leg over his shoulder and behind his head. She was holding his hand affectionately. A little girl of about the same age was in the background, clothed in a tutu and caught unawares by the camera.

The door of the trailer opened, giving Adam a start. He quickly closed the book and put it back where he'd found it, under the magazines. He shoved the photo underneath.

Bijou looked magnificent.

'*Mon ami* … What are you doing?' she purred in her intoxicating voice.

He smiled nervously. He could not lie to her, but he sensed that she would not be pleased that he'd been looking through that book. She might accuse him of snooping. He hadn't meant to snoop. He had come across it innocently. Maybe it was nothing at all, but something told him to keep quiet about what he'd seen.

He continued smiling at her, terrified of upsetting her. He was relieved when her expression softened. '*Mon ami*, come here,' she said, walking over to the bed, and gesturing for him to join her. 'You love me, *non*?' she asked.

He nodded. 'Oh, Bijou. You have no idea how much I love you. I have never loved anyone before you. You are everything to me.'

He had so hoped that she would want him to stay with her,

and she had been adamant that he not tell his mother where he was, but how long could he keep this going? As each day passed he fell further in love with her, and slipped further into a state of guilt about his selfish abandonment of his mother.

'The ticket will be secured.'

A knot formed in his stomach. He would do anything to be with Bijou, but he was nervous. He had known her less than two weeks and already he was planning to run off with her. For good. The idea was exciting, but troubling.

Go with your heart. Don't be a coward.

Perhaps he was not as brave as the heroes in the novels he loved. He wanted to be a great adventurer, but …

Bijou moved in close to him and he felt a warmth spread over his skin. As she began smothering him with little kisses his concerns became less urgent.

'Oh, darling …'

Who cares what anyone thinks, he decided. *Who cares?* His parents had never let him do anything exciting. With uncharacteristic bitterness he remembered how his mother had admonished him for his desire to travel instead of going straight to university when he finished school. Just because she'd chosen that for her own life, why should he? He was his own person. He had his own life to live. Where did she get off telling him he had to go to uni? Adam didn't want to be a chartered accountant like his late father had been. He didn't want to be surrounded by boring numbers and papers and files and the dusty smell of libraries. He didn't want that. He wanted something more.

He wanted *life*.

Again, the feeling in him shifted, and his youthful anger was quickly overtaken by the weight of his guilt. His mum deserved better. She would be so worried already. And when he did call her, how would he explain where he was? How would he explain her missing things? Had his mother even noticed? How could he make her understand what he was going to do with these strangers?

But Bijou was not a stranger. Adam loved her.

Love is never wrong.

She pulled away from him a little, her eyes intensifying. 'You have your passport?'

He nodded. He had brought his EU passport, and left the Australian one at home. His mum hadn't even known he'd obtained the second passport, thanks to his father's English birth.

It seemed that Bijou could sense that something was wrong. '*Mon ami*, you look sad.'

'I …' he began, then faltered, concerned that he might put her off the idea if he said the wrong thing. 'I think … maybe …'

He trailed off, trying to choose his words carefully. He didn't want Bijou to think that he didn't love her. He did love her, so, so much. It wasn't puppy love like he'd had in Year Eight. Not a crush. This was true love. He didn't want to risk anything ruining that.

He sat upright on the corner of the bed, not wanting to seem weak. 'My mum will be really worried. I should call her first, I think. Just to let her know that I'm okay. I won't tell her where I am, I promise.'

'You said you wanted to run away with me. You don't wish to? You don't wish to come away with me, my lover?'

'No, it's not that. No … don't be upset,' he pleaded, trying to reassure her. He had been afraid of this. What if she rejected him, like Patrice?

'You promised me you wouldn't,' she reminded him.

He had. She was right. At the time he was furious that his mother did not want him to go out. His late father had always insisted that he stay home at night to study, saying he needed to improve his marks, insisting that he follow in his footsteps as a successful accountant. After his death, Adam's mother continued to enforce that discipline. But Adam did not want the life of an accountant. Or a teacher. He wanted to escape, he needed to escape, and he had promised Bijou he would escape with her. That was only a week ago, and already he could see that it would be more difficult than he had imagined. It would be hard for him to carry through his plan of forsaking all he knew. The conundrum of what to do was troubling him more by the day. He was torn.

'I love you, Bijou,' he said. He clung to her hand.

'Good. Then get the champagne. We will toast our trip.'

Paris.

The knot in his stomach pulled tighter. He hesitated.

'Oh, my beautiful darling, my beautiful delicious boy ...' Bijou purred, softening his hard thoughts — unravelling them — as she clung to him, looking impossibly beautiful and arousing, and smelling of freshly applied perfume. It was something by Nina Ricci, she had told him. None of the girls he had met before could wear a real perfume from France. None of the girls his age would do or say the things Bijou did, he felt sure. No one could do what she did to him. She was like nothing he had ever experienced before. Her sophisticated scent curled into his brain and rested there, as she took possession of his body.

'*Je t'aime,*' she whispered, her fingers caressing him, running over his hairless chest, pulling his shirt open. With her other hand she gripped his hipbone gently, then slid her fingers across to feel the form of his erect penis. Her fingers seemed to know exactly how to touch him. He throbbed and grew even more painfully hard. The excitement of her presence was almost too much for him to bear.

With the last of his mental clarity he tried again: 'My mum will be getting so worried ...'

Bijou cut his words off with a moist kiss that tasted of strawberries. She always tasted so good.

'You don't tell her anything, darling. Come away with me!' she murmured. 'Live! Love! In Paris we will drink champagne and have adventures and make love all day ...'

She slid her silky hand into his pants and touched him, running those long, delicately painted fingernails through his pubic hair, then teasingly caressing his hardness one centimetre at a time. His mind turned to mush.

'Oh, my lover,' she whispered in his ear as she stroked him. 'We will flee this place and live happily in Paris. You mustn't contact anyone. Stay with me. Will you stay with me?'

He nodded, and licked his lips.

'Stay with me ... only me ...' she sighed, her lips gobbling up little portions of his naked skin, trailing lower, lower ...

She unbuckled his belt. '*Je t'aime*,' she whispered again, tugging at his pants and sending him into ecstasy.

CHAPTER 27

The diaries. I have him.

It was already late and Makedde Vanderwall did not expect to sleep. She pulled into the garage of Loulou's building, excited about what she'd soon be reading. In the passenger seat beside her was a satchel full of photocopies of Adam Hart's every intimate diary entry for over a year. It weighed a tonne. Marian had insisted that she photocopy all 356 pages and leave the originals at the office in case they became of police interest. Mak was fairly certain that the past two hours spent photocopying on that clunky old machine were among the most tedious of her life. But now, finally, she had a night of reading ahead — reading Adam's mind. She had been sleeping badly as it was, but tonight she fully intended keeping herself up with coffee. It was a pity, though, that some of the most recent pages appeared to be missing. She'd noticed at least three ripped paper edges, torn close to the binding, in the latest diary. Either Adam had felt confident to leave all but his final entries behind, or someone else had found the diaries and ripped the pages out.

Mak hauled herself and the satchel up the stairs.

Bugger.

A dozen long-stemmed roses were waiting just inside the front door.

She sighed and plonked the heavy satchel on the steps while she put the key in the lock and let herself in. With a sense of sadness, she saw the writing on the little card attached to the flowers. It was addressed to her, as she had feared. And she recognised the writing, too. *Building security is not so great here*, she thought. Someone must have let him past the front door. Her ex could be pretty good at talking his way into places when he wanted to.

Juggling the flower bouquet and heavy bag, she teetered down the hall and unlocked the door to Loulou's apartment.

At the sound of the door a pleasant voice rang out. 'Hello.' Bogey emerged wet-haired from the bathroom in a T-shirt and tight black jeans. 'Oh, you shouldn't have,' he joked, seeing the bouquet.

Mak smirked.

'Here, I'll help you with your flowers.' He searched around in the cupboards and found a water jug. He cut the roses down to fit, and when he was done they looked beautiful, each silken petal a wonderful luscious red. Their fragrance was intoxicating. It was a shame, because Mak was not sure she wanted them, considering who they would be from. She pocketed the card, not wanting to look at it.

'I didn't wake you, I hope?' she said. It was after eleven.

'No. I don't sleep much, and rarely before midnight.'

'You don't seem to,' she agreed and laid the photocopies of Adam's diary on the kitchen benchtop. She began preparations to brew a large pot of coffee.

'I'll do that,' Bogey offered.

'No, it's okay. You're too kind.' She realised she felt tense in his presence. Andy's flowers had put her on edge. She'd always found Bogey attractive, though she'd never acted on it, and now she felt guilty enjoying his company. It was silly.

'I'm glad you're here. We haven't really had a proper chance to catch up,' she told him. 'Things were pretty crazy when I saw you last.' She had been living with Andy in Sydney, party-crashing the Cavanagh heir's big thirtieth, and recovering from her motorcycle crash. 'How are things with the shop?'

'Going well. I think I'll have a few pieces in a couple of galleries here later this year.'

'That's great news.'

'And how are you? I heard that things in Canberra —'

'Didn't work out. Yeah. Andy and I split. It's for the best.' She found her eyes drifting to his flowers on the coffee table. She felt the urge to throw them out. 'I'm sorry we lost touch when I moved.'

'I understood. It's okay. I just hope you're okay. If there's anything I can do to help, please let me know. You might want an extra set of eyes looking out for properties, or —'

'Thanks. You don't have to do that.' Mak felt flat. It was as if Andy's note was burning a hole in her pocket. 'I insist on taking the couch tonight,' she went on. The coffee was ready and she poured herself a cup. 'I'll be up for a few hours reading as much of this diary as I can.'

'That bedroom is yours. I belong on the couch. I insist.'

Mak sighed.

'Really. I insist,' he reiterated. He looked at her over his vintage-style black-rimmed glasses, and she knew she could not convince him otherwise. It didn't seem right that she would be on the comfortable bed, working, when Bogey was stuck sleeping on a saggy pink couch.

'It's probably against regulations, or something, but I could help with the reading, if that would make it easier for you,' he went on. 'I have a pretty light couple of days coming up.'

Mak paused. It was tempting. She ran a hand across her forehead. 'There must be something wrong with you,' she finally said. 'You are too …' *Perfect*. '… nice.' She took a large swig of hot coffee and felt her blood warm. 'I'll let you off this time, though.' She smiled.

Hours later, Makedde's last cup of coffee was cold and her eyes hurt. She sat perched on Loulou's bed, riveted to Adam's diary.

Absent-mindedly, she raised the cold, half-full cup to her lips, sipped at it with disgust, and set it on the floor. It was nearly two. She'd lost track of time.

Adam Hart, she'd discovered, was a young man who lived in his mind. As she'd suspected, he had written his every intimate thought in his diaries. Unlike his impossibly neat room, his journal was a swirl of ideas, disconnected thoughts and observations, things he'd read online or in textbooks, things he'd overheard at uni, things he had dreamed and imagined. For a beautiful-looking young man, who was obviously smart, he was surprisingly antisocial. He seemed to have few close friends, and kept mostly to himself. But he had a life rich with adventure in his mind, and his diary entries were filled with references to everyone from Jack Kerouac to Harry Houdini.

His mother — and Patrice — had been right about him being a teetotaller. He made mention of it in his diaries. He didn't smoke or do drugs either, and he felt alienated amongst those who did, particularly Patrice, his former girlfriend, whom he mentioned in several entries. From his diary it was clear that he could see the end long before Patrice broke it off with him, and he had tried to stop the inevitable. He complained that she accused him of being 'uncool' and a wimp.

Naturally, Mak had focused much of her attention on the most recent pages — the ones leading up to the missing pages. And she had hit the jackpot.

I took Mum's pearls today and Grandad's gold watch. I feel ashamed, but at least Grandad won't miss it. Maybe he would even be happy for me? I'll need it for money, perhaps, though I hope not to have to part with it. Still, I need to be prepared. I don't know how long I'll be gone. I don't know what I'll do for work. I don't know if I'll ever come home.

Adam was a runaway, as she had sensed. And he had stolen from his mother to fund his adventure. She would be mighty displeased. Or maybe she'd already known? If Mrs Hart wanted Mak to be able to do her job, she was going to have to start opening up about who her son really was.

It was too late to phone anyone, so Mak sent a text to one man she knew could help.

HI PETE. I NEED A LOOK AT SECOND HAND DEALERS BOOK. STOLEN PEARLS AND GOLD WATCH. ANY HELP? M

To Mak's surprise, she got a reply only a minute later.

Oh shit, I woke him.

LUNCH AT 12? USUAL SPOT?

Oh no, not the usual spot, was her first thought. Pete had no palate.

YES. MY SHOUT. THANKS, she replied.

If it was Adam who had ripped out his final diary entries, why had he not ripped out this admission of theft, Mak wondered.

Unless he had not been the one to rip the pages out at all.

CHAPTER 28

It was five minutes past three in the morning when Luther Hand slipped into the quiet lobby of the sprawling Top Hotel Praha.

He scanned the vast reception desk and over-lit lobby area from under a grey ponytailed wig and the brim of a black fedora. His round glasses, with clear, non-prescription lenses, served only to alter his appearance. A tired-looking brunette receptionist worked the desk in an unattractive burgundy uniform. She was talking on the phone in the hushed tones of what sounded like a private call, and took no notice of him as he traversed the lobby. Through a small forest of potted plants, he noted a businessman sitting across from a woman who looked too finely dressed to be with him, both perched clumsily on curved leather seats, leaning in to one another. They appeared to have emerged from the hotel's casino, and were now debating whether the evening's festivities should conclude in a hotel room upstairs. Luther was all but unseen, and certainly unnoticed, as he made his way across the shiny, tile-patterned floor to the bank of elevators.

When the first elevator door opened, he noted that he was not alone. An older man stepped back against the elevator wall to let Luther enter. Hopefully, this would not pose any problems later. Luther could wait for another elevator, but knew he could just as easily encounter someone else. He had already been seen.

The doors slid shut as Luther pressed the eleventh-floor button, the trapped air smelling lightly of spirits, sweat and deodoriser. A circle of red already glowed around the number eight on the panel of buttons. The carriage began to ascend with the muffled sound of shifting gears and cables. His companion stared straight ahead like a wax figure, gripping his briefcase as if it held his life. Perhaps it did; nothing would ever surprise Luther.

People avoided looking at Luther Hand, and this man was no exception. Luther had cut an imposing figure since he was as a young boy, and he had become used to this effect. He was unusually tall — a full 30 centimetres taller than this stranger — and broadly built. It was also clear there was something amiss about his face. The surgery he had endured at a clinic in Kuala Lumpur some years before to try to correct his facial irregularities had not been altogether successful. His face was stretched, and his acne scars still visible. Even if one did not take in the detail, his disturbing presence was felt, the misshapen proportions of his face sensed in the peripheral vision. A type of human survival instinct made people avoid catching his eye. Professionally speaking, that was beneficial to all involved.

Recently though, Luther had privately begun to wonder if he was a man at all. Perhaps he was some kind of ghost.

When the doors opened for the eighth floor, the other passenger slipped out like water. Luther caught a glimpse of him slowing near his door and fumbling for his key, then the doors closed and pulled the stranger from view. The elevator opened again on the eleventh floor, but Luther did not exit there. He travelled to the sixteenth floor before stepping out of the lift into a warmly lit corridor extending to his left almost to vanishing point.

Room 1602.

The hallway was empty, the guests tucked into their rented beds, sleeping soundly on bleached sheets that had enveloped a hundred other strangers. Luther turned right and walked several paces, nearing the east wing. Arrived at his destination, he listened briefly at the door. Room 1602 was quiet within. He pulled on his leather gloves, and checked his supplies with a speedy precision that barely required movement.

The keycard he had been provided with slid into the lock with ease, the mechanism opening with a faint whir. Within seconds Luther was inside the dark room, with the door shut behind him. The air was stifling. He knew the layout, and in the inky blackness moved straight to the king-sized bed near the window, where his two marks slept. They would barely have had time to register the noise of the door, let alone comprehend the light shining in their faces. Luther held his pocket torch in one hand and a Czech-made CZ-83 with its reshaped trigger guard and a long cylindrical silencer in the other. The man's tired eyes opened to a squint, confused. Luther quickly confirmed the identity of the man as his primary mark, pressed the end of the silencer to his forehead and pulled the trigger.

Boff.

The sound of the shot was muffled, flat, final.

There was a small noise from the woman in the bed, like that of a yawning bird, as she flinched and began to come awake. 'Hmmm?'

Boff.

Her hands clenched slightly, then released. Her head lolled to one side. She became still. A shot to the brain was a quick way to extinguish life.

Luther briefly pondered whether the man had seen the end coming, and whether or not he had let on to his wife that something was amiss — his wife, who now lay lifeless on the hotel bed like an angel in a growing halo of blood. He gently closed her eyelids. She was attractive, pale and feminine. The blood contrasted blackly against the white of her nightdress. She looked peaceful, Luther thought.

Someone in her husband's agency had clearly wanted to simplify the employee structure. He had outstayed his welcome and his usefulness.

When will I outstay mine?

Lately his mind had become infected with such thoughts. They were fleeting, but unhelpful. He did not have the time or need to ponder such things. It was not his job to ask why names ended up on his list, what their stories were, whether what he was doing was morally right or reprehensible, or why both the man and his wife were on his list. And so he quickly pocketed the couple's wallets and passports, turned up the heat on the thermostat, then gave the room one last thorough check, stopping only a moment to admire the quiet violence he had effected.

He left the man's eyes open. Small specks of blood across his cheek picked up the colour of the blood vessels. They were already glassy and dull.

Luther flicked off his torch, and listened at the door with one ear that had been unwillingly trimmed at the top by the blade of a scalpel. It was quiet in the hallway, and confirming as much through the peephole, he slipped back into the corridor.

Barely five minutes had elapsed.

He left the *Do Not Disturb* sign on the door and exited the hotel the way he had come. The receptionist had not finished her conversation. The couple on the couch had not finished their negotiations.

In the enormous Top Hotel Praha, the occupants of room 1602 would not be discovered for at least ten hours. The warm room would aid in their decomposition, and make the time of death harder to pinpoint. Despite the fictions peddled by forensic television shows, science could not yet fix the time of death more accurately than within the range of a few hours. When the slaughtered couple was found, there would perhaps be speculation that they'd been robbed, but any experienced investigator would see that they had been executed. Burglars did not shoot point-blank to the forehead while their victims slept. Burglars needed to be disturbed in order to kill.

Luther's client had wanted to make a statement.

That's the way it was. Some wanted death to appear accidental. Some wanted ostentatious acts of violence.

Whatever they wanted, Mr Hand could deliver. He slipped back into the Prague night, invisible, not really a man, a ghost.

When he returned to his accommodation, a blank message was waiting from Madame Q. He replied with the agreed single word: COMPLETE.

It was time to head back to Mumbai. He had a couple of days off. Maybe he could find someone to spend his time off with? Perhaps Ms Rosalay had a new girl who would not merely shake with fear in his presence.

CHAPTER 29

'So, you are missing a string of pearls? And a gold watch?

Makedde was walking quickly through downtown traffic, dodging and weaving through business-suited commuters, a full head taller than most. The streets were slick after a brief summer shower, and the footpaths seemed more chaotic than usual; a discordant symphony of rustling umbrellas and briefcases, mobile phone conversations, footsteps and car horns.

Over the din of the lunch rush, Glenise Hart seemed flabbergasted by the discovery that her things were missing. 'Well, yes. The pearls and watch are gone. I didn't realise. I ... don't understand. How did you know?'

Adam had written of many things in his diary — his desire to escape the mundane life his late father wanted for him; an attraction to one of his female teachers; the 'life-changing' meeting with a mysterious new woman; and his guilty conscience about stealing from his mother to fund his new life. Mak told Mrs Hart only as much as necessary for the moment, not wishing to upset the shocked woman further.

'Well … the pearls are just … money. But the watch is important. It was my father's,' Mrs Hart explained. 'Oh, I am so upset about this.'

'I'll do my best to get the items back, but I can't give you any guarantees. I'll need full descriptions, if you can provide them. If Adam tries to hock anything, we may be able to locate him. If I were you, I'd check for anything else of value that might be missing. Gold bracelets, diamonds, even small stereos, anything transportable by bike.'

'Oh, I really don't want Adam to get into any trouble with the authorities,' Mrs Hart wailed.

'Of course not.'

'I've built up a little nest egg since the insurance settlement. Makedde, I could give you a bonus if you bring him back safely. I really need him home.'

'Don't worry about that; I promise you I'll do my best to get Adam back for you and keep the cops away.'

Keep your nest egg, she thought. *You'll need it for the therapy.*

Mak hung up, feeling bad for Glenise, and the death of her illusions about her son.

Ten hours after answering her text message, the private investigator Pete Don was waiting for Makedde at his usual table, a corner spot in a McDonald's on George Street in Sydney's CBD. Mak had hated the restaurants ever since her class had toured the kitchen areas and freezer of the local McDonald's in her home town in Canada during a school excursion when she was twelve. The uncooked fries had looked to her exactly like the white severed fingers she'd seen at the morgue with her dad days earlier, and the frozen McNuggets like something worse. The association had stayed.

Mak strode in, not looking at the food the customers were shovelling in. She slid onto the yellow plastic seat opposite her friend and former tutor at the Australian Security Academy. 'Hi, Pete. It's great to see you. It's been what, eight months or something?'

'Too long.'

'I'm so sorry I woke you up with that text last night.'

'No worries, Mak. I never sleep at night,' he teased, leaning across the table to look at her.

'Sorry if I look a bit baggy, but unlike you, I actually *need* sleep.' She'd stayed up until four, and her body wasn't overly happy about it. She had something like a caffeine hangover, her brain throbbing dimly behind blurry eyes. 'I thought you'd get my text in the morning.'

He smiled. 'It ain't so bad being woken up by you.' He sipped at a coffee in a styrofoam cup with a golden 'M' branded across it. 'Anyway, how's my most promising student faring in her new career?' he asked.

My new career. God, this is my career, isn't it? I am never going to end up a practising psychologist.

'Any psychos chasing you?' he only half joked.

'No. Not lately. Pete, do you still have contact with someone in the pawnshop records? The second-hand dealers book thing?'

'You got some stolen property issues? Yeah, I know a guy.'

'Any chance he could look out for something for me? A gold watch and some pearls?'

'Sure. But there are lots of watches and pearls that go to Cash Converters every day.'

'The pearls are choker-length, single-strand, white: fairly non-descript, I'd say. But the watch has an engraving.' She slid a note across the table with Mrs Hart's description:

Jill & John. Amor Vincit Omnia.

'A wedding watch. Good,' he said. 'I can have him keep an eye out. No guarantees of course.'

Pawnbrokers and second-hand dealers had to register all goods pawned or sold. Each dealers register listed the time, the date, name and address of the person bringing the goods in, a description of the goods and the price paid, and could be perused by the police on demand. People had to produce ID to pawn goods. So if the watch or pearls showed up, they could help locate Adam, and a stop order would be put on them so they couldn't be sold. A lot of thieves pawned goods using false IDs and hoped that no one was paying attention to the second-hand dealers register.

'I owe you, Pete. If this watch or necklace pop up it might help me break this case. The kid's name is Adam Hart. He doesn't have a driver's licence or passport, so if he tries to sell the stuff he'd have to use some other ID. Or get someone else to do it.'

'Ah, tough case with nothing to track him.' Pete stuck out his lower lip. 'I saw one place that thought a library card would do. Not quite legal.'

'Exactly. He'd probably try to use something like that.' She stood up. 'Okay, what am I getting you for lunch?'

He lit up. 'Deluxe Brekkie Roll, a hashbrown and hotcakes. And another coffee.'

She raised her eyebrows. 'Breakfast? You are one hungry PI.'

'That's me. Been doing all-nighters watching some babe who's supposed to be doing the nasty with her real estate agent.'

'Oh, the world is a romantic place, isn't it?'

Mak came back a few minutes later with a tray steaming with food. She had ordered herself some pretty average-looking raisin toast and a bottle of water.

'Thanks, Mak. Not eating?'

Mak smiled and picked at her toast. 'Pete, did you ever think about … getting them back?'

He looked up from his hotcakes. 'Getting what back?'

'You know. The ones who did that to your face.'

The word was that Pete had spent a long time in hospital after the beating he'd received on getting made during an undercover assignment back when he was still a cop. He had been left for dead, and barely got out of the hospital alive.

'What, you don't like it?' he joked, wiggling his free-form nose around like the foot of a rubber chicken. 'It's not sexy?'

Mak put her toast down and stared into his eyes. 'Really.' She was serious.

'Look, the thought occurred to me, but I didn't act on it. I knew better than to act on that impulse because it would have been a really, really bad idea. I let justice take its course. Two of the top guys are dead, shot by rival gang members, and another three are in the pen. That's justice enough.'

'And what if justice hadn't been done?' she pressed.

He took a mouthful and only half chewed it before speaking. 'Makedde,' he mumbled, 'I would be very careful where those thoughts lead you.'

'Who said anything about me? I was asking about you.'

Pete knew better, and she could tell. While he tucked into a hashbrown the shape of a flattened kidney, Mak cut to the chase. 'Have you seen Damien Cavanagh around since he got back?'

'We don't exactly hang in the same crowd,' was Pete's reply between chews. A bit of grease slicked his lips.

'I'd never insult you like that, Pete,' she said, and smiled. 'But to be serious for a moment, his presence doesn't go unnoticed round the clubs. He still enjoys slumming it, doesn't he? The strip joints in the Cross? Surely he hasn't given that up? And that black Diablo isn't the kind of car that blends into the background.'

'He's been hanging round the Cross. He still likes the shows.'

Strip shows. I knew it. I bloody well knew it.

'And the young girls?'

'A mate of mine used to work Paper Tiger, and according to him Damien doesn't appear to be hooking up with the known local traders. He'd have new contacts.' Paper Tiger was the codename for an operation to bring down the organised crime rings that trafficked 'sex slaves' into Australia. Most of the women were from poor villages in Asia. Some were underage, like the Thai girl who had died in the Cavanaghs' house and had been seen with Damien. The Paper Tiger task force had been disbanded in 1995, but as far as Mak knew there were still numerous active investigations. The problem certainly hadn't gone away, although convictions were tough to secure because the victims were often deported or wouldn't testify.

Mak sensed that Pete had more to say on the subject. She waited, and they ate quietly for a while, the restaurant buzzing around them with kids, teenagers and office workers grabbing lunch.

'I think he has a new guy in the Cross. Some promoter.'

Mak's eyes widened. 'Go on.'

'This guy, James Wendt … he's the son of some famous entertainer, I can't remember who. Anyway, he and Damien have been spotted together a lot lately, and this guy has a record. He did time overseas.'

'Drugs?'

Pete shrugged. 'Who knows?'

'Thanks, Pete.' At least she wasn't the only one who cared what Damien Cavanagh was up to.

Mak felt her heart speeding up. She wanted to know everything about this James Wendt, and Damien's movements. If he was back to his old tricks she might be able to get some evidence this time. Better evidence. Enough to lock him away. She tried not to show too much interest, although Pete could surely guess.

'Be careful, kid,' was all he said.

Mak smiled. She looked out the window and watched the stream of pedestrians and traffic bustling on their way.

'Well, look at that,' Mak said suddenly. 'That guy. In the hat. Him. I saw him yesterday in St Ives. That is the same guy. I've seen him, like, twice in two days.'

A man was leaning against a telephone pole halfway up the street smoking by himself.

'Are you sure?'

She nodded. 'St Ives, on the street outside the Murphys' house. And now. Why is he still standing out there? Why not sit down somewhere?'

'Well, plenty of office workers come out for a fag.'

'Not in baseball caps.' It was more a feeling than anything else. Of course she could not be certain that it was the same man, but it didn't *feel* right to her, him standing there smoking in a baseball cap on George Street while everyone rushed past. He didn't look like an office worker or one of the local rough types. He didn't look … *right*.

Pete craned his neck until he spotted the man. 'Mak, what kind of case are you doing, anyway?' he asked, sounding concerned.

'Just a runaway, I'm pretty sure,' she said. 'I'll get him.'

'I'm sure you will. Nothing else? No other cases? You sleeping with any married men at the moment?'

'Fuck off,' she said.

'I thought not. Well then, I can't see why anyone would be tailing you.'

Try the Cavanaghs.

'They ever catch the guy who tried to rob you last year?' Pete went on.

Makedde had arrived home on her motorcycle and had encountered an attacker in the hallway, an apparent burglar, in a balaclava. The man had been huge, and had a knife. Her motorcycle leathers had saved her. He had tried to stab her, but the blade didn't penetrate her jacket. That was before Mak had run out into the street, sped off on her bike and gone under a truck.

'Burglars don't normally pursue their victims for blocks in car chases,' Mak said with certainty.

'Right you are,' he agreed. 'Suspicious as hell, that was. And the police didn't find prints?'

'Not one.'

Pete crumpled his empty wrappers in his scarred hands, and got rid of their tray. Sitting down again he spoke thoughtfully. 'The guy out there, he could be a coincidence, or he could be another guy with the same stupid cap. That burglar, though, he was no normal burglar, you're right about that. Mak, I think you might find yourself a target so long as everyone knows you're gunning for Damien Cavanagh.'

Mak opened her mouth to protest, but she couldn't lie. She thought for a moment. 'I am gunning for him, Pete. I can't help it. He's a monster.'

'I know. You're probably right there too. Just be careful, okay? If you have to snoop around, be subtle. Watch yourself. Cover your tracks, cover your legal bases, and keep your neck in. Don't put yourself in danger for anything or anyone, okay? It's not safe for you. I hope I taught you that much.'

She nodded. 'You did. I'm not stupid.'

'I would never accuse you of that.'

She had finished her bottle of water, and she rolled it back and forth across the tabletop, frowning. 'Can I touch it, Pete?' she finally asked.

She could only mean one thing. He smiled, and she leaned over and touched his collapsed nose affectionately. Without cartilage it was just like putty in her hands.

'I should go. I got an insurance case. I'll have my guy check the database this arvo,' he said. 'Maybe your watch and beads will pop up.'

'You're the best.' She blew Pete a kiss as she walked out. The man in the cap was gone by the time she stepped onto the footpath.

Mak arrived unannounced at Marian Wendell's offices, eager to check Adam Hart's diary. She'd had an idea.

'How is my Secret Weapon?' Marian asked. She was bent over her desk and waved Mak in with one hand.

'Now, I don't want you to get cross with me, but I need to make some marks on Adam Hart's original diary.'

Marian looked up. 'You what?'

Makedde snatched a pencil out of her purse and held it up. 'Just with pencil. If it doesn't work, I'll try to erase it again.'

By now Marian was frowning. 'If *what* doesn't work? What are you going to do?'

'Trust me,' Mak assured her. 'I stayed up all night reading his diaries. Something was happening to him towards the end. I think he wrote about it, and the pages were ripped out for some reason ... by someone.'

'A pencil rub?'

'Yeah. It's worth a try.'

Marian sighed, and handed her the keys to the filing cabinet. 'Those diaries could end up as evidence if this kid doesn't turn up okay.'

'I know. I'll wear the gloves.' The cotton evidence gloves were soft and white, like something a gemmologist would use to handle diamonds.

Makedde hoped that by rubbing pencil lead lightly across the remaining blank page, she might be able to make out some of what had been written on the final pages that had been torn out. It was a pretty unsophisticated trick, but it sometimes worked.

'Let me know if you get anywhere,' her boss said, and shooed her from her office.

Mak took the diaries into the waiting room while Marian worked the phones, keeping updated on her agents and their cases.

'Okay, don't make me look stupid here ...' Mak murmured, opening the last diary to the torn pages and rubbing the first blank page very carefully with the edge of the pencil. Immediately she could see there were a few spots where Adam had pushed his pen hard enough into the page to make an indent, but it hardly made the entire entry legible; rather, the edges of some letters started to appear. By the time she was finished, three strings of letters had emerged.

THEAT

JOU

OVE

Theat, jou, ove?

Mak stared at the letters, willing her brain to find the connection.

CHAPTER 30

The subterranean Visy Theatre in Brisbane's Powerhouse descended into a hush.

The intimate stage was almost bare, waiting. Eyes were fixed upon it. The evening performance was well underway, and the next act would soon emerge. Adam Hart sat grinning in the back row, his heart lifted by a new sense of love and possibility.

And excitement.

In seconds, there was a dramatic whirl of colour as a performer strode across the stage in a splendid Victorian costume of deep burgundy and ebony, the coat long, and the shirt finished with a tie of black lace ruffles. *Lucien*. As he paused and came into focus, the audience could see that he wore dark eyeliner, and on his right eye lines of black flicked up into stripes like painted eyelashes, right to his eyebrow. The man's face was sharp, but exceedingly handsome, his mouth delicate and small, his eyes large and dark, framed by exquisitely arched brows and dramatic cheekbones. His hair was deep brown and dishevelled, and worn long around the ears, without any of the shiny falseness audiences had begun to associate with Vegas-style magicians, who seemed always to sport too much hairspray and dyed facial hair, almost as if it were a trade requirement. This man brought to mind the golden era of Victorian magic. In no time he had the small Australian audience in the palm of his dexterous hand.

Lucien the Illusionist.

Silently, Lucien extended a hand from one of his long cuffs, his palm up and fingers elegantly curled, his fingernails painted black. He beckoned stage left where a burlesque-attired assistant appeared carrying a small silver tray. In fishnets, corset and veil, she was an alluring cabaret throwback. Gracefully, she produced from the tray a small, flat object. The magician gripped it carefully between his painted fingers, and walked a dramatic arc along the footlights, holding it up. It was a razor blade, and it glimmered dangerously in the lights. To demonstrate the blade's lethal authenticity, Lucien beckoned again to his glamorously dressed assistant, who pulled a handkerchief from the top of her corset. She held it in front of her with both hands, pulling it taut. With one swift swipe, the illusionist sliced through it with the blade, leaving it in two pieces. Satisfied that he had proved his point, he stood centre-stage and placed the blade on his tongue.

And swallowed it.

The audience winced and gasped.

Adam Hart did not wince. He had seen this act several times already, and he now sat watching carefully, a man enchanted and awed.

As if eating the razor blade wasn't enough, the assistant now held out the plate again, placing one delicate hand on her rounded hip, as if to dare the magician to take another. He picked a second razor blade from the plate and placed it on his pink tongue. So convincing was the illusion that Adam actually tasted faint metal in the back of his throat as he continued to watch for the magician's deceit. You simply could not swallow razor blades and expect to live. Adam knew that. Still, the effect was captivating, and unsettling. He racked his brain for how it could be done. He knew something of the technique, but only from books.

Onstage, the illusionist swallowed, uncomfortably it seemed. He coughed. In minutes he swallowed four more razor blades in the same fashion, stopping halfway to again prove their lethal edge by slicing a dramatic 'X' through a paper scroll. When next his burlesque-attired assistant returned she removed her necklace. She handed it to the magician, who held it up to examine it under the lights.

Incredibly, he ate it.

Lucien took a sip of water, gargled, and with a series of motions of his mouth and throat, one hand on his stomach, he reached into his mouth and — *voilà!* — as he opened his mouth wide, he grasped the end of the necklace. There was a razor blade dangling from it, then another, then another, all evenly placed. The string of blades came out of his mouth with surprising elegance.

He held it up to rapturous applause.

Sleight of hand ... sleight of mouth ...

Adam applauded with the crowd. Looking around, he saw eyes wide with the wonderment of magic, hands pounding together. Of course the audience logically knew that no one was really able to eat deadly razor blades only to attach them to a necklace within their body and pull them out in a perfect string, unharmed — but they had not picked the method, nor did they really want to know how he did it. It would be like spoiling a Christmas surprise. This was the unspoken contract between magician and audience — honest deceit.

How Adam wished he could one day be on that stage.

Now, Lucien made his exit with a wave of his dramatic cuff. He would appear again to tantalise with more of his illusions later in the program. The intimate theatre plunged into claustrophobic darkness as the curtains closed, leaving the audience with nowhere to look. Immediately the air was thick with conversation about the last act. In their seats couples touched blindly and whispered exclamations of wonder.

'*Did you see that ...?*'

'*Razor blades! How did he do it?*'

Within this cloak of darkness, Adam sat silently, electrified, but wearing a smile. He had no wish to debate the magic of Lucien the Illusionist with anyone there, and he knew better than most what they had seen. He instead turned it over and over in his head like a child with a Rubik's Cube. He was awed. He'd seen countless videos of routines, but this was truly the best live act of its kind that he had witnessed. He hoped that Lucien would open up to him, perhaps pass on his secrets.

Perhaps he would even invite him onstage.

When Adam watched the show he temporarily forgot his own woes and internal conflicts. It took him out of himself, and Adam Hart indeed wished to be far from himself, far from anywhere he had ever been.

There was activity near the stage.

Bijou.

The next act was about to start.

A familiar warm red glow peeked through the curtains and spread across the crowd. The lush red theatrical curtains were pulled back. The musicians — Lara, the drummer, and the contortionist-guitarist — had reassembled, looking artfully dishevelled in their tatty, old-fashioned tuxedos.

Again, Adam marvelled at how the performers could play so many roles, and show such a range of skills. He could still hardly believe that the troupe had only seven performers; there seemed so many more. *And there is about to be one more.* He applauded along with the crowd, feeling the soft wings of butterflies building up in his stomach. Much more than the saucy burlesque act, and even more than the master illusionist, the next act was his favourite. It was a classic play of the Grand Guignol, a gruesome tale of love and revenge.

Le Baiser dans la Nuit.

The Final Kiss, starring the most mesmerising beauty he had ever seen.

Bijou, my lover, la femme assassinée.

Adam had to watch the play carefully. Bijou was grooming him for the starring role.

CHAPTER 31

Here we go.

Mak had already worked a full day on barely a wink of sleep. In addition to meeting up with Pete, and pencil-rubbing Adam's diary, she'd checked out the Théâtre des Horreurs website, following up on the flyer she'd found in the diary. It had some interesting, undated photographs of their performances, but unfortunately it looked like it was not updated frequently. She'd also hoofed around St Ives interviewing Adam's neighbours, with little result. She'd clocked off at seven to work on her own extracurricular assignment — seeing what Damien Cavanagh was up to. She had again started with her trusty computer, trawling the internet for hits on the man Pete Don had mentioned, and quickly found references to James Wendt and his stint in a Spanish jail for drug trafficking. He had only just been released and was already looking well connected in Australia. She had printed off a colour photograph of him and folded it into her purse.

Waiting, waiting …

Now in a black figure-hugging satin dress and heeled leather boots, Mak was prepared for a night of either continuing to sit in her rental car bored to tears for a few more hours, or following Damien through the sleaziest dives in Kings Cross or to a meeting with the questionable Mr James Wendt. She realised that she so desperately wanted to catch him up to no good, it bordered on perversity. After three hours stuck in the car with an increasingly pained bladder, she was ready to jump at any chance of a lead.

Around midnight, the waiting game was finally over. Damien Cavanagh pulled out of the driveway of the Darling Point house, impossible to miss in his black Lamborghini. He was without a minder. Mak followed him at a distance, wondering what the heir to one of the biggest fortunes in Australia might do on a sleepy Wednesday night. He drove himself into the city and stopped in an alley outside the Metro, a rock venue. Mak rolled the window down, and heard music pouring out. Patrons were still arriving. Two women in tiny dresses and fishnet stockings passed the man at the front door and teetered up the steps inside.

GOOD DRUGS BAD WOMEN, a poster outside the theatre declared, promising international burlesque acts. Mak thought the name of the gig inappropriate for Damien, who seemed more interested in *bad drugs* and *good women* — good, underage, innocent women. In fact, the whole gig seemed a little too cool for a spoilt rich kid. But burlesque was sweeping the world with new-found popularity, thanks to Dita Von Teese, and it seemed that even the rich and infamous were interested. She wondered if James Wendt was inside, enjoying the show.

Mak watched from the car as two men rushed down the steps to greet Damien. One took keys from him to park his flashy Diablo somewhere safe. The other passed him a black eye-mask and led him inside.

An eye-mask? Dress-ups?

A vote for anonymity, she expected. Well, she had some tricks of her own. Mak found a park a couple of blocks away, pulled a black pageboy wig out of the glove box, and struggled for a few minutes to tuck her blonde hair underneath it. She lacked the fishnets and Mary Jane shoes that would make the burlesque theme work, but after hiking up her dress a couple of inches and slicking red lipstick across her mouth, she looked like she was part of the scene.

She locked the car and strolled up the street towards the venue, making a show of herself as she approached the bouncer.

'Hi,' she purred confidently.

'Ticket,' he replied, unaffected.

'Do I need a ticket?' she asked, bringing a finger to her mouth. 'I'm with our friend … you know, in the Diablo. I had to make sure it was parked.'

Recognition. 'Go on up. He'll be waiting.'

Or not.

Mak ascended the staircase, her head already beginning to feel warm from the wig. At the top she pulled her dress back down to her knees out of habit. *This is Damien's crowd?* The venue was packed with an eclectic mix of rockabillys, goths, goggled steampunks, men in long velvet coats and rockers with greasy hair and ill-fitting jeans. The few straight-looking types stood out like freaks. In her black dress, she was positively boring. Half the women were in knickers and corsets.

Mak made a beeline for the toilets, pleased not to be wearing the head-to-toe latex dress some poor woman was struggling with in the next cubicle, and emerged seconds later feeling greatly relieved. She strolled into the main hall, and saw that the fashion was far from the only entertainment.

On a bare stage, an emaciated MC with slicked hair, Jagger-lips and the long face of a young Tom Waits was slipping the suspenders off his shoulders and undoing the buttons on his ivory dress shirt with exaggerated drama. His shirt soon hung open to reveal a lean, white stomach. His lips quivering obscenely, he made an announcement into the old-fashioned microphone. 'Ladeeez and Geeeeeeentlemen, I will now perform a fan dance. And, of course, later this evening we have the much-anticipated international burlesque performer — BELLADONNA!' There was violent applause at the mention of the name, and with this the MC pulled his shirt wide to expose a concave chest with two black 'X's of duct tape covering his nipples. He caressed the 'X's lasciviously and pouted his engorged lips.

Brilliant.

Now the MC brought a stand-up floor fan over. He plugged it in, and it blew gusts of air at him while he performed a satirical striptease, with liberal suggestions of auto-eroticism. Mak laughed out loud. The man was a sensational tease.

She looked around.

Where is Damien?

Mak's stature assisted her in scanning the crowd for the man in the mask. Perhaps he had a contact there, someone who could hook him up with whatever he desired?

A rockabilly band next took to the stage, amped up to maximum volume. They began performing a song that appeared to be about cocaine use — perhaps fittingly for the Snowdroppers, as they called themselves.

Just as she was getting into the music and working her way from one side of the room to the other, looking for Damien Cavanagh or James Wendt, Mak noticed with discomfort that a man at the nearby bar, sober as a stone, was looking at *her* intensely. He had dark eyes, prominent eyebrows, a handsome face, thin lips. She had been prepared for leering drunks or awkward conversations with oddly dressed strangers, but not this. He was too focused as he approached her, too sober.

'Do you come to gigs like this a lot?' he asked. Immediately there was something Mak didn't like about him. Something she didn't trust. Just behind him, a buxom redhead leaned against the bar with her bosoms lifted proudly, hoping to catch his eye, or hers, Mak could not be sure.

'*Are* there gigs like this a lot?' Mak replied with incredulity. She doubted that, but then she had been out of Sydney for a while. She continued to scan the crowd, hoping the man would leave her.

Her attention was again diverted, this time by a flash of flame. 'Absinthe, darling.'

It was the redhead, holding a glass towards her.

'Hi,' Mak said.

Already the woman had the flesh of her shoulder pressed against Mak. She blew her own flaming drink out and sucked the shot back in the time it would take any normal person to inhale a raindrop. Mak took her cue to quickly extinguish her little fire. Steadying herself, she tossed the absinthe shot down her throat, barely touching the warm lip of the glass. It stung, and left a hot aftertaste of liquorice.

Oh, wow …

'Thanks for the drink. That's very cool of you.'

'You looked like you needed it. There's a clique that put on things like this every few weeks. Different venues, different names. You should really come more often,' the redhead told her. 'You're so pretty you should be onstage.'

'Thanks,' Mak said awkwardly, still keeping an eye out for Damien and Wendt in the gyrating crowd.

'Did you see that French troupe when they were in town?' came another voice. By now the strange man was being distanced from her, and she was grateful for it.

Mak looked over her shoulder. Her new friend was a tall, thin, serenely attractive woman in full gothic attire: white face, black lips, glossy black hair falling down her back to a nipped waist encased in tight corsetry. Mak had moved forward to place her empty shot glass on the bar, and was now frozen mid-lope, like a gazelle in an artist's study.

'Do you mean Le Théâtre des Horreurs?' Mak responded. 'No, I missed them.'

Perhaps this is Adam Hart's kind of place? Somehow, that was hard to imagine.

'Shame.' The black lips pursed slightly. 'Moira Finucane is on next week at the Speigeltent. I hope I see you there.' She spoke the last sentence with a small flicker of a smile. Now it dawned on Mak that she was alone at a bar, being flirted with. It was familiar, of course, though much more fun in this crowd. Nothing like her other work for Marian.

Mak returned the woman's smile, flattered. She wondered if accepting the absinthe shot had been such a good idea. She could have turned it down, but it would have seemed rude. Now her brain was more than a little fuzzy. For a few seconds she searched for something to say to the woman, who she felt was infinitely cooler than she was. 'Yeah,' she finally managed, feeling hugely unimpressive, and perhaps even unworthy of the get-up that had piqued the woman's interest.

'You make a pretty brunette,' the lady goth persisted.

'Thanks.' *The wig is obvious. I knew it was obvious.*

Before Mak could compliment her in return, the woman walked away to join her group, a glass of dark liquid in her pale hands. She left behind the faint scent of incense. In seconds, the man had slid into her place, and to Mak's horror, he leaned in close and spoke into her ear. 'You've been busy since you got back in town,' he said.

She flinched.

Had she heard that right? *Back* in town? That was not standard pick-up chat. 'Pardon me?'

His look was direct, but he didn't answer. She was sure he had heard her question. *What's going on here?* He seemed uninterested in repeating his question, and she did not want to play games.

'Oh, I see, you've been reading the papers, huh?' she mumbled, not caring whether he heard her over the loud music or not. He was like the man on the bus, commenting on the news articles. How annoying. Now she wanted to leave. She turned, but was intercepted.

'You shouldn't be following him,' he said, gripping her forearm.

She yanked her arm away. 'What?' Her head snapped around to face him eye to eye. His thin lips looked mean. *Cruel.* At this distance she could smell him, and he smelled of cheap cologne and dirty money.

The Cavanaghs. The Cavanaghs have sent him. He's following me. The bastard is following me.

'Where's your baseball cap, arsehole?' she said. 'I'm out of here.'

'What's up? Is this guy bothering you?' Her buxom red-haired admirer gave the man a vicious shove, which he didn't react to, and grabbed Mak by the hand, hauling her away from the bar, nearly causing her to trip. Now Mak noticed a full-sleeve tattoo of swirling waves and koi. The woman had muscle.

Holy shit. This is getting crazy.

The man held his hands in the air, palms up, and didn't follow, but Mak suspected she would see him later, if he was indeed the man in the baseball cap. Mak felt she had already outstayed her welcome. She was halfway down the staircase when her flame-haired protector spoke up.

'But Belladonna hasn't even gone on stage yet!'

'I'm sorry. I have to go. Thanks for the drink.'

The bouncer noticed her on the way out. 'Leaving so soon?'

She said nothing.

Mak arrived home humiliated. It should have been easy to follow Damien Cavanagh around for a few days, and figure out who his main contacts were, and what they were known for. If he was up to his old tricks, she'd soon find out. But what was the story with her being tailed everywhere? Did Damien really have security looking out for her?

Dammit.

She marched down the echoing hallway and fumbled with her keys. The door opened for her, and she found herself looking at Bogey, unshaven, his black hair slightly ruffled. In her boots she was slightly taller than he.

'Hi, are you okay?' he asked.

'Sort of.'

It was one in the morning, and he was still awake. There were sketchpads on the coffee table. He noticed her looking at them. 'Just working on some design ideas for a new chair,' he explained. 'Kick your boots off and relax. Would you like a drink? I made myself a rum and Coke. Would you like one?'

'Sure,' Mak answered. 'Tonight was a damned disaster,' she said flatly, and sighed. 'At least a woman bought me a drink, so I guess it wasn't a total failure.' She plonked herself heavily on the sofa.

Bogey took her coat and placed it carefully over the back of a stool, walked to the stereo and turned it on. It was tuned to a station playing a Nick Cave tune: 'Into my arms … oh love … into my arms …'

'Is the music okay?'

'I love Nick Cave. Love him.'

'So what happened?'

'It was stupid of me. I was trying to follow Damien Cavanagh, and I got made. Bad.'

There was the clinking of ice, and the sound of bottles. 'Is he still up to no good?' Bogey asked.

She looked up. At least someone sympathised with her side of things. 'I don't know yet. That's what I hope to find out.'

He handed the drink to her, and sat next to her on the sofa. 'I think you are very brave,' he said.

Their faces were close, and without a word she locked her lips to his — the first time she had ever kissed him; the first lips she had kissed except Andy's for what had been years. He tasted delicious. His mouth was soft, his lips like pillows, and so much warmer than hers. His whole body seemed unreasonably

226

warm and magnetic to the touch. They lunged at each other like lovesick teenagers for a moment, kissing and holding each other, until she pulled back, awash with guilt. Was it because she had wanted this so much while she was still living with Andy? She had only just broken with him, and already she was prepared to leap into this other man's arms? Was this what her heart was made of? But, of course, he wasn't just any man.

'I ... um ... should taste this drink,' she said, and laughed.

He smiled. 'Sorry, I didn't mean to ...'

'You didn't do anything. That was me. I wanted to kiss you.' She picked up her drink and downed half of it in one gulp. 'I really like you, Bogey.'

Bogey took her in with childlike wide eyes. He put his hand in hers and looked at her with silent intensity. He clearly did not want to push her into anything she might regret, but his desire was palpable.

Again she leaned close, this time pushing her hips to him. The hollow of her lap connected with his hipbone, and they kissed again, falling back against the couch. She felt him throb and grow. He was straining hard against his jeans, and feeling that mound of warm sexuality aroused her further. She straddled him and positioned herself gently against it, straining slightly.

Delicious ...

The heat between them grew, their kisses ever deeper. She felt herself letting go, feeling like she wanted to consume him completely. In that moment Mak cared little for regrets or expectations. She didn't care about what anyone would think.

She sat up, still straddling him, and smiled. He smiled back, unsure. Her dress had rolled up to her waist. She stood up and took his hand and led him to Loulou's bedroom.

'Sit down,' she ordered.

He sat on the edge of the bed, obedient.

In one movement she unzipped her tight dress and pulled it down to her thighs, letting the bundle of fabric drop from her hands. She stood in front of Bogey in her bra and panties, feeling bold and unashamed, feeling almost like someone else. He watched, entranced, with that same wide-eyed expression. He did not move. When she bent to pull her panties to the ground, his plump Cupid's bow trembled, and he leaped to his feet, sliding his arms around her waist. She carefully took his glasses off and placed them on Loulou's bedside table. Naked of his spectacles, Bogey appeared even more entranced. *Vulnerable*. She brought her mouth to his, and their tongues connected again, tangled eagerly. With increasing urgency, she found herself pushing against his growing erection with her hips, wanting more and more of him. There was a tension in her that was relieved only when he knelt before her and finally — beautifully — took his moist tongue and licked the soft cleft between her thighs, teasing at first, and then harder, followed by a gentle suckling that sent her into gasps, fading away into a temporary, death-like peace.

Mak did not know how long she swayed on her feet, pulsing inside. When she regained herself, a surge of desire reanimated her. He was sitting on the edge of the bed with his forehead leaning against her bare stomach, his eyes closed. She pushed him back and slid his black leather belt out of his belt loops with a forceful tug, the end flicking his exposed stomach. Instead of tossing it aside, she seized his wrists and — silently daring him to refuse her suggestion — she looped the belt over his wrists and pulled it back around his waist, binding him. In seconds she had his dark denim jeans unzipped and thrown to the floor. The firm tent in his boxer shorts displayed clear arousal. He was hers.

Her mouth ravaged him, and before long she had removed their last scraps of clothing and climbed on top of him. Time was nothing. It neither passed nor stood still. She felt their bodies joined together, and at the point of orgasm her shoulders began to shake, her thighs, her lips. She cried out and warm tears collected in the corners of her eyes and rolled freely down her cheeks. In that instant she became deeply aware of a well of grief and sorrow, previously unacknowledged. In a blink she saw a black hole of loneliness in the centre of herself, terrifying and impossibly huge.

Bogey sighed beneath her, snapping her back into the physical world. He pulled out of her quite suddenly, his hard penis pouring warm jets across his naked stomach. She had a flash of his upturned face and his tattoos and pale skin, and she pressed down onto him, melting into him, sweat and moisture pressed tight between them, intermingling. Though her body still tingled with a deep pulsing pleasure, she worried about the glimpse of that giant dark hole of emptiness. She worried about what had been opened up, what it meant.

He rolled her to his side, still bound to her, limbs entangled. There was only the sound of breathing. No conversation. Nothing to distract her. For long minutes her vulnerability felt intolerable.

Accustomed to Andy's habits in recent years, Mak prepared herself for Bogey's physical departure, followed closely by the toss of a towel to clean herself, or worse, tissues, or the sound of the shower starting. But he remained against her, their bodies touching. He watched her, and seeing her tears, spoke no words. Thoughts rushed through her head — urges to weep, to flee — but he only held her tighter. His warm semen was slick across their bellies and felt somehow comforting.

Communion.

CHAPTER 32

'Jolie! Come, come. Mr Roberts is here, and he wants to see you.'

Ms Rosalay stood in the doorway and held out her long fingers, gesturing to the young woman, who rose from the lounge chair as if manipulated on strings.

'You remember what I told you about Mr Roberts?' Ms Rosalay said, her brown eyes glittering.

Jolie nodded. 'Yes.' She felt confident. 'I'll get ready, then.' She tried not to take notice of the sudden interest of the other women in the waiting room. Some looked up from their preparations, their reading, the television that was softly speaking in the corner. None spoke. She supposed they would ask her about him afterwards.

Jolie was not her real name, but no one in this place used real names. She liked to call herself Jolie, after the movie star. Her real name was Faith, and she was from Idaho, but she didn't think that sounded very glamorous so she kept it to herself. 'Jolie' had been working in Ms Rosalay's establishment in Mumbai for only two weeks, and so far she thought she was doing pretty well. The money was excellent. One client had even given her a $500 tip, which was quite a compliment, she thought. Her mum in Idaho thought she was working part-time as some rich businessman's secretary while she studied at the SK Somaiya College of Arts, Science and Commerce.

It was something like that.

Ms Rosalay had told Jolie about Mr Roberts. She had said he was a nice man, and paid very handsomely, but that some of the girls did not work out for him because they had some kind of problem with his appearance or something, and found it hard to perform their services satisfactorily. Jolie thought that sounded ridiculous, but then, she hadn't seen him. The important thing was that he paid top dollar, and he wasn't violent or into any of the weird stuff that she wouldn't do. In fact, Ms Rosalay said that what Mr Roberts wanted was for a woman to stay with him for the entire night, so he could sleep with them in his arms afterwards. She thought that sounded kind of sweet.

Jolie sauntered to the bank of well-lit mirrors in the waiting area, leaned in and checked her reflection. She ran a tongue across her white teeth, and slicked her mouth with another coat of clear lipgloss, making her lips glisten alluringly. With her index finger she pressed against her eyelashes to curl them up further so her eyes would look even wider. She applied another coat of mascara to accentuate the look. When she was done, she stood back and patted her hips a little self-consciously. Jolie wore an ankle-length silk dress in the elegant, sophisticated style Ms Rosalay approved of. It was a dark blue that set off her golden skin, and the design with its thin spaghetti straps and low plunging back offered tantalising glimpses of Jolie's curves. At 155 centimetres she was petite, and wore designer platform sandals, her toenails immaculately polished in a cherry red. She spun before the mirror, ran her fingers through her hair, took a breath and stepped into the parlour.

Ms Rosalay was waiting. She handed Jolie two fresh glasses of French bubbly. 'The private room,' she said, and pointed her long fingers towards the entrance to the small alcove. 'Remember what I said.'

Look him in the eye when you talk, but don't stare. Whatever you do, don't stare.

The main room was a dimly lit place, comfortable and warm, illuminated with stained-glass table lamps and burning candles. A grand piano, now unattended, was the centrepiece. The walls were papered in dark, sensual colours, with subtle hints of carnal red. Incense filled the air. A few customers were chatting with some of the other girls, sitting as couples on lounges and sipping champagne. Most wore suits, and two men were in military uniform — no doubt they were of high rank to be able to afford such a place. Despite the troubles Mumbai and the financial markets had experienced in recent years, business was steady. The women of Ms Rosalay's parlour were renowned as the most beautiful in India, and such a promise would always hold its currency. They came from Canada, Australia, Japan, Russia and America to work there. There were blondes, redheads, brunettes. The majority of the customers were wealthy foreign businessmen, mostly Englishmen and Americans. The establishment was a far cry from the infamous brothels of the Kamathipura red-light district. Rosalay prided herself on civility, service and class. She liked her girls to look classy, too, and have a good grasp of English and some Hindi. Jolie was trying to learn Hindi.

She glided past the other couples with her drinks, and arrived at the entrance to the private room. She pushed the curtain aside, smiling.

Don't stare.

The man waiting for her, the man who called himself Mr Roberts, was one of the most startlingly nightmarish creatures — *men* — young Faith had set eyes on. She was Faith now. Her persona of Jolie had somehow vanished, along with her confidence and her ability not to stare. She had never seen anything like him in Idaho, or in her travels. Even sitting, his hulking size positively terrified her. His hands were thick, the size of dinner plates. His neck was knotted, his chest broad. But it was not just that. Most of all it was his face. There was something wrong with it.

'Hello, Mr Roberts,' she said, trying not to betray her revulsion. Her smile had faltered.

'You can call me Luther,' he told her, and cast his eyes downward.

His nose had been broken, she noticed. It sat strangely on a face already pulled and puckered with scars that ran from one side to the other like train tracks. Part of one ear was missing. She could not stop staring at him.

'Why don't you have a sip of your drink?' Luther said, looking up at her.

This was her line. This was what Ms Rosalay taught them to say. But she wasn't saying it, he was. She could not stop staring. *The scars.* He had them all over his face. What would his body be like? He would dwarf her. He was easily three times her size, and most of it muscle.

'It's okay, I'm not going to hurt you,' he said, and looked down again. He sighed heavily, annoyed.

'I ... I ...' she began, but the words wouldn't come.
'Go,' he said. 'I want to be alone.'
Faith backed away, apologising and shaken.
Ms Rosalay would be upset.

CHAPTER 33

A rogue sunbeam strayed through a gap in Loulou's curtains and struck Mak across the eyes.

Ugh.

She brought a hand to her face to shield herself, rolling over to escape its brightness. Inches away, her rock-and-roll poet, Humphrey Mortimer, lay deep in sleep, curled in the foetal position, facing away from her. Mak's eyes drifted to the red digital numbers of the alarm clock — 7:11 it flashed — then sleepily ran over the ink on the smooth skin of her companion. Her eyes lingered on a tattoo of a coffin etched on one shoulder — no doubt one the motorcycle gang had branded him with as a teenager. He had packed a lot into his twenty-nine years, almost as much as Mak had packed into her thirty. She had once been told that she had 'seen a lot of action' for someone not living in a war-zone, and it was a good observation. Andy, too, had a seen a lot. Perhaps this was the common factor between these two vastly different men she was drawn to. They understood life's extremes better than most.

Andy.

She frowned.

Mak had not opened the card that had come with the roses. In truth, she did not want to know what he had written. His words would hurt, that much she knew, and for now that was knowledge enough.

Her lips curled up again at the sight of Bogey's black-rimmed glasses sitting on the bedside table next to a half-drunk glass of rum and Coke, the ice cubes long since melted. She spotted a tangle of jeans and her dress crumpled on the floor. His studded leather belt was still wrapped around the bedpost … something about his wrists having been bound in it … Or hers?

A touch surreal, all of this …

Bogey was beginning to stir. One hand released its grip on the pillow and reached for her soft flesh. His fingertips found her and ran over her ribs and the side of her breast, leaving a light tingle in their wake. Mak lay back and stretched her arms above her head. His eyes still closed, Bogey rolled over to lie in her ample chest and curled his arm over her shoulder.

Mak's eyes were still heavy, her mascaraed lashes bent like spider legs from being crushed against the pillow. They had not slept much. It was way too early to wake.

As long as you get up before nine …

They lay like that, naked, limbs entangled, bodies dewy with sweat that smelled of sex and warm candy.

Crickets. Big ugly crickets nattering away at her ears …

Ugh, stop it …

Makedde opened her puffy eyes to see her phone jumping around on the bedside table, making its cricket-like buzz. As she reached for it, it stopped. She blinked and tried to clear her vision.

Bogey lay sleeping. She still could hardly believe he had arrived in her life again, much less that she was waking up in his arms. He mumbled something and rolled onto his back next to her. She took the opportunity to revel in the sight of him. From day one he had been interesting and attractive to her, and his dishevelled morning hair only made him more appealing. That square jaw and those black brows framed his handsome features wonderfully. His plump Cupid's bow was extended in a sleepy pout. And the things they had done together ... the way it had felt.

Crazy.

Her phone began to ring again.

Shit, Marian, can't you see I'm busy ...

Marian Wendell was a woman of order and habit. If a phone call woke Mak up, it was generally Marian calling for a morning case update, as she often did with her active agents. Not taking the call would be a sign that something was wrong. Mak leaped up, and for the first time noticed her nakedness. She grabbed Bogey's black leather jacket and wrapped it around herself.

'Marian, hi,' she said softly, scanning the floor for useful articles of clothing. 'Just hang on a minute.'

'Where are you? What's going on?'

'Nothing's going on. Just a sec ...' She pulled on a pair of jeans, realising too late they were not hers. Bogey's blue jeans hung off her waist in eighties rock video style.

Nice look.

She glanced over her shoulder, and seeing that Bogey was still sleeping despite her ruckus, she stepped out the bedroom door and stood in the kitchen. The sun was streaming in through the window, warm across her feet. It would be a hot day.

'Sorry about that,' Mak apologised.

'What is happening?'

'I couldn't talk, that's all.' She thought of making excuses about being in a meeting, a restaurant, something like that. But this was Marian she was talking to. It wasn't worth trying to fib. 'Now, for the update on the case.' She tried to clear her head of remnants of alcohol, of sleep deprivation and her strong desire for a coffee. And of Bogey in the room behind her.

'I'm not calling for a case update,' Marian said, surprising her. 'I know you'll call in. No, I'm calling to let you know that Pete Don called. Mrs Hart's missing gold watch showed up in a Brisbane pawnshop yesterday.'

Mak stood rigid. 'Really? Brisbane? That's great.' *Why didn't Pete call me?*

It was then Mak noticed the flashing light on her phone. She had an unanswered text. Something else she'd slept through.

'He gave them his valid ID. An EU passport,' Marian continued.

EU passport? This was news. Mak hadn't known he had a passport with him.

'Only got five hundred, poor kid,' Marian said. *He isn't doing a good job of covering his tracks. That's good.* 'The client is over the moon that her son's okay. She wants you to fly to Brisbane and bring him home right away, before he gets in any more trouble.'

'Business class?'

'Economy.'

Mak smiled. She'd known.

'You leave this afternoon.'

When Mak slipped back into Loulou's bedroom, Bogey was beginning to stir. His eyes were wet-looking and shiny, just a touch bloodshot.

'I'll get you a coffee,' he said, sitting up. His pecs formed attractive curves, his nipples small and hard — rather distracting for Makedde. 'Eggs?' he suggested.

She smiled. 'No, don't be crazy. Relax.' She looked around, experiencing an odd mix of feelings. She wanted to leap back into bed and kiss those pink nipples, those beautiful lips. But she also wanted to be alone. Safe. It had all moved very quickly and she didn't know what it meant or if it was meant to mean anything at all. The blur of the night's activities came into focus. Yes, the sex had been good, fantastic even, but there had been something else. She had felt a terrifying closeness to something. Something …

'Mak, I …' Bogey began and stopped.

Makedde froze. This seemed serious. Serious was not good. Not now. What would he confess? Something horrible? Her chest tightened.

He tried again. 'I've thought about you every day.' His voice was croaky, breaking like an adolescent's. She sat on the bed next to him, wanting to hold a finger to his lips. She wanted to tell him to stop. 'I didn't want to get in the way between you and … I still don't want to get in your way,' he continued. 'But I want you to know that it took every ounce of my strength not to call you every day since I saw you last, just to see how you were.'

Mak felt overwhelmed. His words should have soothed her, but they did not. Panic set in with the intensity of something like vertigo. Panic about what? She could sense his vulnerability, and she did not know what to say. She had wanted him, dreamed of him while she was still with Andy and could do nothing about it. Now, here he was, and she had not been expecting it.

She gently kissed his forehead, her fingers running through his thick black hair. 'I have to go to Brisbane,' she told him, and pulled away. 'I've had a break in the case.'

Makedde packed an overnight bag, walked up to the main street and hoisted one arm into the air to hail a cab.

Traffic flew past and she felt eyes on her. The warm wind whipped her hair. Perspiration began beading on her forehead. Every cab that passed her was busy. *He is in Brisbane. I have him.* Maybe she would have the case completed in the next couple of days?

Oh, come on.

Her confidence waned with every passing blast of exhaust. She thought about walking back to the apartment and phoning for a taxi. She had thought this way would be quicker.

'Oi!'

A sedan pulled up in front of her. It was not Bogey's car. The window rolled down slowly, and a waft of cool air-conditioning drifted out.

'Get in,' a man said softly. 'I'll drive you.'

Cars began honking. The driver was blocking traffic.

'Mak. It's me,' the man said, a little more forcefully. 'Get in.'

She took a deep breath and ran a hand across her face. Another gust of wind blew against her, tangling her hair. He pushed the door open for her. Mak gripped her keys in her hand, steadied herself for whatever was to come, got in and slammed the door shut behind her. How else would she find out what this was all about?

'My name is Ben, by the way,' the man said, driving on.

It was the man from the Metro; the guy with the mean mouth. 'Hello, Ben. Have you been hanging round here all night waiting for me to come out?' Makedde asked with faux civility, her arms crossed.

'Not quite, but close enough,' he admitted and turned a corner.

'So what do we do now?' she asked him, deadpan.

'Where are you going?'

'Airport.'

He looked at her bag. 'Back to Canada?'

'No. So, this is part of your standard stalking service, is it?' she said. He didn't answer. 'Driving the target to the airport? You know, Ben — if that is your real name — I thought you were an undercover cop when I first saw you at the Metro. You didn't exactly blend in. But I was wrong. You're a private investigator, like me. Aren't you?'

He smiled.

'Have you been hired by Damien, or Jack?'

'Neither.'

Of course you'd deny it, because you're working for rich arseholes who don't think anything of killing people, and that doesn't sound so good. 'I'm not convinced you've been doing surveillance for long, Ben. I made you at St Ives. Same car, and wearing a baseball cap. And then there was the McDonald's on George Street, wearing that same stupid baseball cap that you were wise to ditch. Much better without it, Ben, if I may say. And

242

you should really quit smoking, by the way.' She unfolded her arms. 'Then there you were last night, in an ill-fitting blue cop suit on a dance floor with a bunch of tattooed goths, blending in like … well, like my redhead friend would in an office. So tell me, where did I miss you?' she challenged.

He just continued to smile, and she squinted at the road ahead.

'You're lucky I'm too tired to feel angry,' she told him. In fact, some part of her found the situation strangely amusing. She wanted to know who he worked for and what they hoped to gain by so obviously tailing her. And why he was so bloody bad at tailing her. A tail shouldn't get made.

'They told me you would be a handful. Look, I'm really not such an arsehole,' he said, seeming pleased with himself.

'Really? Are you it, or do they have a team following me?' she asked, hostile now, watching his face carefully. A flash went through her mind. This guy driving her through the gates at Darling Point into the Cavanagh house to meet his boss. Now that would be a interesting conversation.

'I told you, I'm not the arsehole you think I am.'

'What does that mean?'

'It means I'm doing you a favour.'

'Is that so?'

'Someone you know needs to have a chat with you.'

'Really? Who?' she asked, infuriated.

He had only driven two blocks and he pulled the car over. Mak saw a flash of red in the side mirror. Her jaw hung open. *Andy?*

Andy's red car was pulling to the side of the road. Mak sighed and recrossed her arms.

For Christsake!

She got out of the car, and walked along the kerb to Andy's vehicle. The other car drove away. Her ex-boyfriend sat in the driver's seat with the window down. 'I got here as soon as I could. I really needed to see you. Please get in. You haven't been taking my calls.' He sounded breathless.

She stood next to his car as if paralysed. Fresh conflict ran through her.

'Did you get my flowers?' he asked.

'Yes. Thank you,' she said. *They mean nothing. Our relationship meant something, but not flowers, which you never used to give me.*

'Mak, I really need to speak to you.'

'So you ambush me?' She shivered. This was stalker behaviour. 'I have somewhere I have to be.' Taxis were flying past on the street now. She needed to get into one.

'Just give me two minutes,' Andy pleaded. 'It's not what you think.'

Not what I think?

'Fine.' Mak sat herself in the passenger seat, overnight bag on her lap, distinctly unimpressed. 'This better be good.'

Andy looked at her with concern. 'Look, I love you. But that isn't what this is about.'

Will everyone please stop talking in riddles?

'You have to stop tailing the Cavanaghs. You're getting in the way,' Andy said solemnly. 'There's a Federal investigation going on. Damien and his father are both under surveillance.'

The whole world seemed to come to a halt. 'Holy shit.' Mak was shocked. *My god …*

'Exactly. You need to pull back.'

'So something is finally being done?'

'Just stop getting yourself involved. You are either going to get yourself more tangled up in this thing than you already are, or you're going to blow it for them. Either way, it's not safe for you.'

Mak shook her head. *I can't believe it.* 'Is it about the girl?' The 'Dumpster Girl', as the cops called her. The underage trafficked prostitute Damien was seen with. She had not received justice for what Damien had done to her.

'It's broader than that. Organised crime. Something international.'

Mak put her hands over her eyes. 'I'm really tired,' she said, defeated. She had no anger for him. She had no fight in her. She just wanted peace.

Andy moved close to her and hugged her as she sat stiffly, remembering the taste of Bogey on her tongue. And then the tears came. They rolled down her cheeks freely, without warning. Andy held her in her wordless grief, her head leaning into his chest, her tears casting off into his shirt like warm drops of rain.

'I'm glad I got to see you. I hope your case goes well,' Andy told her softly. 'You really did do a great job with the Cavanaghs. I'm sorry I couldn't tell you that. Not even Jimmy knows. It's highly confidential.'

'Jesus, Andy.' She was exhausted. She looked at her watch. 'I have to go,' she said in a whisper. She was aware of his closeness, their intimacy. It was somehow comforting. 'Thanks for letting me know. Just … with the flowers and stuff, give me a break, okay? Things got really bad between us. I can't … can't deal with that sort of thing right now. Okay?' She gathered herself and stepped out of his car. 'Bye, Andy,' she said.

The wind grabbed the door and slammed it harder than she had intended.

Shaking, Mak hailed the first vacant cab that approached.

CHAPTER 34

'No excuses. There aren't any. I don't deserve any. I'm not worthy of forgiveness. If only you knew how much I've cried …'

Adam Hart felt queasy as he read the lines nervously to his reflection in the mirror of a cramped toilet cubicle. He tried to get the hesitation and emotion just right. A tingle of excitement electrified him at the thought of what he was about to do. He would soon be performing on a stage. *Paris*! He would begin with some acting parts, and work on his magic routine. Perhaps he could even work with Lucien onstage? As a double act?

'When you said "I'm leaving you" I thought I'd go insane — it was my entire life. I lost my head. People can become ferocious when they're —' he said, then mouthed Jeanne's lines, '*I'm going to punish you.*'

He had finally been accepted into the troupe. He was in.

I can do this.

This was to be the finest time of his life, if one of the scariest. The most romantic, exciting adventure he had ever embarked upon. He was doing it. He was on his way. *You are nineteen. A man. A real man.* He liked the idea of being a real man. He felt he'd been held back until now, but nothing would hold him back any more. His dad was dead and his mum couldn't tell him what to do.

He was free.

There was a noise outside the bathroom cubicle, someone impatiently knocking on the door.

'Are you okay?' came an unfamiliar voice.

'Just a moment,' he said, disappointed.

Adam was going to be an actor, and he was nervous about his debut. He had been practising in front of every available mirror since Bijou gave him the part. He had read it for her, and aced it. She had given it to him, just like that! '*Magnifique, mon amour ...*' He would be a star! And almost as exciting, Bijou had told him that the contortionist, Arslan, had suggested the part for him. He was finally being accepted. A miracle. He would not let them down. Adam planned to study the lines for the rest of the flight, albeit silently.

Once he touched down, he would have less than seventy-two hours to prepare for his acting debut on Sunday night in a new twist on the classic Grand Guignol short play — *The Final Kiss*.

CHAPTER 35

Makedde Vanderwall was loose on the streets of downtown Brisbane, armed with a map.

She felt she nearly had Adam. She would begin with the pawnshop and then try to determine his whereabouts.

What exactly are you up to, Adam? Did someone harm you? Charm you? Or are you just so desperate to get away from home that you've stolen your mum's jewellery and pawned your grandad's irreplaceable watch?

Behind her professional drive, she was still troubled by her run-in with Andy. Her tears had disturbed her. There was emotional attachment there, even if it was the kind of emotion that caused them frustration and fights, rather than closeness and harmony. Some people, though bonded, seemed destined to never quite make it.

An international investigation?

She imagined herself on the radar of the Feds who were following Damien Cavanagh. She felt a fool. But at least something was being done.

Mak pushed open the door of Rick's Pawn Shop, to the

sound of a tinkling bell. The shop was filled with glass cases bursting with trinkets and gold chains, watches and clock radios. A depressing number of gold wedding rings were up for sale. Mak noticed an old-fashioned surveillance camera trained on the entrance, and another on the spot where a customer would stand at the counter.

A hirsute, heavy-set man appeared through a doorway screened by a curtain of rainbow streamers. She had not seen one of those since she was a kid.

'Can I help you?'

'My name is Makedde. And you are …?' *Rick?*

'Phil.'

'Phil, I appreciate your time. There is a stop order on a watch you have here. A gold watch with an engraving saying *Jill & John, Amor Vincit Omnia.*'

'Yeah. What's that mean, *Amor Vincit Omnia?*'

'Love conquers all,' she told him. 'It's Latin. Can I have a look at it, please?'

'You the cops?'

Mak passed him a business card. 'I'm a private investigator, working for the owner of the watch.'

He disappeared and returned with a gold watch.

'Look, I didn't do anything wrong,' he explained nervously.

'I know that.' She held her hand out and he gave her the watch. It felt heavy in her palm. She flipped it over and read the inscription. It was the one.

'The young man who brought the watch in, he identified himself as Adam Hart?'

'Yeah. The kid had a passport. I didn't do anything wrong,' the man repeated nervously.

Mak smiled.

'This is my brother's shop …' he continued.

She caught his eye and flashed him a pretty smile. She had obviously been too forceful, too direct. She leaned against the counter casually. 'Cool,' she said. 'You like working here, Phil? Is it fun?'

'Fun?' he repeated, his eyes wandering a bit. 'Not fun, really.'

'Oh. Do you remember much about the guy who brought the watch in? What he looked like?'

'Not much,' he said. 'But he was a good-looking kid. Tall. Blond hair. Didn't look like most of the customers here. Clean-cut kind of kid, you know.'

That's our boy. There was no need to check the security tapes. Mrs Hart would be pleased to know that her son was indeed alive and well, if a thief. Unless he was under duress from someone else …

'You have a great memory, Phil. That's a good description. Very accurate.' She leaned closer and smiled. 'Did he bring anything else in? Some pearls?'

Phil shook his head. 'Nuh.'

'And what happened when he came in?'

'I gave him some cash. Hey, if I can't sell this thing my brother says we have to get our money back.'

'How much?'

'Five hundred.'

She forked over the cash and he handed her the watch. Incredible. He had just sold it to her and it had a stop order on it. He obviously didn't know the difference between cops and private investigators.

'Thanks, Phil. You've been really helpful. Do you remember, when the boy came in, was he with anyone?'

'No. Alone. But there was someone outside, smoking a cig. At the café, right over there.' He pointed across the road. 'I knew they was together because he joined her for a drink.'

'What did she look like?' Mak asked, feeling a rush of excitement. This guy had been paying attention. Perhaps there was not much else to do when business was slow.

'Like a movie star,' he gushed. 'Kinda like you.' He added this as an afterthought. It didn't sound like a sincere compliment.

'He was with a woman? Do you mean she looked like me?'

He shook his head. 'No. Dark hair. But yeah, she was a *looker*. She didn't look like she was from around here,' Phil said.

'How do you mean?'

'I dunno,' he said. Mak waited patiently while he searched for a reason. 'Like she ain't a local.'

Mak had to ask. 'Was she white?'

He nodded.

'But she didn't look like she was from around here. How is that, exactly? Was it the way she dressed?'

'I guess that was it. She was dressed real elegant. Like a movie star.'

'Was she short, tall? Younger, older?'

'I dunno. Just like … a movie star. Yeah, she had great legs. Heels. Everything.'

A brunette with great legs. That was something. She wouldn't get any better description out of him, and Adam's mysterious companion had not entered the shop, so the tapes wouldn't help.

'Thanks, Phil. You've been very helpful.'

Mak walked out with Mrs Hart's missing gold watch in her hand. $500 was nothing. Glenise would be happy to see it back. Now all Mak needed was the boy.

She felt confident, on the scent. The café across the road was an upmarket place, with an interesting, well-planned menu. Mak took a seat and ordered a coffee.

Well, isn't that something? she thought.

There was a large sign across the road announcing the shows currently playing at the Powerhouse Theatre. Along with a famous comedy act, it seemed a vaudeville-style troupe was in town—

LE THÉÂTRE DES HORREURS.

Sydney, and now Brisbane.

He had run off with a brunette with great legs. A dancer, perhaps. *Brilliant, Adam. Just brilliant.* And he had pawned the watch right across from the theatre. What a boy. Wherever the woman with the great legs was, Adam would be close, Mak felt sure.

She sipped her expensive coffee and smiled to herself.

Bingo.

It was four o'clock when Makedde strolled across the foyer of the Brisbane Powerhouse Theatre, keeping her eye out for anyone of Adam's description. It was quiet at this time of day, still hours before the evening performances. She stepped inside the air-conditioned building and stopped beneath a graffiti drawing of a staggeringly oversized mosquito. She looked it up and down, not quite able to admire its artistry. Mosquitos had declared war on Makedde Vanderwall back when she was a young model in Hamburg. She had woken to find herself covered in bites — on her right arm, shoulder and side of her face, including some inside her ear, the side which had been exposed while she slept. Needless to say, that had not been one of her more fruitful modelling trips. Mosquitos had been her sworn enemies since, so this piece of art was not hitting the right notes for her.

A pamphlet told her the theatre had been built in 1902 as a power station, and its exposed brick and concrete refurbishment reminded Mak of some of the places she'd frequented in Berlin. She passed a bar illuminated by dangling exposed light bulbs, and a restaurant with an open kitchen, chefs already fussing over plumes of steam. A few patrons had gathered, sipping coffee and champagne. She scanned the sparse crowd for Adam Hart. What a simple case it would be if he just wandered past! It was a stroke of luck that his grandfather's watch had shown up so quickly on the register. Were the still-missing pearls around the neck of his new lover, perhaps?

Mak walked up to the box office, far from the threat of the graffiti mosquito. A woman of about twenty was behind the counter.

'Hello,' Mak said, and smiled. 'I'd like a ticket for Le Théâtre des Horreurs. For tonight please.'

'I'm sorry. You must have your dates mixed up. They were on last night.'

Mak frowned. 'I saw the sign …' She looked out the front windows of the building and saw the sign being changed. *Oh, come on!*

'It was one night only. Can I interest you in Tim Minchin, perhaps? He's playing the larger theatre here, and there are a couple of seats left.'

'No. Um, can you tell me … where are they playing next?'

'I don't know, sorry,' the young woman said, and Mak, quite unfairly, wanted to slap her.

'Can you check? I mean, is there any reference to any other shows on their schedule?'

The woman shook her head.

'Have they packed up already?'

'Packed up?' She seemed confused as to why Mak would want to know. 'Yes, this morning. Why?'

Because everything happened this morning. While I was distracted.

Damn. Mak had so hoped to find Adam Hart in Brisbane, and she could no longer be sure he was even in town.

THEAT

OVE

JOU

Was that a reference to Théâtre des Horreurs? Adam was with them. He had to be.

She had to track down the Théâtre des Horreurs tour dates on the net, and find where they were bound for next.

They can't have got too far … I hope.

CHAPTER 36

On Friday, Paris time, nearly two weeks after disappearing from his mother's house, Adam Hart found himself in the 1st arrondissement in Place Vendôme, staring up at the central column, a replica of a phallic obelisk Napoleon had erected to celebrate victory at Austerlitz. Small European cars dashed back and forth as the cold winter wind carried light rain across the square. He felt empty.

Jetlag was not the reason.

It was his lover, Bijou's, birthday. All morning Adam had watched as enormous bouquets arrived at her small apartment in Montmartre. She had received each extravagant bundle of flowers smiling coquettishly, pocketing the cards before Adam could read them. Three small packages had also arrived. He did not yet know the contents of two, but one had contained a delicate necklace with a single emerald stone. He had been mortified when she had placed it around her throat without pause. Who would send her such a lavish gift? Jealousy had welled up in him, bringing him near tears. He had gone walking.

Adam had to do better.

He stared wide-eyed at the grand Ritz Hotel across the square, feeling a pauper, an outsider. Within those walls, rich men would be giving sparkling jewels to their partners, their wives, their lovers. Dotcom billionaires and supermodels would be sipping expensive champagne in the Vendôme Bar, whiling away an idle afternoon. A couple stepped out the front door, under a neat ivory awning, the woman wearing a luxurious fur. The man held an umbrella for her, and a long black car pulled up to receive them.

Adam could stand it no more. He looked away sullenly, turned and walked down the Rue de la Paix with his hands shoved deep into empty pockets. His eyes moved from the wet footpath at his feet to the glimmering shop windows he passed, and back down again. His leather boots were soaked through, and he could feel the ends of his toes beginning to turn numb. The rain became more fierce, cold drops of water running down his temples.

A strange, pulsing panic took hold of him. He felt on the edge of something exhilarating and dangerous.

Adam reached Number 13 and his boots stopped moving forward. He looked up. The shop window winked at him with its hundreds of carats of diamonds, sapphires and emeralds, and he gazed at the display in fresh wonder. Those kinds of jewels — who wore them? The likes of Bijou, that was who. He was struck with a frustrated longing of a kind he had not before experienced. He wanted to buy something for her, really wanted to buy something like the lavish jewels his eyes had locked onto — but he couldn't. He didn't have any of the money left from selling the watch. Never before had he been made so soberly aware of his deficiencies. Adam absent-mindedly touched the wallet in his back pocket, turned on his heel and entered the store.

'*Bonjour, monsieur.*'

It was a relief to be sheltered from the weather. No sooner had he stepped into the lush interior than a woman dressed neatly in a black suit greeted him politely. Recognising his accent, she spoke to him in heavily accented English. '*Monsieur*, you will catch your death.' She ushered him into an old-fashioned powder room — the entire store was old-fashioned — and he patted his damp hair and clothes down with a towel. When he emerged, the woman had a delicate cup of black coffee waiting for him. She offered him a seat, and took her place behind an ornate gilded desk, smiling pleasantly. Catalogues of jewellery were laid out in front of him. He sipped his coffee. It was strong and invigorating.

'That is better, *non?*'

He nodded gratefully.

The woman was beautiful. Though she was not Bijou, Adam had to admit that she really was extremely attractive and elegant. Her dark hair was worn in a chignon and her makeup was flawless, accentuating the fine features of a refined older woman. Understated diamond earrings adorned her ears. He noticed a solitaire on her ring finger. He wished he could afford to purchase something like that for Bijou. He would ask her to marry him, if he could dare to, if he could offer her something more than the nothing that he had.

'My name is Colette.' She offered him a cool, velvety hand.

'I'm Adam.'

'Adam, welcome to Cartier. How may we assist you?'

He shifted in his chair. The building was very old, and extended across two floors, with staircases reaching to an open mezzanine above them. The carpets were red, the fittings gilded and luxurious. Numerous glass cases on both levels contained priceless objects of beauty, and on the walls were framed portraits of queens, princesses, models and actresses of former days. The ceiling was an elaborate skylight, the panes of glass thrashed violently by the increasingly heavy rain. Overwhelmed, Adam focused on a catalogue. 'Um, how much is that one,' he asked, pointing to an image of a small ring. His beautiful host referred to her own catalogue, one elegant finger tracing the page. Finally the price was indicated at the end of her polished fingernail. His heart sank. He could not buy Bijou such a gift. It was impossible.

'I was thinking of something … simple,' he said, and swallowed nervously.

She smiled gently. 'Perhaps a necklace, or a bracelet?'

He nodded, hopeful.

'Would you like a glass of champagne while I bring you some items to look at?' she asked him, rising from her chair.

'*Merci*,' he responded awkwardly, his heart speeding up. She motioned to someone, and barely one minute later an immaculately dressed man delivered a fresh, chilled flute of effervescent champagne, then disappeared again. Bubbles rose in the glass, and broke on the surface. Adam took a sip and with pleasure felt the cool liquid travel down to his stomach. He began to feel better, *successful* even. Though he was a tall young man, and it was only a single glass, Adam had been a teetotaller most of his life, and had only experienced champagne since meeting Bijou. He still did not realise how slowly it ought to be sipped, and the alcohol went to his head immediately.

'I have brought you a selection of items I am certain you will like,' the woman said, returning. She looked at his glass. 'Would you like another?'

He nodded then stopped himself. '*Non. Merci.*'

Adam was, nonetheless, emboldened by the glass he had enjoyed, and had begun to believe he could achieve his desire of purchasing something for Bijou which would impress her. On the velvet tray Colette placed before him, he saw a thin bracelet without embellishment save for a small square charm with a tiny stone in it. He felt sure that this would be within his price range.

'How much is this one?' he asked.

'Oh, a wonderful choice, sir. This is our classic charm bracelet in white gold. Very elegant.' Again the price list came out, and that elegant finger scanned the page and stopped on a number — 1500 euros, considerably less than the ring had been, but still far more money than he could afford. 'The charm is 900 euros,' Colette explained. This was a further blow. He had assumed that it was included in the bracelet's price.

'Actually, I was thinking of a ring. Something plain,' Adam said abruptly, now fighting a fresh sense of desperation.

'*Oui, monsieur,*' was her reply. 'Of course.' She excused herself.

When she returned, the expensive charm bracelet was gone, and in its place were several women's rings of minimalist design, none extravagant, and each placed lovingly across the velvet-lined tray. The gold shimmered.

'Um, this one,' Adam said, and pointed eagerly to a delicate ring with a distinctive circular design carved into the gold. It was one of the few items without any precious stones. 'Can it be engraved?' he asked. If he could not afford even a tiny diamond, perhaps having something engraved would make it more special?

'I would see to it personally, with no charge,' she assured him.

'How long would it take?' he asked nervously.

'I could have it ready for you tomorrow.'

Damn. He would miss Bijou's birthday. Perhaps he could give it to her before their debut together on stage?

The beautiful saleswoman presented the catalogue to him, and again her elegant finger traced the page until it found the price of the ring.

Adam frowned. It was nearly as much as the bracelet. Blood began pumping in his temples. He felt on the edge of tears. What could he do? He could not return to Bijou empty-handed.

On Sunday he would be performing. Bijou was giving him her love, her confidence, the chance of a lifetime. He had to give her something in return. Something worthy of her. It pained him that he might not even be able to purchase the simplest item in the boutique.

'Do you believe in the significance of history?' the woman asked, quite out of the blue, as he stared forlornly at the catalogue and the small, gleaming ring. He nodded. 'I would like to show you around this building, our headquarters since 1899. There are many interesting rooms and displays …'

Adam found himself trailing behind her as she ascended one of the grand staircases to the mezzanine. He saw portraits of dark-eyed Indian princes with long feminine eyelashes who were weighed down by hundreds of carats of diamonds, and a woman, a Spanish actress, smoking an extravagant cigar and posing in a large-brimmed hat, her ears, her tanned neck and the length of her arms swathed in bejewelled golden crocodiles and snakes. In a case next to him, the very same crocodile necklace reposed, its emerald eyes gleaming. Adam had never seen such things, and he asked many questions.

Bijou ought to be immortalised in such a place, he thought.

He was barely aware that everywhere they went, his new friend carried the small velvet tray, displaying the shiny ring.

CHAPTER 37

On Saturday, Glenise Hart waited in line at the supermarket near her home, pushing an overflowing trolley.

She felt a stab of loneliness, contemplating the groceries. She could not escape the fact that she was about to buy a lot of things she did not need. The household was not running out of supplies as quickly as usual. Adam's favourite snacks still lined the cupboards, and her shopping trolley was brimming with stocks of food necessary to satisfy her son's young appetite, stocks she didn't really need. But Glenise was still shopping as if everything were normal. Though it had been almost two weeks since Adam had disappeared, she had not told anyone except the police, the investigation agency and the Murphy family, who'd recommended them. No one at work needed to know and, anyway, she would not have been able to handle their questions and concern. Glenise was barely containing her fear that she had not only lost her husband to a freak accident but had also pushed her only child away.

You will be alone.

'G'day,' the check-out boy mumbled.

'Hello,' Glenise responded, with a cheer she did not feel.

'That will be two hundred and thirty six dollars and fifty cents. Cash or credit?'

She dutifully handed over her credit card.

'Credit or savings?'

'Credit, thank you.'

Normal. Everything was so very normal. She would return home with the groceries to the same home that until recently had been inhabited by both her husband and their son, and try to feel normal about it.

The check-out boy swiped her MasterCard, and tapped his fingers a few times while he waited for it to go through. The fingers stopped and he frowned. 'It says your card is declined.'

Glenise blinked. 'Pardon?'

'Your card has been declined. Do you have another one?'

Glenise frowned. How could the card be overextended? By her calculation it should have at least another $3000 on it, more than enough for this grocery expedition. Despite the fact that her late husband had previously balanced the bills, she was very good at doing the family accounts herself, and there were never purchases made that she didn't know about or could not account for. There had to be some mistake.

'Can you try it again?' she asked, confused.

'Sure,' the young man said unenthusiastically.

He swiped the card. He waited.

'Sorry,' he said simply and handed it back.

She reddened. For a moment Glenise did not know what to do. Her thin veneer of normality had been torn open.

Adam.

Of course. She peeled her wallet open again and pulled her American Express card out of its slot. 'My mistake,' she said, smiling stiffly. 'This one should work.'

Seventeen minutes later, Glenise was on her home phone, barely breathing as she waited. She had been on hold for what seemed an eternity.

'Sorry to keep you waiting, ma'am.' The voice on the other end of the line sounded slightly concerned. 'There was a fairly large purchase made outside Australia on the card in the past twenty-four hours. In euros.'

There was a long pause, interrupted only by a crackle of static. 'Ma'am, are you there?'

'Yes. Can you give me details please?'

'The payment was made to Cartier in Paris. I'm afraid the exchange rate isn't very good at the moment. The total came to $3482.75 Australian.'

Adam!

'Ma'am, do you want to report the card stolen?' the woman asked.

Glenise paused. 'No. No thanks. It's fine. I remember now. Cartier in Paris. Oh, yes. Silly me. Everything's fine. Thank you for your help.'

Glenise hung up, and quickly pulled herself together. This was good news. She knew where Adam's card was, and that meant she knew where he was likely to be.

Shakily, she picked up the phone and dialled Marian Wendell and Associates Professional Private Investigations.

CHAPTER 38

Makedde drove to St Ives more or less straight from the airport knowing only that the news about Adam was urgent, and that his mother believed there was a chance he had been located. She hoped for Glenise's sake that was true, and that he was safe and well. A day and a half in Brisbane had done nothing to bring him home.

She rang the doorbell, and the door opened immediately. Her client must have heard the car pull up.

'He's in Paris. My boy is in Paris. Get him for me,' Glenise said, gripping her arm tightly. She appeared even more high strung then before.

Paris.

'Are you certain?' Mak asked, her heart speeding up.

Le Théâtre des Horreurs. It had to be the troupe he was following. She'd checked on the net and the troupe that had been in Sydney and then Brisbane had completed its Australian tour and could well have returned to its base in Paris. Was Adam there, too?

He is serious about this.

'Come in, sit down.' Glenise hustled her into the living room and sat on the edge of the couch, eager. 'He used my credit card in Paris.'

'Is he in trouble? What was the charge for?'

'Something from Cartier.'

'Cartier? The jeweller?' *My God. He wants to marry someone.* 'Glenise, do you know what he purchased?'

'No. The lady from the credit card company just said it was from Cartier. It cost more than $3000! I was afraid to ask more questions in case I aroused suspicion and the card got cut off. I don't want Adam to get cut off! I need him to come home. *I need you to go and get him for me,*' Glenise pleaded, her voice rising. The corners of her mouth turned down. Her eyes glittered. Mak worried that her client might be on the edge of tears, this one time she'd forgotten to bring tissues. 'Bring him back, please.'

Paris.

Paris was one of Mak's favourite cities. She had modelled there in her teens and early twenties and had not been back in almost a decade. Naturally she would jump at the opportunity to return.

Mrs Hart went on. 'I don't think he'd come back with me. I need you to do it.' Mak watched as the woman wrestled with some internal conflict. 'I wasn't totally open about everything. The truth is, things have been very difficult at home since John was killed. Adam has been, well, playing up a lot, and we've had some terrible fights. I'm afraid I must have pushed him away.'

Mak nodded sympathetically. 'I'm sorry to hear that things have been difficult. It's hard to lose a spouse, and hard to lose a parent.'

Glenise's voice wobbled. 'Please, find my son and bring him home.'

Mak promised to do all in her power to find Adam and persuade him to return. She would be on the next available flight, and the first place she would be looking was wherever Le Théâtre des Horreurs was performing. That brochure was not a coincidence. Not if Adam had been in Brisbane and was now in Paris at the same time as the troupe. He had written about them and ripped out the pages. Or someone else had. Wherever they were, wherever the brunette with the 'great legs' was, Mak believed she would find Adam.

But what if he doesn't want to come back?

CHAPTER 39

On Sunday afternoon in Paris, Arslan the contortionist sat folded into his old stage box, spying on the world inside Bijou's luxurious bedroom.

This was an oft-adopted position for Arslan, and the pose — though requiring great discipline — comforted him. Over the years he had trained himself to maintain this secretive confinement for hours at a time, his entire frame fitting neatly inside the small, knee-high box. It had several spy-holes through which he could observe the room around him. The box had been replaced — for stage purposes — with a more ornate and beautiful one, of brighter wood, which stood out under the spotlight. Arslan was still attached to his dark old box, however, for reasons Bijou was not aware of. Often, after being temporarily replaced by another lover, he would return to Bijou's sleeping quarters to be near her in this way. Such was the case now. The young lover who had most recently replaced Arslan was in Bijou's bedroom with her. *Adam*. In less than an hour they were all required to be in the little theatre to prepare for their first performance back in Paris. Instead of getting ready for the evening's show, Bijou was half-listening to her new young lover while she tinkered at her impressive, Hollywood-style dressing table.

'I know you said you don't ever want to marry. But I wanted to show you my commitment,' the boy said. He was earnest in both words and appearance, attired in smart trousers and a pressed shirt. He looked serious, and gripped a small package.

'*Oui?*' Bijou responded, turning from the mirrored vanity where she had been powdering herself.

'*Oui,*' Adam repeated, his pronunciation appalling, Arslan thought. 'Bijou, um, *amour. Je t'aime.*' He handed her the box, which was beautifully wrapped in vibrant red. 'Happy birthday.'

Arslan's eyes narrowed.

'What is this?' Bijou asked coyly, her eyes sparkling with delight. She was now perched on the edge of her vanity stool, her silk dress falling open to reveal her shapely legs. Arslan could see her back reflected sensually in the mirror behind her. Her dress had a deep 'V' that exposed her spine to the waist. He vividly remembered having effortlessly liberated her from it on numerous occasions, when he had been her preferred companion.

'You deserve the most beautiful things in life,' Adam said earnestly.

Arslan shifted a few millimetres in his box. He had given Bijou a spectacular bouquet of roses this year for her birthday. He could see them in the corner of the room, standing proudly, and colourfully. What would this gauche boy buy her? And two days late? Some horrible perfume?

He watched as she untied the bow, and slid the ribbon off the box.

'You are so kind,' she told the boy, and planted a soft kiss on his forehead. She peeled the paper back to reveal a red jewellery coffret.

The boy clasped his hands together tightly. 'I love you, Bijou,' he said as she opened the little box, her delicate mouth opening in surprise. 'I wanted to give you this on your birthday, but —'

And now, to Arslan's horror, Bijou was smiling, delighted. 'Oh, my dear Adam! It is *magnifique!*' she exclaimed.

Arslan could not see! He tried to shift position, only to discover, naturally, there was no room to manoeuvre. He could not see what was in the box, but *her* eyes were wide with wonder at whatever it held. She was overjoyed. What had this fool given her?

'*Magnifique!*' she repeated.

Arslan felt himself panic. He wanted to leap out of the box and snatch the thing away. What was it? What had he given her? A ring? Was he proposing?

Bijou reached into the box and lifted something from it. It glittered in her hands, and he could make it out now — a beautiful piece of jewellery. A ring. It was small but undeniably elegant. Arslan could make out the store name on the jewellery box.

Cartier.

'I love you,' the fool told her. 'I love you.' He was on his knees now, embracing her legs and resting his head against her soft thighs. 'I had it engraved. It says *Amor Vincit Omnia*, and your name. Love conquers all.'

Bijou was speechless. The boy took the ring and gently placed it on her hand. It took him a couple of tries before he found the right finger. *Clumsy boy.* Now he sat back on the bed and admired the gift he had chosen, while Arslan strained to get a better view of Bijou's reaction.

She reached for an ornate hand mirror from the vanity table to better admire herself, to admire her slender fingers, now complemented by this shining piece of jewellery.

'You are the only woman I have ever loved,' he told her, back on his knees.

'*Je t'aime, aussi,*' she replied, admiring the way the gold sat against her skin. She leaned towards Adam and kissed him hard on the lips.

Arslan's stomach churned. She appeared so passionate. This was different. He could sense it. Could she actually be falling for this boy?

'I will wear our pearls tonight … the pearls you gave me in Sydney.'

Pearls?

She removed an antique-looking set of pearls from the drawer of her vanity, and the boy took them from her with care, placing them around her slender throat with a lover's touch.

Now more than ever, Arslan wanted to kill this interloper.

The boy's fingers trailed maddeningly down her nape, down her exquisite back, and she twisted on her stool to gaze up at him. 'Run away with me,' she blurted.

Arslan blinked. *What did she say?*

'I'm so tired of this life, these shows, this ungrateful troupe. Let's go away.'

'But what about your career? You're a star, Bijou!'

Bijou turned back to the mirror. Watching her young lover's reflection, she dabbed rouge on her cheeks and lipgloss on her sensual mouth. 'I've had enough,' she said firmly, 'enough of this life.' She put down her makeup. 'Always travelling, always working, always looking after those kids.' She threw her arms in the air. 'Enough of it! Enough of them. I haven't been treated properly for years. We'll do this show together, tonight, you and I. And then, we leave.'

What was she saying?

Arslan's English was far from fluent, but he could not mistake her meaning. Was she being literal, or was this some tale she wished to make the boy believe?

'Don't worry,' she said. 'We'll have enough money to live on for years.'

Arslan's face darkened. She meant it. Bijou was going to leave him, and the rest of them, to be with this foolish boy she had taken up with. She was going to take all their money, his money, his twin sister, Yelena's, money. She was never going to give them, or the rest of the troupe, their proper share. She wasn't hanging onto it for them, doing what was best for them. She wasn't looking out for their interests. She was going to rob them and abandon them.

After decades, Bijou was leaving again.

Non! Maman, non …

Inside his small box, Arslan felt the sting of hot tears. He saw himself leap from his secret place like a jack-in-the-box to strangle his mother with those pearls, but he did not move or make a sound. His torment remained contained, just as *he* was, in the little box. He stayed folded in the tiny box just as he had been taught as a child. Like the others, he and Yelena were the spawn of Bijou's affairs over years of travelling in vaudeville. His biological father was a Russian-born contortionist, a defector. Arslan had no memory of the man, no photograph. He and Yelena were not allowed to speak his name. And from the earliest age, they were not allowed to call her '*maman*', either. Bijou had them, but they never had her. She had come and gone from their lives as it suited her, and denied them normal motherly love. Her sexual love for Arslan had also come and gone.

Maman …

After a decade of travelling as a troupe, finally giving them all a place to belong together, Bijou was going to leave them again.

Arslan could not let her do that.

Bijou and her lover left her apartment for the theatre, and as soon as the door clicked shut, Arslan opened the top hatch of his old stage box. He crawled out limb by limb, and gracefully touched his feet on the hardwood floor as a spider would. Inwardly, he shook with grief.

He was quick to make his way to the quarters he shared with Yelena, to change and grab his things for the performance, aware that he would need to race to the venue — only a few blocks from the corner of Montmartre where all the troupe lived in close proximity — to arrive on time. But before he left, he stood by the doorway with his eyes shut tight, struggling with a decision.

Maman …

Back in his own apartment, he walked quickly, determinedly, to his single bed and lifted the mattress. His hand hovered near a vial of liquid he had hidden there. His body froze momentarily while inner turmoil raged. Finally he picked up the vial and pocketed it.

CHAPTER 40

It was past nine o'clock on Sunday evening, Paris time, when Makedde entered the Cité Chaptal, a little cul-de-sac in the sleazy red-light district of Pigalle. She had rushed from Charles de Gaulle airport to drop her bags at her Montmartre hotel, and literally run the few blocks to the theatre. Slightly out of breath, she stopped on the cobblestones and frowned, lifting her furry collar to her chin.

This is it?

She looked at the address she'd scribbled down for the venue the troupe would be performing at — the site of the original Grand Guignol theatre, from which they took their inspiration — and looked back at the street sign. *Yes, this is the place.* She'd read up on the history of the troupe and its Parisian base and was disappointed to find that the infamous alley now appeared to be much like any other Parisian laneway. It was nothing but a plain cobblestone street leading to a small theatre with an uninspiring façade.

The original Théâtre du Grand-Guignol?

The venue had first acquired a reputation in 1897, when

the French playwright Oscar Méténier bought the little building, a former church, to present his naturalist plays. Méténier was a police employee who spent the final moments with prisoners who'd been sentenced to death. His controversial plays reflected his experiences, and were known for their violence and horror. Mak had previously been aware of the place only through the celebrated diaries of Anaïs Nin, one of her favourite writers, who frequented the Grand Guignol with her lover, Henry Miller, in the early 1930s. *What a place. What a history.* Yet in the cold Parisian evening, the geographical heart of this unique genre of horror was deceptively banal. The original theatre had been closed in the 1960s, and was at present being used as an acting school called Theatre 347. Various plays were performed at the venue from time to time, with Le Théâtre des Horreurs evidently the only troupe trying to revive the Grand Guignol genre.

Mak's flurry of research on the troupe had resulted in numerous contradictions and mysteries — stories of fainting audience members and outrageous publicity stunts — but she was certain of one thing: five years earlier, right in the alley where she stood, a young man named Jean-Baptiste Trevillie had been attacked with acid after watching the Théâtre des Horreurs' adaptation of *The Final Kiss*. It was evidently a brutal copycat crime. The quiet cobblestone alley had been witness to both history and horror.

Mak felt a vibration in her pocket. Distractedly, she raised her phone to her ear and listened to a voicemail message. Familiar, comforting tones reached her from across the world. 'Hi, Mak. It's Bogey. I'm back in Melbourne. I hope everything's going well in Paris, and that it isn't too cold for you. Look, I wanted to say there's a big design fair on in

London this week. I was going to fly over for it, and I thought, perhaps, if you're still in Paris …'

Mak smiled, temporarily forgetting her case.

'… I could come over and see you for a few days before you have to head home? If that would be something you'd be into … or …'

'*Oui*!' she blurted aloud, as if he could hear her, and hung up, giddy.

Bogey? In Paris? That was a wonderful thought.

She would call him later. In the meantime, she hoped to catch the second half of the show Le Théâtre des Horreurs were performing. Hopefully, Adam Hart would not be far away.

Was he already nearby?

Makedde paid her money and took her seat alone in the little theatre in the Cité Chaptal during the brief interval.

The theatre was intimate, almost claustrophobic, with a small stage masked by a heavy red curtain. Above her, two enormous angels hovered eerily, a patina of dust and the wear and tear of age showing on their stern faces and billowing robes. Makedde could faintly smell traces of mildew and smoke beneath the stronger scent of overly perfumed patrons. The room was filled to about half capacity. Mak heard a mix of languages and accents as mid-week theatre-goers, tourists, Grand Guignol fans and lovers of the bizarre clustered in the former chapel. A metal spring showed through the fabric of the seat to her right, and she could not help but feel that the tattiness of the venue somehow lent further charm to the atmosphere. This space — so much more interesting than the bland exterior — had really *seen* things.

The lights were dimming, the evening's performance about to continue.

Out of the darkness, a warm red glow seeped through the curtains and spread across the crowd. The old theatrical curtains were pulled back to reveal a band dressed in old-fashioned tuxedos, bringing to mind another era. The drummer, a woman with close-cropped hair, wore an amusing 1920s-style moustache. Her drum kit declared: LE THÉÂTRE DES HORREURS.

Mak was terribly curious about the content of the show, but this was much more than a night of bizarre theatre for her. The real action, she hoped, would be backstage or in the audience itself. Where would Adam Hart be? In the dressing rooms? In the audience? Or would she need to follow one of the performers after the show to find him? Her first order of business was to get herself backstage. Neither the vaudeville troupe nor the venue appeared particularly high-budget or security-conscious. Mak felt her skills would be more than up to the task. As two eerily similar-looking burlesque artists slinked onto the stage holding signs that declared LE THEATRE DES HORREURS and THE THEATRE OF HORRORS respectively, Mak stood up and began to make her way to the back of the theatre.

'Madame?'

It was an usher, wearing a cross look, evidently displeased by her impolitely timed exit.

Mak held her stomach, as if in agony. '*Où est la toilette*?' she asked with an urgency that implied food poisoning.

With a sneer, he pointed her in the right direction, and she followed the signs towards the washrooms. At the end of a dark corridor were the facilities — unisex in the old-

fashioned French style. And on the other side, a door marked
ACCÉS INTERDIT.

Prohibited access.

Mak grinned slightly, and pushed the door open …

CHAPTER 41

Time for the hard decisions, Jack.

Jack Cavanagh sat across from The American, who waited patiently for instructions. Jack took his time, staring out his hard-earned office window, reflecting.

His career had already been an accomplished one by any standard, but he feared slowing down. Slowing would necessarily involve handing over the reins to someone else. He had long hoped control of the business would stay in the family. But it was clear that handing the Cavanagh empire on to his 31-year-old son, Damien, would be extremely problematic, despite his Wharton education and all his grooming for the position. Damien was his only child. What could Jack do? The shareholders would jump ship before Damien even got the chance to drive the whole thing into the ground himself.

Cobwebs and tar.

Jack Cavanagh had built his influential empire from the ground up, and had imagined that by retirement age he'd be able to enjoy a certain satisfaction at what he had built. He knew what it was to work hard. He was the son of a janitor, not a mogul. He had watched his father toil excruciatingly long hours to save for his education. His father had been a smart man, but a man without opportunities. Jack had wanted to make his father proud.

Somewhere along the way, the dream went wrong.

Cobwebs …

'Jack …?' The American prompted.

He looked at The American with his mouth turned down, his guts uneasy. 'I need you to …' His voice quavered. He tried again. 'Yes. We need Mr Hand. We need Ms Vanderwall gone.'

She was a problem. She had followed his son, and was agitating her police friends. And now, finally, she was out of the country. She had to stay gone.

Mr White, The American, nodded in response. 'I'll take care of it.'

Across the globe, in Algiers, Madame Q sat before a bank of computers ranged across an antique French oak table. An assortment of flowers arranged with expert aesthetic skill filled the crystal vase next to her. The Mediterranean Sea spread out before her, hot African sun beating on the white-painted windowsill.

It was from this tranquil North African location that she conducted her business through a careful web of contacts on a digital network fuelled by need, greed, power and secrecy. Madame Q was an agent of death for cash. For the right price she was able to facilitate hits for wealthy corporations and individuals. She was not interested in politics. She did not deal with governments. Ideals did not concern her. Ideals were best left out of it.

A message came in, from one of her Australian clients, Mr White.

REQUEST. SINGLE. LOCATION PARIS. HAND AVAILABLE?

Before she had a chance to reply that her agent Luther Hand would be available for the usual fee, another message arrived with an electronic beep. It was from the colleague who called himself Rob.

INTERPOL, was all it said.

Madame Q frowned. She knew what this meant. For some weeks she'd been receiving warnings that an Interpol net might be closing around her operation. So it seemed it was true?

She returned to Mr White's request, and responded quickly. CONFIRM. SECURE FUNDS BY THIS AFTERNOON.

She would have to get the funds as fast as possible in case she got another update from Rob and needed to vacate her office in Algiers in short order.

Madame Q would set Luther up for the job, and hold as much of the money as possible. If the Interpol threat was real, Luther would be left to his own devices.

VANDERWALL.

Mr White's reply was a name, not a code. Madame Q paused. She swallowed, her mouth feeling dry. This was a reference to a previous job, an assignment that had become complicated.

HALF RATE was her offer. Tense, she waited for a response. Half rate was still substantial; the client was wealthy and she hoped she could retain them after the dust had settled.

CONFIRMED. FUNDS DELIVERED ONE HOUR.

CHAPTER 42

Mak pushed the door open and found herself in an unlit area backstage at the little theatre in Cité Chaptal.

Yes …

She had worn her favoured rubber-soled boots, and they did not betray her presence as she moved furtively through the darkness in near silence, passing the ghostly shapes of unused sets and lighting equipment, covered with filthy white sheets. There was a skerrick of light ahead, and Mak moved towards it. She could hear the performance taking place only metres away onstage.

She had to find the dressing rooms.

Where are you, Adam?

Mak rounded a corner and stopped in her tracks.

Shit. Caught out.

She had stumbled upon a young man. The two locked eyes. Her heart leaped into her throat, but Makedde soon realised that he was even more alarmed to see her than she was at being discovered by him. He had been leaning over a props table, and when he heard her, he whirled, and nearly knocked over a rack of clothing.

Adam?

The man she had startled was perhaps thirty, and much darker than Adam. The nose was different. This man was handsome in his own way as well, she thought, but there was a hardness about him, especially in his eyes, which were dramatically lined with kohl. He had none of the freshness she'd seen in the photographs of Adam. Even with dyed hair, this could not be him. *Dammit.* For a second there, she had thought it could actually be that easy. How foolish of her to imagine that she could solve the mystery of Adam Hart's disappearance by spotting him backstage on her first night in Paris.

The moment lingered strangely, neither speaking.

'*Pardon* …' Mak said, and flashed her best disarming smile.

The man — who was not Adam — continued staring at her with something like suspicion, even fear, and it dawned on her that his alarm had to do with his being interrupted during some type of sensitive moment. His manner was strangely furtive: he gripped something in his hand and walked slowly backwards, a look of naked guilt in his expression. Mak stole a glance at his fingers, but could not make out what he was holding.

'*Parlez-vous Anglais?*' she asked clumsily, in her most non-threatening tone.

Rather than grilling her — the impostor — on her reason for being backstage, the man scampered away, and a piece of clothing fell off a hanger where he had been standing. A white doctor's coat. His reaction struck her as so odd that she stood confused for a time, before hanging the coat up on the props rack again. Next to it was a satin dressing gown, and a suit jacket, both with the curiously worn air of stage costumes.

Mak paused, unsure what to make of the kohl-eyed man's response. Would he bring reinforcements to boot her out?

CHAPTER 43

Arslan is mad.

Lucien the illusionist sat before a mirror, practising his magic close-up, tilting the mirror at every possible angle to see what the most observant audience member could. He would be onstage for his next routine in twenty minutes.

'*Oui,*' he whispered to himself in an occasional chant of approval as he deftly moved the coin from finger to finger.

Lucien needed to keep his hands soft and nimble. The techniques of sleight of hand required daily practice, and he had grown to look forward to this peculiar ritual of his, and taken to practising this way in times of stress. The concentration it involved took him away from the petty rivalries that inevitably sprang up amongst the 'family' of the troupe, the problems of money and sex and the horrors of the unknown. The future. In his act he could pretend to predict the future but in reality he had no such insight. He did not know where they would end up. He did not know what would become of him if the troupe disbanded. He did not know his future. What he knew was that he could do this:

pinch drops, French drops, the Downs coin roll — his coins rolling down each hand effortlessly, bobbing up and down like ponies on a carousel. Precise. Perfect. Total control.

As a child he had discovered magic. It was the only thing about him that had ever held his mother's attention. And when she went away, it was his escape from loneliness.

Arslan is mad, he thought again.

His half-brother had always been prone to madness. His twin, Yelena, was quiet and lacked confidence, but Arslan had enough boldness and aggression for all of them combined. It was because of their mother. It was her fault that he was that way. They all knew.

French drops, pinch drops …

The show would go on, as it always did. For a while there would be an extra member of the family. And then he, Lucien predicted, he would be gone. Perhaps.

The show will go on …

Lucien dropped his coin. He scowled. A stranger was backstage; an attractive blonde. She did not belong here. He stood and approached her.

'*Pardon, monsieur.* I was just looking for the ladies room, and I seem to have got myself all lost …' Makedde lied, shrugging her shoulders playfully.

Damn.

This isn't Adam, either, she thought, faced with a slender man swathed in a Victorian coat who stood glaring at her, clearly unfriendly. He looked somewhat like the man she had startled only moments before: dark, handsome, exotic; he even wore the same black kohl around his eyes. But this man was not about to scamper away. Mak recognised him from photographs on the troupe's website. He was the resident magician, Lucien. She had disturbed his rehearsal, and he appeared plenty angry about it.

'I am lost,' she lied again, shrugged and tried to push past him, palms in the air in a gesture of peace.

He grabbed her elbow.

'Hey!' She thought to kick out, to scream …

Just then, there was the sound of the quick clicking of heels, and two petite burlesque dancers appeared, rushing through the narrow backstage corridor clad in corsets, fishnets, small top hats and platinum-blonde wigs. They looked like twins. When they saw the magician holding Mak's elbow, their eyes became wide.

'Hi,' Mak said, and smiled broadly, acting the role of dumb tourist. 'I like your outfits.'

'*Qui est-elle?*' they asked Lucien in unison, stopping. *Who is she?*

Mak had to think fast. If she drew too much attention to herself, or her search for Adam Hart, she could send him into hiding. '*Toilette?*' she asked, and giggled, pointing her finger this way and that, indicating that she needed directions.

Together, the dancers pointed back the way she had come.

Mak took the opportunity to flee the magician's grasp. She left the eclectic trio with their mouths open, hands on hips, as she made her way back to the doorway through which she had entered.

Dammit.

Crestfallen, Makedde returned to her seat. She felt a wave of jetlag wash over her. She needed to stay awake through the remaining performances, but it could get tough. She'd been running on adrenaline since arriving, and now that she had not located Adam backstage, nor spotted him in the watching crowd, the tiredness took hold of her. Perhaps he was not even at the theatre, she thought. *Bugger.* That meant she would need to wait at the stage door in the winter cold, possibly for hours, just to be sure. And again the next night, and the next, until she had some luck.

She had barely missed him in Brisbane and, for all her attempts to contact him online, Adam remained beyond her reach. According to Tobias, he was not responding to anyone. Mak had to reason with him in person if she was to bring him home.

Onstage the burlesque dancers entered, parading before the curtain with placards which announced the next item in the program.

The Final Kiss.

Mak perked up a touch. She recognised this as the play that had been suggested as the sick inspiration for the acid attack in the alley outside the theatre five years before. It was somewhat surprising to her that the troupe continued to perform that particular play, all things considered, although the piece did have a revered place in the Grand Guignol tradition. *Le Baiser dans la Nuit*, or *The Final Kiss*, was considered a Grand Guignol classic, the plot inspired by the infamous acid attacks dubbed '*crimes passionels*' that took place in Paris in the early 1900s. The combination of shocking violence, sordid affairs and jilted lovers made the acid attacks front-page fodder, perhaps in the same way the Stiletto Murders in Sydney had managed to grab sensational media attention in

Australia. The heinous nature of those crimes and the beauty of the female victims, some of whom were models and actresses, fascinated the public. It seemed there would always be an insatiable appetite for beautiful victims cruelly cut down. *Schadenfreude*. The original version of *The Final Kiss*, Mak knew from the troupe's website, had a central character who was a glamorous model, though the plot was more complicated than simply that of victim and perpetrator. The beauty, in fact, was shown to be a beast.

Mak was surprised when the curtain parted to show a female character with her face wrapped in bandages, her long dark hair hanging glamorously down her back as she was attended by a doctor and a nurse in a homely setting, something like a small living room. Normally, this role was played by the male. It seemed this one-act adaptation of the famous Maurice Level play had swapped the roles of Henri and Jeanne.

'Her attacker had a very cool head. Exceptionally cool,' the doctor was telling the nurse assistant, as she helped him change the dressings. Thus far, the poor woman patient had said nothing, though her body language made clear her physical discomfort. Audience members strained to one side in an unsuccessful attempt to see the woman's disfigured face.

His coat …

Mak recognised the doctor character's white coat as the one she had picked up and put back on the props rack after her strange encounter backstage. The doctor was not played by the dark, nervous man she had seen, but by a stockier, fairer actor who spoke English confidently for the largely tourist audience in a mixed American-French accent.

'Leave me!' the woman finally cried, her patience apparently at an end.

The nurse and doctor reacted to her outburst as if it were expected. They finished changing the bandages and slipped out the door without a sound. Slowly, the patient stood and turned to face the front of the stage. The audience collectively held its breath. What they saw was a beautiful woman: a fine, hourglass figure dressed in a silk bias-cut gown, a vision of feminine allure under the stage lights. But above the glistening pearls around the woman's neck was nothing but white bandages, her face covered like that of an Egyptian mummy. The audience watched her with grim curiosity as she moved slowly across the set. Her presence was electrifying: what, and whom, was under that gauze?

This is her, isn't it? Bijou.

Mak suspected that under all those bandages was the beautiful actress Bijou. Mak had seen Bijou's face in the posters outside the theatre and all over the troupe's website, and in the flesh, onstage, her figure and manner were spectacularly feminine, though of course her face could not be seen. Could *this* be the woman Adam had fallen for? Not a dancer but an actress. She had been a stage performer for many years and would be much older than Adam. Patrice had been older, but this age gap was much wider. What was she like? Why did she choose to hide her beauty for this performance? Mak supposed that this role-reversal was intended by the troupe to be more impactful for the audience, knowing that not only had the woman been horribly injured, but that a special beauty had been purposefully destroyed. In this adaptation of the play, the beautiful woman had spurned the man by breaking their engagement, and he had brutally disfigured her in retaliation. This had been a more common element in the real-life *crimes passionels* cases. It seemed to Mak a less ironic choice than the

'Beauty is the Beast' theme of the original 1912 play, in which the vicious, beautiful model disfigured her male lover, a theme which would have been a surprising gender reversal in its day. Tonight's performance, however, brought to mind actual cases in countries like India, where acid attacks still occurred.

There was a knock on the stage door, and the woman moved to answer it.

A man stepped onto the stage. Mak sat up and blinked.

Oh!

It was a handsome young man. He stood in the doorway in a dinner jacket. Mak sat forward, her heart speeding up. She fixed her eyes on him, and blinked again, disbelieving.

Adam.

It *was* him. Mak felt certain. He had the same wavy blond hair, the same youthful good looks. He had not bothered with disguises or an accent. Adam Hart sounded and looked just like an Australian onstage in Paris, straight out of one of Mrs Hart's family photographs. Mak felt the urge to run up and snatch him away. *There he is!* He really had run off to join the circus. *Amazing.* And he was performing with them. If it were not for the fact that he had been stealing from his mother and worrying her sick, Mak might have felt happy for him. She would have understood if those accounting textbooks had become too much for him, and he'd had to break loose.

But she had to bring him home. Now she had found him, all she had to do was convince him to leave the Paris stage behind to come back to Australia to live with his mother.

This could be a hard sell.

'Jeanne …' he cried, bringing his hand to his mouth, reacting to the sight of the beautiful woman wrapped in bandages, his acting highly melodramatic.

'Come in, darling,' she enticed through the layers of cotton. The sound of her voice sent a chill through the theatre, at once an alluring purr and a repulsive hiss.

Mak watched the scene unfold, wondering how the dynamic would work. Adam looked so innocent it was hard to imagine him inflicting this damage on his former fiancée. He did not look like a monster. The dialogue continued, the awkward exchange between former lovers, the man, recently acquitted of an irreversible crime, and his victim. The tension tightened expertly, Adam holding his own impressively, the two locked in an unnerving conversation.

Finally, unexpectedly, she grabbed him.

Mak knew what would happen next. The play demanded it.

'Look at me,' Bijou urged him. 'Look at what I have become ...' As she said these words, she unwound the bandages, strip by strip, exposing a face nightmarishly disfigured and eaten away. The audience gasped, as did Adam. 'Now I'm going to punish you!'

Mak squinted. The pearls. Were those Glenise's pearls? *This is her. This is the woman with great legs. The 'star'.*

Mak watched, riveted. Adam was pinned against the couch, and though clearly stronger than she, his character was so overwhelmed by the vision of horror he had created by his own hand that he sat dumbfounded as she drew a vial from her pocket.

'We'll be the perfect lovers ... made for each other!' she screamed at him.

My God.

The vial.

That face sprang back into her mind: the man backstage, the look of naked guilt, the hand closed around *something* ...

Makedde had no time to think or to question her instincts. Before she even realised what she was doing, she was running up the aisle towards the stage. 'Stop! Stop the play! Someone stop her!'

The actors looked up, startled. Members of the audience cried out in confusion, some yelling for Makedde's mad progression to the stage to be halted. She hurled herself up onto the elevated proscenium and landed on her knees. A man ran out from behind the curtain and tackled her before she got any further. Mak fell hard onto her right elbow, sending pain shooting up her arm, but she managed to reach out and grab Bijou's ankle with her left hand.

'No! It is real acid!' Mak yelled at her, and the vial slipped, having already been opened, ready to be poured on Adam, ready for the climactic moment of violence.

No!

The contents of the vial spilled out on the stage, but instead of coloured water touching the skin harmlessly, the contents splashed Makedde's hand with a sharp burning.

Acid!

There was confusion; scorching, searing pain. The skin on Makedde's hand was puckering, blistering in agony. She cried out and grabbed her wrist, standing.

The pain hit with blinding force, and she screamed at the top of her lungs. All around her, the sounds of chaos dispersed for a moment, the theatre audience dropping into stunned silence. With her vision blurred and blood pounding in her temples, Mak looked out across a hundred eyes, each looking back at her, blinking, confused. The full realisation of what had happened came to her. She was onstage. They could not know if it was some strange act meant to shock them.

'Help me!' she shouted, beginning to feel woozy. 'A man swapped the vials! This is no joke ...' Her voice trailed off and she sank to her knees.

CHAPTER 44

Arslan sat in a perfectly motionless panic, his arms and legs folded tightly into the standard position of an enterologist.

Honte ... honte ... Shame ... shame ...

From his hidden vantage point in the old stage box, Arslan watched as the *gendarmes* grilled Bijou about the dramatic incident that had taken place during the performance of *The Final Kiss*. There had been a shocked audience of witnesses in the theatre, and the French police had been tipped off that Arslan himself had swapped the stage vial of harmless coloured water for one containing real sulphuric acid. The woman who had leaped onstage was a private detective who had seen him make the switch before the show. He still did not know how she had ended up there, backstage that night. How had she known what he would do?

'*Non ... c'est terrible!*' Bijou was crying, highly dramatic when emotional. She trembled and wept, one hand to her pale forehead, her distress genuine even though her demeanour inevitably brought to mind her persona of Grand Guignol scream queen.

She knows. My mother knows.

Finally, the Australian boy was gone. He had been questioned by police and then fled France, back to his own mother's arms in Sydney, and he would not be coming back and getting between Arslan and Bijou and their enduring bond. This was what Arslan had prayed for, though it had not eventuated at all as he had hoped. With Jean-Baptiste, his last real rival for Bijou's affection five years earlier, the troupe had remained undivided. His mother had been stoic in her resolve that none of them were responsible for the acid attack in the alley after their show, and it must have been a psychotic audience member who had wrought the terrible violence in homage to their play. She had been saddened by the fate of her severely scarred and maimed young lover, and they had soon after separated. But all was changed now. Bijou and the troupe were estranged from him, and from each other. Fractured. The *gendarmes* were suspicious of Arslan. He was *wanted*, and would have to remain on the run for who knew how long. Worst of all, his mother was not protecting him this time. She was not trying to dissuade them from making their harsh judgements against him.

She knows.

The two officers questioning Bijou stood in her living room, looming over her diminutive figure while she alternately wept and pouted, perched delicately on her floral, gilt-edged sofa. He could catch glimpses of them, and hear their every word, from his hiding place in Bijou's bedroom. For her part she was not confirming the gendarmes' suspicions that Arslan had wanted her to throw acid on her younger lover, disfiguring that beautiful face of his, and tearing him from her forever. But she was not denying it.

'Where is your son?' the shorter officer persisted.

Bijou winced. She hated being labelled a mother, and certainly *his* mother. Few people knew their true relationship.

'*Je ne sais pas.* I don't know,' she said with conviction. And she was telling the truth. She did not know. As she had never known about his hiding in her bedroom, his watching her, his watching her between the sheets with her other lovers, his eternal watching …

'Madame, we found sulphuric acid in his apartment,' the officer explained. 'His fingerprints were on the vial, along with yours. Can you think of any reason he would want to have this man injured? What was his motivation? Was it professional jealousy?'

Bijou began to cry hysterically, her mascara running.

'Where is he?' the other one demanded once more.

'If you are protecting him we may have to assume that you planned this with him —'

'I would never hurt Adam! Never! *Jamais*!'

Arslan peered through his spy-hole at the woman he had always loved, flanked by the police, talking about him as if he was a monster, his love worthless. Never had he felt more alone than at this moment.

'Not professional jealousy …' she said, and the police leaned forward. 'There is no finer contortionist than my darling Arslan.'

He felt his chest swell slightly in the confines of the box.

Je t'aime, Bijou.

His mother turned her back from Arslan's viewpoint, and he watched her shoulders rise and fall in jerking movements. She was sobbing uncontrollably. Rarely had he seen her lose composure at all, but now she seemed to go to water.

'No, he loved me. He wanted to hurt him because he loved me!' she cried.

'Jealousy?' one of them said.

She continued to shake, sobbing. Arslan wanted to comfort her. 'We were lovers. Oh, God help me. God help me …'

He could feel the shock ripple through them. 'Your … son?'

They know.

She cried even harder.

'Madame, try to remain calm,' one of the officers said.

'Do you have any recent photographs of him?' the taller officer asked, offering Bijou a tissue.

She dabbed delicately at her eyes, sniffling. '*Oui*. In my photo album. The photograph is perhaps twelve months old.'

She stood up, straightened her dress and walked into her bedroom, right towards Arslan. His eyes grew wide, his heart in his throat. Did she sense he was there? Could she know?

No.

Bijou searched through her stacks of things, oblivious to his presence, and finding her large leather-bound albums of photographs and news clippings piled under a heavy trunk, pulled at the corner of one of the albums with an ineffectual tug.

'It is here,' she called, and turned to the officers. 'Oh can you help me?' she asked, adopting a look of feminine powerlessness.

'Of course,' the taller officer said, and entered the bedroom.

Arslan felt his panic rise, sure that he would be discovered. If they found him they would drag him off to prison.

Arslan could not see what was happening, and he dared not try to change position. There was the sound of books being moved then something heavy being shifted. The man grunted slightly with the effort, and placed the trunk directly on top of Arslan's box.

Immediately, as the trunk was placed on top of him, Arslan realised what had happened.

Emprisonné!

His fingers flexed. He opened his mouth as if to say something, but remained silent. He could do nothing.

Trapped. I am trapped.

An hour later, and in no danger of immediate discovery, Arslan tried to push his way out of the box as he usually did. But he could not get out. He put his muscles into it, but the thing on top — whatever it was — was too heavy. He tried to shift it with rocking movements, but it barely rocked a millimetre.

He attempted to rock the stage box off its shelf, but he hadn't enough freedom of movement to build momentum.

Slowly, his extremities were becoming numb.

Arslan brooded silently, trapped within the box, imprisoned by a circumstance of his own making.

Maman.

CHAPTER 45

Makedde waited in Charles de Gaulle airport with Adam Hart on her arm, feeling strangely like a stern schoolteacher. She was determined to watch him board the Air China flight, just to be sure, and after two painful hours of waiting the first boarding call had sounded.

It was 9.45 a.m. and she hadn't had much sleep. Most of the night had been spent in hospital and with the police.

'I'm curious about something,' she said. 'Why are some of the pages of your diary ripped out?'

The young man hung his head and spoke to the airport tile, looking younger than his nineteen years. 'I'm so embarrassed. I didn't think...' He trailed off, reddening. 'I guess if anyone *did* find the diaries, I wanted to protect Bijou.' His jaw quivered as he spoke her name. Even with all that had happened and all that he had learned — even with the now public knowledge that Bijou had once had an affair with her own son Arslan — Adam still loved her.

Of course he ripped out the pages himself.

His mother had blamed Patrice for his running away, and

he wanted to make sure that no one blamed Bijou, or knew where he could be found. It seemed that Adam really had believed in a happy-ever-after with his new lover. It would no doubt take him some time to come to terms with the shocking turn of events.

'Again, I really am so sorry about your hand,' Adam told her.

'It's okay,' she managed, but barely meant it. The burn, though only the size of a twenty-cent piece, was exceedingly painful. The damage felt *alive* somehow, moving in her skin. It covered her left hand from the base of her pinky finger to the edge of her palm, and the skin beneath her bandage tingled and ached like terrible sunburn. According to the doctor, it might never heal properly. She would have a scar to remind her of this case forever.

Imagine if all *of the acid had spilled across your hand, instead of a drop?*

She had been very lucky. And Adam had certainly been lucky as well. What if she had not acted so impetuously? He was seconds away from having his lover, Bijou, unknowingly disfigure him for life. If Mak had not seen the man — the contortionist Arslan as it turned out — acting suspiciously near the props before the show, she would not have figured it out in time, and the acid would have covered Adam's face. Nothing could have stopped it once it made contact with his skin. No more handsome face. No more chance for normality. His mother, Glenise, would have welcomed home quite a different son.

'Makedde?'

'Yes, Adam?'

'Thank you,' he said, and embraced her childishly.

'Go on,' she said, dismissing him, and waving him towards the gate. '*Bon voyage*. Fly safely.'

Adam waved as he disappeared down the gangway to his plane. She stepped away, ready for the trip back to her hotel, feeling sorry for the young man. Though it was Mak who had been burned, he had learned a painful lesson. She hoped his reunion with his mother was a good one. They had both been through a tough couple of years. After all that suffering, they deserved to find some happiness.

With a fresh dose of caffeine pumping through her and a stomach happily digesting one of the best croissants she had ever eaten, Mak slipped into the elevator at the Hotel des Grandes Écoles with the satisfaction of a job complete.

Done. You did it.

The elevator door shut with a squeak, and the cramped, rattling lift ascended to her floor. She stepped out into the narrow hallway and flattened herself against the wall to let a maid in a traditional black-and-white uniform, carrying a feather duster, pass her. The corridors smelled of scented cleaning products.

'*Bonjour*,' she offered as the woman brushed past her chest.

Mak could not understand the smiling woman's rapid-fire reply.

She opened the door to her room with a large, old-fashioned key, stepped inside and locked the deadbolt behind her out of habit. She threw herself on the hard bed, grinning wildly, her arms and legs flung out in her preferred starfish pose. It was not just the café au lait that was buzzing pleasantly around her system, but the excitement of having completed her case, and completed it well. Adam would soon be home safe in Australia, unharmed, apologetic and reunited with his grateful mother, Glenise. And he would return with her pearls, too. Mak was relieved. She had felt an increasing foreboding, fearing something terrible would happen to him. Thankfully, this was one case that would not end in the kind of violence and tragedy that seemed always to plague her.

She rolled over and grabbed her phone. It would be evening in Australia.

It rang four times. *Don't get too giddy.*

A warm voice came on the line, full of concern about her injury. Bogey. She'd just managed a thirty-second call to him the night before to let him know the case was wrapped up and she was okay.

'Hi there.' She laughed nervously, hating that she was so girlishly enlivened by the idea of talking to him. She hoped he couldn't tell over the phone. The case was over and the first thing her mind had seized upon was romance.

There was silence for a few seconds. 'You sound so far away, Mak,' he said.

'I am!'

'What's the hotel like?'

'It's not bad. The room's tiny, but I think all rooms in Paris are the size of a closet. But why would anyone spend time in their room when there's Paris to explore?'

As soon as she said the words, Mak regretted them. Her mind immediately went to one very compelling reason to stay indoors. She imagined Bogey in her bed, perhaps lying across the crisp white sheets with his tattoos spread on his naked skin like fascinating constellations to be explored in minute detail. Every centimetre of skin, every tiny hair, every pore …

'Are you boarding soon?' she asked excitedly.

'Yes. I'll be in London in about twenty-four hours. I can come across on the Eurostar as soon as you're ready for me.'

'I'm ready.'

'You are? Great! Congratulations, by the way, on another case solved.'

Mak smiled. 'Well, it is nice to get a happy resolution.'

'You know, your work on the Murphy–Wallace case was pretty impressive too.' He had followed her progress carefully on that one. When they had first met.

She had been feeling elated, but at the mention of the troublesome Cavanagh case, her mood darkened. 'Don't … really, don't get me started about all that,' she said, perhaps a bit too sharply. 'Tobias didn't end up doing time for a crime he didn't commit, but other than that, there's not too much positive I can say about that case.'

Just like that, the Cavanaghs were back in her head. When she got back to Sydney she intended seeing what she could do about tracking down that incriminating video. The police had it, and she wanted to see it again. She even had wild ideas about leaking it to the press, or maybe onto YouTube. Perhaps the only way to circumvent those who were holding back the investigation was to go public. If the Cavanaghs really were innocent of her every accusation, if there was some other explanation for what happened … well, they would have no trouble clearing themselves and they certainly had the money to secure top legal representation. They should at least be put under scrutiny. If they weren't, it made a mockery of the justice system.

'Mak, I'm glad you're over there right now. You're probably safer.' A touch of concern had entered Bogey's voice. 'There was an article in the paper yesterday about the

Cavanaghs. Apparently the name "Cavanagh" and some employees of theirs came up on a database in some raid on an international organised crime ring. It's a big scandal, as you can imagine.'

An edgy electric current slipped up her spine and she shivered. 'An international crime ring?'

'Apparently. There wasn't a lot of detail. Something about a crime ring with some connection in Queensland. That's all the article said. And everything was prefaced with "allegedly", of course.'

Andy. He'd said the feds were onto them.

Mak wanted to call Karen and find out if she knew anything about it. 'How is it that you read this in the paper, but no one told me?'

'I shouldn't have mentioned it. I'm sorry,' Bogey said. 'You really don't need to be thinking about those issues right now. You're in *Paris.* Are you going out sightseeing today?'

'Naturally,' she answered, her mind only half on the conversation. 'Eiffel Tower, Champs Élysées ... the Louvre, the Arc de Triomphe ...' She reeled off the destinations, feeling far away, her thoughts in Sydney, not Paris.

The line was silent for a moment as Mak gripped the phone too hard, and stared blankly towards the hotel window, not seeing the charming drapery or the Paris sky beyond.

An international crime ring. Corruption. This could be it. They might actually get their just deserts.

'I'm glad you told me,' she went on. 'I want to know more.'

'I'm sure the police are onto it,' Bogey replied, trying to reassure her. 'Tell me about what's happening over there. Have the police found the contortionist? How is what's-her-name

… Bijou? How's she coping?' Bogey was clearly trying to get her off the topic of the Cavanaghs.

He was right — there was nothing she could do about the Cavanaghs over here in Europe. Still, the idea would stay with her until she knew more.

'Arslan is still missing, and wanted for assault. I'll tell you more about it when I see you.'

Mak felt a little thrill of desire, thinking about seeing Bogey in only another day or so. How wonderful.

'I wonder where he'll turn up?' Bogey mused.

'I think I mentioned before that one of Bijou's lovers was attacked under similar circumstances about five years ago. That assault is still unsolved, but the police now believe that it might have been Arslan. The victim was only twenty at the time, around the same age as Adam Hart.'

'And they say Arslan is her son? Weird.'

'You're telling me,' she said. 'It seems that Arslan must have been overcome with jealousy of these young lovers, and I think that the only way he could get his mother's attention back was to maim the competition, or even try to murder them. Who knows if Adam would have even lived?'

There was such a strange dynamic amongst the troupe. It seemed they lived out of each others' pockets twenty-four/seven, and had done so for years. Anyone could be driven crazy living like that.

'It's hard to understand exactly how it works, but from all I've seen the loyalty within the troupe is fierce. When the first kid was attacked they probably swung into action to cover up what had happened and make sure none of them was implicated, guilty or not. Keeping the troupe together was a matter of survival for them, and loyalty. It does seem Bijou was devastated. But the theatre is all she knows. And with her Grand Guignol performances she's become a bit typecast — she isn't offered other roles. This is it for her. Her life is that troupe.'

Mak wondered once more what Bijou would do now. She probably wouldn't be charged with any crime. But surely this would be the tragic end to the strange nomadic lifestyle of the Théâtre des Horreurs? What would she do without her children? Would she find a new toyboy to replace Adam? Would she support her son if he was found?

'I think one of the strangest things is that all seven of the performers are blood relatives, half-siblings and such, but they were never billed that way because of Bijou's vanity. She didn't want to be seen as the mother of the other performers, but as more of a queen. An ageless queen. Even now that her history with her son Arslan has been found out, it is not technically a crime in France. Did you know that? Socially it is totally unacceptable here, definitely, but not a crime.'

'You mean the incest?' Bogey asked, puzzled. 'Incest is a crime.'

'Not in France. Napoleon made incest legal a couple of hundred years ago, for uncertain reasons, and the law was never changed back. Once Arslan was old enough, Bijou could take him as her lover without fear of legal repercussions. And she did.'

'Incest is legal? Are you kidding me?' There was notable shock in his voice, and Mak was not surprised.

'In France it is legal. Probably in some other countries too, I don't know.' She paused. 'Well, they hid their relationship for good reason. It isn't exactly the done thing.'

Mak wondered if Bijou denied her maternity of the troupe more for the sake of her professional image, her vanity regarding her age, or to protect her on-and-off sexual liaisons with her son Arslan? Probably it would be for all three reasons.

'Anyway, enough rabbiting on about work. You're coming to Paris, and that's much more exciting right now.'

'I was wondering … have you ever wanted to go to the Moulin Rouge?' Bogey asked.

'My whole life,' she answered.

'Would you like to go with me?'

She grinned broadly. 'Yes, I would,' she exclaimed, a little uncomfortable with just how much joy the thought of seeing him gave her. 'I'd love to go to the Moulin Rouge with you. Actually, there are some beautiful places I'd like to show you. Have you been to Paris before?'

By the time Mak hung up her heart was pounding with excitement. He was more than just an excuse to enjoy Paris for a few more days. A romantic week with Bogey Mortimer was a destination in itself.

What a splendid reward for a case solved.

Mak slipped on a coat and a pair of gloves to brave the winter cold, and before long she was able to forget all about the bandaged wound on her hand, and the close call that had caused it.

Today is a great day to be in Paris, she thought and, with optimism lacking in recent years, set out for some sightseeing in the city of love.

CHAPTER 46

Paris. Paris!

Grinning like the tourist she now was, Mak took several steps from the kerb, and closed her eyes for a moment. Then she looked up.

Wow!

She was directly under the Tour Eiffel, its mighty beams weaving symmetrically into cool, overcast skies above her, a tower of intricate iron lace. A small breath of appreciation escaped her.

'*Mademoiselle! MADEMOISELLE!* One euro!'

Mak could not take the time to appreciate the beauty of the famous French monument from that position for long. In seconds she was being hassled by a young North African man selling tiny glowing Eiffel Tower replicas. And then another one. And another one. She had no interest in a 10-centimetre-high flashing Eiffel Tower. But it was a cloudy midweek day, and the young hawkers did not have many other potential customers.

'One euro!' came the cries, ever more insistent, and a swarm of souvenir sellers gathered round her, many only reaching the level of her chest.

Mak quickly spotted a short queue for the trip to the top of the tower from the closest pylon. '*Non, merci,*' she told her unwanted friends, and quickly broke away. Framed by the giant structure, she strolled purposefully through the scattered crowd, ignoring the pushy young men and their gaudy trinkets.

Once in the queue, she quickly relaxed again, safe. She paid her 11 euros, and stepped through the doors of the elevator that would pull her to the top of the structure. A couple was already inside. She smiled at them, and they nodded. Then kissed.

Mak had not been up the Eiffel Tower since she was a teenager modelling in Paris, and it seemed little had changed.

Buttons were pushed on a control panel by a solemn attendant, and the elevator began to move, rickety and slightly off-kilter, the four of them raised rung by rung up the giant structure in the little cubicle to the rhythmic sound of gears turning, catching ever more thrilling glimpses of the city through the webs of iron, enough to feel something like vertigo.

'To top? Top closing twenty minutes,' the attendant told them in broken English. 'Weather.'

They arrived at the first level of the tower, and were escorted to a second elevator. The kissing couple joined her, along with a second, older couple who had been waiting on the lower platform. A very tall man slipped in last, seeming almost to fill the rest of the carriage on his own. The elevator doors closed and they ascended. This elevator seemed smaller, and more fragile. Hundreds of metres in the air, it turned slightly on its side, perhaps only a few centimetres off balance, but enough to make Makedde hang on.

The doors opened at the top, and the little group of tourists spilled out. The platform was nearly empty. Mak had expected tourists at every turn, but then it was February, and a windy, overcast day. As she walked straight to the railing, she felt almost as if the view — what there was of it — was for her, and her alone. The wind was biting, and she had to pull her collar up over her chin while she gazed through swelling cloud at the fast-receding vista. It seemed this was probably not the day to take in the visual splendour of Paris, but she still fed a coin into the binoculars bolted to the viewing platform, and bent to take in the magnified view. She wondered if she'd be able to pick out the Moulin Rouge, perhaps even the Cité Chaptal and the historic little theatre.

Dammit.

The glass was fogged up.

In the distance dark clouds were moving in, a blur of approaching rain visible. The weather would soon turn.

I am being watched.

Makedde felt eyes on her, and the power of the gaze made her look up from her inspection of the fogged eyepiece.

Several paces away stood the very tall man from the elevator. He wore a hat, scarf and wool coat of black, and small clouds of mist formed just beyond his lips in the icy air before being whipped away by the winter wind. Yes, he was watching her. Mak had a trained eye for detail, so that even with his hat pulled low across his brow, it was obvious to her that the man had some unusual disfiguration of the face; a kind of pulling of scarred skin, which suggested an unsuccessful procedure by a shonky plastic surgeon. Usually such unnatural pulling around the cheekbones and eyes was to be found only in wealthy older people of certain circles. She had seen it often enough in the fashion world on socialites and designers. But this man was no older than forty and did not look the part. Far from it. Perhaps, she thought, he was a boxer or a fighter of some kind, or had suffered in some sort of accident. His nose was crooked.

Feeling expansive and unthreatened, now on holiday in beautiful Paris, Mak smiled politely at the stranger and began a slow stroll around the railing, bracing herself against the wind and the approaching storm.

She looked right at me. She smiled at me.

Luther Hand stood on the viewing platform at the top of the Eiffel Tower, baffled that he had been locked momentarily in a gaze with the woman he was hired to kill.

Makedde Vanderwall.

Appearing unperturbed and only mildly curious about his scrutiny, she had offered an easy smile and turned her head to continue her appreciation of the clouded view.

She isn't scared of me.

Luther had instructions to eliminate Makedde for an Australian client who could not risk her return to Australian soil. Madame Q had wired a payment to his account and made available a new black Mercedes containing a case of money and the tools necessary for the operation. The car was parked a couple of blocks from the base of the famous tower, ready for her. He would need to dispose of her body discreetly.

She looked right at me and was not alarmed.

Luther wandered the platform, watching Mak in his peripheral vision and pretending to take in a view that he had seen many times before. Paris was not a romantic place for him. It was a place for work, like everywhere else. After a few minutes Mak walked back towards the elevators. She would be heading back down the tower with everyone else. The top level was closing.

The next elevator arrived and they both stepped in. Alone. The elevator operator ignored them.

He was all but alone with his target, but he did not let his attention betray him.

Mak.

Luther had encountered her twice before, and despite this, he was sure that she did not recognise him, nor did she sense his sinister purpose. She had never before seen his face. She had no reason to be able to identify him.

'Beautiful, isn't it?' she said casually.

Luther looked around. She had addressed him. Their eyes met again and she held his gaze fearlessly, seeming at ease in her surrounds.

He nodded in reply, and looked away.

Mak.

The tiny elevator rattled and shifted as it descended to the next level. They both swayed in sync with the old carriage, which squealed and hummed. At the next platform, the doors slid open, and Luther stepped out after she did. He walked to the elevator that would take them to street level, following a few feet behind her. Four tourists got in, and the carriage delivered them safely to ground level.

Mak was the first out.

Luther watched her walk away.

He did nothing.

CHAPTER 47

Makedde walked below the cold, rainy streets of wintry Paris, navigating the dank domain of six million dead Parisians.

The Empire of the Dead.

After the Eiffel Tower and the Basilique du Sacré-Coeur, Denfert-Rochereau Ossuary, famously known as the Catacombs, was Makedde's favourite Parisian icon. She had visited the web of underground passageways nearly a decade earlier when she was working in Paris as a fashion model, and, being Makedde, she'd long had the morbid tourist destination at the top of her list of places to revisit. Walking amongst the bones of six million long-dead Parisians was a unique experience, and had affected her enormously on her first visit. Makedde had seen death many times in many settings, but there was something about the seemingly endless corridors of anonymous femurs and skulls, the display of all those naked bones placed namelessly, sometimes haphazardly and other times in meticulous, near-artistic stacks, that spoke to her of her own smallness, and mortality. She found it strangely reassuring to face the facts so largely ignored aboveground.

Underneath, we are all just bones. We are all the same. We are all dying.

There could be no better *memento mori*, or reminder to value your moments of living.

THE EMPIRE OF THE DEAD, the sign above the entranceway said, and with a sense of both fascination and respect for her surroundings, Mak made her way through *les carrières* of Paris, the old limestone quarries famously transformed in the 1780s into a place of reburial. In those times Paris had been suffering disease due to insanitary burials and overcrowded cemeteries, and officials decided to move thousands of bodies from their marked graves to the abandoned quarries, to be placed in anonymous stacks.

Skulls. Stacks of skulls.

Each of those hollow eye sockets had once framed the outlook of some living person, some unique life. Mak found that she was as fascinated by the place as she had been as a twenty-year-old seeing it for the first time.

With her mind fixed contentedly on her sightseeing, and the anticipation of Bogey's arrival, Mak did not foresee her fate. And the bones could not warn her.

Mak was not alone.

She had been followed.

Oh!

A whirl of movement caught her eye, and she turned too late, her motion arrested by a stifling set of arms, her neck locked within the crook of an elbow, pressure behind her head, squeezing ... she was in a chokehold ... the chest behind her felt as solid as a slab of boulder. Immovable. Impenetrable. And she was being lifted, her heels off the ground now ... and her toes. She wanted to cry out but had no breath. Her arms, which now felt strangely autonomous and almost detached, had at first flailed at her attacker, but her stabbing fingers met only with the unyielding flesh of solid muscles, no eyes to scratch at, no soft tissue to grab. Her own eyes remained open, though half blind with a fog of increasing moisture, and the throb of pain and pressure in her head.

Time stretched to slow motion as she frantically kicked at her surprise attacker. She tried to punch, to gouge, but all the while the pressure on her neck increased painfully, and she could not breathe. Every single molecule of her being switched to blinding panic, the sensation of death — of drowning — weighing hard on her nerves, urging her for action. *Do something! Breathe!* But she had no air, she had no air, no air, no air … *no air* …

Time seemed to stretch on, breathless, while her brain fought against its inevitable disconnection from vital oxygen.

In reality it only took a few seconds.

Mak was unconscious.

Seconds or minutes or years later, Makedde Vanderwall woke disoriented, and disconcertingly euphoric, her muscles tingling warmly throughout her limbs. *Discombobulated*. A deep tiredness weighed against adrenaline-fuelled elation. Her heart beat in an odd rhythm. Strange. *Where am I?*

She was slung over a man's shoulder. The man seemed huge, monstrous.

Nothing felt right.

What's going on?

Disorientation soon made way for electrifying fear.

Arslan. My God, is it Arslan? Is he trying to kill me? No, this man is too big.

She had been choked unconscious, she now realised, and she was only just waking up. How long had she been unconscious? How much time had elapsed? She had not even spotted her attacker before he had his arm around her throat. If she had not even spotted him, had not even made a dint in him with all her struggling, then he was capable and meant business, and she was in terrible danger.

She was somewhere in low light, and she could make out the heels of the man's shoes as he walked along an old stone pathway. They were underground. He had choked her unconscious and was carrying her.

Skulls.

There were skulls everywhere she looked, their empty eye sockets staring back at her in the low light. *The Catacombs.* She was still in the Catacombs. Not far from where she had been standing before she had suddenly had the oxygen choked out of her.

'Hey!' she shouted, although the cry came out strained. Her throat throbbed, as if she had been axed in the Adam's apple. She tried to punch the man again but could only reach his hamstring.

No!

There was a jab of something — a needle; it sheared through her jeans and into her buttock. She let out a short cry.

Blackness folded around her abruptly, sending her into a much deeper, much longer sleep.

Impassive, the fleshless faces of Denfert-Rochereau Ossuary's dead watched Makedde's attacker bear her away.

CHAPTER 48

Bogey woke with a start.

Mak.

He found himself strapped into an economy seat on a plane bound for London. His limbs felt stiff, and his mouth dry. He had no place to stretch his legs out. Bogey blinked and looked around him. Passengers up down the aircraft were dozing, their mouths hanging wide and slack. The man next to him had a reading light on, washing him in a white circle of light. The man cast an uncomfortable glance his way, and Bogey realised with embarrassment that he had made a strange noise as he woke. He was a nervous flyer, and had never taken as long a flight as this one would be. He was only four and a half hours in.

The flying, however, was not the root of his uneasiness.

For reasons he could not justify, Bogey had woken in a strange terror, deeply concerned about Makedde's wellbeing. His sleep had been intermittent, his armrest already pummelled by a violent restlessness. Distress soaked his every pore and nerve ending, as convincing and real as any legitimate panic.

Mak.

He had every reason to be smiling. He should have been excited by his fast-approaching arrival in London, then Paris. He had every reason to feel elated to soon be seeing Mak, a woman who, should he be honest with himself, he had fallen for when they first met.

Instead, he felt panic.

Bogey rubbed his eyes and replaced his glasses. He put his seat upright, and remained that way for a few minutes, willing his heartbeat to slow to a normal pace. Out of habit, he reached for the packet of cigarettes in his leather jacket before remembering that he did not have any. He had no matches either. Neither would be helpful on a flight. Bogey was trying to quit. It did not seem to be working. In his mysterious rush of panic, the urge to smoke was strong.

It wasn't guns that killed people, it was the bullets. Not the cigarettes, but the matches.

Makedde did not smoke. She never had. He wanted to quit for her.

By now it would be night-time in Paris, where Mak had said she would be sightseeing for the day — the Louvre, the Arc de Triomphe, the Eiffel Tower. She had promised to show him these places if he had time out from the Form Art and Design Fair. *Of course I have time.* The truth was that London was an excuse to get to Paris to see her. She was the reason he was heading all the way to the design fair. He was not exhibiting his work there, and would most likely not be able to exhibit for another couple of years. She was the reason. He dared not tell her, but she probably already knew.

Bogey found he could not take his eyes from the inflight phone that was staring him in the face from the seatback in front of him. EASY CALLS IN TWO STEPS, it said.

Just call her and see if everything is okay. Bugger the cost.

In moments he had swiped his credit card into the seatback and the headset was ringing. The receptionist at Mak's hotel answered.

She put his call through, and it rang a dozen times. With each ring, his distress increased.

'*Il n'y a pas de réponse.* There is no answer,' she said.

Bogey took a breath and swiped his credit card again. This time he dialled her mobile.

'Hi, you've reached Mak. I'm sorry I can't come to the phone right now …'

It went straight to her voicemail.

Strange.

He had expected her to be back at her hotel by now, or at the very least answering her mobile in a restaurant or café somewhere. Why was it turned off? By his calculations it was already ten o'clock Paris time, yet she could not be reached. Was the stab of worry he felt motivated by fear for her, or fear of a misunderstanding? He recalled their last conversation, and tried to think of anything he might have said wrong. Was he pressuring her by suggesting he join her in Paris? Did she know that he had not intended travelling across the globe to London to attend the show this year, that it had always been a dream of his, but that he was not planning to go until he had something special to exhibit? Did she know he was only going as an excuse to see her, removed from all distractions, in the world's most romantic city? Would that knowledge make her uncomfortable? She had just come out of a significant personal break-up. Perhaps this was all too much, too soon?

No.

Mak is in trouble.

Bogey resolved to continue calling her until she answered. He knew he would not be able to go to sleep again until he heard her voice and knew she was okay. His fingers reached again for the packet of cigarettes he did not have, and he sat back, worried and trapped. He tried to reassure himself that she was at a show, or a cinema, and had therefore turned off her phone. She would soon turn it back on. She was fine.

Mak is in trouble, he thought again.

It would be another twenty hours before touchdown at Heathrow.

CHAPTER 49

Mak cracked open her heavy eyelids a millimetre, as far as she could manage. She was in a dark, unfamiliar space.

Below her was something like a bare mattress, and around her was wrapped a heavy set of woollen blankets. She could see her breath in the air. Her nose felt cold, though her eyes were warm and puffy. She did not know where she was, or how she had got there, and nearly as urgent as this confusion was the tornado of pain in her head, and her throat, which ached as if she had been punched in the trachea. She pulled a leaden hand from under the blankets and caressed her aching neck. *Thirsty. Unbearably thirsty.* With effort, she struggled to sit up, and immediately felt a deep throbbing in her muscles. Her head felt almost too heavy to keep upright.

My ankle?

Makedde's ankle felt strange. With dread, she pulled the blankets away and looked at it. The room spun. *No!* There was a heavy cuff locked around her flesh. A metal cuff and a chain …

Scream.

Scream!

Makedde's mouth opened to shriek, but she caught herself before she uttered a sound. It was only a well-honed survival instinct that kept her quiet. For the moment she was alone. But she might not remain alone if she made a noise. She had to use caution. Anyone she would meet in this situation was not likely to be on her side. She had to figure a way out before her captor — or captors — came back.

Nothing to be gained from screaming right now. Nothing at all. Look. Listen. Remain calm. Figure this out. You can figure this out …

Waves of dizziness bombarded her. She was being beckoned back into unconsciousness. She struggled to remain alert and take in some of the detail around her. She was in a cold, dank space that smelled of mould and fermentation. She could see that the ceiling was low, perhaps not much more than two metres high. The floor was made of stone. The walls were stone. She saw wooden shelves of bottles on both sides of her. *A cellar?* She was not in the Denfert-Rochereau Ossuary any more. Could she be somewhere nearby? She hoped so. But probably not. Mak sensed that a lot of time had elapsed. Perhaps hours, perhaps even a day or two. Yes, it was at least a day. Her mouth was dry, her stomach felt hollow. *My God, where is this place?* There were no windows. She could not tell the time of day. A bit of light crept in from the top of a narrow, steep staircase of the type you found leading to attics, she thought. Was it artificial light, or sun seeping through? She could not tell.

Her eyelids felt heavy. They threatened to shut. Mak had been drugged. She was imprisoned, and she had been drugged.

Arslan.

Could he have been following her? Could he have tracked her down and drugged her? He was dangerous and he was on the loose. She was in danger.

As it is at the moment, you can't get far. No windows. One door. You are chained. And you don't know why.

The world within and without her dissolved into a terrifying, ill-defined fog. Her body didn't feel right. Her brain stopped co-operating, stopped being lucid. And now her eyelids were too heavy to stay open any longer. She forced them open with her fingertips.

It isn't safe to sleep.

Stay awake …

Stay awake!

A black void crept in around her, suffocating, stifling, more powerful than her determination to remain wakeful. The corners of her vision blackened like the edges of an old photograph. Gradually her fingers dropped, and her warm, bloodshot eyes shut of their own volition.

Mak felt her neck go limp as she slipped again into unconsciousness, the fingers of one hand wrapped around the heavy iron ankle cuff that kept her prisoner.

CHAPTER 50

Luther Hand inserted his key and silently unlocked the heavy padlock on the cellar door.

He paused.

The padlock was new, and looked out of place in the rustic surroundings of the dilapidated farmhouse, where everything seemed to have been in place decades before his arrival. He let it swing on the hook with a rattle. He pushed the door open with his boot, and listened.

Silence.

Had there been any witness to this moment, they would have seen that Luther's ravaged face did not betray any emotion. Beneath the surface of his cold countenance, however, conflict raged. With the door ajar, Luther peered inside at the short, steep set of steps that descended to the wine cellar. The stairs disappeared into relative darkness. His eyes took a moment to adjust, and once he could make out ghostly shapes of stone and wood, he stepped inside and listened again. Luther felt a strange tightness in his stomach, a kind of queer adrenaline. He took pleasure in standing in the cool dark, listening for stirring below. He felt satisfaction. Strangeness. Even something like fear.

He could hear nothing.

Is she asleep?

There was no need to sneak up on her now, not as he had in the Catacombs.

Luther pulled a cord that dangled just inside the doorway next to him, and a bare light bulb flickered to life, casting a pale white glow into the space, illuminating the wooden steps and old stone walls. Now he could hear movement below, a weak shifting. The light had startled her out of a doze. She was there just below him. She was awake. Wasting no more time, Luther walked solidly down the staircase. It was not until he reached the bottom that he looked at his captive.

Makedde Vanderwall.

The bare bulb cast a circle of light on the floor where she sat. He'd taken her boots off to fit her ankle with the heavy iron cuff. The right leg of her jeans half obscured the cuff, from which a slack trail of chain ran to one dusty corner of the cellar, and an iron ring on the wall. The chain was solid, and quite sufficient to keep anyone in one place, even the likes of Mak Vanderwall who had proved resourceful in the past. She wore her black top and winter coat, which he had emptied of its few contents — a mobile phone, some cash, an old-fashioned hotel key and a small notepad and pen. He'd covered her with blankets, and she now wore them around her shoulders and over her toes. She was huddled on the bare mattress, knees bent to her chest and back against the wall. It was cold down here, cold and dark.

There was much about this moment which was odd for Luther. For starters, he had rarely been interested in keeping people alive. On the handful of occasions in his career when he'd been required to do so, he'd arranged a similar setup, finding a cellar or storehouse, usually equipped with basic medical supplies and the most common tools of persuasion. Waterboarding. Electric shock. Those targets would always be eliminated once the required information was elicited. This was not Luther's area of expertise, and such jobs had been rare. He was an expert killer, not a torturer. That sort of work was generally left to those with military training or a particular interest in the field. It was not Luther's interest.

And this was different. Luther was not being paid to keep Mak alive. He was being paid to kill her.

He stood near the edge of the mattress, and observed the vision of her at his feet with an odd cocktail of feeling. *Exhilaration. Strangeness.* He had killed a handful of women in the course of his professional duties, but he had never before had a living woman captive in his care. Since he was a small boy, his contact with women had been limited, and once it was clear that his mother would be safer believing him dead, he had lost touch with the one woman in his life who had cared about him. Women hired for their company were his only option, and if it were not for those women that Ms Rosalay introduced him to, he would not have had any intimate encounters at all. It was not that he didn't like women. Luther loved women, and he was attracted to them. The problem had always been that they did not like him. He repelled them. It was only the girls at Ms Rosalay's establishment who were nice to him. But frustratingly, most of them were not very good at masking their distress at his appearance. When they saw him — his size, his face, his scars, his crooked nose, his half-torn ear — their eyes filled with an alarm and disgust they could not hide. Some of the younger girls even cried when he got close. That was not what he wanted. Luther didn't want to make women cry. He had no violence for them. That was not why he was there. He wished to avoid violence outside his work, and inflicting unwanted fear caused him a deep personal sadness.

So, Luther's experiences with women were few. Yet here he was with a woman at his feet. *This* woman …

Will she recognise me now? Will she realise we have met before?

Makedde was still weakly shifting, seemingly disoriented. Possibly the drugs had not worn off, he thought. She was moving though, and eventually, from under the dishevelled mane of her blonde hair, a pair of bloodshot blue-green eyes found him. He did not register any expression in them except exhaustion. He did not register any recognition. Her beautiful eyes were puffy and red, mascara making dark smudges across her lashes. She was contained. This woman would no longer be swinging a motorcycle helmet at his face, breaking his nose. She would not be kicking him, scratching him, fighting and fleeing. He had her. Six years after she first crossed his path, Makedde Vanderwall was finally helpless before him, and this fact delivered mixed emotions. For Luther this issue had become significant. The desire to contain her had crept up on him. Even in the Catacombs, he had not been sure what he would ultimately do with her, or how much his chosen method of elimination was motivated by professionalism.

We have a history, you and I. We have a history.

When Luther had first laid eyes on this woman, he had been in the early stages of his career. He had been roughing people up for cash, and not very good cash at that, certainly nothing like the five- and six-figure contracts he could now demand. Back in those days, his clients were lowlifes. The work was unsophisticated. Mak had been a Canadian visiting Sydney to work as a fashion model, and Luther had at first been hired to merely spook her: move things around in her apartment when she wasn't there, confuse her, leave threatening messages, with the ultimate aim of scaring her back onto a plane to her homeland. It happened that one day he was concealed behind her couch and saw her in a state of undress. She'd had no inkling he was there, and she had moved through her apartment disrobed and radiantly naked. *You are beautiful*, he had wanted to tell her, but waited instead for a safe way to exit before being discovered. That week Luther lost the top of his ear to some unseen protector in her yard at night, in an incident he still did not understand. The man had come out of nowhere. He had used an extremely sharp blade. Luther had not been fast enough to respond. Even with all his many scars and the injuries he had received over the years, losing part of an ear was not something one soon forgot.

But that was years ago.

If he had not lost a chunk of his ear in a backyard in Sydney — sliced off by some protector of Makedde Vanderwall — he would not have fled to Queensland and might not have come to the attention of Madame Q. He might not have graduated to the international scene. So, in a way, this disoriented woman at his feet was responsible for his elevated career, his success.

Strange.

It was a surprisingly small world, and five years and many jobs later she had ended up on his hit list for the first time. It was a different world for Luther by then. He was a high-end professional hitman. But she had proved more resilient and unpredictable than expected. She broke his nose in the hallway of a townhouse in Sydney, fled by motorcycle, and crashed. But she survived the accident. Her survival had been one of his extremely rare professional failures, and now the same client wanted him to kill Makedde Vanderwall before she could return to Australia. This time he would not disappoint. Mak would not be going home.

As time had passed, Luther had begun to build Makedde up in his mind. In his dreams she had become almost mythical. She was the one who got away.

Here she is.

Mak did not look so magnificent and mythical now. She had slumped over again, exhausted. One slim hand was stretched out towards the wall, palm up. Her perfectly formed lips were dry and cracked. Those intense blue-green eyes had once again shut.

I must feed her. She needs water.

Men like Luther Hand did not end up in the company of women like Makedde Vanderwall. He knew that. Still, she had left an impression on his life. A deep impression. Part of him had been pleased when she had survived the motorcycle crash in Australia. It should have disappointed him. It meant he had failed at his task. And yet, it did not seem a worthy fate for her.

He left Makedde huddled on the mattress in the cellar, his mind strangely conflicted. He needed to gather himself and make a plan. Luther locked the cellar door and made his way into the kitchen. He checked his work phone. There was no message waiting from Madame Q, which puzzled him only momentarily. He thought for a while about what to do, and then, having decided his next step, he sent Madame Q a message with the agreed single word, to indicate that the job was done, and Makedde Vanderwall was dead.

COMPLETE.

CHAPTER 51

Makedde Vanderwall felt clear-headed and eerily calm.

With deliberate movements, she resumed her cross-legged position on the bare mattress that had become her narrow domain. It was no coincidence that her repose resembled that of a person meditating. She was captive in the cellar of an old building, her ankle chained to a wall, and if she had any chance of getting out, it would require mental alertness. Until now, focus had been proving difficult. Her temples still throbbed lightly from a gradually retreating headache. Her tongue felt furry. The strained muscles in her shoulders ached. Her socks were caked with dust. Her lips were cracked, and she thought she tasted blood.

Think.

Think.

She was, for the moment, successfully swallowing her panic.

Mak had deduced that she was trapped in an underground wine cellar, and as soon as the drugs had worn off and she became sufficiently lucid, she had checked for her mobile phone in her coat, hoping for emergency reception. Finding her phone missing, along with her money and keys, she had done a meticulous search of the space she was trapped in, moving in a grid pattern from one side to the other as far as the chain would allow her, in much the same pattern as she had methodically searched crime scenes. *This is a crime scene. The victim is you*, she thought darkly. She had carefully scoured the ground for bits of wire, safety pins, anything sharp, anything she could use as a weapon. So far she had found nothing save for dust, alcohol and splinters of wood. She could smash a bottle and use it to slash at her attacker, but she would be easily overpowered by a man the size of the one she remembered seeing briefly standing over her — if her recollections were at all accurate. Her only vision of him had been blurry and dark. She had examined the bottles on the shelves, and found that they were mostly French red wine, and some cognac, which gave her hope that she was still in France, perhaps not far from where she had been attacked. But where exactly? And why? Some of the vintages were impressively old. She wondered how often the place was frequented. Not often enough to be a commercial restaurant cellar, by the look of things. In fact, it didn't look like the place had been frequented at all recently. Except to make her a cosy little bed, of course.

She was desperate to remove the heavy iron cuff around her right ankle. During her schooling for her Certificate III in Investigative Services, she had learned how to pick locks. She was not particularly practised at it, but she knew she could bust out of handcuffs, given time and the right tools. But where to find the tools? A simple bobby pin could open handcuffs, and she could do that behind her back without even looking. She felt that a similar trick should work for the cuff that bound her. Now she wished she was in the habit of putting her hair up.

Fuck.

And she wished she had taken the time to study her new lock-picking book.

Increasingly, she sensed that she had arrived in her predicament via an experienced hand, or perhaps even a professional's. Since becoming more lucid, she had not had the opportunity to lay eyes on him. She did not know his plan, his reason for keeping her, or if he was acting alone. But the attack in the Catacombs had been quick. *So quick.* She hadn't time enough to react, and that was rare for her. Until the past couple of hours, time had been a blur. She had obviously been drugged, but she could not guess with what. A needle had been jabbed into her buttock, and she thought she felt a bruise there when she shifted position on the mattress. What she could remember was that there had been a man. A man had done this to her, he was responsible for her captivity, and was clearly intent on keeping her here against her will. He'd supplied her with water. He'd given her blankets. He had not yet done physical violence to her. She had vague flashes of memory about him, but those recollections were slippery and she did not trust them because of the effects of whatever drug he had sedated her with. She was sure, however, that the man was not Arslan. The man she had seen possessed a completely different build than the contortionist, or any of the other performers for that matter. They were all wiry and lean. Her impression was that the man who was keeping her was quite enormous in size. In her unreliable recollection he took on monstrous physical characteristics — a huge body with a thick, knotted neck and a scarred, odd-looking face, the details of which were patchy. She thought she remembered his hands as being the size of dinner plates, meaty and muscular. In the few memories she could grasp of her captivity, he had visited her once or twice, and each time he was a dark blur, misshapen and strange, a Mr Hyde to someone's Dr Jekyll.

She knew these recollections were not entirely reliable.

It isn't Arslan. It's someone else.

But who? Why?

Was this someone acting for Arslan, or the troupe?

The facts that Makedde had some sense of certainty about, the important facts, were that there appeared to be only one person holding her captive, it wasn't Arslan from the theatre troupe, and that the man who was keeping her here and had come into the cellar had not been wearing a mask. Nor had he blindfolded her. He had allowed her to see him, and that was a very bad thing. That meant that her release was not part of his plan. She was not gagged, which led her to believe that her screaming would not cause her captor any inconvenience. She would not waste her breath on screaming until she heard other voices, other footsteps, and given the opportunity she would then scream with all her might, and not stop. Her situation was clearly one of life or death, and she would take no half-measures. Mak had killed a man before, and she was willing to do it again. She did not have romantic notions of perishing. She would have to get out, and to do so she would probably have to kill the man who had attacked her in the dark Catacombs, amongst the bones and the dust. And anyone else who might be working with him.

Mak had no intention of letting him get his way, whatever it was he had in mind.

She breathed deeply and looked around her with a gaze sharpened by anger at the injustice of her predicament. *Wine bottles, cognac, wood, stone, drain in the floor, wood staircase, bare light bulb, cuff and chain on right ankle* ... It was with determined clarity that she juggled the elements in her head, over and over, seeing which ones could go together, which ones could affect her position, could be combined, could be used for something. This peculiar perspicuity was a familiar state of being for Mak, having emerged from horror a handful of times in her life already. *You are the clear-headed one when things go wrong, the one for whom the world decelerates to slow motion once the gun is drawn, the car is veering off to impact, the exchange turns violent.* She had a strange clarity in those moments, her adrenaline running like a constant beam of focus, static-free. Was that why terrible things kept happening to her? Because she was able to take it? Was that why she was a psycho-magnet? It was a survival mechanism that some people possessed, that ability to sever all emotional connections for a time, suspending grief and confusion so they might better find a way out of danger. It was common in fire-fighters, paramedics, surgeons, high-ranking soldiers ...

And psychopaths. She had met those.

Can you feel it? Can you feel Thanatos pulling at you, urging you to return to the soil?

This was life or death, and there was no time for self-doubt. There was no time to wonder how she could be so unlucky. Self-pity would get her nowhere, and whatever the reason for her ability to keep panic at bay, Makedde would take advantage of her cool head to do whatever was necessary to escape from this place.

There was a bowl beside her, half filled with water. It was a plastic cat's bowl, sitting low and open on the cold stone floor, with little feline pawprints painted around the circumference along with the name MINETTE. A few splashes of water were drying on the stone floor around it. Desperately thirsty, she had already drunk from it.

Drink, her body told her.

Mak eyed the water dish, and with a defeated sigh crawled across the mattress until her chin was at the edge. She tipped it up with her hands and licked at the dish like an animal, relieved at the sensation of the moisture on her tongue and trickling down her throat.

Relief.

It was while she was in this position, her coat pulled halfway up her back, and her legs kicking out, that the door at the top of the stairs opened again.

Mak froze.

She thought to suddenly right herself, so that the man who'd imprisoned her would not have the satisfaction of seeing her in such a humiliating position, but it was too late. He was already looking at her. Calm, and taking a deep breath to further steady herself, Mak rolled over and sat up. A droplet of water rolled from her mouth to her chin. She wiped it away, and strained her ears for outside noise — traffic, voices, anything. So far, she had heard nothing but a single set of footsteps and the creaking of floorboards. One man.

Fucking arsehole.

Her dirty-blonde hair hung over her eyes, and she shook her head to flick the hair out of her line of vision.

There he is.

The man walked down the creaking stairs towards her, the same man she remembered, and his appearance was as menacing in life as it had been in her nightmarish and confused recollections. To her alarm, she found that he appeared every bit as large as she had remembered. She guessed him to be closing in on two metres in height and weighing in at around 115 kilos. This was the man who could well be acting alone to imprison her here. *But why?* Perhaps he was waiting for something? *But what?* Again, he wasn't wearing a mask, and now that Mak was fully cognisant, she took note of his features, which were at best irregular. She recognised in him the hallmarks of facial surgery. Perhaps he had been in a fight and had tried to correct some scarring, but that hardly made sense, considering that his nose was crooked from a break. Had he been injured in the ring? He had perhaps been a boxer, or a fighter? She imagined that his very appearance would have aroused considerable fear in his opponents. Why the facial surgery? Was it reconstructive? Was he vain? Insecure?

The Eiffel Tower.

In an instant the recognition hit. This man had been at the top of the Eiffel Tower on the viewing platform. He had been in the same small elevator as she was, on both the way up and down. She recalled the immensity of him, and the strange features of his face.

He had followed her.

Who are you?

The man stood in front of her, and Mak worked to swallow her fear and panic. She sat cross-legged on the mattress and tried a smile. It was a measured smile, not out of place, just a pleasant face to begin an interaction between strangers. She had to think of this as an opportunity for interaction. Getting angry was not going to make him let her go. Screaming would get her nowhere until she heard the movement of other people in the building. No, she would have to reason with this man, she would have to understand him. She had to figure him out. She had a PhD, didn't she? All those years of study that she was not really using, perhaps they weren't for nothing. Perhaps. Even as she thought it, she worried about the feebleness of psychological methods when pitted against a man-mountain intent on keeping her in captivity and … well, she didn't know what else he intended, but he surely felt that what he had in mind would not be something she would co-operate with. But until she could get him to uncuff her ankle at least, she was not going anywhere. For one dark moment she wondered if she would sever her foot if she had to, if she had the knife to do it.

Yes.

Mak looked up at the man, steady. She kept her mouth fixed in its small smile, her head level to appear non-threatening, as if the simple fact of her captivity was not enough.

'Thank you for the water,' she said, gesturing to the bowl. Her voice was croaky. 'I was very thirsty,' she ventured.

He didn't respond.

Don't try too hard at first. You don't want him to think you're being manipulative. He might get angry at you and do something.

The huge man was no longer looking at her. His eyes were wandering around the space — the mattress, the blankets, the bowl, the floor.

What is he looking for?

'My name is Makedde,' she told him. 'Makedde Vanderwall.' There was no point in being anything but honest about her name, and it was good to identify herself, to let this man know she was a personality, a human. She hoped she could build up some rapport so that it would be more difficult for him to dehumanise her later. And if there was someone he was holding her for — a second party, a friend, a client, a partner — perhaps she could get him to side with her. There had to be a reason he hadn't hurt her yet. She hoped the reason might set her free.

'What's your name?' she asked him gently, as if this were a normal exchange in polite company. 'May I ask?'

His eyes moved to her again, but he didn't respond.

'I don't mean to be any trouble, but I'm very hungry. Is there anything I can eat? I can pay for the food. There was some money in my coat. Or I can make it myself, whatever is easiest for you. I can make something for both of us if you like. I don't want to be any trouble.'

Makedde felt disgust run through her at the sound of her pleading, the reality of her pathetic situation. *Daddy, I'm hungry. Please can I have some dinner?* She felt like she was six years old.

'I remember you,' she said, hoping to forge a bond.

At this the man reacted visibly. He backed up a pace and a kaleidoscope of emotions rippled across his uneven features. She could not be sure what he was thinking. Had she said something that would help or hinder her?

'Yes, I remember you,' she repeated. The elevator. She remembered now.

★ ★ ★

Does she recognise me?

Could she?

Had Makedde felt his eyes on her back when he'd seen her undress in the apartment in Sydney? Was there any way that she could have known it was him hiding there, watching her? Did she know that it was *he* who'd been wearing the balaclava and had been sent to kill her, *he* whom she had smashed in the face with her motorcycle helmet, *he* who had — with a broken nose — pursued her on her motorcycle through the streets of Sydney. He had watched her come off her bike with mixed feelings. He had been sent to kill her, and she looked like she would not survive the fall. It would be a positive result for his client. And yet, he was aware of something else. How *unsatisfying* it would be to have her gone, and even to have her death escape him, to have it come accidentally, dealt by fate.

But she didn't die. Fate brought her here instead.

Luther had never been an attractive man. His physical size was imposing, his features beaten up. He'd already once had his nose straightened in Bangkok by a surgeon who owed him a favour. After Mak broke it with her motorcycle helmet, it had the shape of a crooked potato. He had not bothered to fix it. He had been reminded of Makedde Vanderwall every time he had looked at his face since.

Makedde.

She was shackled, hungry, helpless. Still, her presence — in his care — both fascinated and troubled him. How could all of these occurrences be coincidence? How could one woman have eluded him? Why did she keep crossing his path? What was her role in his life fated to be?

Now here she was, more mythological creature than woman. She had escaped his clutches too many times. No one else in his career had ever done that.

Mak cocked her head to one side, appearing more curious than fearful. 'I do remember you. Hello,' she said.

And no woman had ever looked at him with that curious gleam in her eye. Not fear. Just curiosity.

Does she know me?

CHAPTER 52

Bogey stepped out of the taxi on the slanted and narrow Rue Cardinal Lemoine with his mobile phone in one hand and his suitcase in the other. He had been holding his phone the entire journey, hoping it would ring.

Mak is in trouble. She must be in trouble …

He placed his case on the kerb and handed the driver a fistful of euros, barely paying attention to the counting of the notes. Makedde had given him instructions to take the Metro from Gare du Nord to the hotel, but she was still not answering his calls, and he had wanted to get to her as soon as he could, and in his worry had run to the taxi stand and grabbed the first available car. He had been so relieved to be in Paris, and closer to her, and on the way to her hotel, that he didn't care about the added expense. He had called her from the plane, and from Heathrow, and since arriving on the Eurostar he had called again twice, and left her further text messages, sure that she would call him any moment to explain that she had been struggling with the kind of difficulties that plague travellers abroad with a frequency explained only by

Murphy's Law — a misplaced number, a stolen wallet, a lost phone or wiped SIM card; something to explain the silence.

So far there had been nothing.

His brow knitted with worry, Bogey stepped from the street through a large doorway to the charming cobblestone courtyard of the Hotel des Grandes Écoles, where a three-storey pastoral cottage welcomed him. He took only a moment to register the beauty of it, before making his way up a series of steps to the door. He found himself in a small lobby where a young woman with silken brunette hair pulled into a neat ponytail was talking on the phone in quick French. She did not look up when he entered. Bogey placed his suitcase in front of the wooden desk and looked around worriedly. He could not see Makedde. Hopefully she was in her room waiting for him, and there was nothing amiss. Perhaps she was playing a joke on him. He wouldn't put it past her to play some sort of joke. Her humour was at times left-of-centre, even morbid.

'*Parlez-vous Anglais*?' he asked, when the receptionist placed the phone back in the receiver.

She raised her eyes and appraised him and his jet-black hair and ripped jeans with a look of frank curiosity. '*Oui, monsieur*,' she replied. 'How may I help you?'

'I'm Humphrey Mortimer, here for Makedde Vanderwall. She is staying with you.'

'You would like to call one of our guests,' she said more than asked, and pushed a house phone across the desk towards him.

'Well, I am to stay in her room.' He held up his suitcase. Makedde had said he could stay with her. 'May I have a key and drop my suitcase off?'

She paused. '*Monsieur*, I cannot give you the key to a guest's room.'

The tiredness from his long flight from Australia, then the train under the Channel, came crashing over him. He took a breath. 'Is there a note for me, perhaps? My name is Humphrey Mortimer, or it could be for Bogey Mortimer.'

'Bogey?' she said with a little smile, pronouncing it *Bow-Gay*.

'Yes. Is there a message for a Mr Mortimer, or a Bogey?'

She shifted some papers around on the reception desk. '*Non.*'

'Okay, I would like to call the guest, Makedde Vanderwall, please.'

She gestured to the phone and he raised the receiver to his ear. 'I'll put you through.'

There were a number of clicks and tones, making it sound as if the system had not been upgraded since France first installed telephone lines. He held the phone tensely until it had rung in her room twelve times.

'The guest is not in,' the receptionist said.

He hung up and took a step back, wondering what to do. The dread he had felt since the flight had increased to a sharper, more focused alarm. He asked again for the room key, and when she refused he felt defeated. 'I will wait for her,' he said simply.

Desperate for a shower and a rest, Bogey made his way back to the courtyard of the Hotel des Grandes Écoles in a fog of worry and weariness. He positioned himself at one of the cold outdoor café-style tables, beneath a closed striped umbrella. A light snow drifted in tranquil poetry before melting on the cobblestones. He let it land on him and melt, while he tried to think of what to do. Outside the large doors of the courtyard, the Latin Quarter buzzed with university students, shop owners and tourists. Hopefully, somewhere nearby, Mak was okay.

Bogey did not want to believe that Makedde would forget his visit, but the alternative reasons for her silence were even worse. He sent her a carefully worded text message.

HI MAK. AT HOTEL AND CAN'T FIND YOU. PLEASE CALL AND LET ME KNOW YOU ARE OKAY EVEN IF YOU DON'T WANT TO SEE ME. PLEASE CALL. BOGEY

CHAPTER 53

On the morning of the third day, Luther Hand woke to sunlight gleaming on the rolling hills of the Burgundy countryside.

The farmhouse he had made his own was south of the town of Vézelay, on the edge of the Monts du Morvan, the 'Black Mountains' of the Celts of old. Now that the weather had cleared, Luther could see expanses of green fields, vineyards and forest undulating towards the horizon, where low granite slopes and plateaux were set against a cloud-spotted blue sky, shrouded in places by a thinning wreath of mist. He could just make out the spires of the Romanesque basilica of Sainte-Madeleine in Vézelay rising above the distant treetops, and catch glimpses of the trail of old buildings sloping down the hill below the church. This was one of the most remote locations in central France, about three hours' drive from Paris, and he had chosen it both for its isolation and its familiarity. Luther had recently eliminated the fleeing London financier, Nicholas Santer, in this very stretch of land. Luther had tracked Mr Santer here with ease, at the least-cared-for and most remote of his many European properties. He had been fast asleep as Luther sliced his throat open — the wound had gaped like the smile of a jack-o'-lantern, Luther recalled — before neatly dismembering him and locking the remains into a small crate buried beneath a garden of fragrant lavender. His body had not yet been found, and the investigation into his whereabouts had not been particularly heartfelt. Evidently the man's wife had discovered that her missing husband's will allotted a large portion of his fortune to the mother of his bastard child. She would rather her husband continue his 'extended vacation' while she lived comfortably with unfettered access to his millions. Luther was generally unaware of and happier without such intimate knowledge of his targets' affairs and the crumbling world their pathetic lives left behind. From one corner of the rundown property he could see the bright hedge of lavender several hundred metres away, bordering the Santer holding. It always brought to mind for a moment that grinning red jack-o'-lantern the London banker had become.

Luther had known he would return to the area, though he had not thought it would be so soon. He didn't know that it would be with Makedde Vanderwall.

The grounds surrounding his small farmhouse were lush green with winter rainfall. An old car in the gravel drive appeared to have been sacrificed to wet weather and rust. As he had anticipated, there had not been any foot traffic in the immediate area over the previous two days. No cars. No one to disturb him. A semi-feral calico cat was flicking its tail and preparing to lunge at a rodent alongside the house. Otherwise the world was quiet and still.

Luther looked across at the clock as the hand clicked to the hour. It was still early, just seven in the morning.

Today.

You have work to do today.

With the effort required of a man whose shoulders were unusually broad, Luther rolled over. The old double bed creaked under the weight of him. As with most European beds, its dimensions were unsuitable, and his feet dangled over the end. A soft beam of sunlight fell across him as he lay still once more, and for a time he didn't move out of it. The winter rays felt pleasantly warm on his skin. He found he liked the sensation. Luther did not care for the sun in Mumbai, where he kept a scarcely used apartment in Colaba, a place he'd begun avoiding in favour of his recently acquired flat in Plaça de Catalunya, Barcelona, about eight hours south-west of where he was now. As in his native Australia, the sun in India bit. The air there was excessively dirty too, polluted with fumes and grit. But here, the sky seemed to have a soft green glow. The sun was gentle. Luther did not spend much time in natural daylight. His work involved a lot of movement at night, a lot of time in planes, hotels, always moving. He was rarely in one place for even a week, such were the demands of his chosen occupation. He did not often spend a week in the French countryside. He did not lie about in a small bed enjoying the morning sun through dusty windowpanes.

For a stretch of time Luther lay with the sun draped over his skin, feeling strange.

A rabbit bounded past the window, and suddenly Luther had the feeling that he was unravelling. He sat up and tried to shake it off.

That's it. You need to finish this. Finish it by sundown and fly out. Madame Q will have new assignments for you.

He had not heard back from his agent. That was unusual.

Luther was beginning to feel peculiarly disconnected from the outside world.

CHAPTER 54

'Drayson, it's Bogey. Have you heard anything from Mak? Has Loulou heard from her?'

Through the phone, Humphrey Mortimer could hear loud guitars, and the noise of a crowd. Drayson and Loulou would still be in party mode.

There was a long pause before a reply. 'Mak? No, man. What's up with her?' He didn't wait for Bogey to explain. 'The festival was rockin'. You should have come with us.'

Bogey passed a sign indicating *Musée Minéralogique* and *Rue Jussieu*, neither of which felt helpful. Nothing about his surroundings was familiar or comforting, and the unexplained absence of the woman he had flown so far to see was a continuing shock to his strung-out nerves.

'Drayson, *listen to me*,' he pleaded. 'I'm in Paris, and I'm supposed to be meeting Mak here. I can't find her.'

The music took over the line momentarily and then faded back when Drayson spoke. 'Oh, man, that sucks. You mean Paris, Europe?'

'Yes. Paris, France. This is serious. I think something has happened to Makedde. She didn't check out of her hotel room. She is just missing.'

Static.

Bogey stopped on the street. The air was cold and unwelcoming, his leather jacket, wool sweater and scarf not enough to offset the penetrating winter chill. French men and women passed without making eye contact, busy on their way to familiar places in a familiar routine Bogey was not part of. He did not speak the language. He did not know whom to ask for help, or what to say. *My maybe girlfriend hasn't shown up?*

'Dude, I can barely hear you. I'll pass you to Loulou.'

There were the sounds of shuffling and more static. Bogey felt so tense he thought he might explode.

'Bogey? Oh, darling, you should have been there! The bands were awesome!'

As he heard these words, he saw a waiter coming towards him enquiringly. He was so distracted he had blundered into the outdoor area of a café. He turned away from the establishment, and the man, and walked the other way, shivering, cupping the phone to his ear. He had not eaten since he'd arrived, he realised. It would not be helping his mental state.

'Loulou,' he pleaded. 'Where's Mak? Have you heard from her?'

'Isn't she at my place?'

God, she doesn't even know?

'She came to Paris for an assignment,' he explained.

There was a pause. 'Yeah. I think she said something about that. She isn't back yet?'

Hopeless. This is hopeless.

'Do you have the number for her friend ... Mahoney? The cop?' he asked.

'Hang on.' Even the notoriously scatterbrained Loulou seemed to realise from his voice that something must be wrong. 'I'll see what I can find.'

CHAPTER 55

Distantly, Mak was aware of a stabbing pain in her lower back, like a sword impaling her lumbar region and extending out her abdomen.

God help me.

She stood, arranged her coat and a blanket around herself, and began her ritual walk. In a grim semicircle, she shuffled across the cold floor of the cellar in her dirty socks, one leg weighed down by the heavy cuff, its chain sliding across stone with an eerie rattle. The stabbing pains in her back continued, joined by the ache of knee and elbow joints, and the throb of her head. She tried to keep the pain distant. She needed her head to be clear to think of a way out, and giving in to pain would not help. She tried to imagine the streets of Paris just beyond the walls of her cellar prison. Perhaps she was not so far away from her hotel? Perhaps she was just across from the Catacombs, and hundreds of people were passing on the streets only metres above her. If she could convince her strange captor to take off her cuff, she could flee. She would be up that set of creaking stairs in a flash, out into the day, and into the crowds, absorbed into the movement and life and chaos of Paris. She would be carried to safety by well-meaning Parisians. She would be saved.

You will not be saved.

Mak had to save herself. Somehow.

Back and forth she moved, pacing bleakly in her bonds, cold and on the edge of hunger. She passed her chamberpot, her water dish, her plate speckled with breadcrumbs. She was alone with her quiet fury, disconnected from normality, dignity, common decency, and even from fear. Perhaps fear, like breath, was rationed out, and it was only very few who ran out of one before the other. Yet here she was, alive, breathing, and absolved of fear, like a soldier after too many battles.

It was strange that life would bring her chronic trouble that seemed never to fade, no matter the skills she learned, no matter the introspection she indulged in. She thought of Arslan, she thought of the Cavanaghs, the Stiletto Killer, those who wished her ill. She shared the earth with dangerous people. Mak had received so much unwanted attention over the years that she could in an instant switch from being relaxed to a hyper-alert survival mode. Her father, the retired Detective Inspector Les Vanderwall, had nicknamed her 'The Hawk' for her tendency to survey her surroundings with cop-like attention to potential danger. She found it uncomfortable to sit anywhere except the 'Clint Chair' in a restaurant or any public venue. The Clint Chair was the seating position that let her keep her back to the wall, an eye on entrances and exits, and preferably had a view of the activity at the cash register as well; it was named thus because it was the seat Clint Eastwood's Dirty Harry would choose.

If Mak did have good instincts, as Marian claimed, then they had certainly been hard won through many dangers and challenges. But where were those instincts when she was down in the Catacombs?

Perhaps you were in love, she thought. *With Bogey.*

She wondered if she would ever see him again.

The door.

Mak halted her pacing at the sound of the door opening at the top of the stairs.

Footsteps.

Here he comes.

Luther was not feeling right.

He had not eliminated the mark, Makedde Vanderwall. '*The mark.*' That was what she was. Nothing more. He would have to kill her. The contract demanded it, and he was a professional. Deviating from the job was when people made mistakes, and he was not one to make mistakes. True, Makedde's strength and beauty had fascinated him once but he had carefully reined in his unprofessional desires.

Not Makedde, 'the mark'. She is only a mark.

He still had not heard from Madame Q. He felt a strange sense of disconnection. Never before had a woman looked at him, *really looked* at his face, and not looked away quickly, struck with fear or revulsion. He could see in Makedde's eyes that she was not afraid of him.

He moved to her, noticing that she did not flinch. She licked her sensuous lips, and continued to gaze at him in a way that puzzled him. It was not a look of fear, or even loathing. But neither could it be called friendly. She *watched* him, impassive.

'Could I have a cigarette? I'm really desperate for a smoke,' she said.

He frowned for a moment. He hadn't known she was a smoker. Luther shook his head.

'Shame. I could use one.' Again, her tone lacked fear.

There was a prolonged moment of silence.

'You've killed before, haven't you?' she finally asked. 'I can tell. It's a look we all have.' She cocked her head. 'We're alike, you and I. I killed a man once. With a shotgun. It was bloody, and violent. A mess. But you know what, I kind of *liked* it. It bothered me for a while that I found it satisfying to blow another human being's head off like that, but you know, he deserved it and I'm okay with that now.'

Luther did not know how to respond. She had certainly seemed skilled when he had attacked her in that hallway in Australia. But he had been wearing a balaclava; she couldn't know it was him. Why was she telling him this?

'You're a hitman, right?' She was guessing, but his expression told her that she was on the right track. 'You are. Do you like it? Is it … satisfying?'

Luther did not know how to answer. Yes, sometimes the job gave him satisfaction, but mostly it was work. He did not care about it so much any more. He did not notice the killing the way he once had.

'I want you to teach me. I want to do what you do,' she said.

No you don't.

'Really. I've been thinking. You know, I can't go back to Australia. You know that. If it isn't you, it will be someone else. They will be sure to get rid of me on the off-chance that I inconvenience them. You work for the Cavanaghs, don't you? You're working as a hitman for them?'

Such information was often kept from him. Everything with Madame Q was separated, boxed off. No one knew who else was involved in a job. No one could tell. And yet, he had known it was them. Few could afford his fees. He had never dealt with any of the Cavanagh family, but he had been summoned to their house previously to deal with Makedde, and he had known it was they who had set this assignment in motion.

'You know they've been caught up in an investigation into an international crime syndicate? In Queensland. They were on some database. You might well be on that database too.'

He flinched.

'I can't go back there, and I doubt you can either,' she told him. 'I'm sure they already think I'm dead, and it wouldn't be hard for you to convince them that I am. That's the only way. If they think I'm alive they'll just send someone else.'

He started, and backed away from her. What was she suggesting? That she become his apprentice?

He needed to leave. He had to be out of her presence before he did something he would regret. He turned and disappeared up the staircase.

'I'm lonely down here by myself,' he heard Makedde say as he shut the cellar door fast.

He locked the padlock and leaned against the door, feeling a rare panic.

CHAPTER 56

On the morning of day five, the killer Luther Hand woke to the sound of the calico cat stretching and flopping its warm, furry body against the glass of the bedroom window. He looked across to the clock. It was past eight.

Today is a day to kill.

Luther was still in control of the situation, but increasingly he felt unsure of exactly what that situation was. It would soon be one week, and he had still not killed Makedde. At first he had just wanted to contain her. He had rationalised that killing her away from Paris would be wise. It would define her case as that of a missing person, a non-crime. Out here, buried under the cellar, her body might not be found for many years — it might never be found. That would be a professional result. Luther had been confident enough about the professionalism of his actions to have not found the urge to have her with him threatening. He'd envisaged keeping her for a day or two, thinking that would get her out of his system. He had believed that would satisfy him.

But no.

Something else was happening that he could not explain.

He sensed that some central part of his identity was dissolving day by day, losing strength and relevance in this isolated place in the countryside. It was as if he could no longer really pinpoint who he was. *Luther Hand*. Or Luther Davis, the son of Cathy Davis? He was no longer acting professionally, no longer acting like Mr Hand. He was taking an unnecessary risk by keeping his mark alive, and he could not even say why. And with the inexorable progress of that internal change, that questioning of his identity, came something else — a kind of awakening to the new. Or a rediscovery of the old.

Five days.

And Madame Q was still not responding. Perhaps what Makedde said was true? Had the Cavanaghs been caught up in an international investigation and somehow led Interpol to Madame Q and her operation? If so, that meant Interpol could have all the information Madame Q had, information about the job. About him.

Luther had always been careful, though. He had never met Madame Q. As far as he knew, she did not know what he looked like. Their communications, like those with his other agents, had always been electronic. There were go-betweens, contacts, package drops. No one knew where he lived, what his birth name was. He could not be tracked.

Luther got up, showered and dressed and went about his morning preparations.

With a cup of coffee in hand, he took out his work phone. There were no messages on it.

The job is dead. Madame Q is gone.

Now certain that his professional involvement was complete, Luther disassembled the phone and destroyed the pieces so they could not be traced.

No one knew where he was. No one, not even Madame Q, had known where he would take Makedde. That was good.

Perhaps he could stay with Makedde for a while. Perhaps he could even bring her upstairs?

Laid out before him on the kitchen table were Makedde's phone and notebook. With a sense of curiosity he switched on Makedde's mobile phone. He would check the messages to see if anyone was yet concerned about her. If not, that might buy him more time. He felt safe in this farmhouse. There was nothing linking him or Makedde to this place. Still, when news broke that she was missing, he hoped to be back in Mumbai.

A text message came in to her phone.

MAK I AM AT HOTEL DES GRANDES ÉCOLES. REALLY WORRIED. I'M HERE ONE MORE NIGHT. NO ONE IN AUSTRALIA KNOWS WHERE YOU ARE. I'M GOING TO CONTACT THE POLICE TOMORROW IF I DON'T HEAR FROM YOU. I HOPE YOU ARE OKAY. BOGEY

Luther felt a weight fall across him. Time was running out. Could the police trace her here? Or him?

He knew what he had to do. Luther delivered fresh water and food to his captive, Makedde, while she slept. He packed up his laptop and briefcase and put them in the Mercedes in the garage, started the car and prepared for the drive to Paris.

CHAPTER 57

The cellar had been particularly quiet.

No creaking. No disturbances. No voices. No visits.

On the afternoon of day five, Makedde woke on the mattress in the stone prison where she had been living out hours of her life, bound by an ankle chain and a waning sense of faith in the world.

She wondered what her future held. She had tried talking with her captor, identifying with him, and had got nowhere.

Will I die in this cellar? Will anyone know of my passing, except this monster who is keeping me?

Only he wasn't a monster. He did have a human side, but it was pushed down deep inside him. He was a large man of intimidating size, and his physicality brought to mind the case of Edmund Kemper, a man of unusually high IQ, a height of two metres plus, and a bulk of 136 kilos, who was raised by a strict mother who apparently suffered from Borderline Personality Disorder, and used to chain him up in the basement because she was afraid he would molest his sisters. She made him into a monster. He viewed himself as a monster, and thought natural sex drive was disgusting and evil. He killed ten people — most of them women whom he raped posthumously — including his own mother before giving himself up to the police. Edmund Kemper had been treated like a monster, and that's certainly what he became. And this man who kept Mak. What was his story? He *was* a professional killer, she was now certain. What was he doing with her? Why hadn't he killed her already? She could see that his face was heavily scarred. What were the scars from? The man who was keeping Mak was not inhuman. He was a man. If she could appeal to the man in him, she might save herself.

But for the moment she had no opportunities. Her ankle was raw. She had no tools to relieve herself of its chafing bondage. He had left her water and food, and he had not come back for some time.

Where is he?

Mak picked up her plastic water dish and drank from it, feeling the cold liquid slide down her throat and into the base of her hollow stomach. She ate the bread, and scooped up the remains of a cold TV dinner out of its foil tray with a spoon. Her nameless captor clearly did not trust her with other implements — glassware, forks, knives. Spooning a TV dinner and drinking out of a cat bowl; she had been reduced to this. Her life had brought her to this point.

Mak put the foil tray down, and became aware of a creeping numbness in her limbs, her brain and her heart. She had, for the moment, lost interest in reversing the spread of that natural anaesthetic. The man who was holding her captive had left her to ponder her fate. He had been gone for a stretch of time that she guessed to be equal to a day in the language of her pre-captivity life. In that time she had really begun to believe that she might never make it out of the dark little cellar alive. Her hope was waning with every passing hour, and her inner strength was crumbling in the face of the futility of her attempts to find a way out. She had being trying to reach her captor, and had so far failed. He had walked away from her, and she was still chained up there, no better off than she had been on day one. He could come back at any moment to finish her off. There were no white knights and no guarantees, and if Mak could not save herself from this place then it was over for her, and this whole strange journey of a life she had experienced would have finally reached its end. At thirty, her life would end in a dank, foreign cellar, after being held captive for a number of days she could not accurately document, for reasons she did not understand.

There are no white knights.

This reality penetrated to her core. Some primal belief, some childish ideal had not fully been extinguished until now, despite her harsh years of experience. Funny, she thought, how, despite everything she knew, some part of her female psyche had still held the tiniest fraction of hope that a white knight would come charging in, as in the fairytales of childhood. An angelic Jesus figure haloed in white light and song. A Prince Charming. Or the more rational but no less naïve idea of the far-reaching, infallible long arm of the law. The cops rushing in at the last moment to save every hostage and put the bad guys in jail.

No. Mak had never been one to wait for miracles. But now that she had truly acknowledged their non-existence, the lack of hope saddened her deeply. She recalled a quote that had always stuck with her — attributed to Helen Keller, she was fairly sure: *Security is mostly a superstition. It does not exist in nature.* There was no security here, in this life of Makedde's, or in the limited world she was bound to in this dark cellar. There was no security. In her life, the few fleeting scraps of security she had clung to had turned out to be sad illusions. Her mother was dead. Her father was far away. Her sister had always been distant. She had no children. No husband. No land. No home. And she would die at thirty in this cellar.

You'll die here.

She was losing her will. Her sense of self-preservation was wavering.

From some distant place, cocooned in her numbness, Mak observed her internal crumbling dispassionately.

You're losing your mind. Really, finally losing your mind.

CHAPTER 58

Mak woke with a start.

She'd dozed off again. She didn't know how long she'd been resting on her mattress, her eyes closed.

She was not alone.

Her captor stood before her, and at the sight of him she felt fear fly through her organs — her heart thumping, her brain jolted. He loomed over her with his incredible physical mass, and the pocket of his pants bulged. For an instant she feared he would sexually attack her. But no. He pulled a packet of cigarettes out of the pocket, and she saw something else too. Something metal. A round metal keyring. There was a small key on it. It would be the key for her ankle. *The key.* And quickly the metal ring slipped back into the fabric of his pocket as he removed a box of matches with his monstrously large hand. If she had blinked, she would have missed it.

'Thank you,' she said, sitting up and rubbing her eyes. 'Oh, thank you. You are so kind.'

He had been away for some stretch of time, and had

returned with a packet of cigarettes and a box of household matches. Where had he gone?

She saw the corner of the door, ajar at the top of the stairs.

'Share one with me?' she suggested, moving over on the mattress in the hope he would join her.

'I don't smoke,' he said flatly.

Neither do I.

'Well, thank you,' she said again, and accepted the cigarette, taking it between her fingers and reaching for the box of matches clumsily, knocking it out of his hand, emptying its contents on the stone floor, half a dozen matches scattering across the stone.

'Oh,' she said, as if embarrassed. 'I'm sorry.' She gathered what she could and put them back in the box. She drew one match across the side of the matchbox and it lit. She held the cigarette between her lips and touched the match to the end. The flame was strong and red. Inviting. Makedde had never smoked a cigarette before, only the occasional cigar, and those had always gone out on her and needed relighting. She was not much of a smoker. With a touch of anxiety, she drew the cigarette smoke in a little and blew it out of her mouth without inhaling too much.

'Thank you so much. I was dying for it.' She coughed, and tried to recover herself. 'I thought I'd quit, but ... I was really missing it,' she tried to explain.

He looked at her, watchful.

Behind his cold gaze she thought she sensed him weighing up the situation. He was a man much larger than her. She was unarmed, and still bound at the ankle. What could she possibly do if she got closer — give him a cigarette burn? Surely his pride would allow physical contact with her, if he at all desired it. He was difficult to reach, she could see that, but was it so impossible? He was still a man. There was another angle she could try.

'I still don't know your name, but I feel I know you.'

He continued to watch her, not moving.

'I'm lonely down here by myself. I hope you don't mind if I talk a bit.' She *was* lonely, and she did want to talk. If she was going to die in this place, she wanted to be heard. There were things she wanted to say to this man, or say for herself, she didn't know which. Mak shifted to one side of the mattress, indicating that she had made room for him. 'You can sit down, if you like. My name is Makedde.' She had told him her name before, but she repeated it so that this man might know her, perhaps even understand her. She needed to understand him, and understand what was happening between them. 'I'd like to know your name, but if you don't want to tell me, that's okay.'

He hadn't killed her yet. He hadn't harmed her. What was in store for her? What was the plan? Was he waiting for something?

He did not answer.

She tried again. 'Have you ever lost someone?' she asked.

He appeared surprised by her question. Mak knew that he was older than her. Chances were that his parents were in their later years, or had already passed on. Perhaps she could reveal some part of herself to him, and he would reciprocate.

'I lost my mother,' she told him. 'She died when I was a teenager. Cancer. It was a rare form of cancer called multiple myeloma. Have you heard of it?'

He shook his head, signalling that finally he had engaged with her. *A cigarette and a shake of the head. Connection.* It was a small miracle. Inside, she rejoiced. She felt part of herself break loose, find hope. She felt emotions begin to surface again.

'I want to tell you this because … because I don't know why I'm here and why you're keeping me, and if I am to die, I want to talk about my mother first. Jane was her name. Jane Vanderwall. She was my inspiration, my everything.' He did not stop her, so she continued in a queer ramble. 'I hadn't heard of multiple myeloma, either. But then I was barely sixteen, and there were many horrors I hadn't yet heard of. Multiple myeloma is more common in older male patients, but she was only forty-three. The doctors didn't see it coming, and neither did we.' Her throat began to tighten as she spoke. She felt the precursor to tears — tears for her mother, tears for Andy, tears for her crazy ruined life that seemed always to deal her the greatest horrors and injustice. She didn't care that she would cry. Why should she hold back? Who could care? Days or weeks down in that cellar, and she could not possibly care any more whether this man saw her cry. 'They gave her a bone marrow transplant. That was her only hope, you know, although, at the time, the risk was extremely high, much higher than it is with the procedures they use now. Her brother gave his marrow. He was her best match. The transplant was so hard. They kept her in the leukaemia ward with the other bone marrow patients, and many of them were children. Everyone there was bald. Some of the visitors were even bald; they'd shaved their heads for their siblings or friends, to show support. She was in there for months, fighting. There was a chart on the wall that I didn't understand. White blood-cell count. Graphs. Numbers. And the whole time, for months, my father refused to leave her side. Even though he has a bad back, he slept in this crappy little fold-out cot next to her, holding her hand. They talked, and she suffered, and they talked some more, and eventually she couldn't speak any more, and he was alone, holding the hand of the woman who'd been his wife — my mother. And, I remember ...' Now a single hot tear cascaded down her cheek. '... I remember how we held hands and formed a vigil around her in her last days. My father, my sister, Theresa, and I formed a circle around her. I held her right hand in mine, and it was swollen and warm, like a balloon filled with hot water. It didn't feel like her. The room smelled strange, the air filled with chemicals I couldn't place. Her face was puffy and slack, nearly unrecognisable. Her eyes were closed and her mouth hung open, with tubes going down ...'

Mak's lips trembled a little but she steadied. Warm tears began streaming from her eyes, flowing uninhibited. She did not sob, but she let the tears fall, not bothering to wipe them away.

'They had her on a respirator by then. And once her own breathing failed completely ...' She frowned, with the effort of keeping her voice steady. 'She'd fought so hard. She did all the right things, and she died.'

For a time Makedde sat still on the mattress, her face streaked and wet. Neither of them spoke. She noticed that her cigarette had gone out. It had bent in her fingers. She had forgotten it during her story.

Her captor took another from the pack and lit it for her. She leaned forward and he placed it in her lips, his fingers brushing her face briefly.

'I'm sorry about your mum,' he finally said. 'I lost my mum, too.'

His voice was deep and gravelly, but cracked a little, perhaps with emotion? Or disuse? She could not be certain he was being genuine. She could not be certain of anything.

She shifted closer. 'I'm sorry for your loss. Losing your mum is hard. No one can replace her. Was it recent?' she dared to ask.

The look in his eye changed. He stood up, disengaged.

Dammit, not again. Don't go away and leave me here …

'You don't have to go,' she said softly. 'We can talk about something else.'

But it was too late. He was already leaving, and with that look in his eye that spoke of some deep internal conflict.

What was his plan? Had the Cavanaghs sent him, or was he acting alone? What was in store for her? When would she be executed, or …?

She needed to reach him.

'Please …'

She needed to reach him before he carried out whatever terrible task he had been postponing.

Mak stood. She put the cigarette on the ground.

'Please don't go.' Her tears were running fast now, pouring down her cheeks. 'I've been here for a long time. I can't tell how long, because there are no windows. But I know it's been a long time. You've fed me. You've given me water. You haven't harmed me,' she said. 'You don't want to hurt me. You're kind. You've been nice to me.'

He stopped at the base of the stairs and looked at her. She saw in his eyes that she was getting some reaction.

'I'm lonely down here.' With shaking hands, she undid her wool coat and slid it off her shoulders. 'I want you to know it's all right if you want to kiss me.'

He frowned, and took a step backwards, all the time staring at her.

'You have me here because ... because you want me here. You *want* me. You've got me. Just don't leave me alone any more, please. I'm lonely. I want you to stay.'

Mak licked her lips deliberately. His eyes watched the movement of her tongue.

She gestured at the chain. 'I can't go anywhere. Just stay with me. Please. You're big and strong.' She said this as one compliments a man, not as one describes a monstrous creature. 'I'm not frightened of you. I know I'm yours. But I'm not scared of you.'

He took a step forward. 'I don't ... scare you?'

She looked him square in the eyes. 'No.'

And it was true. She was no longer scared. She had discovered the darkest parts of herself, and she wondered if she could ever truly be scared of anything again.

'I don't want to be alone any more. Stay with me. Hold me.'

He moved closer, and she did not flinch. Her right big toe began to tingle, precisely where the surgeon had carefully reattached it. It had been severed by a scalpel at the hands of a murderer. Andy Flynn had saved her that time. There would be no saviour now. There would be no happy ending. It was too late for happy endings.

'I want to. Please ...' she whispered into his ear and pulled him close. Her lips were dry, cracked, and they met his and found new moisture there. She unzipped her jeans with one hand, running her other around his thick, knotted neck, over his skull, feeling the scars beneath the fuzz of his short hair. He was missing part of his ear. She licked at the lobe, and ran her tongue across his scarred cheek.

'I want you.'

He hesitated for only a moment, and then his hands were busy. She covered his scars in kisses, and heard his belt buckle drag along the stone. He had unzipped his pants as well, and they slid to his knees.

Just a little more ... a little bit more ...

He leaned over her, naked from the waist. She wrapped her legs around him, and pulled him in, feeling a thrilling revulsion electrify her every nerve. She could feel him straining against her pelvis. She locked her knees behind his back, feeling with her thighs, her shins, her toes, feeling him and his clothing with sensual dexterity.

'I want you,' she whispered.

He pulled at her jeans, sliding them down from her waist.

More ... just a little more ...

He got to his knees and yanked her pants off. She licked his broad hand and he rubbed it between her legs. In seconds he penetrated her roughly, and she moaned unconsciously from a mix of revulsion and disturbing womanly pleasure and pain. She clung to him as he thrust into her again. She wrapped her arms around him, her fingers running over his back, his thighs, his legs, her own bare feet. Her toes moved too, and found the metal ring she sought, half exposed in his pants pocket. He thrust again, and let out a grunting exhalation. His pleasure was building fast. She didn't have long. She raised the key ring with her foot until she could grab it with one hand and insert the key in the cuff. 'Yes,' she moaned. It turned. The lock turned. He was losing himself in her, his mouth on her neck, on her chest, his thrusting increasing. She was there below him, receiving him, but not there, not receiving him, receiving her own plans, her own survival. Now her ankle was free, and she was running her fingers down his pants leg, her hips in the air, him leaning into her.

Click.

There.

With a sudden jerk she pulled away from him, throwing herself backwards. He was a confused bull, lunging at her and the air between them, his penis wet and angry, pointing. He had been so shocked that she had been able to slip past the edge of the mattress, just out of his immediate reach. She rolled backwards through a fast and awkward somersault, and arrived, momentarily dizzy, with her heels against a wall of shelves and wine bottles. He recovered himself quickly, however, and with a strange look in his eye moved towards her with his arms outreached in a gesture of pain, desire and confusion.

He reached the end of his chain.

Mak had her back to one of the floor-to-ceiling racks of bottles. She rose to her feet, and pulled her jeans back up and adjusted her T-shirt to cover herself. She pushed the greasy hair back from her drying eyes. Face stony, and with her mind focused to a sharp crystal, she reached behind her for one of the bottles at her back. She swung it off the shelf and smashed the top of it on the ground at her feet, sending splinters of glass skittering across the stone. Her captor flinched and prepared himself for an attack, expecting her to slash at him with the sharp edges of the bottle, but that was not her plan. The bottle broken open, she dumped its contents at his feet, soaking his pants, his shoes. Moving quickly now, animated with her purpose, she took another bottle from the shelf, smashed the top off and threw the alcohol at him.

Instinctively, he tried to dodge the airborne wave of stinging cognac, and it landed down one side, the rest splattering on the mattress behind him. She repeated this game, dousing the mattress, dousing him, smashing bottle after bottle while he went mad with his confinement, his chained ankle beginning to bleed.

'Bitch!' her former captor screamed, blind with rage. He had not even pulled up his pants, and the sight of him aroused, dishevelled, dangerous — yet helpless — struck Mak in that moment as darkly comic.

Her clothing was already hopelessly filthy, and now she pulled her T-shirt off completely, standing unashamedly in front of him in her bra, half-naked but no longer touchable. She doused the fabric in a third bottle of fine cognac, emptying it, and thinking for the briefest moment how strange it would have seemed to the purchaser of these bottles that his fine, carefully cellared cognac should be used to soak a woman's T-shirt. When she was done, one end of it was as wet as if she had dumped it in a bath. The fumes stung her eyes.

Fire, motherfucker. Fire.

The match was just where she had managed to toss it, when she'd knocked the box from his hand, beside one leg of shelving, beyond the reach of the chain that had held her, and now held him. Sick with triumph and sorrow, she trembled slightly as she took the tiny match in her hand. It was dry. *Thank God it's dry.* It was dry and perfect. That tiny red tip — no larger than the pinky nail on a newborn baby — held the key to her captor's destruction. She caught the look of understanding in his eyes when she held it up. He panicked and leaped towards her, the chain going taut and pulling his right leg out from under him, sending him sprawling at her

375

feet. He pulled his leg to his chest — once, twice — and she saw a puff of dust come up from the corner. He was going to try to pull the chain from the wall.

Mak ran the match across the rough stone floor.

It lit.

Kill or be killed.

She touched the flaming tip to the edge of her cognac-soaked T-shirt, and watched the flame spread across it, almost invisibly at first.

His eyes were on the shirt now and the growing flame that was running up the fabric towards her hand. He knew instinctively that it would find him, and that he only had a second to prepare for it. He scrambled backwards on his knees like a huge dog. She threw the shirt with a swoop of her arm and it landed with a wet slap across his face. He flicked it away, but he was covered, a flame ran blue across the material, across him, and when it hit his hair, it too lit in an almost invisible flame, which soon rose with deadly magnificence. Mak doubted that she had ever seen anything so magnificent, so powerful, so heroic as that growing cognac flame as it danced, and its host danced with it, hopping, squirming, clawing at his face and his burning clothes and not yet letting out a sound.

Eat fire, fucker.

Makedde walked to the wall, took the old wooden shelving in both hands and in one — two — three pulls, wrenched it from its position. The shelf teetered forward and fell in slow motion, crashing across the floor in a chaos of shattering glass, liquor and splintering wood, the edge of the shelving hitting her burning captor hard in the ankle as he struggled to get clear of it. She saw him holding his face and rolling on broken glass next to the mattress, which now rose in flame. He was trying to put his clothes out. His hair was still burning. She felt strangely disconnected from the scene, disconnected from everything but her bright clarity, her survival.

Eat fire, fucker. Eat fire.

Numb, shaking madly and with sweat beading on her skin from the building heat of the cellar which had so long held her in deathly cold, Mak turned and made her way up the staircase, scarcely seeing the steps, her feet knowing just where to fall. The edges of the staircase were catching now, slowly, with a line of low flame that ran up the treads in a zigzag. She was untouched by it as she leaped from stair to stair. She was apart from it. And behind her, a deep animal moaning began. The man's skin was melting under flame. His hair was burning away. The chain rattled as he struggled and rolled, trying to put himself out. She did not turn to look. *It is you, or me.* She reached the top of the stairs, and found that the door to the cellar was still ajar and opened at the slightest push. It swung open on its hinges. There was a shiny new padlock resting on one side, the key sitting in the lock.

How much of my life did he take? How much of my life did he spend?

There was a cracking sound. It was the wooden stairs, already breaking with heat and flame. Smoke was billowing out with a horrible smell — wood and dust and flesh burning. He was burning alive down there. Burning and chained. His flesh would be burning off his bones.

She did not look.

Makedde closed the cellar door behind her, locking the smoke in, and muffling the sounds of the crackling flame, the searing death below. She snapped the padlock shut, and with dusty bare feet walked across the uneven floorboards of an old farmhouse and out into a winter evening in the countryside of Burgundy, cold, moist grass pushing up between the toes that had held the key to her escape.

CHAPTER 59

Makedde Vanderwall stood barefoot and dishevelled on the gravel driveway of the remote farmhouse, emptied by a deep exhaustion. It was only the queer adrenaline of survival that continued to animate her with unnatural energy, propelling her until she was safe from immediate danger. But when would that be? Where? Through stinging eyes she saw shades of green stretching in all directions, the sky glowing an overcast white. Wood fences intersected the fields like stitches. *Stitches and scars. Stitches and scars.* Mak recognised nothing of her surrounds. On a hilltop in the far distance she could see glimpses of an ornate church of some kind, and what looked like a small village. Here and there were cottages dotting the expanse of fields. If Paris was nearby, it was hiding very, very well.

As you stand here, he is burning and suffocating in that cellar. He'd had so many scars. You touched them. You kissed them.

She would be haunted by those moments, and yet she was alive. Behind her, the farmhouse was smoking.

Leave this place.

Leave everything, Mak.

There were no fire trucks, no cop cars, no neighbours rushing to her aid. She could not tell how far away the next neighbour lived. She was alone. She wanted to keep moving until she was far from the place of her confinement. She thought of Bogey waiting for her in the hotel room in Paris. She wanted to be there. She wanted to collapse into his arms, and not move or speak for a tremendously long time. She needed transportation. Right in front of her in the driveway there was a car. It was rusted and old. The tyres were flat. It might not even have petrol in the tank. *Hopeless.* It looked as if it hadn't been used for years. She could run to the nearest neighbour's house. Perhaps call the police.

No.

She remembered how little the police had done for Tobias Murphy, for her slain friend Catherine Gerber. Never mind her father's convictions, never mind how she'd been raised to believe in justice and truth. Never mind Andy Flynn. Never mind the Cavanaghs. No, she'd had enough of the police and their *justice.* She'd had enough of playing by the rules while others flaunted their immunity.

Leave this place.

Leave everything, Mak.

The farmhouse appeared to have a garage attached on one side. She ran to it, and tried the tilting door. It didn't budge. She moved around the side and found a smaller door. It was unlocked. *He must have driven here. He must have a car.* She threw the door open, and with a sense of a prayer coming true, she found herself looking at a black Mercedes, just sitting there, waiting for her to jump inside. At the sight of it, she nearly cried with relief.

Oh, yes. Finally. Yes.

She opened the car door and searched around the driver's seat before realising that the keys were actually in the ignition, clearly ready for her captor to make a quick getaway if he needed to.

But he was not going anywhere. She was.

In the back seat there was a briefcase. Perhaps it held the man's identification. The case was locked.

There was a crash of glass as the windows of the farmhouse blew out. The fire was gaining strength. She had to leave, and fast. There was no time to retrieve her phone, her wallet.

Go, go …

With a renewed sense of urgency, Mak leaped into the driver's seat and turned the ignition. She groped around the dash for a remote to open the garage door, and not finding it, pulled open the glove box. Instead of a remote controller, a Glock pistol fell out onto the passenger seat next to her. She blinked at it. There was a wallet in the glove box, and a passport — no, *four*. There were four passports in the glove box of the car. She had no time for this. She had to get away before the garage went up in flames.

Mak leaped out of the car and found a chain pulley alongside the garage door. Using all her strength she pulled until the door lifted outwards. Light streamed into the dark space. Relief. She was nearly there. She could speed off and leave this horrid place behind …

And then Makedde saw something that made her freeze in her tracks.

Out of the corner of her eye, a familiar sight. Something that didn't belong here. Something she didn't want to see in this garage, in this farmhouse, in this horrible place. It was the tips of a pair of shoes. Pointy shoes. Black pointy shoes.

She choked.

No.

Silently, tears began to fall from her eyes. She did not even notice them. She did not wipe them away.

Black shoes were poking out from a bundle wrapped in plastic. Familiar shoes. *Wrong. This is wrong. This can't be.* Her instincts registered the horror before her brain did. She clambered towards the shoes, and kneeling, began to unwrap the plastic sheath. It was the shape of a body.

No.

No!

She tore at the plastic, desperate. Pulling away the layers of her grim find, she began to make out the features of the dead body inside.

Black hair. Glasses. Leather jacket.

Bogey.

Bogey, Bogey, Bogey, Bogey, Bogey …

She had known the instant she saw those shoes that it was Bogey, and that he had somehow tried to save her, that he was dead now, because of her, and it would be the final nail in her coffin. In that moment she knew with certainty that she could never return to a normal life. Not with what she had seen, what she had experienced. Makedde loved this man, she had found new love with him and he had shown her new possibilities, new emotions, the chance of a new life. It was precisely because he loved her that he was now there in front of her with his throat cut open. His eyes were open, unseeing, sunk back into his pallid face. His beautiful lips were dotted with smears of blood. He had been dead for at least a day in that garage, or days, while she had been chained up in the cellar just below him, wishing so badly to be near him.

I'm going to go mad.

Perhaps she *had* gone mad already. This life of hers was madness. Everyone who had ever told her that things would be okay — *Everything will be okay, Mak* — was wrong. Everything in her world was wrong. A trembling began all through her body, and she found herself temporarily unable to act. She wanted to crawl inside his plastic shroud and hold his body, and die there with him, let the flames engulf them both. She realised the danger. If she kept standing there looking at Bogey's body she would die.

Numb, moving like an automaton, Makedde walked to the car and popped the trunk open. Inside, she found cash, jewels and what she recognised to be a sniper's case and the tools of a hitman. The man who had abducted her had been a professional. She had known it, and now she knew in her guts that the Cavanaghs had set the man loose on her, and that they would not be satisfied until she was dead.

With an unnatural strength powered by adrenaline, Makedde lifted Bogey in her arms, and bore his body to the open car. With a tenderness too late, she laid him in the trunk, gently closed his stiff eyelids, and kissed his cold lips. She closed the lid and took a breath. Around her, there was more glass smashing, and the sound of cracking. The garage was heating up. The blaze outside was getting bigger now. The whole farmhouse would go. It was time to leave.

Makedde got into the driver's seat, gripped the stick shift, put the car into gear and drove.

Blind to everything save the winding road before her, Mak drove through the French countryside for hours without stopping until sheer exhaustion made her pull the car over. She fell asleep across the front seat with the doors locked, the loaded Glock near to hand, and the stick shift digging into her ribs. She woke thirsty, bruised and in darkness, a blood-streaked leather jacket wrapped around her. The Mercedes clock glowed the hour of 10:10.

She remembered driving away in the car. At some point she had woken, shaking violently, and had removed the jacket from Bogey's cold body and wrapped it around herself for warmth, along with his scarf, which was now bundled in the back seat, dark with dried blood.

It took her a moment to orient herself, and seconds later, the tears began. She ignored them. She wasn't interested in tears. She was interested only in revenge.

The man she loved was dead in the trunk of the car, and she had enough weapons, jewels and cash to make a new life, under the radar, a life where the Cavanaghs and their thugs could never find her.

They wouldn't need to.

She would find them.

It was not the life she had wanted, not the life she had asked for. It was the life she had to lead.

EPILOGUE

In his thirty-two years of performing autopsies, Dr Auguste had never before come across a fully grown man folded neatly into a small box. Puzzled, the Chief Forensic Pathologist ran through the case notes in his mind as his assistants removed the ornate wooden panels of the contortionist's stage box, within which the deceased was tightly folded. With considerable care, the panels were cut away, leaving the exposed remains on Dr Auguste's autopsy table, balled up like a bloated fist.

The deceased, apparently, had been an accomplished contortionist.

Mr Arslan Gosulja had been missing for just over two weeks, and appeared to have been dead nearly that long. Sheltered from the elements, his body's decomposition had not been rapid, but had clearly taken hold. The once slender physique had ballooned to the shape of the box, and the deep black-purple discolouration of post-mortem lividity was evident along all the lower extremities, strongly suggesting that he had died in this position, trapped in the box.

Dr Auguste could not help but imagine his final days. Within the first twenty-four hours the man would have felt a desperate hunger and thirst, and increasingly unbearable pain in his muscles and joints. Delirium would surely have set in early. He would have experienced giddiness and hallucinations. His tongue had split open from dehydration. As he neared death, his eyelids likely would no longer close, and he would have spied the dark world around him through the holes in his box, helpless. There would have been little else for him to do in the hours leading to his death than watch his mother, the notorious and disgraced actress Bijou, while she went about her routine, covering her grief and bewilderment in an alluring layer of powder and perfume and jewellery, believing her son to have abandoned her. Terribly distraught, she had called the police when she became aware of the terrible smell in her bedroom.

The assistants manipulated the deceased across the table, laying the remains flat. Removed from its deadly container, the body moved easily, rigor mortis having long since passed. Had this man expired from dehydration, a form of positional asphyxia, or death due to one of the complications of prolonged immobility, such as a pulmonary embolism or the pressure effects on skeletal muscle? It might prove difficult to determine.

'*Passez le scalpel*,' Dr Auguste ordered.

The case, which became famous once Bijou's scandalous relationship was leaked to the papers, was one of the strangest in Dr Auguste's illustrious career. He later sought out and purchased a handsome out-of-print book on the subject of contortion and *entérologie* — or 'packanatomicalisation' as it was sometimes called in English — and it sat on the shelf of his office for many years.

He never did find the time to read the text, nor did he again come across a case involving such strange practices, but whenever a visitor noticed the book he retold the story of the curious man in the box. Of all the confounding aspects of the case, the single question that continued to trouble Dr Auguste was this: having voluntarily placed himself in the box, why had this Arslan Gosulja not cried out to his mother for help once he had become trapped and recognised the seriousness of his position? His death would have been agonising. And he had been just a heartbeat from her for days.

Silently watching.

THE END

A NOTE ABOUT THE GRAND GUIGNOL

I conceived of writing about my fictional troupe, Le Théâtre des Horreurs, after watching a documentary about Paris in the 1920s, a time when the Grand Guignol was patronised by the likes of Anaïs Nin and Henry Miller. Sadly, I discovered that the theatre at 7 Cité Chaptal, though still standing, bears little resemblance to the notorious venue of the Grand Guignol, which performed 'naturalistic' horror plays there from 1897 to 1962. Investigating the tiny theatre in Paris (at the time of writing it was the International Visual Theatre, staging plays for the hearing impaired), I was saddened to find the original interiors gone, including the oft-written-about carved angels left over from its earliest days as a chapel, and no reference to the theatre's incredible past except for a little plaque on the corner of Cité Chaptal and Rue Chaptal making mention of its once notorious and yet seemingly near forgotten past. In this novel I have taken literary licence by restoring the venue to the splendour of its heyday, angels and all — my homage to what once was.

ACKNOWLEDGEMENTS

It can be very difficult to be close to a writer finishing a novel. I would be truly remiss not to acknowledge my friends and family, and thank them yet again for the incredible patience they have shown in supporting my writing, particularly over the three years it took me to complete *Siren*. I would also like to thank HarperCollins *Publishers* Australia, and particularly Linda Funnell, for the ongoing support of my work. Thank you so much for believing in me. Thank you also to Bolinda Audio, who, like HarperCollins Australia, have been there with me since my first novel was published in 1999. And thank you also to the readers and publishers around the world who allow me to do what I love for a living.

I have the good fortune of having the most wonderful literary agent, Selwa Anthony. Thank you for your guidance and friendship from day one, and for making my dreams of becoming a published writer come true. Thank you also to Mitch Kaplan and KSGB Literary Agency in Los Angeles for the support and belief in me. Big thanks also go to Michael Schenker and Rob Dorfmann at 2 Roads Pictures, Craig Schneider of Pinnacle PR, Martin Walsh and Chadwick Management, Saxtons, Sisters in Crime, Karen Phillips, Di Rolle, magician Adam Mada, contortionist Arslan Gusengadzhiev of

Zumanity (who is nothing like the twisted Arslan character in *Siren*, despite the name), SWAT leader Doug Martin for correcting my 'mash', 'Big' John McCarthy for choking me unconscious for Makedde's Catacombs scene, and West EFX for literally setting me on fire for research for my farmhouse scene. I was gratefully unsinged. I am also grateful for the assistance of Chief Forensic Pathologist Dr Jo Duflou, forensic polygraph examiner Steven Van Aperen, Carl Donadio of Once Blue, Tony Zalewski and the Australian Institute of Public Safety, and Mike Evans and the Australian Security Academy where I completed my Certificate III in Investigative Services in 2008.

I would like to acknowledge French writer Maurice Level, author of *Le Baiser dans la nuit*, translated as *The Final Kiss*, and first performed at Le Theatre du Grand-Guignol in 1912, and the invaluable book on the Grand Guignol, *Grand-Guignol: The French Theatre of Horror*, by Richard J. Hand and Michael Wilson, University of Exeter Press, 2002. The fragments of play dialogue I've used were adapted from translations in this book. I would also like to acknowledge American writer Jack Kerouac and his novel *On The Road*, quoted in this book.

And to my gloriously patient friends Alison, Gloria, Mindy, Liz, Amelia, Desi and Robert, Manual, Tracey, Misty and Alice, Nafisa, Lionheart, Joel, Erica and Stephen, Linda (Miss J Forever), lovely Hugh for the quote, the Literary Salon crew, the Hillbillies and the Poets, and especially Berndt, Dorothy, Nik and Annelies. I thank each of you for showing support and for being there for me in your own way during these recent roller-coaster years. I love you all.

To Dad, Lou, Jackie, Dave, all the Moss, Carlson, Bosch, Hooft, Hartman and Sellheim clans — love.

Mum, I never forget you.